The Shadow of Wildflowers

The Shadow of Wildflowers

Alta Ione

The Shadow of Wildflowers

AUTHOR'S NOTE:
This is a work of fiction. Names, characters, places, and incidents are the product
of the author's imagination or are used fictitiously. Any resemblance to actual
persons, living or dead, businesses, events, or locales is entirely coincidental.

Front cover design by RaeJean Spencer Hasenoehrl using images from Freepik.com
and Pixabay.com.

Back cover design for paperback by RaeJean Spencer Hasenoehrl using artwork by
Lindsee Hasenoehrl Baker

Please visit us online at altawrites.com.

Digital eBook ISBN: 978-1-7369030-0-1
Paperback ISBN: 978-1-7369030-1-8

Mom and Dad, this one's for you.

Thanks for giving us roots and wings.

In the night of death,
hope sees a star
and listening love
can hear the rustle
of a wing.

- Robert Ingersoll

Prologue: The Hanging
Thurmond, Montana — May 1873

The woman stood atop the platform. A tattered handkerchief dangled from her hand. A noose hung from her neck.

"Drop the hankie when you're ready," the sheriff quietly told her.

Her eyes darted back and forth from the sheriff to the crowd. She gave no indication that she understood the man's instructions.

"Do you have a last request?" the sheriff asked.

"My baby," she whispered. "Please, let me hold my baby one last time."

The sheriff looked to the gathering of women standing front and center of the crowd. Saloon girls, all of them, their hands clasped one with another. A presence of unity for their workmate standing white-faced before them.

"Bring up the child," the sheriff called out.

Mother Damnable held the infant in her arms. This child was not the first baby born to one of her saloon girls. Nor would she be the last.

The woman moved forward, the swish of her long red skirt achingly stoic against the play of horror going on before her.

The sheriff walked to the front of the platform, kneeled, and reached down for the child, a newborn just three weeks old.

Mother Damnable cradled the baby a few seconds longer, pulled the blanket from its face, and handed the bundle to the sheriff. She looked to the baby's mother and called out, "We love you, Louisa. We love you."

The saloon girls took up the cry. "We love you, Louisa." "Be brave." "We'll take care of your little one." "God is with you."

The calls filled the air. Louisa heard none of them. Her only focus was the sweet baby in her arms. She rocked her child, promised that she'd watch and guide from heaven, then bent her head to kiss the tiny forehead.

Before Louisa's lips touched the baby's skin, the gallows' floor dropped. The woman's body followed. The noose cinched out life.

The baby fell from the dying woman's arms. Its body hit hard against the edge of the floorboards before it fell through the trap door and to the ground.

The mother's body flopped to and fro for three minutes, perhaps four, then hung limp against the grey sky.

On the ground, just past weeds and timbers, lay the motionless body of a child cheated of mother and life.

Mother Damnable was the first to run towards the child.

"Stop right there, woman." The voice, unmistakable with its hint of Irish brogue, thundered above the crowd's outcries. "Pick up that child and you'll be the next to swing from the gallows."

Niall McNally stared down the woman he'd warned as he ambled up the steps to the top of the platform. His limped cadence lashed through the crowd's hushed whisperings as he took his mark—an actor on his stage—and surveyed the crowd with lightning eyes.

His stare finally settled on Mother Damnable. He uttered one word. "Pathetic."

He continued the few steps towards the woman dangling from the yard arm. The sheriff, on his knees and hunched over after his futile attempt to save the falling child, was babbling repentant nonsense. McNally shoved him from his prayer stance with his boot, then kicked him twice in the ribs before retrieving the dropped handkerchief from the floorboards. He turned his attention to Louisa and took a knee so he could study his sacrificed pawn face to face.

"Poor lass." McNally traced the handkerchief across Louisa's greying cheek. "The sheriff didn't have a chance to place the hood over your lovely head."

He looked past her ankles through the square hole.

"And it doesn't look as if your little one fared well, either."

He leaned in and whispered into the dead woman's ear. "So sorry, my love. Had you born a son, well, things might have turned out a bit differently for both of you."

McNally turned back toward the crowd and tucked the handkerchief into his coat's breast pocket.

"Show's over, folks. Go back to where you belong."

2

Mother Damnable tripped over her skirts, landing in the mud as she raced to an opening between the gallows' support beams. In the darkslatted shadows underneath the floorboards, a blond bear of a man had already swooped up the child.

"Don't you touch that child, you monster!" She snatched the baby from his arms. "You're a henchman for the devil himself."

The mud sucked at her shoes as she rushed from the confines of the gallows, cocooning the baby and hushing its fears as if death's ravens hadn't already spread their wings over the child.

"Bbut, ma'am, the baby's bblanket!" the bear man called out, grabbing the blanket from the mud as he followed the woman out onto the sidewalk where a new rain was already rinsing dirt and blood from the child's pale face.

"Mma'am, here's the bbaby's bbblanket," he said. He tried to pass the blanket to the woman as she marched towards her wagon.

"Get away from me, you demon! It's vile enough that you hired on to execute that poor, innocent girl. But dropping that door while her babe was still in her arms? You just earned your own kingdom of brimstone, you filthy mongrel."

"But, mmma'am, the mmother would want her baby cccovered."

Mother Damnable turned and kicked the man. She kicked some more and swore and spit in his face, the baby in her clutches all the while, until Kate, one of the saloon girls, forced herself between the two and grabbed the woman by the shoulders.

"He didn't do it, Mother. Stut didn't kill Louisa or her baby."

"Of course, he did."

"No." Kate's eyes pleaded with her employer. "I couldn't watch Louisa say goodbye to her baby, so I turned away. That's when I saw Niall McNally step forward and pull the lever to drop the trap door."

The bear man trembled and bit at his lips.

"Stut?" The girl touched his arm. "Tell us true what happened. You've always been good to us saloon girls. I know it wasn't you."

His body shook harder.

"It's mmy ffault! He hired mmme to be the jjailor. I pppromised to be a ggood jjailor. It was my jjob to be the hhhangmman, ttoo."

3

"Look at me, boy," Mother Damnable demanded. "Who pulled the lever?"

"Mmmme."

She grabbed his chin and forced him to look at the baby held in the crook of her arm. "Tell me who pulled the lever. If you lie to me again, young man, I'll take a pistol to your horse's brains."

Stut turned away.

Mother Damnable grabbed him by his collar. "Who. Pulled. The lever."

"Mmr. McNnally."

Mother Damnable released the shirt from her hold and grabbed the blanket still in Stut's hand. She worked the blanket around the baby and began bouncing the child as though to give it comfort.

Through the fringe of her dark lashes, she caught sight of the bear man's trembling lips. She flinched as he reached to dab away the mud spilling across the baby's tiny lips and chin.

"Mmma'am, you bbetter llook at the bbaby. I think she's bbbreathing."

* * *

Mother Damnable rushed to the buckboard wagon holding the coffin. Kate and Stut followed.

The other saloon girls had loosed Louisa's body from the hangman's rope. The young mother now lay within planks of funereal pine.

"Shoo. All of you, shoo." Mother Damnable held the baby close, hoping no one would witness the small movements the child was now making.

"All of you, get back to work. Except you, Kate. You stay here and drive the wagon." The baby began to whimper and Mother Damnable covered the sound with shouted out orders.

"Funeral will be tomorrow at dawn. Now go on. All of you. Back to work."

* * *

4

Only three people knew the child lived. Only the manchild with the thick stutter could ride well enough or fast enough to smuggle the child to a nunnery far south of McNally's mining town.

But Stut realized a better plan.

Darkness and pelting rain kept the trail west void of travelers. Stut shielded the baby as best he could from the rain and the mud kicked up by his horse's hooves.

As long as the horse kept its pace, the baby seemed satisfied to sleep. When the baby did fuss, Stut soaked his handkerchief with milk from a mason jar Mother Damnable had provided and held it for the baby to suckle on.

A day into the journey, Stut realized the baby hadn't squalled in some time, so he tethered his horse to a tree, nestled the baby into the recess of some rabbitbrush, and walked towards a group of cows feeding in the distance. Quietly, he approached a cow nursing its calf, hoping she'd let him near enough to squirt streams of milk into the empty jar. The cow was suspicious of his maneuvers and trotted away, her calf by her side.

Stut followed suit and quickly realized he was on a fool's errand, so he moved on. He apologized to the baby and when she was unresponsive to his message, he flicked her on the cheek.

The baby crinkled her face and let out a soft mewl.

Stut mounted the horse and urged it forward. Time couldn't be wasted.

He had made this three-day ride to his parents' home station before. This time, he made it in two.

The moon smiled down as Stut laid the baby with the red fringe of hair on his parents' doorstep. Before he knocked on the door to rouse them from their sleep, before he dashed into the woods to shield his parents from the hardships of his past, he tucked his ash-scrawled note beneath the baby's blanket and whispered the words he'd written: "Ma and Pa, I finally done something right."

The Table
Leeds, Idaho — August 1890

Jake didn't care that caked mud from his work boots flew across the kitchen floorboards. He paid no attention to the dust cloud from his coat as it hit the ground. His head hurt, his back ached. And the smell of supper sent bile to his throat.

He rubbed his eyes and turned from the doorway towards his mother working at the stove. The sight of the kitchen table stopped him in his tracks.

"What the hell is this?" he flatly asked.

"Language, Jake."

He crossed the room and grabbed a plate from the table. "What the hell did you do?" he demanded.

Miss Jayne refused to turn from her chore, fearing what she'd see in her son's eyes. "I set the table for supper, Jake. That's what I do. I cook the food. I set the table. We eat. It's nothing more than that."

"Nothing more than that?" He flung the dish across the room. Then the coffee mug. Miss Jayne flinched at the shattered sounds.

"And everything will be just fine as long as supper's on the table," Jake sneered.

He yanked a ladder back chair from its position at the table and sent it sprawling across the floor.

The thunderclap of wood was echoed by Jake's slamming of the door.

Miss Jayne slumped against the dry sink. She didn't fight her tears. They came hard and fast as waves of pain and grief and despair mixed in with memories of blood and sweat and fear.

She was tired of pushing back emotion, exhausted by the task of nobly carrying on. So, over the past week, she'd given in to tears. They were the only constant in her life beyond the graveled pain in Jake's voice. And hatred. She could certainly count on the hatred that shadowed her son's days. And his nights.

It was the tears she counted on most as she mourned the loss of Jake's wife and two babies. Floodgates of pent-up rage and confusion. Nightly squalls of salted frustration and loneliness. Redemptive, succoring, unabashed tears that soaked up her face and left her exhausted for the sweet strains of sleep.

If she mourned, perhaps she would move on.

She wished Jake would shed tears to turn the corner of his own grief.

Instead, he simply became a man she didn't dare begin to know.

Miss Jayne's despair was interrupted by the opening of the door. Jake stalked in, an axe in hand. She screamed as her son's first swing matched metal to wood. One magnificent arc through the air. One chair destroyed.

The table was next. With thunderous abandon, Jake swung the axe, the metal chinking away at hardened pine. Miss Jayne's knees buckled, landing her hard on the floor. Part of a table leg flew across the room, narrowly missing the woman's forehead as she clawed her way across the floor to the safety of the fireplace.

Miss Jayne huddled in the corner. Her arms covered her face and muffled her screams. She didn't see Jake light the fire. Didn't see the first embers fly. It was the frenzied barking of Jake's dog that opened her eyes to this fiery reality.

Bristle danced back and forth just outside the door, yapping, howling, eyes tracking Jake as he pitched chunks of splintered wood at the flames.

Cinders caught flight, danced, swirled.

From the corner of her eye, Jayne caught sight of the curtains burning at the dry sink's window.

She grabbed at the stone hearth and pulled herself upright, rushed to the sink, and threw the bucket of dishwater at the fabric's flames. Smoke seeped from her target and grey flecks of burnt homespun took soft flight.

She swung around in time to witness Jake hunch down and reach his hand into the flames.

His eyes held steady on the searing orange and red that explored his fingers, his palm.

Calloused skin soon blistered.

Shock, disbelief, the insanity of the moment slowed Miss Jayne's thoughts and reaction until finally—*finally*—she took action, pushing Jake away from the fire, grabbing the dishwater bucket, and racing past Bristle to the well outside.

With the bucket full, she fled back to the fire and threw water on Jake's hand, then at the flames.

A second, a third, then a fourth bucket of water finally conquered the flames, their demise evident in the eerie sizzle of retreat.

Billows of smoke clouded her view of Jake, of Bristle, of hope.

Bristle's bark quieted to a whimper as he edged his way into the kitchen, tail hung low, eyes alert, scruff raised.

Next to Miss Jayne, the dog pressed his shoulder firmly against her skirt. She bent down and cradled the dog tight as she choked against smoke and fear.

Jake remained on the floor, his weight balanced on one arm, his rage still racing. His brittle blue eyes surveyed the scene, and after a barely perceptible shake of his head he struggled to his feet and staggered. He raked his uninjured hand through his hair as he realized the damage before him.

"What have I done?" he questioned himself. "What have I done?"

Jake staggered again, this time as he walked through steaming ashes towards the door. He leaned against its frame and gulped in night air. A heartbeat later he was gone.

* * *

The woman knew the dog wanted to follow his master. She also knew Jake needed to roam.

"Stay, Bristle. Stay."

She was grateful that the dog obeyed.

The two slept outside. Miss Jayne, wrapped in a smoke-choked blanket, propped herself on the porch stairs. With her head settled against a railing beam, she fell into a restless slumber.

Occasionally, her head bobbed up as she strained against sleep to search the horizon for Jake. The night air held nothing beyond stillness and cricket chatter.

Bristle settled on the ground close to Miss Jayne's bare feet. He, too, searched the distance for his man.

Nighttime's chill was the least of Jake's burdens.

He grappled with his demons most of the night, stumbling over clods of dirt and hardened furrows, finally dropping to the ground in the middle of his unturned corn field. Plant shards scraped his forehead peak to brow. His shoulder shared the same bloodied injury after its hard landing on the remnant corn stalks from last fall's harvest.

The night sky slowly released him from his drunken stupor. No alcohol filled his veins. Just grief. Guilt. Sins of anger layered with self-contempt.

As he sat up amidst dirt and toil and unplanted fields, he flashed back to the fire. It burned hard. Burned deep. Stung his hand and smelled on his skin.

He wished to remain there, to become part of the soil. It was all he had to offer.

Ashes to ashes. Dust to dust. Fodder for the crows.

Burnt Pine

The house smelled of burnt pine. Remnants of the table were now a charred epitaph of loss. Its greyed dander mingled with the sunlight streaming through the front window. Its soul lay as soot on the possessions of the living.

Miss Jayne spent the morning sweeping up ashes—the recollections of family meals and card games at night. One dustpan at a time, she slipped the cinereous memories into a yellowed pillowcase, threadbare, but up to the task. At the edge of the field behind the barn, she let the ashes go and watched the char scatter across clumps of bindweed and puncturevine.

Next, Miss Jayne scrubbed at the floorboards. The fire had burned through some, left others stained black. Of course, this portion of the floor was ruined. Of course, it would need to be replaced. Still, she scrubbed.

After the scrub water was tossed out back, the rag hung to dry, Miss Jayne faced the rest of her home. She wiped down the grey that had filtered across each room, though she avoided Jake's room. She wouldn't, couldn't, enter that space. She pulled out rugs and draped them on the clothesline and beat out the stench of smoke as best she could. She washed curtains and bedding and placed them to dry.

At dusk, Miss Jayne found her way to the front porch swing and settled into weariness, her rasped eyes diligent in watching the darkening horizon, scanning the distance for her son.

* * *

Jake's night sequestered in the field had brought him sleep. The first real sleep he'd had since his son died.

Mid-morning's light pulled at his thoughts, though he resisted consciousness for quite some time. When the jagged numbness in his arm became unbearable, he rolled onto his back and faced the sun. He groaned when he heard Bristle barking in the distance. A few minutes later, the dog pawed at Jake's shoulder and licked his face.

"I'm awake, Bristle. Leave me be."

Bristle licked him again.

"Criminy, dog." Jake swung his right arm over and grabbed his dog by the scruff. "Just let me be."

The two faced off. Jake held his position, propped on his left arm, right hand tight on Bristle's scruff. Bristle showed no fear.

"Fine, you win." Jake let go of the dog and settled back to the ground. Bristle lay next to him, his head on Jake's leg. Eventually, Jake rested the back of his blistered hand on the dog and took comfort from his friend while he contemplated heaven, hell. And home.

* * *

Jake and the dog made slow progress back to the cabin, stopping midday alongside the river to quench the dog's thirst and clean Jake's wounded hand. His left palm and fingers were a mixture of sootskin and blood. Blisters resided next to raw flesh, a disparity that traveled around his thumb and across his wrist. The wound blazed with pain and any hint of breeze pierced his skin like a thousand shards of glass until Jake's jaw clenched in anguish and he gave in to soothing the pain with the cool water of the river.

Kneeling on the bank, injured hand submerged in the slow trickling water, the other inch thick in mud, Jake studied his face in the languid current. His dark hair fell in hanks, wavy from humidity and miskeep. Crease lines had ventured above his brow, aging him past his twenty-four years. Stubble shadowed his jawline and he distrusted the eyes staring back at him, for their deep-set fatigue held an angry mindset he was unaccustomed to. And yet, those haunted, hollow eyes were indeed his, he was sure, for each blink of the eye reflected in the water, each chaplipped grimace in the neighboring ripples, matched the actions of his own face.

He'd near forgotten what it was like to look at oneself. The hand mirror he'd given Hannah on their wedding day remained face down on their bureau, untouched in the room he couldn't bear to walk into since her death in January.

The only other mirror in the house was in his mama's room. The last time Jake saw that mirror, it was draped in black cloth. Who knew if his mother had yet lifted the veil of mourning from the mirror's surface, though he supposed she had, considering her decision to set the supper table.

Jake's gut wrenched at thoughts of the table. Worse yet, his actions towards the table. And his mother.

She was moving on, ready to uproot herself from a slag pile of loss to land faith first onto cultivated soil.

She'd been meeting with the local traveling preacher, a man who strummed his faith through Presbyterian teachings with a Pentecostal twist. After each meeting she'd come home with religious chatter flinging from her tongue. Talk of redemption and forgiveness and God's gift of grace.

In the past month, religion had become her favorite subject. She talked about it all the time, tossing out breadcrumbs of scripture into Jake's path, hoping he'd peck at one, then another.

Did she think he'd feast on over-reckoned miracles until he was bellyful of conviction with his ass in a pew each Sunday?

She'd talk about Abel and Lucy Morteson and their struggle to have a child. For years Lucy was left barren and, like Abraham and Sarah of the Bible, the couple prayed to be blessed with a child.

The miracle finally happened and six weeks ago a brown-haired, brown-eyed boy was born to the delighted parents.

Jake was well-aware of the baby's entrance into the world, and word at Buckley's Tavern told that Baby Morteson resembled neither of his blond-haired, blue-eyed parents. Folks in town sure did notice the baby was the spitting image of Ernesto Garcia, the Mexican who'd roamed through Idaho looking for work and was hired on by Abel to clear fields in the acreage above their home.

Some miracle. Abel wasn't able, but someone else sure was. Perhaps Abel would see heredities more clear when his son showed summer skin all year long.

One day after church, Miss Jayne had gushed on and on how Lorraine Jefferson hadn't seen her wedding ring since spring planting. Lo and behold, in early May when Lorraine was bringing in the harvest of early season vegetables, she spotted something shining within a tangle of green.

"It's as if the angels plunked that ring right there in the spinach patch just for her to see," Miss Jayne had said.

"Maybe if Lorraine had plunked her ring on the bedside table before choring in the garden, she wouldn't have lost it in the first place," Jake had replied.

Breadcrumb after breadcrumb, the sermons tumbled down like snow in a blizzard. His mother's latest proclamation was just three days ago.

"Fear can keep you up all night long," she'd said, "but faith makes one fine pillow."

He had tuned her out and set to work chopping firewood.

So far, a pillow of bitterness suited him just fine.

Lye Soap

Jake, his burnt hand bandaged and awkward, replaced the floorboards. He oiled the hinges on the front door, cleared out a wasp nest looming near the garden, and trampled the twenty or so mole hills that had popped up in and near trails to the barn and corncrib. He tidied up the tools he'd left astray the past few weeks and put to order the outbuildings and stacked last year's cut of firewood close to the cabin.

Miss Jayne was grateful for these things, these indications that Jake was becoming himself again. She presumed this returned appetite for work was fed by a guilty conscience. Perhaps that guilty conscience would help him set trusting eyes on the future.

On this morning three days past the fire, he'd already filled up buckets with lye water dispensed from the ash hopper and set up a kettle atop firewood ready to be lit. He'd also gathered the crocks of lard she'd saved and rendered the past few months, then taken them outside where she and Irene Bauer would work together making lye soap from the ingredients.

The task of soap making was long and arduous, not to mention foul-smelling, and Jake usually complained that it would be easier and wiser to simply buy cakes of soap from the mercantile in town.

On this day, Jake kept his peace.

Anton Bauer dropped off his wife and their seven-year-old son Hyrum just as Jake lit the firewood. Morning was slipping away quickly, and Anton had little time for small talk before his trip to town, so he abridged his usual banter to *guten tag* and a reminder for his son to *achten sie auf ihre manieren*, which Jake took to mean, *behave yourself.*

Jake hadn't known Hyrum would be tagging along. Usually, the women used this day to catch up on gossip and provide Irene a much-deserved break from her thriving household of children.

The boy could hinder his plan.

Jake called out to the boy who was busy chasing chickens. "Hyrum, I need your help. Come on over."

Hyrum reversed course and ran towards Jake.

"What can I help you with, Jake? I'll bet it's hard to do your chorin' with your hand all bandaged up."

Jake looked from the boy to his hand and back again. "My hand's fine. I'm headed out to do some hunting. Would you mind taking care of Bristle for me? He's training to be a farm dog, not a hunting dog. Don't want him getting hurt."

"Can I take him down to the riverbank?"

"Nah, best stay clear of the river. You two play near the house and far from where your ma and Miss Jayne are working. Don't want either of you getting close to that lye water. And be sure to keep hold of Bristle's rope." Jake secured a rope to the dog's collar. "Like I said, I don't want him running off towards me while I'm hunting."

"I'll take real good care of him, Jake. I promise."

"I won't be back until nightfall. You'll be back at your farm by then, so I guess this is goodbye." Jake swallowed hard and, almost an afterthought, he tousled the boy's hair. "Take good care of my dog, son. Take real good care."

* * *

With his rifle in hand, Jake crossed the barnyard and veered around a stand of Ponderosa pines. He didn't look back at his mother or the boy or his dog. And he didn't find relief in the shade from the torturous sun.

Truth be told, he preferred the torture. He deserved every ounce of condemnation the sun could bring.

Lying about a hunting trip was just one more transgress to add to his pile of sin. What he was about to do would topple that pile and spill it across the devil's front doorstep.

There was no going back. He hurt too much. There was no going back.

Jake continued his route past knapweed and blue asters and scrub brush until he reached the cemetery plot. He had faced the first cross daily for seven months now. He had cursed it. He had blasphemed it. Once again, he stared at it, willing it to change forms, to be a desert mirage lost on a country farm. Despite Jake's wishes, the cross remained a leaden memory of burying his wife and newborn daughter.

The front brim of Jake's hat was soaked through with sweat, and the metal of his gun could burn virgin hands. He laid both the gun and his hat on the ground then checked this first cross—the largest cross—for sturdiness. It stood firm. As firm as the day he planted it. The second, smaller cross had not faired the same. Planted just two weeks ago, it stood tilted, like the lopsided smile of his little boy. Jake moved to straighten it then changed his mind. The stance of the cross was a fitting tribute to his blond-haired son.

Retrieving the gun, Jake walked between the two crosses and sat at the edge of the mounded dirt. In front of him lay a valley chosen to be the final view for his family and it felt right for Jake to see this view as he settled himself between the graves of his son Jackson, buried six days shy of his fourth birthday, and his wife Hannah, who held their newborn daughter in her arms.

The grass and clover had spread across the first grave and a few mid-summer daisies were in bloom at the base of its cross. Jake had taken great care in watering the plot and removing any bramble weeds that might spoil the soft carpet wrapped across Hannah and the baby.

Jackson's grave still lay bare of the carpet of green. The intrusive star thistle that flourished in this part of the country would be the first thing that would try to thrive in this ground. Jake raked his fingers through the soil, intent on interrupting any thistles from growing in the next few days.

He could stop the barbed plant this time, but in a few days, the wicked weed would take control of this tiny family plot.

Jake planted the butt of his rifle into the ground. For the time being, the stock of the gun would rest against his leg. Before he could carry out his duty, Jake needed time to condemn himself. And to condemn God.

A viperous prayer simmered in Jake's mind. Seven months of blame towards a God that would take away two of the most precious parts of his life. Two weeks of blame for himself—the father that could not save his son from a crushing wagon wheel.

Jackson's grave was testimony of this father's inability to protect. And the family's kitchen table, once caked with Jackson's blood, was this father's daily undoing. The town's doctor had tried to save the child. Tragically, no medical degree, no sawblade, no makeshift surgeon's table could save the leg, or the boy, from gangrene.

16

Memories choked Jake's thoughts and sweat traced lines where tears should have been. He wiped at the wetness, replacing it with the soil from his son's grave. The memories were too vivid, so Jake focused on the sounds around him instead. At first, he heard the same starved silence that had filled his cabin for the past fourteen days. Jake couldn't handle any more of that harrowing quiet. He listened more intently, greedily soaking in any sounds that would silence his memories without drowning his intent.

Nature's whisperings would keep him sane long enough to pull the trigger.

Quail in the distance, a murmuring river, the drone of bees searching sustenance. Jake would carry these sounds to his grave, though he expected the last thing he would hear before the blast of the gun would be his own heartbeat pounding in his ears.

It was time, before courage betrayed him.

Jake moved into position. His hands were resolute, having mentally practiced the motions of placing the gun and stretching his arm and pulling the trigger.

He placed the tip of the rifle barrel into his mouth, flinching as the taste of metallic smoke coated his tongue.

Who knew so many of his senses would be tied to this one final act?

Yes, he expected his heartbeat to be the final sound he would carry to the grave. But even the pounding of his heart couldn't drown out the woman's screams carried on the wind.

The devil's greed begged him to stay, rifle firmly planted in the soil, trigger at the ready—no, trigger pulled back and gun fired. A stronger greed kicked him into action. The screaming continued and as he rounded the cluster of trees in his race towards the cabin, he collided with the neighbor boy, no doubt sent on a mission to find Jake.

Jake grabbed the child by the shoulders and stooped to the level of the boy's horrified face. "Hyrum, what happened? Is somebody hurt?"

"It's Miss Jayne. Lye water got all over her face. I think she's hurt real bad."

Jake sorted through the boy's rushed words. Realization erupted. Jake raced to the house with Hyrum following behind, the little boy's legs no match to Jake's frantic speed.

* * *

17

"Quick. We need to get her inside," Irene said as she poured a bucketful of well water over Miss Jayne's eyes.

It killed Jake to watch his mother's face contort in pain as the water splayed against the mottled blisters that had already formed around her eyes, across her forehead, down her cheeks.

"Jake, we need to get her face wrapped to keep infection from setting in. There's fresh linens inside."

Unworldly, muzzled screams busted through his mother's tightgripped lips. Her screams took Jake back to his wife's childbirth cries. The battered, agonizing, horrific wails that accompany the delivery of life, though in Hannah's case, the battlecries were followed by the silent strains of their blue-faced child, then Hannah's own silence.

"Jake?" Irene questioned him, still pouring water over his mother's burning wounds.

"No, we're taking her to Doc," Jake countered. He ran inside, grabbed some tea towels, then delivered them to Irene. "Hold these over her face. I'll get the wagon."

Irene knew there was nothing more that the doctor, as well-schooled as he was, could do to help her dear friend. She also knew that Jake's son might still be alive if Doc had been available to treat the boy directly after the accident rather than four days after the fact. That perhaps Jake's wife could have been saved by university-trained hands.

Still, she hesitated.

"I'm not taking any chances, Irene. She's all I've got left."

Irene shielded Miss Jayne's face with the towels as she led her friend towards the wagon. Jake had already raced to the horse corral where he barked out orders to Hyrum to help hitch the team.

The boy hurried to keep up with Jake as they grabbed halters from the tack room and quickly put them on each horse. As they pulled the horses to the wagon, Jake mentally ticked off the time it would take to hitch the horses and be on the way.

Too long. We're taking too long.

Jake began on one side, hitching O'Malley on the left. Sweat and frustration and his bandaged hand made the usual job nearly impossible, and he cursed as he finished adjusting the leads.

He checked again on Miss Jayne. He could see spots of blood seeping through the layers of the towels that Irene gently held to his mother's face. He cursed again and moved to the right side of the wagon, intent on hitching Lou, but he found the job already done. Hyrum checked the bit in Lou's mouth while a girl—a girl Jake had never seen before—made the last of the lead adjustments.

Once the team was ready, the girl backed away from the scene, her eyes paralyzed on Jake, her chin quivering.

Jake stared back until the mystery girl ran off into the woods.

The Stranger

The news from Dr. Matthews was bad. Severe burns to the skin would leave his mother's face and hands scarred forever. And blindness. His mother had suffered irreparable blindness. The caustic lye had damaged her corneas far beyond the possibility of healing.

A few hours ago, Jake had gleaned from his despondency the will to end his life. Now, from his mother's blindness, he needed to recover the will to live.

Jake returned home. He mustered his way through evening chores, replaying the day, always ending the scene with the screams of his mother and the mystery girl's haunted eyes. Several times, he searched the horizon of fields and trees and rolling hills, never once capturing sight of the girl. He had seen her, hadn't he? He had stood across from her, bewildered by her presence. Hyrum had seen her. Irene had seen her. Miss Jayne had seen her. No, Miss Jayne would never see her. Jake threw a fist at the cabin wall. Miss Jayne would never see anything again.

The knock at the front door was barely audible and Jake questioned whether the trespass was in the control of humans or if the ghosts of the day were playing more unsavory tricks. The second knock was more powerful, more human-like, and Bristle danced at the doorway, irreverent to his role as a guard dog.

The mystery girl stood just outside, a gangly waif lost in a dress three times her size. In her hands she held Jake's rifle.

Her eyes searched the ground as she cautiously handed the gun to Jake. "I didn't want the boy to find it. Might hurt himself."

Jake took the gun and placed it against the wall. His eyes didn't leave the girl.

"Your mother? Is she all right?" The girl continued to stare at the ground, her voice as thin as her waistline.

"She's blind."

The girl quickly looked up, her face bewildered.

20

"I'm—I'm sorry." Her eyes drifted back to the floor. "I'm so sorry." With those whispered words, she was gone.

* * *

The girl ran. She ran long and hard, all the while denying the pain ripping through her lower leg. Once she reached her crude campsite, she fell to the ground grabbing her leg, her pain released as a mangled groan.

"Why? Why did you blind the woman?" She screamed her hatred to the moon, choking back sobs and gasping for air. More quietly she demanded, "Why? Why? Why?"

The pain in her leg was searing. All day, fever had sent her from flashes of heat to aching moments of chilling cold. She checked her leg, gingerly touching the wound. How could such a small cut create such cursing pain? Back home, a thousand miles away and a lifetime ago, her grandfather would have known what to do with the cut, the blood, the pus, the fever. Here, in the middle of someone else's wilderness, the girl had no boiling water, no poultice, no magic herbs to ward off infection. The only thing she could do was keep the wound clean, bind it with fabric torn from her dress hem, and wait.

* * *

Jake paced in front of the fireplace, hands clenching and unclenching as his mind raced between thoughts of his mother and the girl.

The girl.

One more complication in his life.

He knew what his mother would do. Find the girl, bring her back to the cabin, nurse her to a healthy weight. Over the years, Miss Jayne had become a surrogate mother time and again, taking in strangers and adopting them as kin.

Jake wasn't like his mother. A few hours before, he was trying to escape the world through the blast of a '66 Winchester. He had no right or desire to try saving some stray. And he certainly didn't have the patience to nurse a drifter that would probably steal him blind.

In a couple of days, he'd take on the role of nursemaid to his mother. That was already more than he could handle.

After an hour of cursing the day, cursing his family's misfortune, and cursing the girl, Jake landed guilt-first into a cauldron of sympathy. He gathered biscuits left over from that morning's breakfast, found some beef jerky, dried plums, and a jar of apple cider, filled a canteen with fresh water from the well, and set out to find the girl. Jake had no idea where he'd find her, though he assumed she'd be somewhere between the cabin and the family plot. Jake would have to track her in the dark.

Turned out he didn't need to. Bristle was eager to lead the way.

Once out the door, Bristle raced to the south, in the general direction of Hannah's grave. Jake tried to keep up but, despite the moonlit path, his speed was hampered by the flour sack filled with food and the wool blanket he carried across his shoulder.

As Jake crested the hill, he could hear Bristle barking in the distance. He followed the sound, carefully cutting his way through a few tree stumps and surfaced tree roots. He entered the thicket of evergreens, losing sight of the walking path as the moon disappeared behind the darkened trees.

Jake relied on his boyhood memories of the woods as he struggled through the fallen limbs and snagging vines. He entered a small clearing as he drew closer to where he'd last heard Bristle. At last, he could hear the voice of the girl as it lilted across the night air.

"I'm glad you're here, boy" she said to the dog. "I really need a friend tonight. Not sure how much longer I can do this." She sounded tired, her words came in bits and pieces. Jake held his position, not wanting to scare the girl. Maybe if she kept talking to Bristle, Jake would learn why she was hiding in his woods.

"Wish we had a fire." She sleepily continued her conversation. "Something to keep both of us warm." The dog lay next to the girl, blanketing her against the deepest cold of the clear summer night.

"Glad you're here to keep me warm."

Jake could barely hear these last murmured words. He waited for the girl to fall asleep before building a small fire under the watchful eyes of his dog.

After the fire was built and Jake was sure the girl was in a deep slumber, he gently tucked the wool blanket around her, noting the paleness of her forehead and the redness of her cheeks. He gave Bristle a good ear scratch and a piece of jerky, then found a stump to sit on and set to watching over his new ward.

Near midnight, the girl woke with a start. Bristle sensed her panic and licked her hand, giving what gentle comfort he could. Jake stayed still, his eyes intent on reading her reaction to him, the fire.

The girl noticed the fire first and Jake watched her eyes follow the sparks of light lifting into the sky. When the girl saw Jake, she sat full up and scrambled backwards in retreat. A seven-foot log stopped her progress and she grunted in pain.

"I brought you some food. Built a fire. Thought you could use a bit of warmth." Jake slowly opened the bag at his feet and tossed her the biscuits secured in a thin cotton napkin. The bundle landed to her right. The girl quickly glanced at the package, then back at Jake. Slowly, she inched her hand towards the package and unwrapped it. For the first time, she noticed the blanket that now hung around her legs.

"Thank you. For the food. And the blanket." She broke off a small piece of the biscuit and cautiously placed it in her mouth. "You've got a good dog." Bristle nudged his nose against her arm, and she ran a hand through the dog's tousled mane.

"His name's Bristle. I wondered where he'd been running off to the past few nights. Thought he'd found himself a girlfriend." Jake gave a quick, half-hearted laugh. "I guess he did."

"He found me a few nights ago. I shared some blackberries with him. Never thought a dog would eat blackberries. Turns out your dog loves them." The girl kept stroking the dog's fur. Bristle smiled back with content. "That night I fell asleep, thinking he'd head back home. Next morning, he was still here. Kept me warm all night long."

The girl took another bite of the biscuit. Conversation stopped. Uneasiness lingered. Jake couldn't take his eyes off the girl. He figured her to be fourteen, maybe fifteen years old. All skin and bones with a tangle of dark, curly hair that overwhelmed her thin face. He tried to remember the color of her eyes.

"I brought some other food for you." Jake again reached down for the flour sack. "Some dried fruit, jerky, cider. And there's water in the canteen." Jake placed the sack at her side. When he noticed the fear return to her face, he made a quick retreat back to the stump on the opposite side of the fire. "There's a tin cup inside for the cider."

"Thank you." The girl reached for the drink, trying to hide the tremor in her hand as she poured the amber liquid into the cup. She took a sip and willed the nourishment to chase away the infection coursing through her leg.

"It's good. The cider is good." She sipped slowly, knowing that the lack of food over the past several days had weakened her stomach.

"Look, mister . . ."

"Jake, my name's Jake."

"Jake, I didn't mean to trespass. I just needed a place to stay for a few nights, until . . ." She cut off her sentence. No use revealing any more information. It was bad enough that someone else had spotted her. Now word would get out that a runaway had been in the area. People would talk. McNally would hear. "I'll be gone by morning."

"Why don't you come back to the cabin? You'll have a nice bed, a warm fire."

"No. No. I can't do that."

"Look, it's cold out here. Dangerous. We've had reports of a bear in the area."

"I appreciate the offer, but I'll be fine. Thank you for the food. I hope your mother . . ." She bit her lip. "Well, I hope your mother recovers best she can."

Jake realized that no amount of coaxing would change the stranger's mind. He also realized that she was putting on a brave front, masking her fear of something or someone. Or both. "I'll head back then. Bristle can stay with you tonight. He'll keep you warm." Jake added a few more sticks to the small fire, making sure there would be enough timber nearby to keep the fire going through the night.

"Mister? I mean Jake. Do you have a knife with you? One I could borrow overnight? I promise to drop it off at your cabin in the morning. Along with the blanket and canteen, of course."

Jake rolled her request through his mind. Why would this girl need a knife? For food? Possibly. For protection? He took the knife and its sheath from his belt. When he reached her side, he knelt on one knee, trying not to frighten her with his height.

"Keep the knife. Blanket and canteen, too. Sounds like you've got a long journey ahead."

* * *

The girl waited several minutes before touching the knife Jake had left at her side. She adjusted the blanket around her shoulders. Bristle stayed next to her, a comforting presence of warm fur and understanding eyes.

She knew that every moment she waited was another moment closer to possible death. She had watched a man die from infection once. Her grandfather had cared for him for several days, cauterizing the wound, applying poultice after poultice. It was more than apparent the man had let the infection go too long before seeking treatment. No amount of medicine or prayer or words from Grandfather's bible could bring him back from his tortured fever. Regardless, her grandfather had tried to save the man's life.

Now she faced the same dire circumstance, knowing if the wound wasn't cleaned out and cauterized, the infection would progress, and her fate would be sealed.

Stop. Don't think of that. She silently chastised herself. Death was not an option. Death meant that McNally would win.

She pulled the knife from the sheath—a Barlow knife, like the one her grandfather had owned—and struggled with the nail nick to pull out the blade. She took a long drink from the canteen then wiped the sweat from her brow.

She forced her mind upon the plan of action. Inch by inch she crept to the edge of the fire and positioned herself next to it. She drew up her skirt and gingerly untied the wrap around her shin, wincing as the bandage pulled at the sticky scab, reopening the wound.

Her stomach lurched—at the sight of the pus-filled blood or the thought of what she was about to do, it didn't matter. Her fate was in the hands of the stranger's knife.

At this point, hesitation would only prolong the pain. The girl plunged the blade of the knife into the flames. The blistering heat gnawed at her skin. She held firm until the steel blade burned hot, then used it to ply through the wound, digging below the scab, through the swelling, until both pus and blood flowed freely over her skin.

Sticky sweat caught in the girl's eyelashes and glinted in the dancing firelight, enough so that she couldn't distinguish between pus and blood. She squeezed the wound, squeezed it as hard as her tired muscles allowed, hoping to drain as much poison from her leg as possible. In the night air, she caught a putrid scent. Was it decay from the woods? The remnant scent of a scavenged animal? Or was it from her wound? The scent of gangrene? No. No, it couldn't be. It was a small wound. Such a small wound.

The girl tore another length of fabric from her skirt, fashioned it into a slip noose, then placed it around her leg just below the cut. She held the knife blade in the flame again. She needed the blade to be red hot to cauterize the wound.

She gulped in air and plunged the flat edge of the knife against the wound, forcing her right hand to hold it in place as her left hand tightened the noose. She fought back the waves of nausea and darkness that threatened to overcome her sensibilities. The knife was in place, the pain screamed through her skin. She needed to further tighten the noose. Needed to keep the blade in place long enough to sear the skin. Needed to make sure the job was complete.

* * *

Jake watched, awestruck by the audacity the girl showed in handling the knife. He now understood the reason for the fever on her brow.

Watching from a distance, he flinched and clenched his good hand and flinched again as he followed her movements, her intensity of purpose. He nearly shouted his alarm as the girl dug the blade deeper and deeper into her skin. Several times he nearly leaped from his position in the woods, ready to take over the makeshift surgery.

With each motion the girl took, Jake flashed back to memories of the night when his tiny son, ravaged by pain and fever, was quieted by gangrene's poison to the point the child barely moved, his heart barely beat. Images of the doctor—finally discovered a few miles away at someone else's emergency—arriving with his arsenal of forceps and saws and knives and suture wire. Fractured sequences of Jake and his mother holding down his son, so weak, so fragile, as the doctor made the initial cut, then stroked the blade back and forth, back and forth, until the amputation was complete. Then the futility of time, of waiting, of praying, of sharing coffee laced with liquor with the doctor so both men could ease their burden of knowing the amputation had come too late.

Jake finished the girl's surgery. The girl woke midway through then lost consciousness again, but not before her screams of pain pierced the trees. He cut strips from the flour sack, bound them around the wound. Wiped the blood from his knife, returned it to his belt. Threw dirt on the fire, watched the embers fade. The night animals could have the rest of the food.

He lifted the girl and threw her over his shoulder. He'd finish his night watch back in the cabin.

The Girl

Jake deposited the girl onto his bed, lit a lantern, placed it near the bedside, and proceeded to clean the skin surrounding the girl's wound. The dim light from the lantern displayed more to the wound than the firelight had. Blood poisoning for sure, but what kind? He looked closer for signs of gangrene, smelled at the wound for odor. Her skin looked different than his son's had. Thank God.

He moved on to washing her hands and arms. The color of dirt turned out to be skin the shade of leather.

Excepting the settler's clothes, someone spotting her in the distance might think she was Indian. Closer inspection of her ink black hair showed a shade of red at her temples and part line.

Jake gently wiped at her face as he tried to place a name to the memory of her eyes. Earlier in the day, when she'd brought his rifle to his front door, he had been startled by their color. Almost mesmerized. But he could neither remember the color or why it had drawn him in.

The girl's clothes were tattered, stained with sweat. The bodice, with its trim of worn lace and sunfaded buttons, hung loose against her frame. Faint reminders of the homespun's print were indiscernible in the quiet light.

He figured he should slip clean clothes on her and place this dress in the burn pile to be rid of the infection's poison.

He retrieved one of Miss Jayne's nightgowns from her closet and decided on the best way to get the girl changed while keeping her modesty intact.

Jake nudged at the girl, waking her enough that she responded to his instructions to change out of her dress while he turned away. She struggled with the buttons of her dress, then slowly slipped off the bodice and let it drop to her waist. The effort of slipping into the nightgown sapped her strength and she slumped back onto the bed with only one arm through a sleeve.

Jake sat on the edge of the bed and slowly lifted her right shoulder. He willed his coarse hands to gentleness as he moved her arm into the sleeve. Holding the base of her neck, he felt raised impressions on her skin. He pulled the neckline back enough for study. He found welts of scarring far too familiar to a cattleman.

"Blinded mercy," he mumbled to himself. "Somebody branded you."

He looked again at the marks. Sure enough, he was able to make out the initials N and M positioned in a distinct pattern.

"What kind of inferno have you been through?" he quietly asked the sleeping girl.

He shifted the girl back onto the pillow. With his eyes cast in the opposite direction, Jake pulled the trail-weary dress past her legs. She grimaced at the movement of her injured leg. He whispered, "Hush, you're going to be all right." Then he eased the nightgown over her lower half. Once she was properly covered, he returned his sights to her slight frame. Miss Jayne's nightgown barely covered the girl's knees. Not a surprise considering his mother stood several inches smaller than his six-foot frame. And if memory served, this girl stood nearly as tall as Jake.

No matter the length of the gown, it would serve its purpose while she slept.

With the girl tucked under a quilt, Jake deposited her dress on the outside burn pile. He would wait until tomorrow to set it ablaze. Tonight, he needed to tame the girl's fever.

Miss Jayne kept a supply of remedies in a box on a shelf in the kitchen. Crushed elm bark and yeast and rosemary and herbs and oils he had no names for were lined up, at the ready for medicinal purposes. The last time any of the jars had been opened was when Jake's little boy needed his grandmother's healing hand.

Despite her vast knowledge of frontier medicine, nothing had saved the little boy's life.

Now Jake would be the one depended on for nursing. This night and for the next few days for a mysterious stranger with black copper hair. In a few days and forevermore, for his blinded mother.

The jars weren't marked, so Jake depended on his sense of smell to remember the ingredients for his mother's fever tonic. He mixed laudanum for the pain and herbs for the fever with heated water from the stove and let them steep. Once cooled, he again woke the girl. He lifted the cup to her lips and encouraged her to sip the bitter liquid. She took in some, not enough. It would have to do.

He removed the bandage from the girl's leg and smeared a grayish brown, almost tar-like poultice across the cut and the inflamed skin. Though deep in sleep, the girl still winced in pain.

Feverish chills swept through the girl's body throughout the night, and she moaned from time to time. Jake let Bristle in and allowed him up on the bed to ease the girl. She realized the gesture and kept her arm draped around the dog's neck while he lay with his muzzle on her stomach.

Jake sat nearby in his mother's rocking chair retrieved from the front room and drifted between concern and closed-eye consciousness until sunrise.

In morning's light, the girl was able to take a full second dose of the laudanum mixture. Just barely. She drifted back to sleep as soon as her head hit the pillow.

After milking the cow, feeding the animals, and stoking the kitchen fire, Jake checked his charge one more time.

"What should I do, Bristle? Take her into town and let Doc examine her?" Bristle spread his forelegs across the girl in protest. "Well, there's my answer. Take care of her while I'm gone, boy. I'll hurry back."

* * *

Doc Matthews' office was set on the edge of town, just across from the barbershop. For years, Willie Shackleford acted as town barber and makeshift doctor, providing a shave one minute, bloodletting the next. Willie also claimed the duties of tooth extractor and wound surgeon, plus folks joked that he could bandage up any mishaps his straight razor might inflict. Willie's dual practice took a serious downturn when the newly matriculated Frank Matthews arrived in town. The barber had never been much of a doctor and, when Doc Matthews put out his shingle, most folks in town steered clear of Willie's services for want of educated care.

Jake avoided the glaring look Willie gave his strayaway patients and the ones who'd never set foot inside his practice by avoiding the main street and approaching the doctor's residence by way of an alley. The alley, just wide enough for a buggy or wagon to travel through, zigzagged behind the livery yard, an attorney's office, the post office, and a dry goods store. Doc's building was situated on the corner of the next block and Jake knocked on the back door, knowing it was early in the day and Doc would most likely be in his residence at the back of the building rather than at his practice situated in front.

Doc's wife Emmeline opened the door, showing off her toothy smile and flour-specked apron.

"Mornin', Jake. Please come in."

"Mornin', Emmeline. How's Mother doing?"

"Fine, she's doing just fine. Frank gave her some medicine to help her sleep through the night and I just finished serving her some breakfast." Her eyes traveled to his injured hand. "You ready for me to take a look at your hand yet?"

Jake shifted, tucking his bandaged fingers into his back pocket.

"Did she get enough to eat? You know Ma, she'll lack on food when her mind starts to worry."

"You, Jake Adamsen, are stubborn. And yes, your mother ate enough for now. Her appetite will return some as she starts to heal." Emmeline gave him an encouraging smile. "Doc and I will take good care of her, I promise."

The two walked towards the kitchen. "Now, how about you, Jake? Could you use a bit of breakfast? I made plenty of flapjacks," she said.

"No, ma'am, I'm fine. I appreciate your thoughtfulness. Right now, I'd just like to spend some time with Mama."

"Of course. I'll show you the way."

Emmeline walked him down the hallway to a door that led from quaint country home to new-fangled doctor's office. Jake knew what to expect of the office. He'd been there enough over the past three years and knew that when Doc Matthews had left the big city on the East Coast to become a small-town country doctor, he'd brought every piece of medical equipment he could muster.

"Wait right here, Jake," Emmeline said. "I'll make sure your mother's ready for visitors."

Jake studied the small room. It was more of an examination room than an office, he supposed. The slender exam table atop a bureau of drawers was padded for comfort and had an extension to accommodate a person's height. Two metal rods were attached on each side of the table near the extension. The rods rose several inches above the table, and each was fitted with an elongated piece of metal that Jake guessed to be some sort of foot press.

He cared not to think what that particular contraption was used for.

Doc kept his rolltop in the corner, piled high with books and papers and a few brown bottles of oft-used medicines. Jake studied the labels. A bottle of Ayer's Sarsaparilla, touted as a tonic water to purify the blood, quicken the appetite, and make the weak strong. Two bottles of ginger brandy with handmade labels, probably Doc's own recipe. Magee's Emulsion, a remedy Jake became all too familiar with during a bout of pneumonia.

The glass-fronted hutch, filled with bottles of Beecham's Pills and porcelain jars of creams and salves and ointments, stood near the exam table. A folding case of medical tools stood open on top. Doc also kept a human skull atop the hutch, which most folks found objectionable. Jake held no problem with it, nor did he spread stories about the other anatomical specimens Doc kept hidden from the public eye.

Here it was, 1890, and folks still feared any knowledge or interest in anatomy.

Just outside the office, two wooden chairs and a spittoon stood alongside one wall, composing the waiting room, though most folks simply waited on Doc's front stoop. That's where Jake had waited for his mother's prognosis. Now, as he waited to see his mother, as the scent of alcohol and tonics folded in on him, he was ready to return to that post.

Doc Matthews walked through the door just as Jake began to make his exit.

"Somehow I knew you'd be here bright and early," Doc said.

"Would've been here earlier if the cow could milk itself," Jake replied. "Thanks again for taking care of Mama for me."

"Of course, of course. I wish the news was better about her condition."

"Me, too."

Jake picked up a book from Doc's desk and thumbed through it, deliberating his next set of words.

"Look, Doc, before I go in to see Mama, I'm wondering if you can help me out with another situation. I've got this foal that cut its leg up. The wound's looking pretty red and swollen. I'd hate for the infection to get worse. Was wondering if you might have some salve I could put on her cut."

"Well, Jake, knowing that you don't have any foals at your place right now, could you be talking about a two-legged, dark-haired filly?

31

One that stands tall and probably weighs the same as a hundred-pound sack of feed?"

"You've seen her."

"Yes, I spotted her south of the Bennett place a few days ago. She was in a gully picking huckleberries, eating them as fast as she could pick them. I'm sure she didn't expect any wagons to be driving down that washboard lane, but I was in the area, so I thought I'd stop in and see how Mrs. Bennett's asthma was doing."

"Did you talk to the girl?"

"No, as soon as she noticed me, she crouched down to hide. I pulled ahead a few yards, stopped and had myself a roadside picnic. But darn it all, I realized I wasn't so hungry and absentmindedly left my lunch pail behind. I left my sandwich, some fruit, and a big slab of mincemeat pie. By the time I returned from the Bennetts', the lunch pail was empty."

"You're a good man, Doc."

"Not that good. I was mighty sad to give up that piece of pie."

* * *

Emmeline returned as the two men finished their conversation.

"Thanks for waiting, Jake. Your mama wanted to freshen up some. She's ready to see you."

The two ventured into the next room. Again, small. Again, purely practical, except for two oil paintings Emmeline had insisted be hung on the wall across from the two beds kept in place for patients. Each painting depicted a field of purple camas lilies that bloomed wild across the prairie.

"Something to nurture patients back to health," she'd explained.

A chair had already been placed next to his mother's bed. Emmeline gestured towards it. Jake reluctantly sat, stood again, reversed position of the chair, and sat down again with his legs straddling the backrest.

"Good morning, Mama." Jake noticed how strands of his mother's golden hair framed the bandages wrapped around her face. "How are you feeling?"

"Lost."

"You know where you're at, don't you? At Doc and Emmeline's place in town?"

"Of course, I know where I'm at. I'm not lost in my location. I'm lost in my senses. Without my eyes, I don't know which way is up or my left from my right."

"Sure, you do," Jake assured. "You just need time to adjust. Your eyes are still talking to your brain. Pretty soon all the rest of your senses will start compensating."

"I'm not so sure about that, son." She held out her hand, trying to find his. "I don't even know where to find you."

"I'm right here, Mama." He reached for her hand and held tight. "I'll always be right here."

"You think on that, Son." She swallowed hard. "No one wants to be hobbled to an old woman with no eyes."

"Don't say that, Mama."

"It's true. People like me end up in institutions, asylums. You should stick me in some tiny room, chained to a bed."

"Stop it. That's not going to happen. I'd never do that to you. Not in this lifetime or the next."

"I'll become some feeble woman, needin' to be spoonfed and diapered like a baby. God, I don't want that. Please don't let that ever happen to me."

"I won't. I promise." With their hands still entwined, he placed a kiss on her fingers. "I promise, we'll figure this out. Somehow, we'll make it work."

Jackrabbit on the Run

Over the next two days, sleep was sparse for Jake. He tended to animals and hauled buckets of water to the garden. In between outdoor tasks, he kept the kitchen stove stoked and a kettle at the ready for boiling bandages and rags. Time inside the house was spent tending to the girl, worrying and wondering.

His worry bounced around like a jackrabbit on the run, bounding one way then the next. His thoughts mostly settled on his mother and the state she would be in for the rest of her days. Life on the farm was already a struggle. How would she find her way around the farmhouse? She wouldn't be able to take on most chores, wouldn't be able to draw water from the well or cook over a fire or help with planting season or harvest.

Whenever Jake did try to catch some sleep, he'd sit in his mother's rocker and focus on a plan, hoping his ruminations would merge with slumber, allowing his sleeping mind to somehow be enlightened in ways his fully conscious mind couldn't. Just as he'd start to nod off, the slightest of movements from the girl on the bed would have him drawing thoughts about her and the backstory she carried.

He didn't sense the girl was a thief, though he was positive she'd filched her share of food to survive, and he realized now that his mother had recently noted missing onions, cabbage, and green tomatoes from their own garden. He'd accounted those losses to wildlife. Miss Jayne had deemed the vanishments more likely from a human hand.

Snitching food from fields and gardens and hen houses—he'd have done the same thing given the circumstance. Condemning a body for the same crime you'd have committed reeked of hypocrisy. Besides, their own garden was bounteous this year, thanks to Miss Jayne's backbreaking work, and knowing the girl snatched huckleberries and blackberries from the thickets that grew dense across his family's land bothered him none. The plants grew of their own accord, and their roots settled this land long before his ma and pa had a snippet of an idea to claim it as their own.

The brand on the girl's neck puzzled him most. Jake considered the possibility that she was some rich miner's housekeep, a servant on the run from an inhumane employer.

"Blast it all," he complained to Bristle, "marking a brand on an employee—on any human being—is simply cruel."

He'd ran other theories about the mark on the girl's neck. Kidnapping, cruel parents, savage husband. One had to admit that darkness too often laid a heavy hand, turning humans toward menace and destruction, plights and brutalities, plunderings and wars. He could only guess what empoisoned this girl to run.

On the second morning, the girl ebbed in and out of sleep for several minutes. The silhouette of lace curtains painted her face with soft swirls of light. Jake pondered the gentleness that lay across her features, the angelic fortitude. Maybe God had sent an angel for this time of need. He dismissed the idea, deeming it more likely that his lack of sleep was manifesting itself as divine lunacy.

And yet.

The girl's lashes fluttered. Slowly she opened her eyes to focus on waking.

When her sight landed on Jake sitting in the corner, she bolted upright.

"Where am I?"

"Calm down. You're safe."

"How did I get here? Where are my things? How did I get inside your house?" She looked around. "This is your house, isn't it?"

"Yes. Well, more specifically, it's my mother's house."

"How did I . . ."

"Here, drink this tea and I'll explain," Jake said. She eyed him suspiciously. "The tea will help with the pain."

She accepted the cup, took a sip, and grimaced at the taste of the bitter liquid.

Jake urged her to take a few more sips. When the tea was nearly gone, he retrieved the cup from her shaking hands and set it on the floor.

"I carried you back from the woods," he said as he settled into the rocking chair. "You fainted while trying to cauterize that cut on your leg."

She threw back the blankets, cringing as she bent her knee for a better view of the wound.

"Is it poisoned?"

"It was looking pretty bad. The medicine Doc gave me helped draw out the poison and take down the swelling."

"Doc? You mean somebody else knows I'm here?"

"Yes."

"I can't be here." She pushed herself out of bed and took a tentative step. Jake caught her when she stumbled.

"Whoa, there. You're in no shape to travel."

"You don't understand. There's no way I can stay here. If he finds me here, it'd be dangerous to you and your ma."

"Who is looking for you?" Jake asked as he struggled to keep her from leaving. "What kind of danger are you in?"

"Let me go, mister. If he finds me here, he might . . . he'll . . ." She yawned, unable to fully finish her thoughts.

"Chasing me. Chasing. Hiding. I can't be here. I can't be home. Can't be anywhere."

"Well, you are here. And now the laudanum is talking. Let's get you back in bed."

She grimaced from pain as she settled onto the mattress and Jake straightened the nightgown around her legs.

"Wait. Where are my clothes? How did I get into this nightgown?" She was too tired to blush.

"Never mind," she murmured. "I probably don't want to know."

* * *

The girl awoke a few hours later. She kept quiet as she studied Jake who stood leaning against the door jamb.

He finally broke the silence.

"What's your name?"

The girl closed her eyes.

"Look, I gotta call you something. Real name, fake name, whatever suits your fancy. I'm just saying that a name would make conversation a whole lot easier."

She thought for a while, afraid the name she'd come up with on the trail would tell too much of her story. It was a composition of her parents' initials.

"Lainie. My name is Lainie."

"Is that a nickname? For Elaine, I mean?"

She knotted the sheet in her fist. "No."

"You got a last name?"

"Not these days."

"Well, Lainie with no last name, are you in trouble with the law?"

"No."

"Runnin' from a husband?"

"No."

"Runnin' from your parents?"

"I never knew my parents."

He studied her face, her eyes. She had secrets following her.

"You're running from someone," Jake said. "It'd help if I knew who to aim the gun at should somebody show up for you."

"I'm thankful for all you've done, giving me a place to stay, taking care of my leg and all, but I'm not asking you for any more help."

"Then I'm asking you for help."

Jake gauged her reaction, then continued.

"My mother is going to need some looking after for the next few days. I've got kin—a cousin named Paul and his Nimiipuu wife, Snow Owl—that I'm sure will be willing to help. Right now, they're working a cattle drive from Texas to Colorado, then back home to Idaho. I have no way of sending them a post or a telegram, so we're bound to the timing of the trail."

Lainie recognized the direction this conversation was going and began to protest.

Jake held up his hand. "Please, hear me out." He walked to the window, pushed back the curtain, and stared into the distance. "In a few days they'll be back to help with fall harvest and to move our cattle for winter grazing. They've been looking to start a family. Maybe settling down here and working their inheritance of the land will give them that chance. Paul can farm and ranch, Snow Owl can care for mother and become a mother herself."

He turned around and leaned his back against the wall. With his arms crossed in front of him, his fists buried beneath his forearms, he sturdied himself for the next point of conversation.

"Until then, I need someone to take care of my mother, make sure she doesn't hurt herself, help her learn how to get around and take on chores that she can do without her eyes."

He tapped his knuckles against the windowsill, not sure if he should spill out the rest of the speech he'd rehearsed over the past day. Disregarding the skepticism he had for his own plan, he continued.

"You need time to heal, a place to stay. You can sell eggs to earn a paycheck. We can benefit each other. After fall harvest, I'll put you on a train to whatever town you want to land in. You won't need to tell me where you're going."

"You're crazy. Why would you trust me to do this? All you know about me is a concocted name."

"I also know you're on the run from someone, and I'm assuming that person is a danger to you. Here you'll be safe."

She let out a huff.

"Look, I don't know your story. I probably don't need to know your story. But whoever you're running from has most likely given up the hunt."

"What if he hasn't?" she snapped. "What if he's still trying to find me?"

"How long have you been on the run?"

She turned away from him.

"How long?"

"Several days."

"And how many miles do you think you've traveled?"

She shrugged her shoulders.

"Do you have a certain destination you're headed to? Some family you're trying to find?"

"No."

"There are a lot of what-ifs out there. Just remember that miles of trails and thousands of acres certainly outnumber all the what-ifs running through your mind. This man has no idea where you're wandering to because you have no idea where you're wandering to. If you consider all the possible directions you could have chosen to travel, the chances of this man finding you are pretty meager."

Lainie pondered his theory. In a way, it made sense. On the other hand, there had been people along the way she had relied on.

Sure, acres of land couldn't talk. Streams and meadows and trees couldn't talk.

But people could.

"Problems need solutions," Jake said. "You staying on for a while provides solutions. For all of us."

Jake settled into the rocking chair and gave the girl time to think. A few minutes later she threw out the words, "What else?"

"What do you mean?" he asked.

"I saw you. The other morning at your family's graves. I saw you." He didn't answer.

"You had a gun barrel in your mouth. You're using me as a means to an end. You're trying to keep me here at the house to take care of your mother so you can go off and blast your brains out."

"You've certainly got a bold mouth."

"I'm just speaking truth."

"You don't know that I would have gone through with it," he said, knowing the words were the tipping point of a lie. "Besides, me leaving this world is no longer an option."

"Oh, please. Don't throw that kind of hogwash at me. You've tasted suicide. You probably ache for it. I sat by your family's graves up on that hill. I read the dates on each cross. Wife and newborn lost on the same day. Your son dead just a few months later. That's a heap of grief to swallow."

"I'm past it," Jake said.

"Sure, just a few days after your little boy dies and a few hours after your mother's tragedy, you are past this yearning for release. Suicide's no longer an option. It's as easy as that."

Jake clenched his fists, stood, and paced the room.

"Look, I don't have any other options," he said at last. "Three days ago, no one in this world needed me. Every ounce of my willpower was poured into my family's coffins. Now that Mama's blind, I need to revive my will to live. And I need to revive this farm. For the time being, I can't do either without you."

The Decision

Jake left the following morning to bring his mother back to the farm. From the doorway, Lainie watched him leave. At this precipice, with one foot inside the cabin, one foot on the front porch, three words chanted in her mind.

Stay or flee. Flee or stay. Stay or flee. Flee or stay.

Yesterday, she had grudgingly agreed to stay at the farm until Jake's kin arrived. It was absolutely the wrong choice, for it didn't matter from what vantage point she looked at Jake's plan, the plan would not work.

Stay or flee. Flee or stay. Stay or flee. Flee. Or stay.

Once again, a history she held no control over was strong-arming her decisions.

Her plight was summed up in one name. McNally.

Jake had correctly guessed Lainie's predicament. She was on the run, but not from a husband or the law. Well, perhaps from the law. She didn't know for sure. What she did know was that twice she had barely escaped the man who had killed her mother seventeen years before. The man who was now intent on killing her.

Because of that man, Lainie had spent nearly a month climbing through thorny bramble as she dodged trail riders and freight drivers. She'd slipped on mossy stones as she forded creeks and rivers with her few possessions held high above her head. She'd slept in the branches of trees at night in fear of two-footed and four-footed predators that lurked below.

She'd survived on little food, zero safety, and plenty of fear.

Beyond the looming terror of being caught by McNally, of being gunned down by his pistol or slashed up by his knife, she feared the freight drivers most. They all drove the same freight trail from Salt Lake to McNally's mining town in Montana. They all carried news back and forth, from town to town, with the most important nuggets, whether gossip or truth, delivered to McNally's front door. They were all fearfully loyal to the man. And they were all duly rewarded for sniffing out any advantage to defeat McNally's enemies.

She was certainly an enemy.

If one freight driver spotted her, if he pinned her down in the middle of the wilderness and hogtied her and tossed her into the back of his wagon and hauled her back to McNally, his reward would be sizable.

Two women, Mother Damnable and a dancer named Kate, had warned Lainie that McNally would be ruthless in hunting her down, for the man's son—the heir to his so-called mining kingdom—was dead because of her.

Lainie had no proof that anyone continued to follow her, but the women's warnings fueled her fear as she held tight to memories of accusations, gunfire, and blood.

She was weak. She was worn down. A warm bed and the promise of food in her belly belied any ambition to put miles between her and the man who had branded her.

The man hell-bent on taking her life.

Was Jake right? Would the land's labyrinth of trails and cutaways, mountains and forests and improvised shelters conceal the path she'd traveled?

Possibly.

Still, there were people. Despite Lainie's best efforts to travel far from towns and houses to remain unviewed, there were times that she had secretly relied on people for food, for clothes, for shelter in a storm.

And there were times when she'd been caught. Snatching trousers and a shirt from a clothesline, sleeping in a hayloft, harvesting a trapper's snare.

She'd nearly taken a backside of buckshot for that.

And barnlooting.

She stepped back into the cabin, shut the door, and let her mind open memories from just a few days ago.

* * *

The Idaho Panhandle — August 1890

She had no intention of barnlooting, but her stomach griped for real food.

41

Lainie scanned the farmyard twice, sucked in courage, and slipped through the barn door. She squinted as her eyes adjusted from the bright sunshine to the building's somber light.

The hayloft was near empty, the walls of the barn were dotted with horse tack, farm tools, and the like. An anvil stood cobwebbed in the corner.

Lainie wandered through the space, peering behind crates, nosing through burlap bags. She didn't expect to find much. She found even less.

One bag stiffened by time and moisture held two potatoes, wrinkled and starting to mold. She broke off the sprouts that tangled together and nibbled them to nothing.

In the corners of another bag, she salvaged seven dried peas. Probably leftover seed from spring planting season. She tucked them in her pocket. Later, she could soak them and give them a bit of life before she turned them into a meal.

A third bag, again empty but worth extra inspection, brought forth a handful of corn kernels accompanied by leftover sandy grit.

Lainie pressed the kernels into her dress pocket and sifted the corndust from one hand to the other, her eyes keen on catching any weevil. Then she thought better of it. A few weevils held more nutrition than this meager supply of cornmeal. Not enough to make Johnny cake batter. Not enough for mush. She pinched the corndust between her fingers and tucked it in her cheek, just like the old men sitting at Hobson's store would do with their tobacco. Theirs would end up in a spittoon or, more likely, as black globs on the floorboards where Mrs. Hobson would, on hands and knees, swab the mess up with her grimy dish rags.

Lainie gagged at the image and quickly turned her attention to the barn rafters. *Focus on the pleasantries,* she reminded herself.

Certainly, Lainie's mind could add some refining qualities to the corndust chaw. A little moisture from her mouth, some time to savor the coarse flavor—why, the softened mixture would swallow down just fine.

She worked the chaw on one side of her mouth, then moved it to the other. When her mouth was dry as burnt kindling, she forced herself to swallow. The mixture inched along her throat, lodging halfway down. She swallowed again and again, wishing for a ladle of water to assist her efforts. She sagged to the floor and let out a frustrated sigh. Her gut still hurt and now she had a knob in her throat.

The rooster chose this particular moment to remind her of his presence.

"Keep crowing, you old coot, and I'll roast you over a fire."

Back outside, Lainie skimmed the horizon and spotted a woman and two small girls working in the garden. The girls had their backs turned south towards the barn. The woman used a hoe, pivoting from south to east in an order of attack against the weeds. Her face was turned to her work, but a glance up could land on Lainie.

The well stood just east of the house at the midway point between the garden and the barn. Lainie had rationed out water for two days, and her canteen had dried up the evening before. Unable to find a creek or a pond nearby, she'd planned to take advantage of the well during the night. But the moonless night left her fearful that she'd blunder in her mission's footsteps and awaken one of the gun-toting members of the family. Instead, she had tucked herself in a burrowed-out hole beneath the barn, fallen into a deep sleep, and missed dawn's opportunity to slip over to the well before the family began their early morning chores.

Lainie's mouth was parched to despair. She anchored the canteen strap over her shoulder and took a tentative step towards the well. Then another and a third. The woman looked up in Lainie's direction, squinted hard, then forced her eyes back to her work. Lainie was sure the woman's eyes had landed on her. No way they couldn't.

She should run. Bolt for the tree line and make her escape before the woman put her realizations to work and grabbed for a gun. But Lainie's feet were grounded, stuck to the earth which held the fierceness of bog mud.

The woman spoke to the girls then left the garden and headed to the house. Lainie raced around the corner of the barn and rushed back to the woods to retrieve her bedroll. Half past the barn, she tripped over an uprooted length of wire and dropped hard, knocking air from her lungs. She scrabbled forward, clawing across the dry ground, waiting for the sound of gunblast.

No sound came.

At the back corner of the barn, Lainie pulled herself up and clutched at the ache in her side. There was simply no way the woman could have missed her. She stood still, tempting fate, reasoning out a plan. She needed water. There was no way to go on without it. If she stayed a bit longer, maybe the opportunity would rise to pull water from the well. Or maybe she'd find herself tied up and hauled to the sheriff.

She couldn't risk it. She couldn't risk it.

Lainie checked the path she'd just followed. No one in sight. She'd beeline back to the stand of trees, grab her things, and run in whatever direction her legs would carry her.

As she summed up courage, words lifted on the breeze. "Girls, come on in and have some cobbler. It's fresh hot from the stove."

She couldn't believe the opportunity that stood before her. It wasn't possible that she, a wandering thief, would be warranted a chance to draw water from the well while the woman and the girls were inside, and the husband was away.

But believe she did. As she quietly reapproached the front of the barn, sight of the woman leaving the cabin stopped Lainie in her tracks. She watched the woman walk to the well, set a bundle on the ground, and pull up a fresh pail of water. The woman left the pail hanging there, dripping wet and such a temptation that Lainie was sure it served as trap bait.

The woman scanned the horizon towards the barn and hollered out, "Girls, go ahead and have a second helping, then don't forget to wash up your dishes."

She pulled the bucket from its hook, settled a dipper into the water, picked up the bundle, and hauled all towards the barn. Lainie made a hasty retreat to the back, unsure if kindness or sabotage was headed her way.

Waiting out her fate, she heard humming, then wordsong. "Do this, and joy your hearts will swell. All is well, all is well."

The song returned to humming. The tune faded as it distanced.

Lainie heard the mosquito-netted door bang shut. She peered around the corner. The bucket of water, the bundle of goods, both lay mere feet away.

Ladles of water. More for the canteen. A loaf of bread. Half a dozen potatoes, ready to be cooked, with matches for a fire. Sweet raspberry cobbler.

Words could never express Lainie's gratitude.

She slipped open her bedroll, unpinned her mother's tarnished brooch from the blanket, and gave it a soft kiss. She pinned the brooch to the muslin that had surrounded the food and nestled it in the pail next to the ladle.

"A blessing on this house," she whispered. "A blessing on you and yours."

* * *

Lainie refused to entertain any more memories. They were weighsome things and she was already a mess of exhaustion and nervous energy.

She tried to accept that Jake's plan made sense. A woman in need of nursing for a time and help around the house for the long run. Another woman—a young wanderer—in need of a place to stay and time to heal. The match seemed tagged by fate.

Or speared for ruin.

She looked out the window down the lane. How long would it take for Jake and the woman to return? How long until she knew if the woman would accept her?

How long until Lainie knew her next footpath in life?

Telling Miss Jayne

Jake helped his mother into the wagon. "Sit towards center, Mama."

Whiteknuckled and grim, she inched her way across the seat towards center.

"That's good, Mama."

Jake turned to Doc and Emmeline. He gripped the doctor's arm and gave both of his friends his thanks.

"Be sure to use this salve on her burns for the next few days," Doc said, handing Jake two small tins along with a bottle of tonic. He leaned towards Jake and confided, "I expect you to also use the salve on your hand. There's plenty for both of you. Understood?"

"How did you know?" Jake mumbled.

"A doctor takes care of wounds with his ears as much as he does with his hands." Doc shared. "Your story is safe with me."

"Miss Jayne, Doc will stop by soon to check on your progress," Emmeline called out as she handed an old cane to Jake for his mother to use.

When his mother didn't answer, Jake offered up another round of thanks, then clambered onto the buckboard. The harsh jostle of the wagon blanched Miss Jayne's face further. He studied her, paste pale underneath bulked bandages at her eyes and along each cheekline. "You're gonna be alright, I promise. Grab onto my arm and we'll be off."

She wrapped herself around his right arm, noosetight and unrelenting. Jake could barely manage the reins under her fierce grip.

Halting progress was made, and the horses tossed back their heads more than once with the gravest of inquiries as to the slow pace of the journey. Regardless, the animals kept to the sluggish duty assigned, for any time Jake motioned them to move faster, his mother's grip tightened, and she burrowed the top of her head deeper into his shoulder.

About halfway home he told her about Lainie.

"I've got news for you, Mama. I need you to listen." She kept her head buried. "Mama, it's time to sit up straight. I need you to hear this."

Hesitation lived in her spine, but slowly she straightened.

"The other night, there was a girl in the woods. She was injured some. Could barely walk."

He looked towards Miss Jayne. Her jaw was clenched tight.

"The girl, she needs our help. I bandaged her up best I could, gave her some laudanum for the pain. Doc gave me some salve for the infection in her leg. She's doing much better, but she's scared this side shy of death. I figure she's been on the road for a while."

"No." Barely a whisper.

"I've asked her to stay on for a time. Help out until you've healed."

"No." This time her response was accompanied by an unremitting shake of her head.

"We need her, Mama. Until Paul and Snow Owl return, I can't run the farm without her. I promised that you'd never go to an institution, and I aim to keep that promise. This girl is what stands between us keeping on at the homestead or you ending up at an institution and me shifting from job to job to pay for your care."

There. The words were out. No misspeak of circumstance. No honey-sweetened swallow of halftruth.

She shook her head harder. "No no no! No one can see me like this."

"I've already asked her to stay on at the house for a time. Figured she'd be of help with chores and whatnot. Figured you could work your magic on her, too."

Jake pulled back on the reins to stop the team. He turned to his mother and gathered her to him. "It's the way it's gotta be. You, me, and this girl named Lainie."

* * *

Lainie was anxious to get on with the day, but the sun moved slow in its journey overhead and the passage of time clopped on with meager haste.

She moved about the kitchen using the crutch Jake had smoothed from a downed tree limb. She'd twice swept the already meticulous cabin, excepting the loft that required steady footing on a ladder to reach. She could venture outside, take on a few outdoor chores, but nervous pride kept her inside where the dress Jake gave her would remain unsoiled.

The calico dress was a work dress, for sure, with spattered grease stains across the bodice and a slightly frayed hem. She worried that any additional damage to the dress on her part would be a sign of disrespect. Then again, no damage to the dress might be considered a sign that she wasn't pulling her weight at the farm. She wondered if the dress had belonged to Jake's wife. Perhaps it belonged to Jake's mother. Either way, she would need to add a few inches of fabric to the skirt to accommodate her height.

A sudden rush of fatigue washed over her. She leaned against the kitchen doorframe, refusing to give in to a desire for sleep. Instead, she let her eyes roam the room. She gave stories to the walls.

The kitchen had a dry sink of copper with a galvanized pail set inside. To its left, a thick, crude wall shelf held prettily patterned dishes.

There was a disparity between this sturdy timber shelf and the fine china assembled atop it that Lainie felt kin to. Unyielding and graceful. Rugged and fluent. Roughhewn woodgrains set off by soft pastel flowers. Lainie wondered if the china pieces were used at suppertime or simply left for show. She counted plates stacked five-deep, seven saucers and seven teacups, two with missing handles. There was a pitcher and other miscellanies, but what caught her eye most was the large platter.

Carmine red on white. Gold edging. Bold fruits and flowers. This dish was nothing like the dainty pieces it stood next to. No, this piece was audacious. Headstrong, even. The design was not that of a timid hand.

She walked to the shelf and reached out to touch the platter, but just as quick withdrew her hand.

Not my place to touch another family's things, she reminded herself.

Above the sink were four panes of glass, two on top of two, that overlooked the yard and a couple of trees. Cornered to that, a bank of shelves stood above a work counter mounted to the wall with doored-in shelves below. Next to that, a cook stove.

Mortar and pestle, creamer, wooden dough bowls, coffee grinder, brass pepper mill, copper pots, cast iron pans. Standard fare for a kitchen. She also noted an elaborate cake form, a well-used waffle iron, a recent-new enamelware breadbox, and a Spong and Co. mincing and chopping machine of which Lainie's grandmother would surely have approved.

It would be too highfalutin to glance through the doored-in shelves, so she'd wait for permission from the woman to learn what treasures and tins they held. For now, curiosity need be kept at bay.

The adjoining front room was warm and quaint. The fireplace at one end left her craving a cool, crisp night with a book in hand.

She admired the slant-front writing desk that stood next to an upholstered rocking chair with a yarn basket tucked beside. The front room's window was trimmed with lace curtains and a walnut-trimmed sofa upholstered in dark had a matching side chair. Centering the furniture group was a dainty round table. Lainie set it aside as precaution to the newly blinded woman's first awkward steps within her home.

Once done, Lainie scanned the side-to-side rooms again. Something was off. She'd noticed that new floorboards mingled with old in the kitchen. The new boards had the complexion of oatmeal while the rest of the boards were nearer the color of mustard honey. The effect was a near optical illusion that tipped the space some, with the dark end heavy and the light end floating such that you believed yourself walking a bit uphill as you entered the kitchen.

A long hook straddled the lighter floorboards. A hook where a lantern should hang. Little by little, Lainie's tired mind wrapped itself about the puzzle that lay before her. There was a full-equipped kitchen for cooking, but no table for eating.

For now, the puzzle of the table and the lantern and the floorboards would lay with chinks missing. There was no one about who could answer the nosy questions churning in her mind and it wasn't her business anyway.

She hobbled to the woman's bedroom, once again checking that nothing stood in the path between the doorway and the bed. She'd already plumped the pillows and folded back the blankets and the broken star quilt so the woman could easily slip into bed to rest. Perhaps she should have left the bed made up, with pillows atop blankets tucked tight. She didn't know.

How does one present such a pretty bed to a blind woman?

The room was tightfilled with a dowry chest along with a dark-stained travel trunk. A standing closet, made of what looked to be walnut, was tucked in one corner. It had double doors with full-length mirrors attached. The carving over top was nice, but the fancy carved feet were too showy for Lainie's taste. She did like the way the bottom section of the closet had two drawers above one long drawer. They would certainly hold a tidy sum of pretty hankies and shawls and such.

Pretty this. Pretty that. It had been a long time since Lainie had summoned up the word *pretty*. And here she'd thought it at least a dozen times within the past few hours.

She didn't want to say the word in front of the woman. Pretty was the last thing a blind woman would want to think on. Lainie would need to watch her words. It had been so long since she'd had someone to use words with, she was sure they'd hatch out all busted and cracked and misshapen.

Lainie was tempted to return to the room where Jake had cared for her, but the layer of dust that coated the bureau, the floor, even the guitar and the fiddle that hung on the wall, was thick with a smothering grief. That morning, as she had dressed and attempted to make herself presentable, she had picked up the hand mirror on the dresser to check her appearance, thus stirring up the dust and the grief attached to it. She had quickly replaced the mirror to its space on the bureau, then blown across the grit that remained, hoping to disguise her meddled intrusion. All she accomplished was to stir up motes and give them new life.

She circled the front room three more times before returning to the front room's window. She practiced out a greeting as she watched for Jake and the woman to return.

Soon she saw dust on the horizon.

Too much dust for a wagon traveling slow.

* * *

Lainie's heart lunged to her throat. Riders. Traveling hard and headed straight towards the cabin. She pivoted from the window, resisting the urge to run. Surely these riders were friends of the family, stopping to check on Miss Jayne or talk farmtalk with Jake. They'd knock on the door and ride away when no one answered.

Bristle was on the front porch. He barked as the sound of hooves came closer and then to a halt. Lainie chanced a glance out the window. Two men dismounted.

One with a familiar limp.

Oh, Lord, tell me what to do.

Lainie left her crutch propped against the wall and shuffled past the front door to climb the loft ladder. Four steps up, her foot slipped. Her chin smacked hard on the ladder rung and her teeth knocked together. She winced from the lightning bolt of pain as she struggled up into the loft.

A knock at the door. Then another.

A child's bed was tucked against one wall of the small loft. She looked underneath the bed. Not enough room to hide. Her eyes roamed frantic through the near bare space. A bed. A dresser. A trunk. Nothing more.

Banging at the door. A deep male voice yelling, "Shut up, dog." A thud. The sound of Bristle yelping and running down the stairs.

Lainie threw open the trunk that was snugged against the end of the bed. It was filled with winter quilts. She pulled them out, settled them on the bed, then hurried into the trunk and crouched over. She fit. She grabbed the top quilt from the bed and managed to center it over her back.

Lainie huffed and strained as she grabbed the lid and pulled it down, pinching her fingers in the process. After the ham-handed struggle, the lid almost shut tight.

* * *

"Break it down," McNally said.

"Ain't nobody home, boss," replied the younger man.

"Don't care. Break it down."

Three deft kicks from the six-foot brute and the door was felled.

"Check the rooms, Sam. All of them. Look under beds. Behind doors. Everywhere."

McNally scanned for clues while the paid help did his duty.

"Deplorable," McNally grunted, mentally calculating the necessities the cabin lacked. No table. No indoor plumbing. An antiquated Winchester rifle in the corner. In his estimation, the place was a hovel.

"She ain't here, boss. Only two small bedrooms. No one in either."

"Well, she's got to be somewhere in this godforsaken town," McNally demanded as he inspected the crutch he found leaning against the wall. "Three people sighted the girl heading towards this place. There's only one road in and one road out."

51

"It's been a few days since they sighted her. Maybe she cut cross country," Sam ventured. "Or somehow met up with Stut."

"No, my bet is she's following the road, looking for handouts from the locals." His mind flashed to the brooch the woman in Calder was wearing when they searched her property a few days before. The brooch had been the first real clue that he was following the girl's tracks. "That girl doesn't have the smarts to live off the land."

"She made it this far. She must have some savvy for the wilds," Sam pointed out.

McNally pushed past Sam and headed to the back rooms. "Go look outside. Check the barn, the hen house, the smokehouse. Hell, check the shithouse. Maybe she's hiding in there."

In the bedrooms, McNally made his presence known. He flipped over beds. Filtered through dresser drawers then threw them to the ground. Smashed mirrors and sliced open pillows. The man took his time, acquainted himself with each item looking for signs of the girl. Then he tore apart the front room and the kitchen.

Sam climbed down the loft ladder. "Ain't no sign of her outside or in the outbuildings, nor any sign of her up that ladder. Nothing but a kid bed and a trunk filled with old quilts."

He quick-surveyed the carnage surrounding McNally. "Thought you was keeping a low profile, boss."

"A low profile has gotten us nowhere, son. What we need is an insurrection."

* * *

The sounds in the house were stifled by the weightiness of the quilt's cotton and wool, but Lainie full-registered the landing of boots on ladder rungs. Her flesh turned volcanic, pumping fear and heat that was roasted acrid in the airless surroundings of the sweatbox.

She would be found.

She would be found.

Jake's knife was in her pocket. Could she reach it? Such a small blade would make for a feeble defense against these men.

She would be found.

She would be found.

The final rungs of the ladder. Boots across the floor. Drawers sliding. Once. Twice. Pulled out and tossed aside. Three more drawers. Open. Shut. Open. Shut. Open.

Please, God. Please, God.

A slit of light as the trunk lid hatched open. Quilt layers shuffled. The lid slammed shut. The trunk shoved aside.

Creaking. Cursing. The thud of something dropped. Something large smacked against the floor. Had he lifted the bed to look underneath it, then dropped it to the ground?

She heard the man descend the ladder. Dark conversation. Outraged boots in retreat. Horse hooves grating against the parched ground. At last, silence.

She was safe. She had been sheltered.

What now of Jake and his mother?

Trouble at Home

Jake reached for his mother's hand to give it a squeeze. "Only a couple more miles, Mama, and we'll be home."

Miss Jayne pulled away from her son's touch. She sat tall with her chin jutted out. Her hands, clenched fierce to the seat, burned with ache. But better to endure that pain than to bounce from the wagon when it hit a hole in the road. Or to link arms with the son who had just betrayed her.

Two miles back, she'd sniped a storm at Jake's announcement about some waif girl taking up residence at their home. It was ridiculous, this notion to bring in a stranger when all Miss Jayne wanted to do was hermit away in her corner of dark.

She had yelled out her fury then brooded in plaintive silence.

All the while, Jake had kept his peace. He wouldn't cave to her demands for solitude. Nor would he back down from his plan.

After another mile or so of silence, Jake saw dust in the distance.

"There are two horsemen coming our way, Mama. Probably wise not to mention the girl."

The riders flew around the bend and stopped just shy of the Adamsen wagon.

"Hello, folks. Good day to ya." Jake noted the slight Irish brogue from the smaller of the two men.

"Hello," Jake said. "New to these parts?"

"Why yes, yes we are. My name's McNally. Niall McNally. I'm out with my nephew looking for someone."

"And who would that be," Jake replied.

"Well, sir, I'm looking for my daughter. I've received word that she has traveled to these parts. I've just arrived myself from back east. Took the train, I did. Wanted to see where my little girl landed here on the frontier."

Jake's eyes passed from one rider to the other. The Irish bull, squattish and wide-shouldered, extended his height with a flat top derby, a well-played stature, and a sharp-turned stare. The younger man, stragglehaired and thick-muscled, sat easy but had unsettled eyes.

"Don't know of any newcomers," Jake said.

"How about you, ma'am," the man asked of Miss Jayne. "She's young. Just seventeen, with a mane of red hair and the loveliest green eyes you could ever see. Those emerald eyes remind me of my ancestral land, don't you know."

"I'm sorry, mister, but my mother is just returned from the doctor. As you can see from the bandages on her eyes and face, she's suffered some injury."

"Jake, I can speak for myself." Miss Jayne turned her face towards the sound of the stranger's voice. "No, sir, I've not learned of any newcomers. And your description doesn't fit any of the young people in town. Now, if you don't mind, my head is aching fierce, and I'd like to get home to lie down."

"Of course, ma'am," the stranger said. "I'm grateful for your time."

The horsemen eased their animals back as Jake flicked the reins to motion Lou and O'Malley forward.

After they'd distanced the horsemen, Miss Jayne quietly warned, "Keep your head forward, Son. That man's expecting you to look back."

"I don't need to look back, Mama. All about, that scene was a lie."

* * *

Jake kept the wagon's pace steady until they were a fair distance from the riders. Once he believed the wagon and the dust his horses were about to kick up were out of the men's sight, he tole Miss Jayne to grab his arm and hold on tight.

He pushed the horses to a faster gait, wanting to push them harder to get back to the farm, but knowing the rapid motion could jolt his mother from the wagon.

He kept check over his shoulder to be sure the riders weren't following. All the while, suspicion hammered in his head.

Back at the farm, suspicion turned to certainty. The front door of the cabin was bashed in.

Jake helped his mother from the wagon and settled her on the front porch step. "Stay here, Mama," he warned. "I'll be right back."

He rushed up the stairs and into the house.

"Lainie," he called out.

The kitchen and front room were in pieces. He threw each bedroom door open to find upturned beds and torn apart belongings. Lainie was nowhere in sight.

Jake continued calling out her name, glancing through each window he passed.

Bristle had come through the open door and was barking like he'd treed a coon.

"Stop it, Bristle. Hush."

Muffled sounds came from the loft. Jake clambered up the ladder to find more chaos. His son's bed was off kilter, its blankets disarranged. Two drawers from the tall oak dresser were plucked loose, their contents strewn across the room. His wife's dowry chest was shoved against the frame of the dresser, its lid lifting and banging against a partially extended drawer that blocked it from fully opening.

Jake muscled the trunk from its position and threw open the lid. He grabbed at the quilt atop the quaking bundle of fear below.

The girl gasped for air.

Jake helped her sit up.

"Are you hurt?"

"No." Her body trembled, and her hair and skin and dress were drenched in sweat. Jake pushed the wet strands of hair from her face as she gulped in air so hard, he feared she might pass out.

"Slow down your breathing. Take in the air slow and easy."

"He was here," she gasped. "He was here."

"I know. Now slow down your breathing."

"He was here. He was here. He was here," she chantwhispered with each gulp of air.

"Slow and easy. Take the air in slow and easy. That's good. Now let's get you out of this trunk."

Jake stood and took firm hold of Lainie's forearms to help her stand. Her legs, weak and numb, buckled beneath her. Jake caught her, picked her up, and settled her on the mattress.

"Sit here and rest," he said, wiping the sweat from her face with the corner of a quilt. "Everything's safe. I promise, everything's safe."

She watched him disappear down the ladder. A woman's voice was calling his name.

"Jake? Jake?"

"I'm climbing down the ladder, Mama. I'm right here in front of you, just inside the doorway."

"What is going on? I don't understand what is going on."

"Shh, it's all right." He grabbed her hand and guided her past the broken-down door and their strewn belongings to the toppled rocker. He set the chair upright and maneuvered her into the seat. "Those men were here. They broke down the door. Tore up the house."

"And the girl?"

Jake's focus was on the sights outside the window. Did he just see movement at the corner of the barn?

"Jake, where's the girl?"

"She's in the loft. Safe. Spooked but safe."

"We've got to get out of here." She aimlessly grabbed for Jake's hand. "We've got to leave this house."

He swiftturned from the window and snapped out, "No, Mama, the men are gone." He tried to soften his voice. "They were traveling towards town, probably already scoured the countryside looking for the girl. They didn't find any signs of her, so they're moving on."

"They could come back any minute now."

"They won't."

"How do you know that, Jake? How can you possibly know?"

"Because I feel it in my gut. And right now, my gut's the only thing I dare trust."

* * *

Lainie heard the squabble. She needed to leave the cabin and spare the family any more harm. She quieted down the ladder, hoping to slip past Jake as he spoke with his mother.

He caught sight of her as she picked up her crutch and stepped outside.

"I'll be right back, Mama." Jake followed the girl onto the porch.

"Where are you going, Lainie?" he asked.

"I can't stay here, mister."

"We have a deal."

"That deal didn't include two men tearing through your house." She stopped her words, fumbled for control. "I'm real, real sorry about all that's happened. It's best that I go. Thank you for all your help but please, forget I was ever here."

She turned away. He let her walk.

"Blast it all," Jake murmured. "Fool girl's gonna die out there."

Bristle had found his place next to the man and whimpered at his words and, seemingly, at the sight of the girl walking away.

"What do you want me to do, dog? I can't force her to stay."

Bristle looked up at him and Jake swore the dog knit together his eyebrows to question the man's words.

"Don't believe me? Go after her yourself, you mangy mutt."

The dog did just that. He scampered down the stairs and trotted to the girl until he blocked her path.

"Go home, Bristle. You can't come with me, so just go home."

The dog continued to block Lainie's path. She moved to go around him, shook the end of her crutch at him to scare him off. He dodged the crutch and blocked her path again. "Stop it, Bristle." She picked up a stick and threw it towards the barn. "Go on. Fetch it. Fetch the stupid stick." She picked up another and threw it even farther. "Fetch the stick! Fetch the stick and take it back to Jake."

The man's name caught in her throat.

"Go on, Bristle, I'll stay here with Lainie."

Jake stood behind her, less than an arm's length away. "Look, I can't promise that you're going to like it here. I've had too many ugly days to be likeable, and my mother is—well, I have no idea who my mother is anymore. Now, with her eyes gone and her face all burned, who knows how she'll cope. But she's always been strong, forged from iron. She's a good woman. And maybe I'll to return to being a good man."

He cleared his throat. "My point is, life here isn't going to be easy. But I can promise you a roof over your head, food in your belly, and safety from the road and from the man that lit his brand on you."

Shocked, Lainie reached up to the searmark on her neck.

"Yeah, I saw it. No one deserves to be marked like that, Lainie."

He moved in front of her. "We saw the men on the road as we were coming home. The one named McNally, with a touch of Irish to his voice, he's who you're running from, right?"

She nodded her head.

"And the other man?"

"I don't know. I didn't catch good sight of him."

"He was tall, thickset. Long dark hair. Greasy looking. He had a long scar on his chin and wore a cavalry hat."

"I'm sorry. I really don't know."

"No matter. Both are gone. Headed towards town, then off to the next town, I suspect."

Jake pushed back his hair then rubbed at the strain in his neck.

"No promises, Lainie. No guarantees that the Irish devil won't ride back and storm through the cabin again. No assurances that the three of us will get along or that we'll make it through the next few weeks without driving each other insane. But you, on the road with your leg wound and cold weather sure ahead, your chances are slim. And Miss Jayne, struggling blind on a farm without anyone by her side while I work the fields, well, she's bound for mishap."

Lainie rubbed her arms and journeyed her thoughts forward. Solitary trails of harsh cold and little food meant she was the only target of McNally's rage. If she stayed in any one place for any length of time, whether it was with Jake and his mother or at some other location, innocents would pay.

"He'll hurt you. Might kill you. I can't stay."

"He won't be back, Lainie. We've got to trust in that. And somehow, some way, you were sheltered up in that loft underneath Hannah's quilt. Maybe that's the sign we all need that you should stay."

She scoffed. "There is no trust. There are no signs. You, of all people, should know that."

"You're right. And you were right yesterday when you said I crave suicide." He walked closer. He lowered his head and his words. "Yes, I've still got the taste of gunpowder in my mouth. If I don't start believing that God's somehow got his hand in all this, I'll be bound for that hill again, rifle by my side."

Lainie squeezed her eyes tight against the image of Jake seated in gravegrass, gun angled to his lips, the air stock still with anticipation of a shockblast.

"Promise me you won't do that, Jake. Promise me."

"No promises. No guarantees." He hated the way she looked at him, with those pleading green eyes. "I'll do my best," he finally conceded. "I'll do my best."

The Meeting

"We're back, Mama," Jake said as he and Lainie reentered the house. Jake lifted the door from the ground and leaned it in the doorway as best he could. One hinge was torn off. Jake kicked it and a chunk of the broken cross latch out of the way.

"Jake? Jake? What is it? Are the men back?" Miss Jayne's voice cracked with fear.

"No, the men aren't back. The door just needs some repairs. I'll fix it later."

"Why were they here? Why did they break into our home?"

She pushed herself from the rocking chair and, with arms outreached, took shuffling steps towards Jake's voice. Jake intercepted her before she tripped over the basket lying on the floor. He guided her to the sofa. "Just sit a spell, Mama. There are a few things scattered on the floor. Lainie's already picking them up, but it will take a bit."

"Stop her. I don't want some drifter touching our things. She'll steal them. Probably already has a pile of our belongings hidden way out in the woods."

"Mother. That's enough."

"The girl is covered head to toe with mange and lice, isn't she? She's already smelled up our house. Can you smell it? Can you smell it? The air is rank with her wrongs. She's probably a squatter, part of a family of squatters, waiting to outstay us, wile away our land from us. How dare you let her infest our home with her disease and misfortune."

"Stop it, Mother. You're conjuring stories that just aren't true. Lainie helped the day of your accident. Lainie is not trying to steal our land or our home."

"Lainie. Lainie. What kind of name is that? Who would give their child such an unseemly name? Come here, girl," Miss Jayne barked out. "Come here, now."

Lainie looked to Jake. Her eyes pleaded with him to delay this first formal meeting. Pinchlipped, he nodded her forward.

60

She crossed the room, leaning heavily on the crutch, and her uneven footsteps strode-thumped across the awkward quiet. She kneeled in front of the woman and the pain from her injured leg jolted through her. She placed some unraveled crochetwork retrieved from the floor into the woman's hands.

"I'm sorry," Lainie whispered. "I'm so, so sorry."

The woman's hand combed the air until it found the girl's face. She gently cupped Lainie's chin with her fingertips.

"I'm sure you are."

Smack.

Lainie winced at the sting from the woman's slap.

"I don't want you here." The mother's whisper was venom. "The minute my nephew and his wife arrive, you are gone. Do you understand?"

"Yes, I understand."

"Now go on and fetch a bucket of water from the well. And take your time about it. My son and I need to have some words."

* * *

"Our home is in shambles, Jake. Get her out of here. Now."

"You agreed that she could stay until Paul and Snow Owl return."

"I changed my mind."

"Mama, we can't send her away. We need her right now."

"She's brought trouble on her heels. I won't have her in my home."

"You're not being reasonable."

"Reasonable? There's nothing reasonable about this day."

Jake paced the room, his boots crushing the glass shards from the gilded frame that earlier in the day had held his parents' wedding picture.

"Fine, I'll send her away as soon as you prove you can get around the cabin on your own. As soon as you can cook meals without setting the kitchen afire. As soon as you pull up water from the well without falling into it. I'll be happy if you can find your way to the piss pot, let alone the privy out back. But right now, we need that girl, so suck up your indignation and deal with the fact that she is going to be here until Paul and Snow Owl arrive."

"How dare you talk to me that way. I didn't raise you to . . ."

61

"To what, Mama? To bust out orders on how to survive? To slap you in the face with reality? To talk like Pa used to talk? The girl stays."

Jake stomped over the door that had fallen back to the ground when Lainie walked out. At the doorway, he threw one more barbed message to his mother: "You're not the only one with darkness boiling before you."

* * *

Lainie remained huddled behind the well for a good thirty minutes before Jake found her there sitting on the frilled grass, her back against the well rock, her hands covering her ears, her eyes shut tight.

He kicked a small rock to make his presence known.

"Food's in the larder," he said. "Have supper ready. I'll be back at sundown."

* * *

Miss Jayne refused the food offered by Lainie. She refused to talk or to lie down. Seated on the sofa, she remained stonefaced, the bandages across her eyes a tourniquet to conversation.

The woman listened to the girl bumbling around the room with her obnoxious triadic gait. Step shuffle thump. Step shuffle thump. "Can I get you anything, ma'am?" Step shuffle thump. "Perhaps a pillow to rest your head on?" Step shuffle thump. "A cool glass of water, perhaps some tea?" Step shuffle thump.

In no way would she relinquish control of her home, her life, to the patronized coddling of this loathsome stranger. She—a woman who had crossed hundreds of miles of desolation rooted to a wagon seat, her blisterhanded grip tugging at leather reins to control a pair of yoked oxen, making due with overburdened odds and minimal supplies—she did not need some misguided floozy making her meals or stirring her cup of tea.

No, Jayne Alexandra Adamsen would not put up with this situation. As soon as Jake realized what a leeching jezebel this girl was, he would regard his mother's words and oust the freeloader from their lives. Of this, she was sure.

* * *

Darkness settled hard the first night Jake, Miss Jayne, and Lainie shared the same home. Jake had repaired the door and secured its latch, but this layer of protection didn't make any of them feel secure.

Miss Jayne continued to refuse food, including the girl's tossed-together supper, but did drink a glass of milk that Jake offered her.

Jake picked at his stew. Lainie grimaced as she heard him crunch through a piece of half-cooked potato. The man stomached a portion of the meal. The remaining food he threw outside to the dog before retreating to his bedroom.

Lainie lacked appetite altogether and recognized after eating a spoonful of the stew that it was indeed throwaway food, barely fit for the pig trough. Her conscience, though, reminded her that she was near starved just four days ago. She couldn't justify this sudden inclination for wastefulness, so she speared another hunk of hide-tough meat and chewed it in earnest.

While Lainie washed the supper dishes, Jake dragged the mattress from his room into Miss Jayne's room. He pulled it to the far side of her bed and dropped it on the floor. It was much too wide for the space, so he butted one edge of the mattress alongside the length of his mother's bed and let the other edge curl up the wall. The extra width of the mattress immediately flopped over, and Jake determined the only remedy was to tack it up. He retrieved a hammer and some nails from the barn, ignoring his mother's pestering questions as he walked past her once and then again to finish his chore. He pounded five nails in place, tested the durability of his craftsmanship, then added four more nails for surety.

From there, he returned to his room, retrieved the blankets and a slashed, half-empty pillow he'd left piled on the ground, and tossed them onto the newly situated mattress.

A third trip to his room yielded clothing from the upended dresser—three dresses, two shifts, a nightgown, some socks and unmentionables, and two aprons. Before he placed them on his—no, Lainie's—mattress, a shudder of realization hit, and he hugged the clothing tight to his chest.

I know this is what you'd want, Hannah. To help the girl. I promise, I'm not letting go of you. I'm not letting go.

* * *

63

The night finally calmed. Miss Jayne found sleep, in part, from drinking a tonic the doctor had provided.

Lainie tugged the blankets to her chin as she attempted to sleep in her new quarters. There was no security from the confining walls. No solace from the ceiling that blocked the stars. No comfort from the steady cadence of her roommate's soft snore. Half an hour passed, then an hour. The swarming of mindchatter and fear and premonition snared her lungs, her chest, and she flung back the blankets to allow herself some air.

Lightheaded, dizzy, covered in sweat, she clutched her head as the minutes throbbed by.

When panic seized again, she crawled from the mattress, inched through the dark, and finally found comfort when Jake's rifle was in her hands.

* * *

From his bedroll on the front room floor, Jake heard the creaking of his mother's door. Open. Then shut. He watched the girl use her crutch to pad across the floor and pick up the rifle kept by the door. She stationed herself at the front window and leaned her head against the window's casement. For the first few minutes, her eyes remained intent on the dark horizon before her. Just past midnight, her eyes began to close, and Jake feared she'd drop the rifle wrapped within her arms.

"The dog will bark if anyone comes near the house," he said.

His words chased away her stupor and she soldiered her stance at the window.

He pulled himself from the bedroll and walked towards her.

"Do you know how to use that thing?" he asked, nodding towards the gun.

She gave a small nod.

"They're not coming back, Lainie."

She tightened the grip on his gun.

"I've had a couple of hours of sleep," he lied. "How about if I stand watch for a while? I'll wake you in three hours and we'll trade off."

Lainie held her stance, keeping her eyes on the black existence before her.

64

"Here," he said, gently taking the gun. "Even a soldier needs sleep. I'll keep a sharp eye out, I promise."

She gave up the gun, sat on the floor in the corner, and fell asleep.

McNally
Along Idaho's Snake River — August 1890

In 1864, Niall McNally took a bullet in the leg at Petersburg. He wasn't sure of the date. June sixteenth. June eighteenth. The date meant nothing. The only thing that mattered was the damnable ball of steel that caught his flesh, then his bone.

The doctor had wanted to saw off the leg. McNally left the old sawbones with a broken jaw instead.

McNally's limp and scar were the only vestige of honorable service he'd shown his country. After months of healing and hating and listening to his mother's sanctimonious goading to walk tall and display his wounded gait as tribute to the Confederacy, he had simply walked out. Out of the family life that sweltered with expectations. Out of a white-columned Greek revival, looted and ravaged by the northern enemy. Out of Virginia, a state depressed by the war and thoroughly useless to his ambitions.

He thought of his mother now as he rode his grey alongside the mighty Snake River. He thought of her ruffles and ringlets and doting manipulation and her family's prominent wealth and prestige. How ironic that the war her family had hailed as the battle cry to freedom had sloshed their acres of land with brewed chicory root and blood-soaked disdain.

"Boss, dust ahead." Sam's words brought McNally back to the task at hand. They had learned from a couple of freight haulers that Bogger Buchanan was box sluicing near Whitepine Canyon. It was time to pay McNally's old friend a visit.

The riders neared Buchanan's slipshod operation. McNally knew what he'd see there. Wooden sluice boxes, twelve-foot long or so, angled to filter sand and stones and gold from the riverbed's depths. Cutbanks and dips and mounds of muck and mud, with stones and boulders thrown aside like cast out strumpets. Five, maybe six workers, their arms and faces and hair slopped over with grit, sludge caked to their clothes, the color of cold mush.

McNally had worked this type of scene years before when the lure of gold outwitted the lingering battlefields in his head. Memories of Petersburg and all the combats before were replaced—no, not replaced, dethroned—by the battle for gold.

At the age of twenty-four he had traveled west, paying his way with the coins he filched from a tin his father had buried before the war. By the time he reached Montana's Nevada City, the place was ready to close down. It was a considerable town of pine logs and shanties dug in the ground, but many of the shanties lay abandoned, the occupants having gone to other diggings or headed back home.

The gulch was torn up from one end to the other with men still working in it, throwing up the dirt like beavers. That's where he ran into Bogger, a fellow soldier from the Army of Northern Virginia, and Stut, Bogger's buttoned-up tagalong who had enough brawn to be worth his keep.

McNally and Bogger formed a partnership and kept young Stut busy with grueling work. When the partners learned all claims were taken up and talk in town was of suckers becoming fast disappointed and quitting the country, they moved on.

Virginia City, seated next door, told much the same story. Better houses and streets. Some buildings made of stone. Most built from hewed pine logs. Some covered with shingles, others with poles and dirt. Many of the houses were for sale or rent. More signs of decay. More reasons to give up on the gold. Montana held more disappointment than a burned-out distillery.

The men stayed anyway, digging up earth to send it sprawling through their sluice box. Hunching over riffle bars to flick away waste rock. Rinsing gritty concentrate, fingers achingly cold from the river water's bite, then panning out hints of gold. After days of this tedious routine, while Bogger slept off backbreaking hours of work and Stut kept guard over their claim, McNally secretly borrowed his partner's meager earnings to fund a long night of poker.

Bogger's unknown investment in his partner's gaming skills proved lucrative. McNally pocketed some of the winnings, spent the rest on a steak breakfast and a drawn bath, and returned the borrowed amount to Bogger's pack without raising suspicion. The next night, McNally quenched his appetite for women and was gone before the evening girl knew she had been robbed of her earnings.

Mining development was moving north towards Helena. McNally stopped short of that, veered west towards Butte, and eventually transgressed his way into a fortune.

Bogger and Stut followed.

When they first arrived, the three turned the earth for a time and found scant of nothing. Wearied from picking and digging, sweating and aching, McNally determined himself a better swindler than a miner. He made his next small bundle using intellect and guile.

With a tidy sum of funds now at his disposal, McNally began to dress for his new role. He purchased the best suit, hat, and boots he could find. He even convinced the salesman to knock down the price because the quality of the sable-brushed cotton simply wasn't as fine as the suiting material sold back in Virginia.

His next business decision was to end his mining partnership with Bogger and hire on Stut as his personal valet and bodyguard. Convincing the tongue-tied boy to sever ties with Bogger took some doing. Who knew the boy would have such scruples? Meals filled with beef or venison or broiled bladebone of lamb didn't sway Stut's loyalty, nor did desserts of currant dumplings or stewed rhubarb with clotted cream, for the boy was accustomed to hunger. A few gold coins with the promise of more didn't stoke the boy's fire to leave his nomad mentor, for he took pride in exchanging his meager share of hard-earned gold dust for necessary supplies. McNally considered purchasing Stut an hour with an establishment girl but was sure the boy would crumple into a pile of red-faced embarrassment at the mere thought of seeing a woman, let alone spending time in her chamber.

The gift of a green-broke buckskin was the boy's undoing. McNally's offer was simple: accept the horse, become my bodyguard. Once Stut accepted the terms of their new business relationship, McNally sent him to a tailor—for the town had no civilized clothing in Stut's size—to be fitted for two white button-downs, a pair of trousers, and a shawl-collar vest to heighten the expanse of the boy's intimidating frame.

Now, with Bogger standing just a few yards before him, McNally was face to face with his past. Twenty-five years ago, it had been simple to dispose of Bogger Buchanan and their ill-suited partnership. It would take a swift bait-and-snare to regain the man as an ally.

McNally and Sam remained unseen as they rode towards the mining operation. The workers' conversation, alongside the sound of water and gravel traveling through the sluice, masked the sound of their approaching horses.

"You catching anything in that burlap table of yours?" McNally hollered out, his Virginia accent slipping into place.

The man pouring gravel into the upper end of the sluice box turned, looked up, and fitted his hand to his forehead to shade out the sun. When he recognized the rider on the grey, he hollered for his crew to halt operations.

"Landamighty, boys, look who's here. Mr. Niall Bullyboy McNally, the patron saint of fisticuffs, has graced us with his presence."

"Still holding that last right cross against me, Bogger?"

"That last right cross broke my nose."

"Seems to me I did you a favor. That newly hooked nose prettied up your face some."

Bogger tossed his bucket to the ground, cueing his men to stand ready for trouble. "What're you doin' here, Mick?"

"I've got myself a dilemma. You're going to help fix it."

"Why would I help you fix anything?"

"Cold Harbor."

Gapemouthed, Bogger stared at McNally. "Why the hell would you bring that up?"

McNally nodded towards the crew. "Mind if your men take a break under that spread of shade while we talk?"

Bogger eyed McNally and Sam suspiciously.

"Go ahead, boys. Take a break. Ol' Mick and I have got some memories to rehash."

"You sure about this, Boggs?" one of the men asked.

"I'm sure. As long as Mr. Tall-in-the-Saddle walks over there with you." He nodded to Sam. "You head over with my men. They'll take good care of you. Just be sure to leave your horse and your weapons here with me and Mick."

Sam surveyed the crew. Each of them burley. Each of them now holding a huge stone in their hand. Two held pistols. One had a knife. He turned to McNally.

"Boss?"

"Go."

Sam slipped off his horse, unhitched his gun belt and laid it on the ground.

"Put your knife next to your guns," Bogger ordered.

Sam leaned over and pulled a Bowie knife from his boot, then stabbed it into the soil.

"Now, go on. Your boss man and I need to talk."

* * *

"How much you earning for specks of gold?" McNally asked as he examined the sandy pulp gathered atop the rough burlap of the sluice table.

"Twelve hundred colors are worth a cent," Bogger replied. "Takes a heap of flour gold to make any money."

"Any coarse gold in this sandbar?" McNally inquired as he pointed to a speck of color in the pulp.

"Enough."

"Liar."

"One piece. About half the size of a tenpenny nail."

McNally laughed. "Glad I got out of this business. Remember the rumors after the war? Montana's clay was going to earn us ten dollars a day. Folks claimed you could pull up a sagebrush plant and shake a dollar's worth of gold from its roots."

"The adventure worked out for one of us, I suppose." Bogger picked up a shovel and a bucket. As he walked to the embankment edge, he called out over his shoulder, "How is the silver mine business these days, Mick? You keepin' up with Marcus Daly over in Butte?"

McNally held his place. When Bogger returned, his bucket filled with earth, he gave his answer.

"Nobody keeps up with Daly, not with George Hearst funding a quarter of the company's stock without ever setting foot on site. The Anaconda Mine has its share of silver, but those boys are banking on copper deposits to turn Butte into the richest hill on earth and Daly into a tycoon."

"You sound as if their copper has the same worth as a pile of cow dung."

"Let's put it this way. As I watch Daly drown in debt over his futile dreams that electrified copper wires will someday crisscross the frontier, I'll be drinking a champagne toast as I celebrate my town's newspaper, public school, eight saloons, roller-skating rink, library, ballpark, and theater."

"No hotel? No bank?"

"Of course, I have a hotel. And a bank. And a hospital."

"And I'm sure you have a thriving red-light district."

McNally held up an imagined champagne flute. "Cheers to the district ladies. May their charms forever bewitch my crews and earn me back my money."

"Sergeant Mick. Pompous as ever."

"With good reason."

"You still chained to Aggie?" Bogger asked, jabbing the shovel into the ground.

"Of course."

Bogger grunted his disapproval.

"I didn't marry her to be my wife. I married her to be my nexus to the business and political sphere."

"Just like your Irish daddy married your well-to-do mama."

"I'll ignore that."

"Why'd you bring up the war? Cold Harbor?" Bogger's face twisted into a ghostly mask of pain.

"Because that is where we became brothers on the battlefield. Because that is where I gave you your life."

Bogger shoved a thatch of hair from his face. "You didn't give me no life, Mick. My dreams still spiral through sheets of blood and gunfire, bald cypress and Virginia swampland."

"The entire Army of Northern Virginia has those images burned in our brains. But you got out. You didn't lose your life. You didn't lose a limb. You didn't end up with a bullet in your leg. You got out. You took the paper pinned inside your uniform and handed it to me. That paper—that paper with your name on it so your dead body could be identified—I took it and I handed it to our commanding officer and I swore that I'd witnessed a Yank slit open your gut."

"Would've been better if a Yank had sliced me from stem to stern," Bogger grumbled, bending over to adjust the boulders that anchored one end of the sluice box.

"You got out of the war. All because of your cowardice. And my lie."

"I got out because the Confederate line was in shambles." Bogger said. Fists clenched, he stood up and eyed the weapons Sam had left on the ground.

"Cold Harbor was a mighty victory for the Confederacy." McNally growled. "Our men were slashing the Yanks as if they were straw in a field, and you ran."

"Our boys were deserting the cause left and right, heading back to their families where they could make a difference," Bogger retorted. "We could see the confederacy crumbling. Me leaving wasn't going to change that situation one bit."

McNally pulled a knife from his belt holster and used it to lift a gold fleck from the sluice box. He studied the flake, then flicked it to the ground. "You may be right. But, unlike you, those rabble Johnny Rebs scampering from the front lines didn't have a daddy serving as a mighty Confederate general."

"The past is the past, Mick."

"Does your family still think your dead? Do they still imagine you bleeding and withering in the blazing sun, lying next to a heap of rotting bluecoats? Being eaten alive by beetles at night until death finally claimed you? Do they picture your ghost wandering through the trees, trudging through swampland, drinking bloody creek water?"

"That's enough, Mick." The man kicked the leg of the sluice box. Sandy pulp slopped over the side of the box and splashed across McNally's shirt and trousers.

"What would The General do if he found out his oldest boy had abandoned his fellow soldiers? Had turned tail on the Confederacy? What if The General at long last learned that his warrior on the battlefield was actually a milksop on the run?"

Bogger rammed the sluice box and McNally stepped out the of the way as it collapsed to the ground.

McNally held up a hand to warn off Sam and the miners. "I know your father's still alive, lawyering down in San Francisco for the Southern Pacific Railroad, traveling the lecture circuit, flaunting his military escapades at veterans' meetings and reunions. I know your sister is married to a congressman. They have two sons at The Citadel. I know your brother is a federal judge with friends in high places. We could wire each of them, let them know that their dearly departed was, in truth, a damned deserter."

"Don't you dare go ruining their lives."

"My, my, your disgraceful actions certainly would sully the family name."

"What d'ya want from me, Mick?"

McNally walked around the toppled sluice box to stand next to Bogger. "Stut is in trouble. He and a girl are on the run." He pulled a tintype of his son from his shirt pocket and held it out for Bogger to study. "Their actions cost me my son's life. If Stut turns to anyone for help, it'll be you. You raised him to be a man."

"Until you poisoned him against me."

"Cowardice has a price." McNally returned the tintype to his pocket.

"And if Stut does find me?"

"You'll bring him back to Montana. The girl, too, if she's with him. Stut and I have a long discussion ahead of us. Then a trial, of course."

"Discussion and a trial, huh? Well, don't that sound civilized." Bogger looked towards his men, let out a huff, then turned his attention back to his former partner. "Why would I mangle Stut's life even more?"

"Beyond keeping your desertion a secret? Beyond keeping your family name on the esteemed side of history?" McNally let out a bemused laugh as he slipped a piece of paper from his vest pocket and shoved it against Bogger's chest. "Because you've been digging for gold for nearly thirty years. Because I can see the rheumatoid in your hands. And I swear to God you're wearing the same shirt I last saw you in."

As McNally walked away, he pulled a handful of silver dollars from his trouser pocket and tossed them at Bogger. "You'll bring Stut to me because the reward printed on that wanted poster that's now in your hands is worth more than you'll ever find in gold."

First Days
Leeds, Idaho — August 1890

Miss Jayne drew the battle lines at dawn. By the time Jake came in from feeding stock, a war of words had begun. Lainie was losing.

"You might as well get along with the girl, Ma. She ain't going away anytime soon."

"She's not staying here, Jake. Certainly, Irene can help me out for a few days until Paul and Snow Owl arrive."

"With her stairstep flock of kids in tow? I don't think so."

"I only want Irene here. Her oldest can take care of the rest of the children."

"Heaven almighty, woman, Irene is needed on her own farm. You know she's busy putting up food and preparing for harvest, just like you'll be—" He let the sentence drift. "Just like you and Lainie will be doing soon."

Miss Jayne's hand flew to the bandages wrapped across her eyes. Jake's sternness caved in.

"Look, you and Irene have helped each other for years with preserving food and cooking up meals for harvest crews. You know how much work that involves, with not a spare minute to wipe a kid's nose, let alone take care of someone else's home." Jake wrapped his arms around his mother and held her tight. "There is no one else to help us now," he whispered in her ear. "Emmeline is busy helping Doc at his office. Other womenfolk are busy with their own families and farms. Face it, we need Lainie."

* * *

After Jake convinced his mother to eat some eggs and bacon, he laid a piece of paper in front of Lainie.

"Here's a list of your duties. Leastwise for today. We'll finish out the list later on, after you've had time to get both you and Miss Jayne settled." He grabbed the last two pieces of bacon. "I didn't list the inside chores like washing dishes and sweeping and such. Figure you know the basics of that."

He turned to leave.

"Oh, and laundry day is tomorrow. I'll help set up the wash tubs this time, but next week you're on your own."

Lainie rubbed her temples as she reviewed the list.

Meals. Breakfast at five, supper at seven or so, depending on when I get home from working the fields.

Might as well fill my lunchpail whilst you're cooking breakfast.

Milk cow morn and night. Separate cream. Churn butter (Mama can help with that).

Feed and water the chickens, gather eggs morn and night, clean out the droppings from the hen house. Mrs. Fischer picks up five dozen eggs every Friday afternoon on her way back from town. The rest can be sold at the mercantile.

Put food scraps in mealworm bin.

Zucchini row needs hoeing. There's at least a dozen baby zukes for frying and some large ones for baking bread. Rest of the hoeing can be done tomorrow.

Pick other vegetables ready for harvest. Tomorrow water the vegetables at their base with the laundry water.

Do you know how to process fruit? Peaches will be coming on soon.

"Oh, my," Lainie mumbled. "And this is just part of the list."

* * *

Lainie tackled outdoor chores in between checking on Miss Jayne, who remained glued to her rocking chair, excepting discreet trips to the outhouse when Lainie would guide her to the privy's door and stand nearby hoping that nothing of a confounding sort would happen while the woman was out of her sight and near a deep, dark hole.

She followed through with Jake's list. Having worked in her grandparents' stagecoach home station her whole life, she was accustomed to all sorts of inside chores, though her skills at the stovetop were minimal because her grandmother had insisted on cooking all the meals for the travelers and the family by herself. Lainie had taken turns with her grandfather milking her family's two cows, straining the milk, separating the cream, and cooling the milk for the travelers and occasional boarders at the station. After her grandfather's health began to fail, she took on the job full time. Caring for a garden was old hat, though this new landscape's temperature withered her energy sooner rather than later. And though caring for the chickens had been fourth on Jake's meticulous list, she repeatedly delayed the chore.

She bemoaned that decision once Jake discovered her act of procrastination.

"Those chickens are supposed to be done near first thing," Jake said.

"Don't worry. The job will get done."

"Criminy woman, just throw some feed onto the ground then open the hen house door. Those hens'll come right out to feed. Then you can go inside to fill the feed and water containers and collect the eggs."

Jake grabbed the feed bucket and started scattering the feed.

"Go open the door," he ordered.

She did as she was told and jumped back as several chickens crowded through the doorway to snatch up their overdue breakfast.

"Great, you're scared of chickens."

"I'm not scared of chickens."

"Fine, then get in there and finish the job."

She snatched the feed pail from Jake, leaned her crutch against the outer wall, and darted into the hen house.

The smell hit hard, and she vomited before she was three steps in.

"Give me that." Jake grabbed at the pail.

"I can do this."

"Uh huh. You're of little use to me if you can't stand farm stench."

"Just get out of my way and I'll finish up here." She grabbed the water pans and dumped the mucky water at the base of a nearby stand of sunflowers. She refilled the pans from the bucket of fresh water she'd left outside the henhouse door.

Once done, she gathered eggs from the nests in the long, narrow building. She let out a scream when one of the chickens, still in its nesting box, pecked hard at her hand.

Jake watched, grimfaced, arms crossed, from the corner of the building. When she vomited again halfway through gathering the eggs, he ordered her outside and finished the job himself.

* * *

76

The next morning, Lainie tackled the chicken chores just after breakfast. She'd mentally willed Jake to leave her alone and tend to his own chores. Instead, he followed her to the chicken coop.

"Don't need your help, Jake."

"Prove it."

"Don't need your attitude either, Jake."

"Tough."

She pulled through the chores, swallowing back bile and whisking away stenchtears with her sleeve. She'd nearly completed all her duties when a hen dropped from its roost and set its spurs into Lainie's shoulder. She screamed and twisted and turned, trying to fight off the hen. She dropped the egg basket in the process.

"There goes a pay day," Jake said. "Clean up your mess."

* * *

Day three of what Lainie now termed Chicken Wars went much the same way as the previous two. Lainie tried. Jake scrutinized. She didn't vomit this time, nor did she break any eggs. Jake fired her from the task anyway.

"No, you said this is my job and I'm going to do it."

"Face it, Lainie, you're not fit for this type of work. Get back inside and stick to housework."

"I can do this. I just need time to adjust. Why don't you just—why don't you just shoo?"

"You are such an innocent," Jake said. "You don't even have the nerve to tell me to go to hell."

"Of course, I do."

"Then do it."

She stared at him and tried to form the words.

"See, you don't have the gall to backtalk me," he called over his shoulder as he headed towards the cabin.

"Don't walk away from me, Jake." She threw an egg, hitting him squarely between the shoulders.

"Confound it, girl. What are you doing?"

She threw a second egg at him. He caught it and stormed towards her. She grabbed a third egg from the basket. Jake snatched her wrist before she could throw it.

"Look, mister, I've cleaned up the tar-wretched vomit of miners bent on spending the half speck of gold they found on whiskey and cigars. I've helped upright an outhouse that some idiot blew off the ground when he decided to set off dynamite behind the laundry house. I've skinned pigs, pulled out their entrails, and kicked away rats greedy for the undigested food landing afoot. If I can't stomach the smell of chicken shit, don't judge me. If I flinch at the sound of a hen cackling or balk at touching pin feathers, do not judge me. There's a reason for my fears. And considering you're a man that can't walk across the new floorboards in your house, I imagine you've got a few fears of your own that turn your insides green."

Neither let go of the other's eyes.

"Well, I'll be." Jake finally let go of her wrist. "You haven't lost your backbone after all. Now that you've shown it to me, go show it to my mother."

Good Christian Woman

Lainie grated zucchini in the kitchen. It was just past noon, and the day was already long and made even longer by her attempts to avoid Miss Jayne as much as possible because she realized her backbone wasn't quite ready to face this particular tough old bird.

Since the two had met, the woman spouted off at Lainie's every move.

Quite the feat considering the woman couldn't see what was going on.

And Lainie cowered at every snipe.

"Good Christian woman, my foot," Lainie said to herself, remembering the description Jake had provided of his mother. He'd used words such as gracious and compassionate and charitable to describe the woman.

Thus far, the descriptors Lainie chose were to the contrary. Names like crotchety nag, irascible inkheart, and sourpuss Sue came to mind.

Add to that the title of calculating conniver. When the woman finally decided to get off her royal rocking chair throne, it had been to shufflefoot her way to the kitchen, handseek the crock of salt, and throw a handful of it into the pot of soup Lainie had just set on the countertop to serve.

Lainie had caught sight of the incident from the corner of her eye, and when she tasted the soup to confirm the crime, a host of invectives flew through her mind.

If Lainie's grandmother, God rest her in peace, knew such name calling was on the tip of her granddaughter's tongue, she would have washed the girl's mouth out with lyesoap.

Admittedly, the girl didn't need her grandmother's disapproval to send shivers of regret down her spine or to realize that, fatefully, lyesoap was the reason Miss Jayne was now blind.

She also didn't need her grandmother to explain that Miss Jayne's fears were spilling over, and Lainie was caught in the downpour.

Within just a few weeks, the woman's spirit had been bludgeoned first by loss and grief, then by injury and blindness. Such tragedy was certain to defeat any woman, at least for a time, including this woman that Lainie had deemed Countess of the Countryside.

Once again, Lainie tasted the memory of her grandmother's lyesoap.

"Enough of the name calling. Enough of the name calling," Lainie whispered to herself as she sifted flour into the bread bowl.

Lainie trudged through ideas on how to work with the woman, on how to plow through this awkward wariness of being with someone who was different from everyone else she knew. The woman was blind, and that blindness made everything about each day seem strained and elusive. The woman's bandages, burns, and scars to come all lent to the story of someone fractured, someone ill-delivered of the normalcy of life.

Yet, just a few days ago, the woman had been just that. Normal.

Before the accident, Lainie had watched the woman from afar for nearly three days. She'd watched her weed and sweep and launder and tend to flocks and flowers. Once the woman returned to the cabin, Lainie assumed the same ambition moved forward, for scents of cinnamon and venison and homemade bread drifted across the land to where she camped.

Oh, how those scents had tempted. To sneak into the house and steal a fresh baked biscuit. Or a spoonful of beans. Or lick her finger clean of bacon drippings.

The woman's activities spoke of hard work, capability.

Then came fate's mindset and the woman's life was changed forever.

One minute, normal. The next minute, blind.

Lainie knew that, more than likely, friends of the woman would fall into the social mores of treating the different as if they were daft. Certainly, Miss Jayne didn't deserve such thoughtlessness, but it would happen. Lainie's grandparents had watched it happen with their son Nicholas, the man she'd grown up believing to be her father.

* * *

Up until the age of three, Nicholas had walked and talked just like the other children in his age group. A month after his third birthday and just days shy of Christmas, a dysfluency registered in his speech and, in time, both parents and son experienced frustration that the boy's messages wouldn't come out.

Repetitions, prolongations, blocks in spoken stride—the three syllables of his name stretched to several syllables as he struggled the sounds together.

Nnnnnicholas.

With each birthday, the stuttering grew worse until the little boy shrouded his frustrations with near silence.

Once happy and outgoing, the boy withdrew into his own world. When schoolmates teased, he'd busy himself with reading and rereading books or straightening chairs or picking up bits of debris from the school's dirt floor. When bullies threw bad humor and obnoxious words at him, he'd walk away—to the corner of the schoolroom, to the backside of the huge whitebark pine, all the way to his tiny room at the home station. He'd walk wherever he needed to avoid an argument. When a bully's fist partnered hurtful words, the wordless boy would never fight back or retaliate. Speech was already out of his control. He wouldn't allow self-drawn anger and fistrage to become out of his control, too.

One thing kept the boy going to school. He loved words, though only his parents and the school marm knew, for the rest of the town had deemed him a stammering simpleton. It took patience to listen to what little conversation the boy would offer, and the consensus of the town, fostered by wagging tongues and busybody proclamations, was this: the boy was a halfwit who would burden those who knew him. Better to avoid that burden and instead save conversation for the youth who would someday make hearty contributions to the town's well-being.

Thus, in the town's diligence to look down their noses and criticize the boy's every move, the people failed to see the earnest hunger for knowledge hidden behind the boy's downcast eyes.

Nicholas accepted his lot in society, though he refused to back down from his passion for words. If he couldn't have words flow from him, he'd have them flow in him, through books and lessons and readings by the teacher. Any words he could see or hear or touch—those were the words for him, and he'd keep them gratefully locked away inside of him, ready to reemerge during times when he was completely alone, which was often. Too often.

Lainie had always frustrated over thoughts of her almostfather's boyhood torment. She had hoped that, as an adult, he was better accepted, if not by society, by at least a few good friends. Though, based on the limited knowledge she did have of his situation, she knew that time hadn't necessarily treated him well.

These thoughts about her almostfather were too hard, too revealing. They were leading her back to a road she wasn't ready to travel. She deviated back to thoughts about Miss Jayne's future.

Would Miss Jayne's affliction leave others sightless to the value of her friendship, her companionship, her talents and teachings? Would she be dismissed as a simpleton, as Lainie's almostfather had been, simply because she lacked the function of her eyes? Why should burns and blindness suddenly position this woman on the side of peculiarity?

Lainie deliberated these questions and thought back to an incident she carried from her childhood.

At the age of nine, she'd met a traveler who had lost part of his right arm fighting Confederates during the Battle of Fort Donelson. She spotted the man sitting at a table, waiting to be served one of her grandmother's meals. She was so discomfited at the presence of the tight-stretched skin across his forearm's stump that she could barely put together a full sentence, let alone serve him his supper.

The man recognized her unease and nearly laughed at her wide-eyed expression. He'd witnessed similar reactions for nearly half his life now, but none from such a delightfully green-eyed girl. So, he dismissed the idea of condemning her response—a tact he might have taken with worldwise adults—and happily accepted the plate of fried ham, mashed potatoes, bacon beans, and spoonbread.

At the end of the meal, he called her to his table. "Girl, I've got a problem with this meal," he'd growled.

Once again, her green eyes opened wide and she gulped hard, wondering what to do.

"My problem is," he continued, "the food was so tasty that I want to applaud the cook. Then I remembered, by golly, I've only got one hand. How's that for a predicament?"

The man appeared overbearingly stern as he stated his problem, and she had mirrored the solemnity of his facial expression to the point that, when he broke out with a smile and gave her a wink, her knees were locked, and she was near ready to faint.

He finally asked, "Are you going to help me out?"

"Help out? What do you mean?"

"Help me applaud the cook, of course." He held up his hand. "Go on, clap hands with me."

She gave him a quizzical look then did as told. The action secured a smile on both their faces.

"See there? I just clapped hands for the first time in twenty years. Want to know a secret?"

She nodded her head and the man quietly shared his wisdom.

"All sorts of folks out there have an infirm of some kind or another. A little help from a special lady like you and they can accomplish things they forgot was possible."

Her smile broadened, and she clapped his hand three times more.

"Now, run on back to the cook and tell her a customer demands to see both of you. Put on your grumpy face so she gets worried some. When you get back to my table, you know what to do. We'll applaud up a storm that will shine light on her day."

* * *

Lainie's memory was interrupted by a knock at the door. Miss Jayne jumped in her seat. Lainie boosted herself onto the dry sink and clumsily lunged out the open kitchen window. Jake answered the door. It was Doc.

"I'm here to check on my patient, Jake. And your patient, if she doesn't mind."

"You'll have to catch my patient first, Doc. She just flew out the window. She did the same thing yesterday when Mr. and Mrs. Callahan paid a visit."

"I don't blame her," the doctor quietly confided. "The other day, two men were headed towards town asking about a red-headed runaway. They came from your direction, so I assumed they'd already stopped here and found nothing."

Jake nodded. "Yeah, they were here. Tore the place up, but they didn't find the girl."

"I'm glad she's safe," Doc said. "Listen, I've been doing a little detective work. Turns out those lowlifes paid a visit to pretty much every farm around."

"Did they hurt anyone?"

"Not that I know of. And from what I learned, if any of our locals have spotted the girl, they didn't confess to it."

"Are the men still in the area?" Jake asked.

"I don't think so. Bud Schewster over at the farrier's shop said they stayed a couple of nights at the hotel, then headed east after picking up their horses. Sounds like they put quite a few miles on the animals. And Jake, Bud said those men aren't afraid to ride those horses into the ground."

* * *

Jake left the doctor alone to examine Miss Jayne's eyes and the burns on her face. He found Lainie hiding behind the smokehouse.

"Doc wants to check your leg."

"My leg's fine."

"All the same, I'd feel a whole lot better if you'd let him see the wound, make sure the infection is clearing up."

Lainie huddled deeper into the shadows drawn by the building and an old elm tree. Her arms were crossed tight and she rubbed at the gooseflesh on her forearms while she banged her shoulder blades against the building's roughhewn wood.

"Look, Doc already knows you're here. He saw you in the woods a few days back. Criminy, the man even left you his sandwich that day. You can trust him."

"I don't think trust is in my vocabulary."

* * *

"So, you're the dark-haired filly Jake told me about," Doc said after Lainie entered the room.

She threw a confused look from Jake to the doctor and back again.

"It's a long story," Jake said.

"Let's have a look at that leg," Doc moved a table chair next to Miss Jayne, who was seated in her rocker, and motioned for his next patient to have a seat.

84

"Now, where is the injury located?"

Lainie didn't respond, so Jake did the talking for her.

"It's her right leg, halfway up on her shin bone."

"May I have a look?" Doc asked.

Grimfaced, with her eyes sighted on the wall before her, the girl lifted her skirt just high enough for the doctor to see the damage beneath the bandages.

She pinched her eyes shut as the doctor gently uncoiled the bandage.

"Still tender, eh?" Doc said, noting that the girl's face had paled some. "It looks to be healing well, though I still see signs of the infection." He applied salve to the wound and rewrapped the girl's leg with a new bandage.

"It's not the same," he said to Jake and Jake nodded.

"Not the same as what?" Lainie asked with a shaky voice.

The question hung in the air.

Jake wasn't ready for explanations about his little boy or the gangrene that had killed him.

Miss Jayne sliced through the silence.

"Doc, you got any idea of someone in town who would be willing to come out and stay with me?" she asked.

"Ma, don't." Jake warned.

"You heard it from the good doctor, this girl's wound is healing up fine. It's soon time she sets out on her own, finding her way to wherever it is she wants to go."

"Lainie is staying, Ma."

"There's no sense in her staying with the leaves ready to fall and snow soon to fly. This girl, I'm sure, has got places to be. So, Doc, I'll be needing someone to care for me until my nephew and his wife get home. How about that Perkins girl? She'd be up to caring for me and taking on chores."

"I believe the Perkins girl is a month shy of delivering a baby," Doc said.

"That would work just fine then," Miss Jayne said. "She can stay here until her youngster is born. By then, family will be here for me."

"Ma, don't be ridiculous. You can't ask that of Sarah Perkins. She's got her own life to lead, her own house to take care of. We already have someone who is perfectly able and willing to help out."

"Now if that Perkins girl isn't up to the task, how about one of the students at the school. Surely Miss Franklin has a pupil that's in grade eight and close enough to being done with her schooling. Besides, school's out for a few more days."

"Mother. Stop it. This instant. You are not disrupting someone's schooling. You are not campaigning for a new caregiver. And you are not ousting Lainie from this house. From what Doc said earlier, those men are looking for her all over these parts."

Jake cringed, regretting his words.

"I have to leave." Lainie hurried from the chair to Miss Jayne's room to retrieve her meager belongings.

"They left town, headed east," Jake assured as he followed the girl.

Miss Jayne interrupted him. "They could be back any day now, and who knows what will happen then."

Jake ran a hand through his hair. "Why would they come back through our town? It sounds like they searched it clear through and didn't find a trace of Lainie's existence."

"But folks know about me now, Jake." The girl stepped back into the front room, her bedroll in her arms. "I can't hide from every one of your friends that stops by. It was hard enough keeping quiet in the bedroom when the pastor stopped in to check on your mother. Word is out to more of her friends that she's been injured, so I'm sure there will be more folks stopping by and wondering who is helping her out."

"Yes, townfolk will hear that someone is taking care of mother. And if they ran into that McNally man, they know a young woman with curly red hair might—*might*—be in the area," Jake said. "You look nothing like the description he gave. You can keep your hair dyed black and you can braid it or cover it or fix it up however you womenfolk know how to so the curl doesn't show."

"I can't hide my eye color, Jake."

"There's more than one person in this world with green eyes."

"And what happens if I stumble about my name or where I come from?" Lainie asked.

"You'll just have to be careful," Jake said. "We will all be careful, won't we Mama?"

Miss Jayne gave no answer.

"If I may interject one thing," Doc said, "you are overlooking an important component of the plan to keep Lainie here, whether it's for a few days or for the long run."

"What's that?" Jake asked.

"Lainie does need to come from somewhere," Doc said. "She can't have simply shown up at just the right time to provide care and help with the farm. That, in itself, would be suspicious."

"Just one more reason for me to leave," Lainie said.

"Let's not be hasty, my dear," Doc said. "I may have a solution."

Doc's Plan

The next morning, Doc posted a note on his office door: For medical emergency, contact Mrs. Matthews at the Adamsen farm.

Once he and his wife arrived at the farm, Emmeline went straight to work blackening the red of the girl's grown out hair with fabric dye she'd picked up at the mercantile. She also kept Miss Jayne preoccupied with stories of the goings-on in town.

"You sure about this, Doc?" Jake asked one more time as the two hashed out details of the plan.

"No, but as you saw in the letter, my associate from college established his daughter's plan for a nursing apprenticeship alongside a doctor. I replied that I would be happy to host the girl, but a recent letter announced that she opted to apprentice with another doctor closer to her home."

"So, the letter asking you to help with the apprenticeship is basically evidence of a reason for Lainie to be here," Jake said. "But the letter states that the girl's name is Janet."

"Easy enough to remedy," Doc said. He dabbed his finger into his cup of coffee, flicked the liquid onto the elegant brown script where the name Janet Kearn was listed, and smiled as the ink bled across the page.

"Darn it all. Emmeline is always complaining about my messiness," he said.

"All right, you solved one part of our dilemma. What happens if someone finds out Lainie isn't really this nursing student? Or if someone discovers your friend's daughter working in another town?"

"Not likely to happen," Doc responded. "My friend lives in Pennsylvania. How many people in Nez Perce County have any dealings with folks living over two thousand miles away?"

"You do."

"That's a valid point."

"I'm just saying that, even though we're on the other side of the country, word from east to west and back again can and does get around," Jake said.

"Have you come up with any better solutions?" Doc asked.

"No. I guess we stick with your plan."

"If we're going to help keep the girl safe and your mother safe, I'd say we don't have any other option."

"You're right. I know you're right. It's just difficult to wrap my mind around all that's happened," Jake said as he poured a second cup of coffee for his friend. "What's the next step in your plan, Doc?"

"As we've discussed, I will make my regular trip to Lewiston to pick up supplies. Lainie will travel with me, hidden in the back of our buggy. Once Lainie and I arrive in Lewiston, she will visit the telegraph office and send me notice through our town's telegrapher that she is to arrive in Leeds by stagecoach sometime within the week. Upon her return, I will make a few formal introductions in town, explaining that she is my medical student who, for the next few days, possibly weeks, will be assisting with your mother's care until your cousin and his wife return home."

"And after that?"

"Assuming that your mother will indeed kick the girl's hind end from her house, as she so eloquently put it yesterday, Lainie is welcome to stay on with me and Emmeline to study medicine."

"What makes you think she'd be interested in studying medicine?" Jake asked.

"A young woman who attempts to cauterize her own wound certainly has the gumption to take on a career in nursing. If after a few weeks of training she has no interest in the field, she's welcome to move on to the next venture of her life."

* * *

The doctor's buggy was fancier than any wagon Lainie had ever been in. It was eight-foot-long or so, painted black, and its front half was fitted with an upholstered bench seat.

The back half of the buggy was a basic box, maybe five feet across and three and a half feet long. The box wasn't deep, nor was it covered, but it served its purpose of carrying medicines and supplies to patients and, when necessary, carrying patients to the doctor's office in town.

Doc termed the buggy as secondhand luxury, for he'd purchased it from an oldtimer physician whose palsy had ripped from him the ability to properly attend to patients. Doc had sanded down and painted the framework of the buggy while his wife reupholstered and tufted the seat in plush grey fabric. The original retractable top that stood over the upholstery had also been in dire repair, so Doc exchanged his services as a dentist with the services of the town's tailor whose dental health was quite amiss.

Lainie should have been excited to ride in such luxury, but the terms of her invisible departure from the Adamsen farm included a trip past homesteads, through town, and along an oft-used road where someone might see her. Thus, her ride in the fancy buggy was relegated to the boxed-in bed where Doc had provided two feather pillows and an old quilt to provide some semblance of comfort for the girl.

Once Lainie was settled, Doc redistributed around her the empty crates for his supply run and the commodities he intended to take to outlying patients on his return trip from Lewiston. Finally, Jake and Doc covered her and the supplies with a sheet of canvas.

For the second time in two months, Lainie traveled in a wagon under the cloak of camouflage.

Time underneath the canvas was sporadic, with Doc signaling her with birdcall when the path was free and clear of people so she could pull back the cover for fresh air and conversation.

When she was tucked underneath the canvas, the hot, jouncing ride to Lewiston left Lainie plenty of time to reflect on another disappearing act.

Escape
Thurmond, Montana — May 1890

Somehow, she'd escaped. The rage. The binding knots. The bullets. Somehow, she'd escaped.

And somehow, she'd landed sanctuary, not in a church, but within a dancehall saloon.

"Praise the Lord, you look just like your mother," a heavily painted woman said to her, rushing her through a long, dimly lit hallway to a back room.

"I knew it was you the moment I saw you walk towards Niall McNally's mansion," a second woman named Kate said. "I tried to get ahead of you, to stop you from entering the property, but a mule team hauling freight got in my way and when I saw you next, you were knocking at the door."

The painted woman instructed Kate to fetch supplies, then she pulled back a rug, revealing a hidden door in the floor. She pulled the door open, urging the girl to climb down the ladder.

"I don't understand. Who are you? How can you know me?" The girl asked her questions as she gathered her skirts and took the first precarious step down the ladder. "And where is Stut? Why did he leave me here?"

The painted woman handed her a lantern. "My name is Mother Damnable. We know you because we saved your life when you were just a babe."

* * *

Within the dark, dank cellar, the girl and Mother Damnable moved through a corridor built of earth and stone.

"Where are we going?" the girl asked.

"Just ahead, we have a room to hide you in," Mother Damnable explained.

"Why is there a tunnel beneath the saloon?"

"Because others have needed to be saved." Mother Damnable's words closed the conversation.

The girl's questions furthered when they entered a small room, again with walls of earth and stone, that held a mattress tick, a stack of folded blankets, a chair, and a table.

Kate soon joined them and set a pile of clothing and some tins atop the table. She informed Mother Damnable that a trusted dove shut the cellar door and replaced the rug. Mother Damnable nodded her approval.

"Quickly, remove your dress while we prepare the dye," Mother Damnable instructed the girl.

"Dye?" the girl questioned.

"Yes, for your hair. We need to disguise you."

"We should iron out her curls, too. We can do that first thing in the morning," Kate said.

The women rushed to transform the girl, answering her questions as best they could.

"Your mother, Louisa, was my best friend," Kate said. "She was beautiful and a talented dancer, but she was too trusting."

"That girl was a butterfly," Mother Damnable said. "Headstrong and naïve, not knowing the difference between nectar and poison."

"We both became dancehall girls here at Mother's saloon," Kate said. "We had good wages, a commission from the drinks we sold, a roof overhead. T'weren't no proper jobs available to us."

"You mean my mother was a prostitute?" the girl asked.

"Absolutely not," Kate said. "The sporting women keep to the brothels, and heaven knows there are enough brothels in this town. Mother runs a respectable establishment. We may show off our knickers while we dance, but we certainly aren't forced to drop them for booze or money."

"So, my mother was married when she had me."

"No. Mother has lost her girls to marriage on many occasion, but that didn't happen with Louisa. Instead, she was lost to the trill-tongued flattery of that menace. Mother warned her, warned all of us, not to trust that man, but Niall McNally knows how to charm the ladies when he puts on his Irish brogue."

"The man had his own missus to charm," Mother Damnable said, "and enough brothel gems that he didn't need to hover around my place."

"It's not your fault, Mother. We all tried to warn Louisa. And you did your best to keep McNally away from all of us."

"I obviously failed," Mother said. "But I won't fail again with that man. He may own this town. But he doesn't own any of us hall girls." She squeezed the girl's shoulder. "And he doesn't own you."

* * *

The girl needed more answers, more time with the women to unravel her past, but time's travail moved quickly and soon she was left underground and alone with a lantern, the warmth of heavy blankets, and a brooch Kate had fetched from her room.

The brooch had belonged to the girl's mother, Louisa. Years before, Kate had smuggled the small piece of jewelry from the jail cell shortly after Louisa's arrest.

At last, the girl knew her mother's name and she used her finger to trace its letters across the cold rock wall.

Louisa.

Her arrest. Why had her mother been arrested? And what exactly had her relationship been to that man? McMurray. No. McCauley. No, that wasn't it either. McNally. The women had called him McNally. In all the absurd, dizzying, rabid circumstances of the day, the man's name kept slipping from her grasp, so she silently spit it out over and over again to embed it in her mind. McNally. McNally. McNally.

Because of this man, her mother had been arrested. Falsely arrested. Then what? The women wouldn't give details. Instead, they told her to take comfort, that her mother was buried amid asters and daisies.

But she knew. She knew from McNally's own words that her mother had been hung. Executed. Murdered for a crime she didn't commit.

And Stut, the women, they had saved her as a baby. They knew her story, her beginnings, her transfer to another town, another life, another destiny. But the women didn't share details. Why wouldn't the women share details?

The girl studied the brooch in the dim light. Sterling silver? Perhaps. She traced the wings of the tarnished dove and pondered the olive branch it carried. *Peace, sweet child.* The words flitted through her mind and she dismissed them, scoffed them, labeled them as nonsense. She adjusted the honey-soaked muslin Kate had prepared to cover the brandmarks McNally had singed into her neck. *Peace, sweet child.* The words did nothing to diminish the searing pain of the burn marks, the newly lit fear, the confusion over her mother and the man this town called Stut.

Her chest clenched as, past the earthen walls and against the moan of wind or the mourn of a wolf, she heard men shouting, horses racing.

She and Stut were the subjects of a manhunt.

Would they be the next to hang?

* * *

A few hours later, Mother Damnable and Kate ironed out the girl's newly darkened hair. A pressing iron with a wood handle was kept hot within a pail of greying coals. Seated in the chair, the girl leaned her head against the blanket-topped table while the two women pulled and plied at her unruly curls, one holding the strands in place atop the blanket while the other moved the iron to and fro.

"You keep mentioning Wallace," the girl said. She grimaced as another section of her hair was pulled taut. "Who is Wallace and what does he have to do with me?"

"Wallace isn't a person. It's a place." Kate set the iron back onto the coals. "Wallace is the mining town we're sending you to. And it's a town that Niall McNally loathes and refuses to set foot in. Mother sends all her frightened doves there."

"It's a mining town in the panhandle of Idaho," Mother Damnable continued. "A woman named Gretchen runs a hotel there. The railroad is nearby, so travelers come, travelers go. You'll be one in a sea of new faces."

"But a mining town is full of men. Surely a woman showing up alone would seem suspicious."

"Trust me," Kate reassured, "this mining town is filled with women boarders. Probably every building with an upstairs is part brothel."

"Wait, last night you condemned sporting women."

"I condemn the brothels and the men who lust for them, yes," Kate said. "But the women? These so-called shady ladies? Most don't deserve that name. They come from the same type of predicament that your mother and I did. Raised on a farm that couldn't support the whole family. Locked up inside a mill, working sixteen hours a day for barely enough money to scrape up a small meal. Widows and abandoned wives needing to care for their children. Orphans needing a home. Many of these women have good morals and good hearts, but they're forced to work any way they can."

"Is that where my future lies?" the girl asked. "In a brothel?"

"Yes and no," Kate said. "Have you ever heard of the Underground Railroad? Secret routes and safe houses that helped slaves cross into freedom?"

"I've heard a little bit about it."

"Mother Damnable, Lady Gretchen, and I, well, we help women in trouble, who've been beaten down and are scared for their lives. We help them escape their world to find a better one. Lady Gretchen's place is part brothel, yes, but it's also a safe house."

"I don't understand."

"Lady Gretchen hides our frightened doves in plain sight," Kate said. "Some work preparing food or serving meals or cleaning rooms and eventually move on to marriage or earn enough money to move back east or prove up a homestead claim. Other doves do choose to entertain menfolk in Lady Gretchen's brothel, mostly because they can make good money and Lady Gretchen does her best to protect them. I know it sounds contrary to escape a man's fist only to be paid to be in another man's bed, but sometimes it's the safer answer."

"We were ill-equipped to save your mother from Niall McNally, God bless her soul," Mother Damnable added, "and we certainly can't protect every woman who gets fist-smacked or is left penniless, but we can sure try. Lady Gretchen's place is part brothel, yes, and some sisters in our cause choose the upstairs life at the brothel for themselves. We don't want that for any of our doves, but we understand when it happens."

"And if it's going to happen, if there's no other way for a woman to get a meal or to thwart destitution, then Gretchen's hotel is the place to go," Kate added. "Her business is fitted with crystal chandeliers and fancy rugs and tapestries and she provides a home that is sure as shootin' more secure than any of us could ever dream."

* * *

Before the light of dawn, the girl stood in the shadows of the saloon's cellar wearing a new dress, shoes a size too large, and her hair pinned into a bun and tucked underneath a heavy scarf.

She understood the reasoning for the scarf when shown her mode of transportation: a farm wagon filled with crates of chickens. Feathers and dander were floating above and around the wagon and the girl turned to Mother Damnable with questions in her eyes.

"Trust, my sweet girl," the woman said. "Just trust."

Kate hugged the girl tight and whispered in her ear, "God's speed."

As Mother Damnable said her goodbyes, she, too, held the girl tight.

"You were just a babe the first time we smuggled you away," Mother Damnable said, her voice thick with emotion. "God saw it right to protect you then. We're praying that this time, He sees fit to protect you again."

* * *

During the first leg of the girl's journey, she was confined within a boarded-up hutch placed in the wagon bed just behind the driver's seat. It held a musty straw floor with hints of miniscule movement. Ants? Mites? Earwigs? In the darkness she could not tell, and she dared not guess. Gauzy threads and matted strands clutched her walls, curtaining them white and leaving little doubt that weavers and spinners of the arachnid sort were somewhere present within the space.

The compartment's air was stiff with ammonia and loam and her own sweat and heavy breath. Soon the girl was clenching her stomach, holding back shuddering heaves of thick nausea.

Auditory warfare pelted through the sweatbox. The incessant chicken calls of her fellow travelers were unnerving. Their staccatos and heraldings hammered through her head and dived at her sanity. She was grateful for the camouflage the animals offered—what fool would unload dozens of chicken hutches piled three high, then traipse through feathers and smelly excrement carpeting the wagon's floorboards to investigate a less than coffin-sized box?—but she wished the massed conversation of the birds would pause and provide her some semblance of relief.

The girl squirmed into a position where her face would be less engulfed by the smell of her own vomit. She wondered how long she could endure this den of stench and stunted movement. Kate had assured that other women—even with their children, their babies—had survived such a journey before. Back east. During slave times. The girl hadn't dared ask how many. Or why. And she hadn't asked Mother Damnable to share more of her family's story about chicken wagons helping black folks get to the River Jordan. Instead, she held tight to the woman's promise that the girl's own River Jordan was lying just ahead.

The wagon finally stopped its travel. The driver and another man loaded the chicken hutches onto a railcar. The girl kept her quiet as the wagon bounced and quaked from the movement of the work.

"More dead chickens than usual," she heard one man say.

"Hotter day than usual," the other replied. "Muggy, too."

"More'll be dead by the time they get to the mines."

"Not my problem," was the response.

When the wagon set in motion again, the girl was sure the driver had forgotten about her but she dared not slip open the lid or hammer her fists against the sides of the box for fear of being discovered. Her only relief came when the man tapped the box three times, which she took as assurance that she would soon be freed from her getaway prison.

Soon, the rumbling and hissing and cursing and footstomps that composed the workingcog clamor of the railroad fell away and the wagon distanced itself from town.

The driver stopped the wagon along a wooded trail and climbed into the wagon bed. Through the small slits of light, the girl watched the man check for onlookers, then open the door of the wooden hutch. He held out his hand to the girl and helped guide her through the doorway and onto the muck-covered wagon boards. She stood, cautious of the numbness in her legs, and picked up her skirts to cross to the end of the wagon bed where the driver gripped her around the waist, lifted her, then settled her on the ground.

"Thank you," she offered, her voice frail, raspy.

He tipped his hat in acknowledgment and returned to the front of the wagon.

She followed.

"Sir, what do I do now?"

He grabbed a flour sack from underneath the seat and passed it to her.

"There's clothes inside. Some food. Canteen of water. Head into the woods and get changed. When you're done, head back to the railway and purchase your ticket. Information about where you're headed is inside an envelope, along with money for the ticket."

He climbed into the wagon and took his seat.

"Sir, what if . . ."

"Forget about any what ifs, miss. You ain't got time for 'em. Follow your gut and you'll be fine."

The Hook House
Wallace, Idaho — July 1890

The girl had landed in Wallace, Idaho in May. She had found her way to Lady Gretchen's Hotel. She was afforded a bedroom with seven roommates and only three small beds. She was provided two meals a day and one bath a week. She hadn't known what her wages would be but was told she'd receive her pay once a month.

From there on, she lived out life as best she could, mopping up spilled whiskey and dried manure and tobacco spit. She cleared tables amidst poker and faro games, washed dishes in scalding water, and traipsed across rutted backtrails with buckets filled high with the day's leftover food to slop the pigs Gretchen kept for eventual use on the supper table. She tried not to blush when she spotted soiled doves leading men upstairs and she kept her eyes on the ground when the dancehall girls lifted their skirts and did indeed, as Kate had put it, show off their knickers. She did all this amidst butt grabs, low whistles, and the overzealous cajoling of wannabe suitors looking for quick love.

Her least favorite job: dumping the dozen or so spittoons into the trench latrine outside the building. Each container held the sickly-sweet smell of earthy leather and rotting teeth. Bile coiled in her stomach from that smell combined with the plop plop plop sound as the mucoused chunks of tobacco sloshed against the hardscrabble ground. No matter how hard she tried, she could never escape the tobacco spit backsplash against her skirt and shoes. The first time it happened, and she grew nauseous from the scent following her every footstep, she slipped into the kitchen to try and clean off the rancid stains. When the head cook spotted her efforts, she received a swift kick to her backside and orders to get back to work.

She was the new girl in town working in this hotel—this hook house—and she saw no better future in sight. When some other damaged dove landed in Wallace, maybe she'd move up the ranks to a job with fewer obnoxious odors and revulsive sounds.

In truth, she didn't believe such a job existed for any woman in this town, unless the woman was tucked away in marriage to a man with few vices, who didn't believe a backhand across his wife's face was a means to marital bliss.

She did her best to avoid the other hook houses and gambling dens—living in one was discomfiting enough—though it was hard to walk anywhere in Wallace without passing one.

The majority of men who came to tunnel through the mountainside were young, single, and desperate for their handful of riches from the mining trade. The women who came to Wallace had the same aspiration of riches with quite few prospects for success; thus, they tunneled through their own entrepreneurial mountains, including prostitution—the world's oldest trade.

Washing laundry? You could earn a bit of money doing that, slaving over boiling vats of soapy water, dipping and plunging, dipping and plunging. The workers' underdrawers and sweatrags and lindsey-woolsey britches all needed cleaning now and then, though the unmarried miners rarely cared about their cleanliness after their fourteen-hour shifts underground. But come washday, they still held on to certain standards. They still wanted their sleeves ironed and their shirt collars starched.

A decent cook with the fortitude to work over a hot fire, no matter the weather's mood, might have a chance to make it in this town, for the miners always needed sturdy meals to eat.

Two weeks after landing in Wallace, the girl had watched a woman with shaggy brows and sparse blonde braids pinned halo style around her head hunch over a cooktub heaped with minced lamb, chopped potatoes, rutabagas, and onions. The woman pinched spices from tins—rock salt, ground pepper, rosemary perhaps?—and handkneaded them into the filling. Then she scooped the filling onto circles of dough.

"You fold it like a wave," the woman narrated, her Irish accent lilting each word. "Top o'er bottom, like a wave rolls in on the shore. Then braid. You must always braid the edge of the crust, like so."

The pasties, fragrant and golden brown, came off the fire grate just in time for lines of men to return to the mines.

"Pasty for you, love?" Halo Woman asked again and again. One by one, each pasty was purchased and slipped into a lunch tin.

The girl didn't know which she craved most—the savory meat pies or the sound of coins landing in Halo Woman's cup.

On the opposite side of the street, a beauty with thick words and raven curls earned honors as the most creative female entrepreneur. Each day she set up a small table draped in black alongside two red velvet chairs. She'd stand, slowly fanning a deck of unusual cards in her hands, and call out, "Is this your lot in life? Or do you have a bigger destiny? Come. Come. See? The images on my cards, they are from a holy book written by Egyptian priests and brought to the old continent by Gypsies from Africa. Come. Let us see your destiny."

Then there were the wives, mavens of tradition, working their days separate and apart from their husband's shiftwork. Make the meals. Bake the bread. Keep the children quiet so the husband can sleep. Shiftwork widows, with their twilight to midnight routines of childkeep and upkeep, scrabbling and scouring, watching their menfolk march off into the mountain, always wondering if they'd march back out.

Shiftwork. Looming shiftwork.

The girl supposed a few women landed positions as operators at the telephone exchange or at the post office building where the town founder's wife had once served as postmistress. Those jobs were limited by number and, if ever a position became vacant, by formal introduction. Employment opportunities were also limited at the mercantiles, restaurants, and the traditional hotels. The saloons and the hook houses were the only places that seemed to have job openings for women in any form of abundance.

At least that's how a girl named Abbie described things. She'd been working as a server for Lady Gretchen since September's flashflood sent waters over the banks of Placer Creek and left men and mules clambering to move wagons through mired streets.

The girl couldn't shake Abbie's words: The only way in here is *for* a man, and the only way out of here is *with* a man.

"Most of us hire on at Lady Gretchen's for short periods of time," Abbie had said. "A volume house is what she calls it. There's probably ten men for every woman in this town, so chances of catching a man to marry are good."

"So, you work in a saloon or a hook house to find a man?" the girl had asked incredulously.

"Sure. This is where us throwaways go," Abbie had replied. "Ain't no menfolk beyond brothers and cousins where I'm from, and not enough farm to keep feeding everyone in the family. My twin sister and me, we was shoved out of the nest real young. Shoot, every time ma and pop got themselves into another baby sitsheation, they'd boot a couple of us older kids out the door. My oldest brother, he ended up in the cavalry. We've got an older sister who hooked up with the circus show and another sister who ended up dead, but she was sickly to begin with. Me and Beth Ann, well, both of us landed here in dear old Wallace and I'd say we're better for it."

"Where's your sister at?"

"Beth Ann got on at the Hayes Hotel. She's a real fine cook. Went pleading for a job in their kitchen as soon as we set foot in this town. The head cook, a Mrs. Fenstermacher or something like that, she didn't believe Beth Ann's braggings about her cooking, so she shooed my sister away. But Beth Ann's ornerier than a rattlesnake with hives and she snuck into the hotel's kitchen that night and cooked eight different recipes while no one was there. That next morning, Mrs. Fenstermacher or something like that walked into her kitchen and it done smell like heaven. 'Better for a hotel to have a good cook than to clean out the bedbugs,' Mrs. Fenstermacher or something like that said to my sister. Beth Ann's been cooking there ever since."

Abbie had rambled on about her and her sister's mining town adventures and, by all accounts, seemed content with this life. She had a roof over her head, never worried for food, didn't have to soothe and shush teething babies, and was quite polished at flirting with Lady Gretchen's prosperous clientele, enough so that she'd received a few silver coins that she had sewn into the hem of her underskirt.

Each depleting day, the girl became more skeptical that Abbie would find a husband before opting for a different working-girl status. She feared that route for her friend. Throughout this town and other towns like it, too many of these working girls, theses soiled doves, fueled their lives with dark whiskey, Fraser's Tablets, and toothache drops. Too many of them had dark circles under their eyes and dark thoughts in their hearts. Too many of them clenched their teeth whenever they moved—she was sure they had bruises to hide—and stared out the window with regretting eyes. Too often, a soiled dove's life was cut short by an overdose of laudanum in some lonely room.

Too many. Too many. Too many.

At Lady Gretchen's hotel, filled with its finery and flair, life was still deceiving. Dangerous. Dark.

And cruel.

The girl was sick of it all.

She was sick of the saloon men, always expecting attention.

She was sick of the box trap of haze that she worked in, with its stench of tobacco smoke, horse hide, and sweat. And she was sick of going outside for fresh air, only to be trapped by blastsmoke and mine vapors and the inescapable taste of black powder and metal that heavily grazed her tongue.

She was sick of the silt that rained down and grabbed at her clothes, her skin, her hair, like chaff to a wattle hog, and sick of the signal bells from the mine—one bell, two bells, three bells, more—and the screaming steam from each ore train as it squealed through the middle of town.

Yes, the town of Wallace, with its tramp miners and Wallace diehards, had truly saved her life. But it wasn't her town. It would never be her town.

And she was sick that she hadn't figured a way out. A way to a new life. A way to a new future. She needed a new sky. A new direction. A new name.

Answers. Possibilities. Some sort of destinate path that would lead her to—to what? She didn't know. But opportunity had to be out there.

It had to be out there.

* * *

"You're serving tonight."

The girl couldn't believe Lady Gretchen's words.

"Nellie's moved on to greener pastures. Some fool man is starting up a creamery. Claims he's going to buy hundreds of gallons of milk and cream from the farmers to make butter and cheese in bulk, then sell it all over the territory. Nellie fell for his pitch. Now she'll be arm deep in curds and whey all day. No matter. Put on your best dress. I need you out on the floor in ten minutes. Callister's got a big meeting going on, so put on your best face. Maybe one of those bigwigs will notice you and hire you on as housekeep."

The girl raced upstairs to the bedroom. She slipped inside, tiptoed past the girls who were sleeping before beginning their night shift, and put on the only other clothing she owned—a fawn-colored blouse with cap sleeves and ruffled trim down the front of the bodice paired with a pleated navy taffeta skirt that tsk tsk tsked her every move.

Might she have the chance to move on to greener pastures like Nellie had? She wished she had met Nellie's new employer. She would have jumped at the chance to work at a creamery.

Back in the parlor, the girl was given her orders.

"You and Cora will handle the miners. Keep their glasses full and their antics to a minimum," Lady Gretchen said. "Lila will be taking care of Callister and his guests. Stay out of her way. That girl is gonna bring in a pretty penny selling top-shelf drinks."

"This is your first time serving drinks, right?" Cora asked the girl.

"Yes. Any advice?"

"I choose which tables are mine. The rest of the swine are yours to serve."

* * *

The girl couldn't avoid the loud words spewed at the so-called table of honor where Callister and six other men butchered through pan-fried steaks as they argued the fate of their mining towns. She wasn't the only one paying attention. A few miners had traipsed in for their evening round of drinks, and their conversation was near stopped as they homed in on the heated debate taking place in the far corner of the parlor.

Snippets of conversation centered around miners, labor unions, and talk of a strike.

"Up in Montana in that town called Granite, they've already built themselves a three-story union hall," one man complained. "I heard they spent over $20,000 on it."

"Ain't no way miners will unionize under my watch," another man barked out.

"Anyone that even whispers the word *strike* will be arrested, with his ass hauled to the pen I've already fenced in," the man with the long mustache and goatee said.

The youngest of the men bolted from his seat and his chair was sent flying.

"If Colonel Wallace was here, he'd . . ."

"Your precious Colonel Wallace was swindled of his property. *All* of his property." This time it was a red-headed man who spoke. His voice was low, controlled. "I will not jeopardize my empire by considering the thoughts of a man whose shortfall of business acumen left him slunking out of town, tail between his worthless, feeble legs. Now, if you'll kindly take your seat, Mr. Daniels, we'll prioritize our response to any unionization threats."

The crimson-faced man picked up his chair, set it upright, and sat down.

"I just mean to say that Colonel Wallace had some very profound insights as to how . . ."

The red-headed man waived the comment away as if it was a bothersome gnat.

"All that's left of that man in this town is the sour taste of his name. Perhaps you should rethink the name of this town." The red-headed man lifted his glass to indicate need of refills for the table. "What about you, Jenkins? What's your take on all this talk of unions and labor strikes?"

"I don't have a dog in this fight. I've got a dry camp. Fewer accidents, fewer fights. Miners in my neck of the woods are just fine with their working conditions. And their pay."

"Then you, dear man, are a fool." Whiskey sloshed onto the tablecloth as the red-headed man banged his glass on the table and again lifted it in the air. "Idaho has just been granted statehood. Montana has been a state for a few months now. You watch. Those steps into the Union's government control will lead people to think they actually want *more* government control. Tongues will wag with talk of safety, better wages, shorter hours. More money in the miner's pocket means less in mine. The winds have shifted, gentlemen. The government is ready to take us for a ride."

"Certainly, safety issues should be considered," Jenkins countered. "At least in some small degree."

"Safety?" The red-headed man stood. "Safety? You want safety, then get an education. You want safety, then become a leader." The man hurled his glass towards the bar. The sound of shattering glass exploded in the room. "You want safety, then get yourself a different life. Now where is my damn drink?"

"I'm sorry, sir." The girl rushed over. "It seems your server has been waylaid for the moment. I'll be right back with your drink."

It was then that she saw his face for the first time.

The red-headed man.

The man from Montana.

The same man who had held her prisoner.

The same man who had tried to have her shot.

The same man who had killed her mother seventeen years before.

She felt the jagged scar at her neckline burn hot with the memory of his branding iron singeing her skin.

Boiling with rage, frozen with fear, she couldn't move away from this man she knew as McNally.

"Wonderful. The feeble-minded hussy doesn't remember her way back to the bar," he jived.

Cora came to her rescue with a tray filled with shot glasses. "Your drink, sir, plus drinks for your whole group. This round is compliments of Lady Gretchen, who would like you, sir, to discuss a business venture with her after your meeting."

McNally took the drink. He eyed Cora suspiciously.

"A business venture."

"Yes, sir."

"With Lady Gretchen."

"Yes. You'll find she is quite astute with financial matters. She has several holdings in nearby mines and, I dare say, is quite influential within political circles. Perhaps she might be of service in swaying opinions concerning unionization."

He tapped his fingers against the table as he eyed Cora's curves.

"Once I'm done harnessing these fools into agreement, it would be refreshing to meet with someone who holds some degree of fiscal integrity. Set the meeting up."

* * *

"Who is he?" Cora hissed out the question as she piled more drinks onto her tray.

"Someone from my past," the girl whispered.

"Did he recognize you?"

"I'm not sure. I don't think so." She pulled at a strand of her recently darkened hair.

"You better thank your lucky stars that Lila is back at their table, flirting and flattering us back into that man's good graces. If we don't keep him happy, he'll find a way to shut us down. Then we'll all be on the lam."

"I can't go back out there, Cora. He'll figure me out."

"You gotta keep working the floor. You gotta smile and flirt and serve up drinks and hide in plain sight. You gotta make like there's nothing wrong at all. If he's got one inkling of recognition about you, the worst thing you can do is look suspicious by flying outta here."

The girl held tight to the edge of the bar.

"Take the tray." Cora kicked the girl's shin. "Take the tray. Don't you go fainting on me. And don't you dare cry. If you made it to Lady Gretchen's, you've got survival skills. Now put those skills in motion."

* * *

The moment Cora led McNally to Lady Gretchen's office, the girl made her way through the crowded saloon to the back hall.

The head cook, a towering woman with a booming voice, caught her leaning against the wall, her hands on her knees.

"Get your lazy bones back to work before I kick you to high heaven."

"Please, let me stay here just a moment," the girl pleaded. "It's my monthly. The cramps are killing me."

"You lazy girls, always looking for a reason to slack off your work."

"I'm bleeding through my rags. Please, just five minutes, then I'll be back on the floor serving drinks."

"Five minutes. Git."

The girl slipped through the back door and raced the opposite direction of the privy.

She hurried past wagons and horses and miners on course to their bar-time rounds. *Don't look back. Don't look back.* She turned at the corner and raced towards the livery. *Don't look back. Don't look back.* Would there be a horse she could afford with the few coins she had in her pocket? *Don't look back. Don't look back.* Of course, she couldn't afford a horse. *Stupid girl. Stupid girl. Don't look back.* She turned around and rushed towards the opposite end of town. *Why is it so hard to breathe? Why is there so much silt in the air? Don't look back. Don't look back.* She felt a burning sensation at the nape of her neck. She rubbed at it, expecting blood from an insect bite. Instead, her fingers found sooty black.

Curious. She slowed her pace and realized the people around her were doing the same. It wasn't the usual silt falling through the air. It was ashes. Black, crepey ashes drifting, dancing, delivering big news.

Two men standing across the street hollered out the first warning. "Fire. At the end of town."

Within seconds, the street was bedlam. Piercing screams. Frightened horses. Orders shouted out.

"Start pumping water!"

"Buckets! We need buckets!"

"Whole town's gonna burn!"

The girl stood transfixed. Several feet in front of her, flames of orange and scarlet hypnotized the sky. Rushing past her, a frenzy of footsteps and fear, some racing away from the fire, others plunging towards it, intent on putting out the flames. All around—north, south, east, west—chaos reigned as the town people surged towards either safety or bitter end.

The girl backed away from the flames. She turned in the direction of safety, her feet directing the path her mind hadn't yet planned, and immediately bumped into a woman whose flight was slowed by the bundle she carried.

* * *

Agrippina McNally knew it didn't take prophecy to see this trip to Wallace would be a boorish waste of her time, but prophecy of a fire would have been nice.

Accommodations at the Central Hotel had been adequate but nothing close to the accommodations she was accustomed to at her own hotel where she had often stayed when she tired of Niall, her husband of twenty-plus years. Where she had lived since her son's murder in her front parlor.

Yet here she was in this wallpapered hovel, chitchatting with societal bovine, drinking tea from cheap china, and staring at gawdy crystal chandeliers while her husband bought rounds of whiskey for a group of mine owners who had no concept of how to thwart unionization or to silence emerging threats of a labor strike.

Her thoughts turned to Beau Johnson, her most trusted lieutenant for monitoring manufacturing output at the Thurgood Mine. Through hard work and covert reporting of her husband's management theatrics, Johnson had earned her trust. He was quick to carry out her orders and voracious for lucre. He had further vowed his loyalty when she declared they would bring in trainloads of strikebreakers at any hint of labor unrest.

The clinking of china brought Agrippina's thoughts back to her guests and their palaver of platitudes.

A Mrs. Charles W. Winford was just finishing her story about a gilded Seddon entry table she had acquired in England when Agrippina smelled smoke, then spotted it eking its way beneath the side door to the dining room. The rest of the group remained unaware. Agrippina calmly excused herself from the group of women. She quietly ordered her butler who stood just outside the dining room's main double doors to quickly follow her. She hastened to her room, gathered her jewelry and her most expensive dress, threw them into a valise, and ordered her man to take the valise, fetch her carriage from the farrier, and meet her in front of the tasteless saloon where her husband held his meeting. She gathered as many of her remaining dresses as she could—she wouldn't allow this fire to thieve away these links to her son—and struggled down the stairway and past the nosy onlookers who had finally noticed the haze of smoke creeping through the air.

All the dresses she carried were black. Mourning dresses in honor of her boy. He'd only been seventeen when he was shot down by a Smith & Wesson 38. She had refused to wear mourning crapes—such an inferior choice—and instead relied on her tailor to create a full wardrobe of velvets and silks trimmed in lace and rosettes, jet stones for healing, and pearl buttons carved from the pearl-gripped pistol that had killed her son.

She hurried along the sidewalk planks, the skirts of her carried dresses billowed out like a murmuration of starlings swooping in the wind. She spotted her husband's bodyguard standing next to the saloon door and boldly called to him from across the street.

"Get over here. Get over here." Her words were lost in the melee of horse hooves and creaking carriages. She freed one hand from her load and gestured wildly towards herself, then the fire.

The giant of a man pointed towards her and she nodded and waved him forward. Another wagon drove between them, momentarily blinding their wordless conversation, but she had caught his look of confusion. Once the wagon passed, she watched his eyes widen when he finally spotted the fire.

He popped his head inside the saloon, and she presumed he barked out a warning to her husband before he dodged his way across the street to where she stood sweltering in the heat.

Before the bodyguard reached her, an inattentive girl backed into Agrippina. The woman was knocked off her footing. Her dresses dropped to the ground.

"Ma'am, are you hurt?" Niall's bodyguard grabbed at her arm. "We need to get you out of here."

At the same time, the clumsy girl blurted out an apology.

"I'm so sorry. I didn't mean to bump into you." The girl reached down and clutched up armfuls of shimmering black in an asinine attempt of apology. The girl pushed the dresses into the woman's arms and apologized again as she crouched to retrieve one last dress.

"Get away from me." Agrippina clamped her arms around her clothes and twisted away from the frizzled imbecile.

A memory sparked in Agrippina's mind. Those eyes. Those eyes.

She spun back around. "It's you. It's you. You killed my son."

The girl's eyes locked on those of the woman. It couldn't be her. It was simply impossible that this woman in black, this demon flesh, stood before her.

"Grab her," Agrippina ordered the bodyguard. "Don't let her escape."

The girl tossed the dress she held into the giant's face before plunging into the crowded street. People and screams and commotion were pouring out of every building. Explosion after explosion of windows came from the direction of the blaze. She could run back through Lady Gretchen's place. No. The path was blocked by that man. That man. How was he here? How were they both here? She spotted the giant racing towards her, slipping between the wagons and the wild-eyed horses that packed the road. She darted towards the farrier. A horse. She needed a horse. But there was no way to escape, even on horse. The streets were too crowded. She turned backed, climbed underneath wagons and past prancing horse hooves, low enough she was difficult to see, and moved towards the fire. Surely, no one would follow her towards the fire.

She was wrong.

Both the giant and McNally had her in their sights. McNally raised his arm in the air. Gun. Shots. No one questioned one more sound amidst the fire-fueled percussions that rattled the streets.

The girl slipped underneath another wagon, bellycrawled her way to the sidewalk. Something sliced her hand. A sticking tommy. The miners jammed them into crevices of rock to hold their candlesticks. She wrapped her hand around its handle, pulled herself to her feet, and pushed her way through the crowd of people that were relentlessly passing buckets of water towards the town's front line of fire defense.

She ran inside a building that had just begun to burn.

The girl felt her way through the smoke. Past tables and chairs. Choking. A thick arm swooped in and clenched around her neck. She bit the arm, then backwards plunged the tommy stick into the giant's gut. Once. Twice. He bellowed like a stuck pig. A third time through the gut. He released her. Fell to his knees. She finally reached the back of the building and felt around for a door, a doorknob. Nothing. No windows either, just a hint of light from a spot on the wall that was poorly boarded. She back-kicked at the wall until the wood finally splintered open. Gasping, she kicked again then pushed at the remaining timber until there was a hole large enough to slip through.

In the distance she saw a wagon racing to safety. She hollered and flagged it down. "Please. Please help me." The wagon sped up and the girl raced after it, all the while begging for help.

The wagon came to a stop. A woman's voice. "Hurry. Hurry, lass, before we catch fire ourselves."

Stut

Trinity Creek, Montana — July 1890

Stut sat back in the saddle and stretched his aching back as he eased his horse into a slow walk along the creek bank. He was wearied of crisscrossing the countryside, of weaving a complicated trail of clues to his whereabouts. He'd been both running from McNally and trying to steer the man's course since the shooting in April.

He wanted McNally and his men to believe his girl was with him, that the duo was fleeing eastward, across Montana's mountains to the plains and rolling hills that would spill into South Dakota. He would endure any circumstance, any pain, to divert attention from the town of Wallace in Idaho, where his girl was hopefully sheltered, and yet he itched to find her, to make sure she was protected, cared for, secure.

An image of Kate slipped into his mind. Lovely Kate, the dancehall girl who had moved so gracefully, who had always treated Stut with respect. She and Mother Damnable had twice protected his girl from Niall McNally. The first time, his girl had been a baby that defeated death. The second time, his girl had been seventeen, and her tragic past had reared its ugly head and tried to kill her.

A seething mixture of hate and regret boiled in his head whenever he thought on McNally. He had been the man's puppet for too long, his sideshow marionette. Stut had spent over twenty years regretting his decision to work for McNally, but the man had offered him something he hadn't been able to afford on his own: a beautiful two-year-old stallion, greenbroke and full of potential.

Stut thought back to his growing up years, when the horses that trailed through his family's home station had been his only friends, visiting as they passed through, never taunting him or spitting at him or landing a punch in his gut. Stut had known them all by name and he had handled them as if they were his own, wiping them down after their long journeys, feeding them grain, checking their legs and hooves.

He'd talked to them in his stuttered fashion, and they had never once minded his awkward ways.

When Stut was fourteen and as gangly as chicory weed, the town bully, joined by his tosspot father, hogtied him and bullwhipped him to an inch of his life. He near crawled the entire way home, where his parents nursed him to health. Stut never revealed who had nearly killed him for fear of the men's warnings of retaliation against his family.

This wasn't the first time he'd been beaten. His family knew it wouldn't be the last.

Once Stut healed, his father gave him a few dollars and an old roan he'd bought from a drifter. His father helped him pack a few belongings. His father paled at this premature goodbye. But his father knew. It was time for Stut to move on before worse beatings happened.

For years, Stut's father had tried to protect him, had tried to keep the browbeaters at bay and the ruffians from attacking. But the bashings had continued. And they had become worse.

Stut left the home station the next morning at dawn. His father pushed a torn-out bible page into his son's hand as he gasped through his goodbye. His auntie wept and clung to her ragdoll. His mother didn't shed a tear, though she did call out, "You was always a good boy."

The manchild, so wise to the ways of a ruffian's fists, was leery of companionship, so the isolation of travel suited him. He wandered for some time, trying to find his place in the world. He ended up working as a ranch hand for several months, and that lonely work seemed to fit.

Until he heard the call of gold.

By the time Stut left the ranch to head for Montana's mining fields, he had grown seven inches taller than he had been at the home station. He'd also gained several pounds of bulk. Pure, muscle-driven bulk. The day before he headed out, the kindly ranch wife, who had twice lengthened his trousers to accommodate his sudden bursts in height, presented him with a newly made pair of trousers and two second-hand shirts.

Stut worked hard in the mining fields but was never able to earn more money than what fit his meager needs, not even when he partnered up with Bogger Buchanan and the two of them combined forces to work more dirt in less time.

Then McNally showed up and things changed for the better and for the worse.

In time, McNally's ambitions turned from dredging dirt to counting cards. And, in time, McNally wiled his way towards a small fortune and pompous plans. That's when he hired on Stut to serve as his valet and bodyguard.

Stut's duties were simple enough. Look intimidating and put the fear of God into anyone that tried to cross his employer. As a bodyguard, Stut never had to beat a man or use his pistol. His intimidating brawn had been enough to dissuade any menace that brewed. Most importantly, within his job duties, he never had to say a word. Not one single word.

He hated the job. He loathed that his role was to intimidate, to become savage when needed. And he detested himself for leaving Bogger, the one man beyond his father that he'd ever trusted. But the gold mining business hadn't served him well, and the new horse eased his loneliness and gave him purpose. Besides, few were willing to hire a man with words as tangled as loose strands of barbed wire.

A few years later, a back injury left Stut harnessed to pain. He was demoted from bodyguard to jailer. Shortly after his demotion, in a heinous act of deceit, a young woman was imprisoned for a murder Stut was sure she didn't commit. As the jailer, Stut was put in charge of building a gallows. On the day of the hanging, he was warned to keep his mouth shut, he was ordered to tie boulders to the prisoner's ankles as she stood atop the hangman's platform, and he was forewarned to pull the hangman's lever, for if he didn't Niall McNally would personally slaughter Stut's beloved horse and chop it into fine bits.

Like a sheep to the slaughter, he followed through with each order. Except the last one.

God save his soul.

God save his soul.

When the sheriff placed the newborn into her mother's arms, Stut turned away. He couldn't watch the impending atrocity before him. When McNally pushed past him and pulled the lever and Louisa dropped and the baby fell from her arms, a flood of disgrace washed over Stut. He could have stopped all of this. He should have stopped all of this. And when he saw Louisa's body swaying from the gallows beam and the dropped boulders hovering above the ground where the baby had landed, shame lashed through his body and he raced to pick up the child and will it some life.

"God, save this soul," he whispered without stuttering. "God, save this soul."

Then followed the blur of events. Mother Damnable swooping the child from his arms. The baby's timid movements. The flurry of action to conceal the child. The desperate escape with the child in his arms.

After months—no, years—of being a coward, it was time to stand as a man.

In the first quiet moment of escape, when he and the baby were far enough from town to be unseen, he huddled under a tree to shield the child from the pouring rain and he fed the child and gave her a name. A name he would never share with another soul. And he called her daughter. This man of misfortune now had a daughter. And he wouldn't fail his child. He owed that much to her mother. He wouldn't take his child to a nunnery or an orphanage. He would gift his daughter to his parents, for they would cherish the one good fate he'd plucked from this earth.

As he returned to Thurmond from delivering his child to his parents' home, his beloved buckskin—exhausted and weakened from their long, arduous journey—broke its ankle as they crossed Thurmond's railroad tracks. Stut pulled out his pistol and shot the valiant animal to save it from misery.

For the next seventeen years, he worked for McNally, all to earn money for the child. His child. His blood didn't run through his girl's veins, but his spirit and his hope did. Each year, as he delivered his earnings to his parents' home station to help take care of his girl's needs, he would hide in the distance and watch for his little girl to appear. Each time he spotted her he feared his chest would near explode from the love he held deep inside.

A couple of otters scampered along the creek bank and slipped into the water. Sight of their actions pulled Stut away from his memories, though he held on to one last thought: Beyond his parents, beyond his aunt, beyond that buckskin horse, there was only one other being in his life that had meant as much to him, and that was the baby girl he'd saved from the gallows.

Had his girl, all grown up and as beautiful as her mother, made it to the panhandle of Idaho? Had she found sanctuary in Wallace? Was she safe at Lady Gretchen's? Safe from McNally? His men? The men of the mining town?

Agonizing questions chewed at his nerves. His horse tossed its head in protest when Stut punched his fist across the pommel of the saddle.

"Sssorry, bboy." He loosened his grip on the reins and tapped his heels against the horse's belly, cueing him into a trot.

He eased the horse into a canter as he considered their next destination: Trinity Creek.

He was depleted. He needed rest and time to determine what his next course of action would be. The Trinity Creek Ranch had become his refuge after he left his parents' home. He wondered if the kindly ranch wife still lived there, not that he'd reintroduce himself, for he needed to live out the next few weeks in obscurity.

Stut planned to hunker down in a small cave on the desolate east end of their property. He needed Trinity Creek to be a stronghold of invisibility where he and his horse could rest. Where he could make plans. Where he could dream of the child he'd saved so many years ago.

Then maybe, just maybe, if he and his girl each stayed invisible long enough, they would be reunited. God willing, he'd have his girl back. God willing, he'd become the father he had always wanted to be.

Emmeline
Leeds, Idaho — August 1890

Miss Jayne figured she would near celebrate the absence of the girl. Instead, she held silence fist tight and barely held conversation with Emmeline who, after several attempts at small talk, busied herself with whatever chores she could find or invent that kept her inside the house near her patient.

With the wheelhouse of gossip churning across the valley, visitors soon began showing up, some with earnest concern and some, Emmeline would realize too late, ready to snoop out the image of the woman's burnt face and bandages to reel in their own chapter of gossip to blather across town.

When the first visitors arrived, packing a prepared ham hock and a fresh loaf of bread for the Adamsen's supper meal, Emmeline near begged Miss Jayne to move from her bed to the front room rocker to take part in some conversation.

"They've traveled far, and during such a busy season," she said. "Surely you can sit proper and say hello."

"I'm injured. I'm tired. And I don't need their pity," Miss Jayne said. She turned her face to the wall, an end to the conversation that forced Emmeline to change her tactics.

"Jayne, you are a pillar of this community. One of the first settlers in this land and a lady who is well esteemed. Certainly, our townsfolk need to see you stand strong, to be iron-willed. Show them your strength and graciously accept their gift of compassion."

"You're talking like a preacher's wife, Emmeline. Don't appreciate that. Not one bit." Miss Jayne threw back the bedcovers and slid her feet to the ground. "And don't you dare start talking to me like a doctor's wife either. Don't need to hear how visiting with folks will lift my spirits and help me heal. Those words are a bunch of bunk when you're the one on the healing side of things. Now help me into my green dress. If I'm going to sit through this mess of nosy talk, I'm going to wear my best color."

* * *

Miss Jayne was courteous the rest of the day as her guests tiptoed through topics of conversation. For the most part, talk focused for a floundering moment on her injuries, to which the woman said little, then shifted to the idle talk of weather, grasshoppers, wheat fields, and corn.

Emmeline made sure the visits remained short, knowing the day was wearisome for Miss Jayne. And she was relieved that the staggered visits throughout the day kept her patient actively engaged in conversation rather than silent brooding about her darkened world.

The framework of the day twisted cruelly when Mrs. Fischer mentioned what a shame it was that Jake's wife was no longer around to take care of her mother-in-law. Emmeline didn't recognize the statement as innocent or filled with intent, but she did recognize the piercing grief that strained the portion of Miss Jayne's face not covered with bandages.

Emmeline immediately reached for Miss Jayne, excused themselves from the room, and led her patient back to her bedroom. She settled Miss Jayne under the covers and hushed away both of their sobs and hiccoughs.

Forty minutes later, after Miss Jayne settled into an exhausted slumber, Emmeline peeked through the doorway. The front room was empty of visitors.

* * *

When she awoke, Miss Jayne's jumbled dreams of her daughter-in-law spilled over into ached memories of the day the young woman died.

In many ways she wished her daughter-in-law had never said her deathbed words. Oh, how those words played over and over in her mind. Today, with no eyes to see, the memory was ferociously visible, to the point that she was again sitting in that bedroom, witnessing Jake and Hannah melt in their handgrip of goodbye.

"Keep Jackson safe," Hannah said.

"I promise. I promise to always keep our son safe," Jake replied.

"He's a handful," she whispered, her eyes near closed from exhaustion.

"I know," Jake gulped, "just like his pa."

"Yes, just like his pa." Hannah's voice was barely a whisper. "Safe. Love him, love you, keep him safe."

Nothing more. Hannah was gone.

And the baby in her arms had never taken a breath.

Jake lost his wife and newborn daughter just as the sun hinted red and orange on the horizon.

Miss Jayne forced her mind to the present. Back then she knew her son would keep his promise to Hannah, for Jackson was all he had left of his wife.

Months later, Jake was powerless in keeping that promise. Little Jackson, ever in motion, tried to climb into Jake's wagon while it was moving. The little boy lost his footing and fell before Jake had a chance to stop the wagon.

The rear wagon wheel crushed the boy's left arm just above the elbow.

Miss Jayne cleaned and treated and bandaged the gash left by the wood and the metal of the wheel before she capably splinted the boy's arm. When infection set in, Jake spent two days desperately searching the countryside to find Doc, to bring him to the cabin where his little boy withered with fever. Gangrene had taken over the little boy's wound. Amputation seemed the only answer.

Once Doc arrived at the cabin, Jake set his boy on the kitchen table, spilled sweetened rum into his mouth, and urged the little boy to drink just a bit more while the doctor tied a tourniquet around the boy's arm above the wound.

Miss Jayne held down the little boy at the shoulders, Jake held his son's legs, and the doctor performed his ghastly duty.

The boy died an hour after the surgery was complete.

Back in Leeds

Lainie arrived back in Leeds three days after her trip to Lewiston. She was dustspun in entirety and after dismounting the stagecoach, she slapped at her clothing, creating plumes of trailweary silt that settled atop the rutted roadway. She fetched her bag from the driver, stepped onto the planked sidewalk, and looked at herself in the station's window. She swiped at the dirt smeared across her face with her sleeve, reconsidered her actions, and pulled out a handkerchief from the pocket of her skirt to finish the task. Once she determined that the remaining dirt was owned by the window and not by her skin, she turned her attention to her hair, pulling out the hairpins scattered within the tangles and lanks of what had been a careful and longsuffering attempt at a smooth, low chignon. There was no way she could redeem the hairstyle, so she handcombed the lengths of ebony into loose waves that settled onto her shoulders.

She fretted over the green of her eyes and wished they were as colorless as they appeared in the dusty window. But truth was truth, and the color of her eyes couldn't be changed, so she snatched the large-brimmed hat, purchased with Doc and Emmeline's money, from atop the travel bag they'd given her and placed it low across her forehead to veil her eyes.

The new blouse and skirt she wore also gave her cause to fret. The doctor and his wife had invested too much time and expense in her, and she agonized that she would never be able to pay back her debt. At least with Jake and Miss Jayne, she was providing her labors as payment for room and board. For Doc and Emmeline, she would probably never have the chance for such payback.

She fetched the bag, gulped in courage, and inquired of the ticket agent as to where she'd find the office of Dr. Franklin Matthews. She quickwalked a portion of the town before realizing her gait was neither ladylike nor unremarkable, especially in front of townspeople who, from first appearances, seemed to bide their time from shaded porch fronts and dingey windows. But the pace of her strides matched the pace of her heart, thudding with awkwardness and hurry.

Lainie slowed her gait and rehashed her vision of how she'd appear arriving in town. She wanted to look poised, confident, unflappable. Instead, she was tucked with tizzy. The smiles and nods she'd planned to share with passersby were difficult to produce. She had tripped three times in rapid succession as she timidly eyeballed the lay of the town. And based on the number of gawking eyes that furthered her faintheartedness, news of her arrival would be chronicled across supper tables and faro games for days to come.

At last, she spotted the sign that indicated her arrival at Doc's office. Awestruck, she took in the breadth of the building. During her walk from the station, she had witnessed a trail of plain-clad shacks and shanties tucked between the occasional well-built framehouse.

Doc and Emmeline's place refused to look withdrawn. It blossomed before her, three shades of spring green with white vergeboard lacing the undersides of gables. The house sat pleasantly lobsided with a portion of the house jutting forward. A porch spanned the building and wrapped around one corner. A rounded tower lofted from the right side of the porch.

Fishscale shingles paneled the tower and were painted such that the top third of the shingles displayed the lightest shade of green, mid-tone green held center, and the darkest green at bottom was near the shade of the burdock leaves Lainie had survived on the past few weeks.

At the crest of the steep-pitched roof, a horizontal group of roof finials decorated the skyline. They shared the horizon with a corbelled chimney on each end of the house. A magpie strutted the expanse of the roofline, cawing out ownership of the space.

Potted shrubs trimmed into globes ushered Lainie up the sidewalk. She kept her eyes on the home's architecture rather than the front door that held the next step in her journey.

She stopped short of the first porch step when a man called out, "You the new help for Doc?"

Two men and a woman were settled on the front stoop to Doc's office. The woman sat on a wicker chair, chin downturned and hands positioned in prayer mode. The older of the men paced back and forth while the younger leaned against the porch railing, scraping at a fingernail with his pocketknife.

"You the new help for Doc?" the younger man asked again.

"Me?" Lainie asked.

"You're the only one standing there, looking all edgicated," he said. "Doc says his new helper is getting all edgicated in fixin' folks. So, are you the new help?"

"I suppose so. I mean, yes, I am. I'm here as Dr. Matthews' nurse, I mean student, I mean nursing student."

"Best you get inside then. Doc's got a mess on his hands after that knifing business."

"Knifing business?"

"Yeah. Kid brother's in there bleeding like a stuck pig."

The older man piped in. "No sense looking green around the gills, missy. Haul yourself inside and help."

Lainie hiked her skirts up and zigzagged around the trail of blood that crawled up the stairs and into the entryway. Inside, she followed the blood trail beyond the newel posts, through a wallpapered hallway, and past four rooms. When the blood trail turned to the right, she turned to the right, stopping short of passing through the doorway where Doc hovered intently over an unconscious man.

The girl's feet planted deep as she stalled for options. Enter the room unannounced? Announce her presence and interrupt the doctor's methodical work? Turn tail and walk out of the house and out of the town?

When the doctor no longer held sharp objects in his hand and began cleaning the man's wound with some gauze, Lainie cleared her throat. "Dr. Matthews? Doctor, the man outside told me to come in. I'm sorry, I'll just wait outside."

"Ah, Miss Kemp." Doc looked up and added, "I presume." He gave her a conspiratorial wink. "You've arrived just in time to meet Bern Pantcher, sniveling fool and part of the acrimonious Pantcher family, of which each member is slightly more miscreant than the next."

"Dr. Matthews, you should watch your words. His family is standing just outside the front door."

"I've said worse to their faces, Miss Kemp. No matter what I say or how many times I patch up one of the Pantcher boys, they continue with their boorish ways. Bloody brawls, knife fights at the tavern, hijinks that should have landed at least one of them in the funeral parlor." Doc tossed the bloodied gauze into a waste pail near his feet then checked the tourniquet tied high on the injured man's thigh. "But no, these boys keep coming up with trouble and I sew them up time and time again. Leastwise when there's too much sewing for their ma to handle which, lately, seems most of the time."

"There is quite a bit of blood out here." The girl swallowed hard. "And all around you." She noted the blood on Doc's shirt, the spray of blood on the wall behind him, the rivulets and droplets on the floor. She turned and began to leave, calling out, "I'll leave you to finish with your patient."

"No need to leave, Miss Kemp. Please, do come over and assist me with the next step in our procedure. After all, you are my new student."

Lainie hesitated, then gracelessly hiked her skirts even higher, tiptoed around what blood she could, and set her bag in the corner. Doc continued with conversation as he completed a portion of what looked to be a delicate surgery. By the time Lainie reached the surgical table, he seemed content with his results.

"I'll have you slowly release the tourniquet as I watch for bleeding. If the artery leaks too much, you'll need to quickly tighten the tourniquet so I can add more stitches."

She hesitated.

"If that tourniquet stays on much longer, he'll lose his leg. Get to it, Miss Kemp."

Lainie moved into position and stared at the belt wrapped around the man's leg. The belt was buckled in place and secured by a brass device. "What do I do?"

"Grab hold of the T screw and very slowly turn it counterclockwise. Just a bit. Good. Good. Stop."

She jumped at the sight of squirting blood. "Tighten. Tighten." Doc called out orders as he packed the wound with more gauze.

Lainie's pulse raced as if she held the Pantcher man's life in her hands. She turned the T screw back to its original position. The doctor added more stitches to the artery, then dabbed again at the blood.

"Alright, let's try that again," he said.

Lainie's forehead wrinkled with concern as she repeated the process.

"Open it up a little bit more. A little bit more. There, that's looking fine." Doc looked to Lainie. "You did a fine job."

"All I did was turn a screw," she said.

"More importantly, you didn't pass out at the sight of all this blood. Now, let's see what you can do with a needle."

"Excuse me?"

"A basin of water is in the corner. Lather up your hands and your arms, scrub long and hard, rinse off, then douse your hands and wrists with some alcohol. Dry off on the towel. I'll remove the tourniquet, check our patient's heartbeat, and prepare the next set of sutures."

She did as she was told, all the while thinking that the doctor was playing some sort of prank on her. She half expected that he'd have the man fully stitched by the time she was finished washing her hands, but when she turned, she realized he fully expected her to take part in the surgery.

"I'll suture the muscle back together while you watch," Doc explained. "The muscle is thick and difficult to pass the needle and catgut through. Watch my technique. It's not much different than that of a seamstress's hand."

Lainie presumed the doctor would hold the foreign-shaped needle in his hand as he began this layer of repair. Instead, he held the needle with a metal instrument and used something called forceps to further advance the sewing project.

"It's bad form to hold the needle directly in hand," he explained. "In using these instruments, we keep the surgical field sterilized, and I don't cut my own fingers while holding and prying the needle."

He looked up from the surgery and smiled at her. He smiled even larger when he noticed the look of concentration etched across her brow. As Doc maneuvered the catgut into knots, he noticed the girl's hands copycat his own intricate moves.

"And now that the muscle is sutured, it's your turn to finish the work."

Doc traded places with the girl and handed her the necessary tools. He encouraged her to lift her right elbow and rotate her shoulders just a few degrees to best place herself for the surgery and shared instruction on how to properly hold the surgical tools.

"Stick the needle in at this angle, close to the edge, but far enough away so the skin won't rip." Doc demonstrated the motion as he talked. "That's it. You're doing fine."

He continued his instruction, patiently encouraging the girl as her brow creased further at her clumsiness with the needle holder and forceps. Her first three stitches were made by tremulous hands. Once she accustomed to the grips on the tools and the pressure needed to suture the skin, she gained confidence and completed the task with a calming breath.

"You have a gift," the doctor said, handing her a towel to wipe her hands.

"For stitching? I don't think so," Lainie replied.

"For grit. You can have all the talent and knowledge in the world, but without grit, talent and knowledge are simply decorations to ooh and aah at. Grit accomplishes things. Makes a difference in the world. Saves lives."

Lainie blushed and hurried to change the subject.

"How'd he get hurt?" she asked, pointing to the man lying on the table.

The doctor threw back his head and laughed.

"Today's injury came about during a cock fight. It seems the brothers attached a homemade knife to the leg of each of their rooster combatants, then threw the birds together and stood back to watch the fight. As fate played out, one of the birds flew at Mr. Pantcher here and knifed him in the leg, nearly severing his femoral artery."

"No. You're making that up," Lainie said.

"I'm imaginative, but not that imaginative. Take a look." He pointed to the far corner of the room. "The rooster's lying there, blade still attached to its leg."

"That's balled up repulsive, Doc."

"Lucky for our patient, Pantcher's family was smart enough to leave the knife buried in his leg, which helped stem the flow of blood. The rooster did his part, too, after one of the Pantcher clan broke its neck to keep it from flapping around. The rooster's weight helped slow the bleeding and its feathers sopped up some of the mess."

Doc walked over to the rooster and picked it up.

"This ol' boy probably weighs a good ten pounds," he said. "I suppose I should deliver it back to the family. They'll probably want to cook it for supper."

Doc gave Lainie instructions to keep an eye on the patient in case he began to wake.

Once again, she had no idea if the good doctor was speaking truth or pranking her. She had a sudden vision of what the patient might do if he woke up, and when he moaned and flopped his head from left to right, she reached across his chest in order to hold down both of his shoulders, then wondered if she'd have the strength to keep him in place if he did wake up.

Lainie could hear Doc talking to the man's family, explaining that the boy had lost a great deal of blood and would need to stay at his office for at least two days, to which three voices threw out argument and an arsenal of foul language.

Doc dismissed the family then walked back into the operating room where Lainie continued her awkward stance holding down the patient.

"My goodness," Doc laughed, "if that boy woke up right now, he'd kiss you full on the lips and claim you as his bride."

She released her grip and backed away from the patient.

"He moved his head. I wasn't sure what to do."

"You are a blusher, Miss Kemp. Quite enchanting, I must say."

Doc checked the boy's eyes. "He'll be sound asleep for several more minutes. You can retreat from guard duty of the patient."

"You don't think he'll remember that I—"

"That you were a kiss away from becoming his bride?"

"Doc!"

"Amusing and enchanting, that's what you are. And I think you're just what the Adamsen farm needs."

Lainie groaned.

"On that note," Doc interrupted, nodding towards his patient, "thanks to the injury of our dimwitted friend, I'm not at liberty to take you to the Adamsen place this afternoon. But I do believe I hear a solution to our quandary. Let's take a look outside."

* * *

Lainie was skittish about Doc's revised travel plans for her. But as she stepped aboard the freight wagon boasting the name of Halifax Timberman's Notions, Sundries and Exotic Junk, she tried to hold tight to Doc's reasoning.

"It makes good sense for you to ride with Halifax," he'd said. "It proves to people that I've officially introduced you to our human telegraph. Halifax will have the whole county knowing that you are my student and that, for the time being, you'll be helping out at the Adamsen place."

A lie, kept secret for seventeen years, had propelled her to this place. And now a new lie would spread across the countryside via Halifax's gossip machine in an attempt to keep her and the Adamsens safe.

* * *

Halifax changed his mapped-out course for the day to deliver Lainie along with Doc's horse, now tied to the back of his wagon, to the Adamsen farm well ahead of sundown.

"I'll need to make a couple of stops along the way, yes ma'am I will, and we'll make good time, lessing of course Mrs. Zimmerman decides to inspect every encyclopedia I've got for sale, though she inspected them the last three visits and complained that she wouldn't buy them since they'd already been looked through and they shouldn't be newpriced if'n somebody has already put their paws through 'em even if the paws were hers and we'll also be droppin' off the new knickers that Mrs. Morteson ordered, which won't take no time at all since she'll be wantin' to show them off to Mr. Morteson as soon as she can, if you know what I mean, so yes ma'am, I think we'll be home free in getting you to the Adamsen place in time to help with supper."

Lainie was fascinated with the man's ability to carry out an entire paragraph of conversation within one sentence and, more impressively, within one breath.

She supposed that she should carry on at least a small fragment of the conversation as they bounced along the rutted road, metal pans and chains clanging loudly enough from the back of the wagon to necessitate Halifax to holler out his words. She timidly asked how he got his name and when she realized he didn't hear her, she shouted out the question.

"I'm from Halifax, ma'am, yes I am. Coldest doggone place I've ever lived and couldn't wait to get my frozen be-hind to warmer parts, yes ma'am. So, I traveled with some Swedes that had landed in Canada, and we crossed the border into these United States on my twenty-first birthday, we did, we did. Real name's Rufus Pervius Sissinghurst, but by golly that's the type of name folks throw rocks at, so I changed it up to something a might bit prettier. Halifax Timberman. Rolls off the tongue, now don't it?"

"It's quite nice," Lainie called out.

"Funny thing is, Sissinghurst ain't my real surname either," he continued. "My real surname is Ellis, but when ma got off the boat from England with me in her arms, and the immigration man started asking her all sorts of questions, she set me down right atop the papers on his desk and I proceeded to leak my diaper, I did, I did, and the man's stack of papers got all wet and my ma was red-faced with shame and the man flew out of his chair and yelled at my ma something fierce and she begged his forgiveness and that's when he told her she'd get some forgiving if she served up some loving and that's when my ma slapped him across the face and the folks in line stood at her side and he saw those folks was fuming mad and he filled out her paper but instead of writing in Ellis he wrote in Sissinghurst for the surname, which is where she was from, and that was that."

Lainie gave the man a smile, realizing that his naming ceremony certainly outdid her own. After all, she had only laced together her parents' initials to come up with the name of Lainie. She felt herself relax a bit as the man prattled on.

Halifax was correct in knowing that the lady awaiting the new knickers would be in a hurry for him to move on. Lainie was grateful that the young woman never noticed that the wagon boasted more than one passenger.

Time was far spent at the next home, however, as Mrs. Zimmerman, surrounded by three youngsters with hands stained brown and yellow by the dandelion bouquets they held onto, insisted on reviewing the complete set of encyclopedias one more time. Her browsing session was hindered by her frequent need to smack her curious children's grubby hands as they snooped through the various sundries Halifax had tied to the outside of his wagon. On three separate occasions she had to pluck one squealing child from inside the wagon, and she ended up holding on to that wiggling, squealing child the entire time she tried to dicker down the price of the books.

Halifax held firm to his price and noted that most of the paw marks in each book belonged to the woman and thusly she should be the one paying a fine for the disrepair she'd caused to his inventory. Above the children's giggles and squeals and wails, Lainie heard the two adults finally reach an agreement, and then she heard Halifax audibly count and recount the payment to be sure he hadn't been shortchanged.

"That woman could pinch a penny from a turnip," Halifax told Lainie as he climbed into the wagon. "Oh, where's my manners. I near forgot to introduce you to Mrs. Zimmerman."

"No!" Lainie whispered loudly. "That's not necessary."

Her attempt at stopping the introduction produced no result and soon she was locked in the sights of the woman who towed one child underarm and led another by the ear like a farmer holding on to the nose lead of a cow.

"Roberta, this is Lainie—what is your last name again?"

While Halifax fumbled through his memory for the last name of his passenger, Lainie fought through her fears and smiled.

"Lainie Kemp. I'll be helping at the Adamsen farm for a short time, then training with Dr. Matthews to become a nurse."

"How long you been practicing that line?" the woman asked.

Lainie blanched.

"Just joshin' ya," the woman laughed. "No need to be so formal in these parts, missy. Ain't none of us gonna bite. Exceptin' this little mountain lion, I suppose."

The woman let go of the little girl's ear and worked at prying open the boy's teeth that now clamped her arm.

"Stop by anytime," the woman called out, pushing away the boy's face as he tried to bite her arm again. "We'll put on the tea kettle and enjoy a bit of girl time."

"That would be very, uhm, interesting. Thank you," Lainie said.

"You both can come in right now. You'll get to meet the rest of the children. And Mr. Zimmerman, he's off in the field working 'til sundown, but if you'd like to stay and chit chat a while, you can meet him as soon as he gets home."

Lainie could hear the earnest need for some adult conversation in the woman's voice.

"I'm sorry. I really do need to get to the Adamsen home soon. With Mrs. Adamsen being injured so." Lainie's voice trailed off.

"Of course. Of course. But please, when you do have a moment?"

"I'll stop by," Lainie said.

"For sure as sure?" the woman asked as she wiped away mud from her youngest who had just eaten a handful of dirt.

"For sure as sure," Lainie said.

* * *

Lainie thanked Halifax for the ride.

"Did you want to visit with Jake and Miss Jayne?" she asked as he untied Doc's horse from the back of his wagon.

"Wish I had the time, yes ma'am I do, but we'll be losing light soon, and I need to make one more stop before I set up camp for the night."

129

He handed her the reins to Doc's horse. "Please wish Miss Jayne a speedy recovery for me. Let her know I'll be by soon with all sorts of new inventory she won't find in those Roebuck catalogs she's so fond of, yes ma'am, yes ma'am."

"I will," Lainie said, wishing he would stay and charm some light into each of the Adamsens' frame of mind. "Thank you."

"Before I leave, a gift." Halifax searched through a box of trinkets. "Ah, here it is."

He handed the girl a small picture frame.

"Do you have a picture of your mama?" he asked, wondering over her puzzled expression. "I imagine you might get a bit homesick being so far from home, and Miss Jayne, well, she's a good woman and she'll mother you out of your loneliness, for sure yes ma'am, but there's nothing like your own mama close by to help you sleep at night."

Lainie had no words.

"What's your mama's name?" Halifax asked.

She wasn't ready to say that name out loud.

"Thank you," she whispered instead.

Halifax tipped his hat, strode back to his wagon, and climbed in. With a gentle flick of the reins, the salesman and his storehouse were gone.

Jake's Memories

Jake heard Halifax Timberman's wagon coming long before he spotted it. The man's emporium on wheels made an unfettered clanking noise as it rolled along, and usually the salesman would blow a whistle as he neared a homestead so anyone who could break free of their outdoor work would know to come running to see the new wares he somehow always had available.

This time Jake didn't hear a whistle and he looked up to see Halifax talking away to the passenger by his side.

Lainie.

Jake moved far enough back in the hayfield to crouch down and hide himself from the travelers. He wasn't in the mood to hear one of Halifax's tall tales. And he certainly wasn't looking forward to having Lainie back at the cabin.

While Lainie was gone and Emmeline stayed on to help, his mother had returned somewhat to the person he'd always counted on. She was still distraught over her lost eyesight and was beginning to realize how prominent the scarring would be on her face, neck, and hands, but she was sorting through plans on how she would do her part on the farm and she talked aloud of those plans, asking for Jake's and Emmeline's approval of her creative insights.

She had asked Jake to buy lengths of rope and lay them in paths outside the house to grasp onto so she could walk on her own to the barn, the laundry line, the chicken coop, and the outhouse. Each rope needed to be a different thickness for each destination so her hands would tell her brain which direction she was headed in. She had asked Emmeline to help her track the number of steps between the kitchen and the front door, the front door and her rocking chair, the rocking chair and the fireplace. Emmeline recorded each entry and the two practiced the routes until both women were confident that Miss Jayne could cover each distance safely without assistance or verbal instruction from someone else in the room.

131

The ladies had also practiced table settings on the countertop, since a dinner table no longer existed, with Miss Jayne's dinner plate set center in front of her, utensils to the left, tumbler to the right. The milk pitcher would always be set two handspans right of the tumbler, the breadtray would be two handspans left of the fork.

Emmeline had worked her magic and Miss Jayne had been devoted to conquering her new world.

That picture was bound to change once Lainie walked into the room.

Jake knew the girl wasn't working out. She wasn't agreeable. She wasn't capable. She wasn't adaptable.

Worse yet, she wasn't Hannah.

Lainie wasn't the childhood sweetheart whose braids he'd dipped in ink as he sat behind her in school. Lainie wasn't the bride with a crocheted veil draped across the daisies tucked in her hair. Lainie wasn't the woman who brought out picnics to wherever Jake was working so the two could eat together and dream about their future.

Yet this stranger would be cooking his meals, wearing Hannah's clothes, tending Hannah's garden.

Sleeping in Jake and Hannah's bed.

He thought back to the day Lainie hid in the cedar dowry chest. A quilt had disguised her location.

That quilt was Hannah's wedding quilt. He'd tucked it into the cedar chest the day after Hannah died.

Somehow, that quilt had protected Lainie. What was Jake supposed to think about that?

* * *

Leeds, Idaho — January 1890

Hannah had been positive their first child would be a boy.

"Only a boy would kick up this kind of commotion," she'd say after a sleepless night.

She had also claimed the baby would grow up to be just like his daddy—a handsome, mule-brained prankster.

After that remark, Hannah found a giant toad in her pillowcase.

Three and a half years later, Jake worked near the cabin each day as Hannah came closer to delivering their second child. He split firewood in the bitter cold, checked on animals, chipped away ice from water troughs, made repairs and improvements to the house and barn. Anything and everything to keep his mind off the worries and excitement that came bundled together with the growth of his little family.

Miss Jayne stayed busy tending to Jackson. This little grandson was a godsend now that her husband was gone. The little boy was full of giggles and always happy to cause a fun commotion. Jackson had taken on his mother's fair hair and complexion. When it came to mannerisms, he was a pint-size version of his daddy.

Morningtime, Jackson would scamper from his bed before dawn to make sure his mama was awake to hear the calling birds.

Lunchtime was meant for adventure. At least on nice-weather days. Since Jake was usually working in the fields or with the animals, Hannah would bundle up a meal to take to her husband. With Jackson underfoot, she would walk to meet Jake. Neither Hannah nor Jake would tell Jackson where the secret picnic destination would be for the day. Instead, they gave him clues that roused the boy's curiosity, kept his eyes on the landscape, and kept his hands out of mischief.

Suppertime was Jackson's favorite time of day. He would excitedly wait at the door for his daddy to come home for mealtime and playtime. Once he spotted his daddy walking towards the well, he'd run out with two towels and both would wash off the day's work, splashing water at each other, chasing each other through the yard, then bounding through the front door like calves racing to a hayrack.

With the coming of the new baby, Jackson had taken on the role of master and commander. He came to the profound determination that the baby would be a girl to be named Joseph. He set aside toys that were meant for babies and insisted that his mum set them high on a shelf where the dog couldn't chew them. He told his grandmum that she'd need to read him extra stories each day, so she'd be practiced up to read to the new baby. And he insisted on being taught how to hold a newborn.

"She'll need to be held properlike, you know."

Jackson's parents laughed at his words.

"And what is the properlike way to hold a baby," Jake asked.

"Like this." Jackson wrapped his arms around Bristle, the pup Jake had found lingering around the barn. Lifting the dog from its sleeping position on the rug to its bungling position mere inches from the ground took some doing, and Jackson panted at the effort. Considering that Bristle was nearly as large as Jackson and that Jackson had the poise of a three-winged chicken, the demonstration wasn't half bad.

"See, you gotta be gentle and make sure the baby's comfy." Jackson beamed.

The boy stumbled a bit as he cradled the so-called babe, but he kept his footing. When the dog began to slip through Jackson's arms, the boy did his best to keep the dog in place.

"Jake, stop laughing!" his wife scolded in between giggles. "Go and rescue poor Bristle."

"Now Hannah, those two are as happy as can be." Jake laughed even harder. "See, Bristle's even waving his paws at us to show how much fun he's having."

"He is not having fun. He's trying to save his own life!" She pushed Jake from the sofa. "Go. Save your dog."

Jake gathered the dog from his son's arms and settled him in his own. Bristle's paws waved high, his tongue dangled, and his tale froze stiff while Jake rocked him side to side.

"See, son, when the baby is tiny, you'll have to hold her like this. With one arm tucked underneath her head, the other supporting her bottom and back. Then you'll gently sway and sing a lullaby."

Jake began a version of *All the Pretty Little Horses* that set the dog to howling and the boy to covering his ears.

"Daddy, you don't sing good. My baby sister's gonna cry if you do the singing."

"Why don't you set Bristle down and let Jackson show you how to sing a lullaby," Hannah recommended.

"Sounds like a good plan, Mrs. Adamsen."

With Bristle safely on the floor, Miss Jayne sitting in her rocking chair with her knitting, and Jackson tucked on his mum's lap, Jake studied the flawless scene before him.

"Alright, son, show me how to sing a lullaby."

In his tender, feathery voice, Jackson sang.

Sweet little baby, close your eyes,
I will sing you lullabies,
Sunbeams await you when you rise,
But now it's time for sleep.

Softly the angels gather by,
Gently the clouds fill the sky,
Sparrows shall call out as they fly,
But now it's time for sleep.

* * *

The day Jackson was able to sing the lullaby to his new baby sister face to face was the saddest day of his life. The baby was born lifeless. Her mother died soon after.

There was nothing Miss Jayne, a seasoned midwife, could do to save either. And there were no words she could share with her son to console his indescribable grief.

Instead of the wail of a newborn, the house held muffled cries and Jackson's goodbye song to his mother and baby sister.

"Sunbeams await you when you rise, but now it's time for sleep."

* * *

Jake built the coffin for his wife and daughter from timbers meant to be used to finish their new home on the bluff. He dug a grave on the hillside where he, Hannah, and Jackson had shared so many picnics. And he waited. Miss Jayne insisted on a proper funeral for her daughter-in-law and grandchild. She sent word to town with a trusted neighbor, requesting Pastor Evans' services and the congregation's prayers.

A funeral was held the next day. Simple. Humble.

For Jake, hollow.

The Return
Leeds, Idaho — August 1890

Emmeline heard the jangle of Mr. Timberman's wagon and expected a subsequent knock at the door. When the salesman didn't knock, she opened the door to check the situation and realized that, by the sight of things, Halifax had once again been called to service to provide a ride from town. This time for Lainie.

"Doc must have a customer," she guessed out loud, wondering who was ill or injured.

She went back to fixing dinner, hoping to finish the busywork before Miss Jayne woke from her nap. She pulled the hambone from the kettle of beans sitting atop the fire, placed it on a platter, used a fork to pull the meat from the bone, then returned the meat back to the soup.

The jangle of Mr. Timberman's wagon again filled the air and Emmeline pondered his unusually quick disappearance. She pulled back the window curtain and spotted Lainie sitting on an overturned bucket across the yard. The girl looked none too happy, and Emmeline could swear the girl was wiping away tears with her bare hands.

She grabbed a dish towel, slipped out the front door, and approached Lainie.

"Whew, the dog days of summer sure turn travel sour," Emmeline said, handing Lainie the towel. "Every time I travel these roads during the heat of day, the dust and the sweat beat at my eyes."

"Thank you," Lainie said, using the towel to wipe her face.

Emmeline pretended to look off into the distance. The girl eventually calmed and reined in her breath.

"Are you feeling up to this? Staying here at the farm, helping out Miss Jayne?" Emmeline asked. "I know you were only expecting to be here a few days."

Lainie shrugged her shoulders.

"Doc and I can help figure something else out. For you. For Miss Jayne." Emmeline sat on her heels and placed her hand on Lainie's.

"Emmeline, can I tell you something? Something nobody else knows and I don't want them to know."

"Of course. I won't tell anyone."

"Dozens of miles from here, I was walking alongside a freight trail, keeping to the trees, but close to the road to give me some direction. It was nighttime, so I didn't expect anyone would spot me. I was so lonely and scared that I'd been begging the Lord to send an angel to walk by my side. I had prayed that prayer for at least a week with no result, no comfort, no reassurance. I finally told the Lord that if I didn't get my angel that night, that I'd give up and find a rope to hang myself with."

Lainie rocked back and forth, gulping in air while she fought for words to continue. Emmeline held her hand the entire time and when the girl calmed enough to talk again, the woman encouraged her on.

"Tell me," she said. "Lainie, tell me your story."

"That night, walking in the dark, I heard these strange moaning sounds. Not human. Not exactly animal either. I should have headed off another direction, I know, but I didn't care at this point which way my life ended. By rope, by animal, it didn't matter. So, I walked towards the sound and when I saw what it was coming from, I couldn't distance myself from it.

"There on the side of the road was an ox, worn out from work and left to die. A few days before, on that same trail, I came across at least a dozen ravens eating at the maggots of two oxen who'd dropped in the path. I swear those ravens bragged about their feast. They bragged and they bragged and they spread out their wings and they bragged some more. I spotted a dead horse, too, with its stomach bloated from heat and yellowjackets swarming its hide. I couldn't hurry fast enough to escape those scenes. The smell of death was loud and fierce. But this ox, all alone and still braying some life, I couldn't leave him. I poured the little water I had into my hand and he sucked it dry and nosed me for some more. I tied my dress sash around his neck and led him into the woods until we found more water. He survived. And I had my angel.

"We walked on for days like that until we landed at a cabin where I snitched some food and left him as payment. I didn't want to leave him, but I didn't want to be a thief either. I figured he could be hitched to a plow and do some good. You know, be an angel for someone new. And I promised him I'd become an angel to someone, if given the chance."

Emmeline nodded her head. "And here you are."

"And here I am. But what if I don't want to be an angel to that woman? Miss Jayne is mean to me, Emmeline. You and Doc and Jake and even Halifax talk about what a good woman she is, but all I've seen in her is pure, bitter meanness. I'd rather be back on that freight trail than be stuck in a room with her."

Emmeline thought for a while. She was well aware of the verbal bludgeoning grief and pain could pull from someone's lips. She'd experienced it as a nurse, attempting to provide sustenance and comfort only to be backlashed for her efforts.

"I suppose angels weather storms within storms," she finally said. "A wildflower seed grows inside them and whatever weather they're given, they grow. They flourish. And they show up when the nighttime festers and the tempest brews hot, and sometimes their wings get singed by scorn or soaked by rain, but they put on a brave face and continue their work, building upon stars and listening love and the rustle of a wing. And when they need relief, when they need to shelter themselves against the storms and their charges, they turn to the wildflower within. They drop seeds to the earth and let the rainstorms serve, and if the wind carries off some of the seeds, so be it. It simply means those wildflowers will grow where somebody else needs an angel."

"What if it's not me? What if I'm not supposed to be her angel?" Lainie asked.

"You'd already be gone if that wildflower seed weren't planted so deep inside you."

* * *

Emmeline checked the pot of beans as Lainie shared news about the injured man and how Doc had performed surgery.

"I'll need to be getting home then." Emmeline bustled about, gathering items into her travel bag. "Care after such surgery needs to be round the clock. I'm sure my husband probably hasn't had any rest. Did any other patients stop by the office while you were there?"

"No. Were you expecting anyone?" Lainie snuck Emmeline's straw hat from the back of the sofa and slipped it underneath hanks of yarn in Miss Jayne's knitting basket.

"We have an asthma patient that usually stops for a weekly treatment when she's in town. And tomorrow morning Doc's scheduled to ride his rounds east of Chapman Creek. Depending on how our surgery patient is doing, Doc may need to reschedule."

"Shouldn't you wait until tomorrow to return home?" Lainie asked, secretly tucking Emmeline's riding gloves into her skirt pocket. "Dusk is creeping in. You shouldn't be traveling the road in the dark."

"I've traveled that road in the dark more than once. The moon is near full so there will be light enough to see the way."

"But you've already cooked supper, so you may as well stay to enjoy it. And you can sleep here one more night. I don't need a bed. I'm used to sleeping on the ground. Having you here just one more night will be a great comfort to Miss Jayne."

Emmeline's heart sank when she realized the girl was mapping out diversions.

"My gloves?" Emmeline pointed to the hint of embroidered glove trim that had slipped from Lainie's pocket.

The girl pulled the gloves from her pocket and set them in Emmeline's outreached hand.

"I wasn't snitching."

"I know."

"Really. I wasn't snitching."

"I know."

"You probably want your hat, too."

"It would help."

Lainie retrieved the hat and picked at the pieces of fiber that snagged at the straw.

"It looks like your hat has a few snatches of yarn attached to it. I'm more than happy to clean it off for you. Just take a seat. I'll finish cleaning it after supper."

Emmeline smiled and moved a strand of hair from Lainie's face.

"She'll come around, Lainie. No ravens. No yellowjackets. Just seeds. Angel wings and seeds."

"Don't go, dear friend," Miss Jayne called from her bed. "Please don't go."

Emmeline rushed to her room. "I'll be back. Soon. You're in good hands with Lainie. She'll help you practice getting around. You two can figure out ways to make cooking work for you. I know how much you love to cook. Show Lainie all that you've learned the past couple of days. Show her, Jayne. Show her that you are still you."

The Wallflower

Lainie grew into the predawn-through-nightsky routine of farm chores. It wasn't much different from her days working at her grandparents' home station, for there were floors to be cleaned, cream to be churned, and mouths to be fed.

But here at the farm, silence sulked in every corner.

And she was the wallflower, soaking it all in.

At the home station, routine had rose with the sun, then scurried into random moments of flurry as travelers added freshness and energy to the day. The work was always strenuous, frenzied, even fulfilling, and at night she would sometimes slip into slumber before her quilts fell into place.

Now, within this home of muted grief, upon this land of persistent loss, she worked just as hard, worked just as long. But she was always weary, always sore, always lonely. And she didn't sleep.

New, unnatural chores were added to her list each day. Checking the woman's dress hems to make sure they weren't soiled from Miss Jayne's awkwardness in the outhouse. Convincing the woman to wash her hair and her body of the clammy sweat that attracted horseflies and mosquitos. Setting up syrup traps topped with grains of rat poison to bait the biting insects. Prodding the woman to do something, anything, beyond sitting in her chair all day or taking long naps.

When Miss Jayne finally dared venture outside on her own using the rope system she and Emmeline had created, she stepped into a badger hole and slammed to the ground. A new morning duty of checking Miss Jayne's walkways for vermin holes was placed top of Lainie's chore list.

Lainie worried about the woman. Several times over the past few days she had watched Miss Jayne claw at the undersides of her rocking chair's arms. The grooves notched out by her fingernails grew daily. One Sunday morning, after Lainie and the woman both swore they could hear the town's church bell ringing and they hurried outside to catch the sound better, the woman returned to her chair, felt the pockmarks in the wood, and puzzled how they had gotten there.

She worried over Jake, too. He was rarely home. Why should he be? The sentiment of home must seem tainted to the man, a nuisance rather than a comfort. Lainie didn't blame him for this need of absence, yet she detested him for it.

Every day she watched Jake rush off in the morning and edge in at night, usually well past dark, usually to a house where his mother was in bed and out of sight.

But not out of mind.

He'd be covered with the day's work, farmweary, barely able to stay awake as he ate his reheated supper. He'd ask groggy, staggered questions. How did she do today? How much did she eat? Any change? Any change at all?

Any change to what, Jake? Her sight? Her mind? Her pride? Her son? The girl wanted to scream the words, to slam him into the reality lived within his home.

The afternoon that Jake slipped off his boots before entering the cabin to attempt a stocking-footed prowl for a pair of pants to replace the ones he'd spilled grease on, Lainie pummeled him with her eyes. He knew he'd been caught trying to slip in and out of the cabin without either of the women noticing him, and her lightning flashes of anger both hit their mark and bounced off his shield of self-pity.

Lainie had felt guilty over that. The man's road home was littered by death and despair. She supposed his absence from home was his armament against the future, his shelter within the storm, and she wondered as Jake lost himself within his work, was his absentee diligence blunting his pain? Or setting the stage for his final exit?

Lainie watched it all. A wallflower waiting for the world to explode.

A wallflower, never knowing if Jake would come home.

* * *

Lainie heard the clipclop of hooves and the sound of wagon wheels heading towards the Adamsen home. "Time to make myself scarce," she said to the row of summer beans she was harvesting.

The girl couldn't yet see the wagon as it traveled past a span of evergreens, so she presumed the travelers wouldn't yet be able to see her. She grabbed the rifle she toted to every outdoor chore and

142

crouched low as she moved towards the garden gate, hoping to go unnoticed as she slipped from the vegetable garden to behind the house, then into the hide and seek shadows of the woods.

The sound of a strange birdcall caught her attention. Doc. From behind a stand of stately sunflowers, she ventured a look towards the road. Sure enough, Doc and Emmeline's buggy clipped along at a nice pace. Both of its passengers waved their hello.

For the first time in weeks, Lainie didn't fear talking to someone.

The girl leaned the rifle against the fence, adjusted her hair scarf, and went back to harvesting the row of beans as she waited for the travelers. Once they arrived, she stood and stretched, slapped the soil from her skirt, and hefted the pail of beans to the stump just outside the garden gate.

"It's a beautiful morning to be in the garden," Emmeline called out as she climbed down from the carriage.

Lainie wasn't quite sure how to respond to that. Beauty was such a foreign word to her these days.

Emmeline drew the girl in for a hug, then stood with one arm draped around the girl's shoulders as she pointed out the marigolds bursting with color and the fat tomatoes ripening on the vine.

"Look at those sunflowers, Doc. Look at how high they reach, their arms held out and holding up the sky. You just know such flowers tell their secrets to the sun."

"And what kind of secrets do sunflowers have to tell, dearest wife?"

"You need to spend more time in the garden, Doc. There are all sorts of secrets waiting to be told. Tales of dragonflies and damselflies in glided flight searching for good souls. Butterflies gathering wishes, then delivering them to the Great Spirit who hears and sees all. The ladybug's promenade to honor Mother Mary."

"My wife waxes poetic," Doc explained to Lainie. "It's part of her early-morning charm. By noon hour, she'll turn into a mere mortal, just like you and me."

"Oh, Apollo, if only you had loved dear Clytie, we wouldn't behold such tournésols in our midst." Emmeline playacted, pulling a sunflower blossom to her face, and taking in its hint of scent.

"And now she's brought in mythology. Watch out, Miss Lainie. There are probably a dozen flowers brought to life by those exasperating Greek gods, and my wife can cite each story, act out each role, and translate each script into French, Spanish, and Portuguese."

"Docteur Franklin Matthews, aren't you the droll one." She grabbed his chin and gave him a playful kiss. "Peut-être devrions-nous accorder notre attention à la fille. Oui?"

"Oui." Doc turned to Lainie and whispered, "I have no idea what I just agreed to."

"Sounds like you could use a few language lessons," Lainie said with a laugh.

"I'll stick with Latin. It's a language that both wearies and warms the cockles of my heart."

"And how are things coming along for you, Lainie?" Emmeline asked, once again using her East Coast voice. "Are you catching the reins of this bold new journey you're on?"

Lainie shrugged.

"We spotted Jake working down near his alfalfa field," Doc said. "He mentioned that he'll be harvesting that field soon. With Paul and his crew still on the trail, who will he hire to help with the work?"

"Locals, I suppose. He hasn't really mentioned much to me, but I know he's worried that if he doesn't get the field cut in the next few days, next spring's crop from the same rootstock will be scrawny." She swatted a honeybee away from her face. "Jake is counting on this late fall cut to winter feed a herd of cows he hasn't laid eyes on yet. If his cousin doesn't come home with at least a dozen cattle to build up their herd, all Jake's efforts to bring this crop in will be in vain."

"Would it be better to leave the field uncut?" Emmeline asked.

"Probably. As he explains it, the fall growth helps moderate the soil temperature and keep the plants for next year's crop in good health. When soil freezes and thaws over and over, it heaves out the plant roots and damages them. But, like I said, he's got to take this chance to keep a growing herd fed during the rough months of winter."

"Those rough months of winter will be here soon enough," Emmeline commented. "I'm surprised Miss Jayne isn't out here soaking in the sun. Is she taking a nap inside?"

"Taking a nap, plotting my murder. I have no clue. I've been banished to the garden."

"Things aren't going well, I take it. I had so much hope that her attitude would turn around by now."

Lainie cut her off with bitter words. "Hope doesn't sit well on this farm."

Doc watched Emmeline's face fill with hurt. He wrapped a protective arm around his wife's waist.

"Emmeline, Doc, I am so, so sorry." Lainie cringed and covered her face in defeat. "We're all tired, frustrated. Words have become our weapons." The girl rubbed at her neck, tried to stretch away the tension from her muscles. "What I wouldn't give for an ounce of relief, a pound of energy, and a good night's sleep."

"Things are bound to turn better."

"That's real nice of you to say, Emmeline, but that's a proverb we're getting mighty sick of hearing. The preacher, the lady from the mercantile, even the Catholic nuns from Saint Joe's parish stopped by. All of them told Jake or his ma the same thing."

Doc changed the discussion. "Do you think Miss Jayne will mind if we go in for a visit?" he asked.

"You can knock on the door, but no guarantee she'll invite you in."

Doc and Emmeline looked at each other.

"Ladies first."

"Coward."

"A coward to the core, my dear." Doc kissed his wife on the cheek. "You go in for a visit first. You've always been good company to her, and she to you. I'll stay outside and visit with Lainie."

Doc watched his wife enter the cabin—she didn't knock—and gave a slight nod of approval. He then grabbed a chore bucket hanging on the garden fence post, set it upside down on the ground near Lainie, and used it as a seat.

Lainie stared at the man and puzzled over the absurdity of the moment. This man, this very tall man, hunkered down on a rusty old bucket with his back hunched, his hands latched around his beanpole legs, and his knees nearly touching his chin.

"You look quite ridiculous, Doc."

"Nonsense. I always look cultured. Dapper. Debonair. Ask any of my wife's flower nymphs, or perhaps that garden rabbit sampling your vegetables. They'll all agree."

He pointed to the section of cabbage where a cottontail was taking full advantage of the breakfast offering set before her.

Lainie chased after it, flapping her skirts to scare it off. "Shoo, you stupid, thieving rodent." The rabbit scampered away. Lainie's anger lost wind as she thought about her own garden thieving.

She walked back towards Doc, settled onto the gunny sack she'd been kneeling on as she pulled weeds, then fanned herself with the bottom edge of her apron.

"Does the air ever move around here?"

"Only when it wants to," Doc said.

"Great, even the air is ornery."

Lainie pulled at the frayed edges of the gunny sack.

"She won't come outside, you know. Miss Jayne won't come outside. Not to check on the animals or listen to the birds or visit the privy."

"Oh?"

"She hasn't come out all day today. She didn't come out all yesterday or the day before that or the day before that. She won't even allow the door to be open, for chance of a breeze. She just sits in her rocker, sweat-soaked, staring wide-eyed at nothing."

"Is she eating?"

"Nothing that I cook. Last night she made a meal out of apple butter. She wouldn't touch the bread I made. Wouldn't touch the ham steaks or the potato hash I cooked. But she dipped into that crock of apple butter like it was her last meal."

"Is she fevered at all? Any signs of infection?"

Lainie broke up a clump of dirt. "No, I haven't seen any signs of infection. But it's been five days since she let me put salve on her wounds. Seven days since she bathed. She smells horrible and looks worse. Doc, I don't know what she needs to turn all of this around."

"The praying folk will say she needs prayers. Oldtimers will say she needs mountain remedies. Most everyone in this town will whip out Bible readings and rosary beads to chase off her demons and find her a miracle or two."

"What do you say she needs?"

"Time. Enough time to get tired of grasping at nothingness. Enough time to realize that there's an awakening, of sorts, at the corner of daylight and despair. Miss Jayne's had a lot to grieve on the past few months. Her steadfast soul has been rebaptized time and again in grace-filled waters. This time, those waters need to run deeper and flow stronger than any she's met before if they're going to bring resolve back to her life."

"What if time just eats her soul and she gives up? Or gives in?"

"Has she made such talk?"

"Not out loud, at least not to me." She considered her own thoughts of giving in. Jake's thoughts of giving in. She cringed at the image of the gun barrel against Jake's lips. "I suppose that's a conversation most folks don't put actual words to."

Lainie spotted Emmeline in the distance, carrying the cabin's chamber pot to the privy. The girl got up and raced towards the woman.

"Oh, Emmeline, you shouldn't be doing that."

"It's no problem at all. It's all part of my nursing duties." Emmeline nodded her head towards the privy door and Lainie ran ahead and opened it.

"But she's not your patient. I mean, well, I guess she is your patient. But I'm the one who's supposed to be caring for her. This is part of my job."

"It's hard for Jayne to ask you for help, Lainie." Emmeline set the emptied chamber pot on the ground. "You're still a stranger to her. A stranger who seems to be taking over her life and taking over Hannah's life."

"Hannah?"

"Jake's wife. See, you've been here for three weeks, and you don't even know the family names."

"I know Hannah's name, from her grave marker. Never once has Jake or his mother used her name in front of me. Or the names of Jake and Hannah's children. They never talk about anything, so it's not my fault if I'm left in the dark."

"Left in the dark. Isn't that the statement of the day?"

"Wait a minute. What exactly did she say to you in there?"

"Ladies, what are all these angry words about?" Doc asked.

"That dear woman's heart is going to burst out of her chest, Frank. She's scared of the what-ifs. What if she makes a fool of herself? What if she can't pray this blindness away? What if she must depend on everyone for everything for the rest of her life? What if her son doesn't love her anymore? What if this girl . . ."

"What? What did she say about me?"

Emmeline ignored the girl.

"You know what else she said to me? 'I don't matter anymore. Not to my son. Not to God. I'm blind. And God has kept me blind.' She's got a crucifix in her hand, ripped out Bible pages crumpled all over the floor, a river of misery thrumming through her veins, and she believes she doesn't matter."

"I'll go in and talk to her," Doc said.

"No, Frank, she doesn't want you in the house. She thinks you and Jake and Lainie have all conspired against her."

"What? That's ridiculous."

"Not to her. She's mulled things over so many times that she's created an entire tragic drama filled with dark, threatening scenes."

"How did you become the innocent in this story?" Doc asked.

"I didn't. She spit nails at me, too. I just listened until she had nothing left to say."

"Well, I've got something to say." Lainie dashed past them and stomped into the house. Doc retrieved the rifle as he and Emmeline followed.

"Jayne Adamsen, we're going to have words, and we're going to have those words right now. I'm sick of you. I'm sick of me. I'm sick of Jake. And I'm especially sick of this blasted hailstorm we're stuck in.

"Now you've got some fine friends who have come to see you. You're going to sit here and visit with them. I don't care if you gripe about me. I don't care if you tell lies about me. You can make them believe that I'm a fool who'd swim across the river to get a drink of water. Say whatever you want. Just get your bellyaching done today so tomorrow we can start living."

* * *

Lainie had no idea what Miss Jayne said to Doc and Emmeline, or what Doc and Emmeline said to Miss Jayne. After delivering her heated speech, Lainie had stormed back to the garden and pulled weeds with a vengeance. After the visitors left, Lainie had returned to the house, slathered three slices of bread with butter, and carried her food outside for a front porch feast. She went to bed early. Very early. Jake and Miss Jayne were left to fend for themselves.

At dawn, the girl had completed her usual chores without a single word spoken, then prepared the washtubs for a day of laundry.

Today, Miss Jayne was going to be put to work.

"You don't need to see the clothes to clean them, Miss Jayne," Lainie said as she guided the woman's hands to the washboard resting in the tub of soapy water. "You've seen enough stains over the years to know where they'll land, so just follow through with the motions. Plunge and soap. Plunge and soap. Scrub against the board, then plunge and soap some more."

"Stop ordering me around. Why are you always ordering me around?"

"I'm not ordering you around," the girl said through clenched teeth. "I'm trying to encourage you."

"You don't listen to me. You just order me around. Do this. Eat that. I don't want a helper. I want to do things my way. In my own time."

"Then do it. The laundry tub's ready and waiting."

"I. Can't. See." Miss Jayne stomped her foot. "I can't see. Not where I'm walking. Not what I'm doing. And you come in here trying to take over my life. And those awful men. If it hadn't been for you, those awful men wouldn't have ransacked my house and ruined my beautiful things. My blood turns cold every time I hear a noise and think it's them."

Lainie understood fear of the men all too well, and for the past few nights she'd contemplated that fear from the blind woman's perspective. Her eyes roamed to the loaded Winchester she'd set on the ground next to the laundry stand. She grasped Jake's Barlow knife tucked in her pocket. He had given it to her the night of their first meeting and she had carried it with her ever since. Would she have the wherewithal to use either the rifle or the knife to defend herself and the woman should McNally show up?

The sound of Miss Jayne's groan brought Lainie's attention back to the task at hand.

"If you're not going to help with the choring, what are you going to do every day? Sit on the burner like a rusted tea kettle, squawking when you get boiling mad, but never serving up a decent cup of tea? All you're giving is a brouhaha of bellyaching, not one attempt to live your life."

"You're one to talk," Miss Jayne countered. "Hiding on our farm, pretending to be someone you're not. I know that you're wearing Hannah's clothes, using Hannah's hairbrush. You're even sleeping in Hannah's bed."

"I'm sleeping on a mangled mattress tick that's nailed to a wall."

"That was Hannah's bed. Jake's bed, too. You can't take him away from me. You can't."

"Jayne Adamsen, you truly have some absurd stories running through your mind. I'm here to help. That's it. Nothing more. I promised Jake that I'd stay here until your nephew returns, then I'm out of here whether you can wash your own skivvies or not."

"I want you gone now. Now." Miss Jayne pushed at the laundry tub until a tide of water backsplashed onto Lainie's skirt. Lainie retaliated, dumping a bucket of rinse water on Miss Jayne, soaking her head to foot.

"You are not a six-year-old, Jayne Adamsen. You are a lady. It's time you remember that."

"That coming from a hussy. I'm ashamed you showed up on our doorstep. Now take me inside. I need to change my clothes."

"Hussy? Hussy? Listen, shrew, you get your squally, sanctimonious self to your room on your own. I've got work to do."

"I can't."

"You're going to find your way inside on your own. You've got a cane. Learn to use it. Then you're going to open your door and find your own blasted dress. You don't need me to choose the color or do up the buttons."

"I can't."

"Then you'll either stay sopping wet or go naked. I've got laundry to do."

* * *

Jake was mending spokes on the hay wagon when he heard the women shouting. "What now," he grumbled.

More shouting.

"Guess we better check in on them, Bristle."

The two returned to the cabin to discover Miss Jayne sitting in her rocking chair, ringing water from the skirt she wore.

"What happened to you?"

Miss Jayne threw her hand up in answer and glared at him like she did when he was a child and about to snitch a biscuit before supper prayer.

"Ma?"

"Shoo. No lunch being served here today."

"Look, Ma, I'm just trying to figure out what's going on."

"Jacob, the good Lord is trying to help keep me from cursing. You're not helping. Now shoo on out of here before you push me any closer to sin."

Outside, Jake found Lainie sitting, wilted on the front porch steps.

"Any clue as to why my mother's sitting in her chair like a drenched tabby cat?"

Lainie stopped the question with her hand and a glare.

"You two are more alike than you think," Jake muttered.

"Not funny, Jake."

"Yeah, it actually is."

"Well, I'm glad you're in a jovial mood because for the rest of the day, she's yours."

Lainie rose from the stairs and stomped down the trail into the woods, whistling for Bristle to join her.

"Great," Jake said with a groan. "I got the grump, and she got the dog."

* * *

Near dark, Jake and Miss Jayne ate leftover bread sopped in milk for supper. Jake laid out his mother's nightclothes, returned to the kitchen to clean up supper's remnants, then returned to his mother's room to assure she made it safely into bed.

From the front porch, he spotted Lainie come up the lane and head off to the chicken coop.

Jake followed her inside.

"What happened today?"

"Is she alright?"

"She'll survive."

Lainie reached inside a nesting box and pulled out two eggs. She added them to the other eggs she'd already tucked in her apron pockets.

Jake checked the next box and found it empty.

He slammed his hand against the box frame, setting the flock into a fuss of cackles and broody growls.

"Shut up," he yelled as he kicked a pile of straw out of his way. "Why can't anything ever go right?"

Lainie backed away, then scrambled out the door.

"Lainie, don't. I'm sorry that I yelled, that I lost my temper."

Jake hurried after her and the girl quickened her steps, spewing out reasons why she needed to get inside the cabin.

"I best get these eggs in. Mrs. Fischer will be by tomorrow to pick them up."

"Lainie." Jake followed her.

"I should have had them cleaned and waxed already." She plunged forward, as if against hard winds.

"Lainie, please, talk to me."

"She's saving them up for wintertime," Lainie fumbled on. "Gotta get them cleaned and waxed."

"Look, forget the eggs already. We've got to figure this out."

He touched her shoulder and she cowered and spun away from him and floundered for a path of flight and found no escape from this hulking man standing between her and the safety of the cabin. The woods. The trail that would take her far from this place.

She was shivering. Shivering with cold and fear.

Jake knew this fear was his fault.

He took off his jacket and placed it over her shoulders, his fingers accidentally skimming the scar at her neck. He stepped back, leaving her a path of escape.

"Lainie, I'm sorry. I shouldn't have yelled and I'm not going to hurt you. I will never hurt you like you've been hurt before. I will never give you any scars."

"Don't. Don't talk about that."

"Understood."

"Ever, Jake. I don't ever want to talk about that man or that woman or that day."

"Of course," he replied, confused about her reference to a woman.

"And don't ever bring up the other—the other times that—oh, God." Lainie choked on a sob. "No one could do that to someone so innocent. No one."

Jake puzzled over what she was talking about. Beyond the brutality she'd experienced at the hand of McNally, what other trespasses had this girl witnessed?

"Go on into the house, Lainie. I'll sleep outside."

Summer's Grip
Leeds, Idaho — September 1890

Summer was beginning to loosen its grip over the land. Heat still plundered the days and sometimes clouds, heavy and layered, stifled the air and suffocated movement. But night skies brought release, enough so that extra layers of clothing were needed to ward off each day's early morning chill.

Miss Jayne tried to imagine how big the chicks in the henhouse would be. She wondered if the cherry trees she'd planted needed to be better staked. She fretted over her garden and whether it was being tended to properlike.

She felt ridiculous, condemned to a dark where she was useless to her family, their farm. She wanted to catch sight of the season's change, the silhouette of flaxen crops against the setting sun, yet she couldn't even see her own hand in front of her face.

Had cottonwoods turned into feathers of gold? Had walnuts begun to drop from her tree? Did red remnants of paintbrush still fringe around fields? She wanted to ask for a report, but neither Jake nor Lainie had time for descriptions. Paul and Snow Owl and their crew of workers still hadn't arrived, so the girl who was to be her helpmeet had turned, instead, into a farmhand.

Day in, day out, Jake and the girl worked and sweated and callused while Miss Jayne was left to sit on the front porch of harvest's landscape. Crops were brought in, food stored, firewood piled up. She heard the action but was never asked to help.

Like the landscape, change lingered over the Ademsen home. Jake no longer spent hours away from the cabin, from the farm, as he did those first weeks after her accident. Miss Jayne was thankful for that, for each time Jake hadn't been within earsight, she had worried that he had walked off to self-inflict his fate.

153

She still worried over her son. She pictured him, six-foot tall, all muscles and tendons and cords. A man who could move mountains. Indeed, had moved mountains in helping to settle this land. And now he was nearly housebound with a sightless mother and a worthless girl.

And she had no way to see if desolation lingered in her son's eyes.

She'd caught hints of healing in Jake's voice. She sensed that his gun would be trusted to drop a deer rather than end his life, but there were no guarantees and Miss Jayne conjured images of Jake abandoning her, leaving her stuck with the girl.

The targeted girl.

How dare he. How dare he think of running away. Of committing suicide. Of leaving her with that tramp who showed up in their lives with trouble on her heels.

Lainie. Stupid name. Stupid girl.

Stop that, she mentally scolded herself. *Don't focus on her. Focus on healing. On learning. On doing things on your own so you can rid yourself of the trampgirl.*

She pushed a strand of hair from her cheek. She no longer wore bandages over her wounds and now ventured to touch her skin and imagine what she must look like with scars and ghost-covered eyes. She didn't dare ask anyone about her appearance. They'd just placate her with heartening lies. Besides, she had no one to look good for. The gawkers and the gossips had all made their visits and moved on to other frontpage news. The only friends who ever came around were Emmeline and the pastor.

It was thoughts of friends—her so-called friends—that left her plastered in suspicion. Surely, they were talking about her at church. The women were always talking about why so-and-so didn't make it to services this week or why the such-and-such family always forgot to bring food for first-Sunday potluck.

If they were always talking about her, why did no one ever stop by?

What of Paul and Snow Owl? They should have arrived by now. Had they heard of Miss Jayne's injuries? Had they disclaimed the woman as kin and planted their feet in another county to avoid her unseeing eyes? How could Paul abandon her? She had raised him since he was five years old.

Then there was Irene. Best friend for nearly twenty years. Five-mile neighbor. Miss Jayne had delivered six of Irene's nine babies and had grieved with her over the loss of two of those babes born too tiny to survive. Why hadn't Irene dropped by? The first two weeks after the accident, Irene had visited five times. Since Lainie had returned from Lewiston and taken over as—as what? Nursemaid? Caregiver? Housekeeper?—Irene had disappeared.

Miss Jayne reprimanded herself for loathing her friend. She knew Irene had family and chores and crops and a future. A future that didn't need some blind woman babbling along and causing a fuss. A future where she didn't need to hold the elbow of a sightless, blustering fool to guide her to a table or a chair or the blasted church pew. A future where she need not sit next to the latest sideshow freak.

My best friend has shittily disappeared, Miss Jayne thought.

She said the words aloud. A second time. A third time. Then she screamed out the statement, "My best friend has shittily disappeared."

No one heard her. Jake and the girl were both working in the field.

"My best friends have shittily disappeared," she whispered, then closed her ghost eyes and began to chant, "I am healing. I am healing. I am healing."

A thought crossed her mind: *If I don't heal, then what?*

The day droned on, a wearisome medley of bird calls framed by silence, suspicions drenched in black. The woman braved to venture through the yard only once and she held on so tightly to the guiderope leading to the privy that she came back with rope burns inside her hands.

She fumbled into the kitchen and handsought a jar of udder balm she kept available for both the humans and the cows. As she rubbed the balm into the pain that seared across her fingers and palms, she thought back to a day when Lainie had tried to interest her with some small chores, things that could be done without sight. The girl convinced her to help wash the lunch dishes. She slowly trusted herself to gently wash the dish in the basin, slip it into some rinse water, and settle it on a towel to dry. One mug slipped from her hands and shattered on the floor. She refused to help further.

Another time Lainie goaded her into kneading some dough. All worked out well until Miss Jayne went to clean up. Unable to see where the dough stuck to her hands, she let her imagination run wild, to the point that she believed spiders were crawling on her skin. Frantically, she rubbed her hands together to remove the sensation, then resorted to flinging her hands and arms about. Jake walked in on the scene and quickly gained control of his mother, holding her in is arms and rocking her back and forth while Lainie cleaned off the remaining dough with a washrag.

Thus far, Miss Jayne's return to everyday living had left her frustrated and humiliated. She was a burden. An agonizing burden no one wanted to deal with.

The opening of the front door latch startled Miss Jayne from the evening halfsleep she had fallen into. Her sound of fright prompted Jake to call out, "Don't worry, Mama, it's just us."

Lainie rushed to the woman and placed her hand on her shoulder.

"You barely touched your lunch," Lainie said.

"I spilled water all over the bread. I heard the cup roll on the floor but wasn't able to find it."

Lainie spotted it under the sofa. "I'll hurry with supper," she said, bending over to retrieve the cup and wipe the spill from the floor with her skirt. "Would you like something to eat while the food cooks?"

The woman turned away.

"Would you prefer honey or peach preserves on your biscuit?" Lainie asked.

No response.

"How about two biscuits? Honey on one, peach for the other."

"Tomorrow you're taking me with you to the field," Miss Jayne said.

Lainie and Jake exchanged concerned glances across the room.

"Mama, I don't know how that will work," Jake said. "Lainie and I need to cover a lot of ground if we're going to finish that field before bad weather starts."

"You're not leaving me alone in this house again," she said. "Not for that long of time. Never again."

"Did something happen, Miss Jayne?" Lainie asked.

"Absolutely nothing. Nothing nothing nothing," she said. "The day was monotonous as a grave and I near buried myself in it."

"Did you work on your knitting?" Lainie asked. "Paul is truly going to enjoy the scarf you mentioned you would like to make."

"He's not coming."

"What did you say?" Lainie asked.

"Nothing. Just know that tomorrow I'm going with you. I'm not wasting another day in this cabin, all balled up and cussed crazy."

* * *

156

Once supper was done and Lainie helped Miss Jayne into bed, Jake motioned Lainie to meet him outside.

"We cannot take my blind mother out in the middle of a hayfield and expect to get anything done."

"Any booze in this house?" Lainie asked. "Load her up, then let her sleep it off while we accomplish something."

"Not funny."

"I didn't intend for it to be funny."

"My father died a drunk. Cirrhosis of the liver."

"Criminy, Jake, this whole farm is one huge Greek tragedy."

"I hadn't noticed."

Lainie rubbed at her eyes, pushing away the edges of a headache.

"Has Miss Jayne ever raked hay before?" she asked.

"Of course, she has."

"Then put her to work."

"Well, there's an idea. Let's take the woman who can't make it from the front room to the kitchen without knocking a hole in the wall and put her in the middle of an alfalfa field filled with rocks and holes and stubble."

"She's a worker, Jake. If she doesn't put herself to use soon, she'll drive herself crazy."

"Are you going to trust her with a pitchfork?"

"If she's far enough away from any living thing, sure."

"What happens if a mouse runs across her shoe? Or a flock of birds rustle up in flight and spook her? She breaks out in a cold sweat at the pop of firewood or the rattling of the door. Last night, Bristle whimpered in his sleep and she bolted out of her chair so fast I thought she'd land face-first on the floor."

"Sitting in that chair all day, fear is going to be her only destination," Lainie said. "She needs independence, you need a job done. We'll succeed out of necessity."

"And if we fail?"

"We'll tell fate to bugger off, then figure out a new plan."

* * *

At dawn, Miss Jayne had been the first up, the first dressed, and the first to wait at the door.

And now, tucked in bed with the sound of a barn owl in the distance, she was the last to find sleep.

That morning, as they had readied for the day of work, she had heard every one of Jake's whispered complaints to Lainie. He'd grumbled about her rocking chair being loaded into the middle of the wagon bed and bellyached that work wouldn't get done. Mother can't do this. Mother can't do that. We're on a fool's errand.

Lainie finally shushed him and told him to leave them both alone.

After they arrived at the field Jake had cut during the night, it was Lainie who jumped into the wagon bed, pulled the rocking chair to the tailgate, and hefted the chair to the ground.

"Leave us be," Lainie said, shooing Jake and his dog to the far corner of the field.

Lainie positioned the rocking chair between two windrows and guided Miss Jayne to it. "Hold on to the backrest of your rocker with your left hand. Use your right hand to hold your pitchfork and use it like a cane. Take three steps back, pulling the rocker with you." Lainie watched to make sure the woman could perform the task safely. "Good, now turn to your right to face the field and use the pitchfork to scatter the row of hay. Kick your foot out now and then to see how far from the windrow you are."

Miss Jayne kicked her foot to gauge the distance between herself and the cut hay. Satisfied with the distance, she pierced the tines of the pitchfork into the dry strands and gave them a toss.

"How was that?" she asked.

"Let me put it this way. You're hired."

Miss Jayne beamed.

"Once you've finished that section, grab the rocker again and take another three steps back so you can scatter more of the hay. I'll be in the next row, making sure you stay on course."

After a few awkward attempts, Miss Jayne found her stride. Lainie saw that the woman's work was by no means perfect, but she was getting the job done.

Several feet into the project, she called out to Lainie, "Is my boy watching this?" to which Lainie had said, "He sure is."

And now, sixteen hours later, the young folk were fast asleep while she, the matriarch of the Adamsen family, was soaring high with excitement.

She had done it. She had proved she could work. She had proved she hadn't completely disappeared behind her scars and blind eyes.

The next day, the trio set off to work, this time with no complaints from Jake.

Five hours into the workday, dust clouded the horizon.

Jake moved closer to his mother as he shielded his eyes from the sun. Two wagons and two riders on horses were headed towards them.

"Who is it?" Miss Jayne asked, snagging Jake's arm and his front suspender with her searching hands. "Are they the same men who tore apart our home?"

"No, Ma, I think neighbors are coming for a visit." He loosed her grip from the suspender and placed a kiss on her hand. "Looks like Anton and a couple of his boys. I think that's the pastor on one of the horses. And there's a couple of others I can't place from this distance."

Lainie pierced her pitchfork into the ground.

"I've got to go," she said.

Jake let go of his mother's hand and reached for Lainie's arm. He snatched the fabric of her blouse sleeve and pulled her back.

"You can't keep running from everyone. Time to meet the neighbors. Just like we talked about, keep your hat low on your forehead to shade the color of your eyes, but be sure to look these boys in the eye so they know you belong."

Pinchlipped, she nodded. After she adjusted her hat and made sure all of her hair was tucked into the scarf she also wore, she returned to raking the hay to help it dry.

"Guten Tag, Jake."

"Good afternoon, Anton. Gentlemen." Jake tipped his hat to the others in the group and greeted them each by name. "Pastor Evans, I didn't expect to see you here in the middle of an alfalfa field."

"We heard news that Paul and his crew have yet to arrive from their travels," the pastor said. "Thought you could use some helping hands."

"Help would be very welcome, but I can't take you away from your own fields."

"Your family has helped each of our families on many occasion," Henry Jefferson said. "We'd be honored to help you bring in your harvest."

"Had we known that Paul and his crew weren't back, we would have come sooner," Anton added in his heavily accented English. "Mein Nachbar, mein Freund, mein Bruder."

"My neighbor, my friend, my brother," Jake repeated in English as he shook Anton's hand. "I appreciate your offer of help."

"Miss Jayne, I should have guessed you would be out here showing your boy how to get the job done." The pastor took her hand and gave it a squeeze.

"Better to be doing than to be dying," she said. "Did you boys bring along some tools? Those summer rains brought us a real nice crop."

"We've brought along all the tools we need," Henry said. "We'll be back to help with your corn harvest, too."

Pastor Evans nodded towards Lainie, who had retreated several feet away. "I see you've got Doc's protégé working hard."

"She's been a big help," Jake said. "We're beholding to Doc and Emmeline for sending her to us."

"What's her name again? Lonnie? LeAnn?" one of the men asked.

"Lainie. Her name's Lainie." Jake motioned to her. "Come on over. Meet some of our neighbors."

The girl turned two more forks of hay as she tried to calm her nerves. She sucked in air, planted a smile on her face, and beelined her way to the group.

"Gentlemen, nice to meet you." The girl looked each man in the eyes as she shook each of their hands.

Hide yourself in plain sight, she reminded herself.

"What brings you out to the Adamsen's place today?" she asked.

"Hard work and the promise of a bounteous harvest," the pastor said.

"Goodness, such enthusiasm."

"Yes, ma'am. Pastor Evans drives us near loco with it," the tallest of the group joked.

"What can I say?" Pastor Evans joked back, "Enthusiasm spins cobwebs into sunbeams and dust motes into stars."

"That's a real nice sentiment, Pastor," Lainie offered as the men groaned and made jokes about his saintlike wit.

"Thank you, miss. As for all of you buffoons who don't recognize top-notch seminary lingo, get to work."

Lanie laughed. "You heard the man, get to work."

"Jake, before I forget, Clyde Hemmings down at the telegraph office asked me to bring this." The pastor handed the telegram to Jake.

Jake read the words then made his report. "Paul and Snow Owl are still a few days away."

"They still working with that man from Pileup?" Henry asked.

"You mean that cattleman from Washington? Yeah, they've been working together for years, though I'm not sure the town's name is Pileup."

"Puyallup," Lainie said. "I think the town you are talking about is Puyallup. Pew, as in a church pew, then all, followed by up."

"You from those parts?" the tall man asked.

"No, no," Miss Jayne dashed in. "Lainie's from back east, aren't you, dearie?"

"Of course, back east, I'm just familiar with a bit of that area because I, I . . ."

"She has a cousin that moved out there. Long time ago. Used to send home letters describing the towns." Miss Jayne verbally nudged the girl. "Isn't that right, Lainie?"

"Yes, a cousin. A very good, dear cousin. Who lived in Puyallup. And other places. Lots of other places."

"Well, gentlemen, looks like you're ready for a good day of work," Jake interrupted Lainie's fumbled words. "Shall we start loading those wagons with hay?"

Shucking Corn

After Lainie's slipup of words out in the alfalfa field, Miss Jayne had insisted the girl return to the house and make lunch for the hardworking crew. "I'll stay out here with the menfolk," she'd said, throwing Lainie a disapproving glare. After Lainie returned to the field with sandwiches, vegetables, fried potatoes, and buckets of water loaded onto a sled she dragged herself, she was tasked with watering and weeding back in the vegetable garden.

When Jake and his mother arrived home that evening, Lainie overheard them arguing about her earlier blunder.

"She near revealed where she's from," Miss Jayne said.

"How do *you* know that? *You* don't even know where Lainie's from," Jake said.

"Well, *I* know where she's supposed to claim she's from." Miss Jayne shook her finger at her son. "And no one back east has the slightest inkling on how to pronounce all these Idaho and Washington towns with words from the tribes. Asotin, Latah, Kootenai, Puyallup. Jake, if our town catches on that we're housing a runaway—a runaway that's toting a huge bounty on her head—we won't hear the end of it."

"There's no bounty on Lainie's head," Jake said.

"Might as well be. That man who's following her has plundered through enough farms in our town that folks probably figure there's a bounty."

* * *

At the supper table, Lainie discovered that Pastor Evans had asked Miss Jayne if she felt up to hosting the monthly quilting social. "Why wouldn't I?" Miss Jayne announced. "I'm out working a field, and the pastor's not sure if I can host a quilting bee. What a preposterous notion."

A week later, still fuming at Lainie's conversational blunder, Miss Jayne made sure the girl knew she would come nowhere near the fine ladies of her church.

"Don't need you accidentally spilling beans about yourself, now do we," the woman told her.

Lainie recognized the woman's speech as a pleasantly edited version of the same speech she'd given Jake earlier in the day. That conversation had ended with the slamming of the front door.

Jake, ever the arbitrator, spotted Lainie doing her chores and promised to have a few bushels of sweet corn awaiting her underneath the shade tree near the house.

"You'll enjoy shucking corn a might lot better than spending time with that gaggle of gooseflesh," he said.

When the women showed up, Lainie kept her distance. She spent the afternoon grabbing hanks of leaves and silk in the solitude of the sultry air.

Through the open kitchen window, she snatched the various welcomings. "Jayne, it's been much too long." "Jayne, you poor, poor dear. If there's anything I can ever do to help, please don't hesitate to ask." "Jayne, I wanted to visit, but life has been so hectic."

Lainie imagined some of the sentiments were genuine. She imagined that Miss Jayne recognized that, too. But no matter the fussed and clucked greeting, Miss Jayne reacted in much the same way. "I'm doing just fine. My boy is taking such good care of me. Now, don't make a fuss over me. Instead, tell me what's happening in your world."

Jake was right. Shucking corn was a godsend.

The women's conversation cantered along and Lainie leaned back on the grass and bit into an ear of sweet corn. The kernels were crisp and soft and spouted juices that lazily trailed from her cheek to her ear. She didn't wipe away the juice. It felt too good. Plentiful. Something to be cherished after scarcity's swarm. Lainie didn't wipe away the words coming from the house, either. She should have, for the conversation wasn't hers to hear. But she had lacked conversation for so long, had so forgotten the busyness and curiosity of voices that she strained to grasp every word, every sentiment, every tassel of gospel and gossip that she could cling to.

"Goodness, Jayne, how long have we been meeting here to quilt?"

"It's been nearly twenty years, right? After all, for many of those years, this was the only house with a wood floor."

"When will Paul and the native he married be back? Are he and Jake still planning to start a cattle business?"

"I don't understand that nephew of yours, Jayne. Traipsing all over the country, chasing cattle from one neck of the woods to another. Paul should settle down and start a family, just like Jake did."

"Colleen! Remember? Jake? His family?"

"Oh. Oh, my. I'm so, so sorry to remind you of your family's loss."

A new voice entered the conversation.

"Jayne, you got rid of your kitchen table."

Lainie counted the lull of seconds. One, two, three, four, five.

"That old thing. Got rickety. Wasn't worth trying to fix."

"That's too bad, Jayne. Your husband did such a nice job building it."

Another chimed in. "Do you remember our last game of Schafkopf? We played it at that very table. I declare, May Hemmings didn't have a losing hand that night."

"And we've always used that table to cut out our quilting blocks."

"Jayne and I used the table while cutting out a few dresses, too. Didn't we, Jayne? Last time, that little grandson of yours sat at the table drawing pictures on his chalkboard."

More silence.

"Jayne, I didn't mean to bring up hard memories. Please forgive me."

The woman's words were interrupted by something flying through the window.

"What in the world? It's a half-chewed corncob. How on earth would a corncob come flying through that window?"

The women left Miss Jayne and rushed to the kitchen window to search out the answer. All they saw was a pile of corn.

"Must have been a bird," Miss Jayne said with a knowing smile. Maybe the girl was worth something after all.

Hints of Progress

Hints of progress. Hints of progress. That's what we need. Lainie had been mindchanting encouraging words for over an hour. There had to be more ways to help Miss Jayne move past her fears, to keep her spunk renewed, to help her remain confident.

And if the woman lost some of her pugnaciousness in the process, all their lives would run much smoother.

Working in the alfalfa field had been a good start and, despite the few moments of awkward conversation at the quilting group, the ladies had brightened Miss Jayne's attitude. She had even become more civil towards Lainie. How long this interlude of civility would last, Lainie didn't venture to guess.

Based on overheard snatches of the quilting group's conversation, Miss Jayne obviously enjoyed needlework. This love of sewing might help Lainie bolster the morale of the woman this town thought so highly of.

Lainie threaded several needles and attached them to scraps of fabric with different textures. She tucked the needles with white thread into a piece of burlap. Needles with blue thread were attached to a piece of flannel. Needles with brown thread were placed in a piece of muslin.

Convincing Miss Jayne to try her hand at sewing was easier than expected. Lainie simply darned two of Jake's socks as poorly as she possibly could, leaving gaps between some stitches and bulges of wool between others. When she handed the socks to Miss Jayne for inspection, the woman insisted the stitches be torn out and the work be redone.

"Get me my sewing basket. On the floor in my bedroom, next to my dowry chest."

"I'm afraid I have a poor hand when it comes to sewing," Lainie said as she handed the woman the basket.

165

Miss Jayne fished around the contents and pulled out what looked to be a wooden egg at the end of a long handle.

"Ever see one of these?" Miss Jayne asked.

"No."

"It's a darning tool. You slip it inside the sock to fill it out, then you make your stitches just tight enough that the seam doesn't get all bunched up."

Miss Jayne held out the tool and tapped her foot until Lainie realized she was supposed to take it.

"Foolishness," Miss Jayne said. "Not knowing how to properly darn a sock. What did your mother teach you as a child?"

"Absolutely nothing," Lainie said. She was surprised by the sarcasm in her voice and quickly added, "I was raised by my grandparents."

"Oh. Well, then."

Miss Jayne didn't know how to finish her sentence, and flustered by the girl's words, returned to sorting through the basket.

"Did your grandmother teach you how to embroider? Do patchwork? Piece quilts?"

"I've done some mending and I can tackle simple seams. That's pretty much it," Lainie said. "Most of the time I was too busy waiting on tables or washing dishes or hauling travel bags to have time for sewing."

"Then you'll need to learn now." Miss Jayne held out several skeins of embroidery thread. "We'll work on quilt pieces tonight. Right now, tear out the stitches you made in the socks and I'll show you proper how darning is done."

As Lainie pulled out stitches, Miss Jayne further rummaged through the basket, all the while looking into its fabric lining as if she could see into every nook and cranny. She pulled out spools of thread in a dozen colors or more and tucked loosed threads into place. She found snippets of fabric that she unfurled and smoothed and reverently folded into tiny square bundles.

A silver tea tin rattled with sound and Lainie assumed it was filled with buttons and snaps. Scissors in three styles, packages of needles, a jar of stick pins, thimbles in wood and silver—the findings each rediscovered by Miss Jayne's curious hands.

Miss Jayne let out a surprised "oh" as she pulled out the last item. She folded both hands around the treasure and tucked it to her chin.

"Oma. Oma." The woman rocked back and forth, eyes closed, as she traveled through memories and time.

"Oma," Lainie said. "That means grandmother?"

"Yes, yes. My oma gave me this when I was eight, perhaps nine. A few months before she left this earth."

She held out the object for Lainie to see. Instead of taking it from her hand, Lainie cupped the underside of the woman's hand with her own. The woman flinched slightly. Lainie kept her own palm in place until the woman relaxed and let her hand settle into Lainie's touch.

"It's beautiful," Lainie said, watching the woman's reaction. "I've never seen a more beautifully made pincushion."

"Opa made it for Oma as a wedding gift," Miss Jayne explained. "He was a sculptor known throughout Bavaria for his bronze work."

Miss Jayne placed the pincushion into Lainie's hand. "He made the wooden carving, followed by the mold, to look just like Oma's cat, then cast the little figurine with bronze saved from a statue he made for the German government. He only had one chance for the cast to be perfect. He destroyed the carving and the mold as soon as the task was complete. You see, if the officials discovered he had used bronze from a government project, even though it was such a small amount, he would have been imprisoned. Opa risked his life to give Oma this small, precious gift."

Lainie studied the lines etched into the bronze and smoothed her fingers over the time-stiffened velvet.

"The memory, it's as cherished as the gift?" Lainie asked.

"Always," Miss Jayne said. "Always."

"Shall I place the pincushion on the table by your rocker? Something to hold onto and bring back memories when the evening grows quiet?"

"Perhaps it's best left tucked away."

The woman placed the supplies back in the basket and asked Lainie for her knitting basket stored next to the rocker.

Again, Miss Jayne pulled out supplies, this time more hurriedly, until she found a length of tatted lace and folded white muslin tied with a ribbon.

"These were for my new grandchild," Miss Jayne said. She untied the ribbon and pulled a baby bonnet from the wrap.

"I tatted the bonnet from silk thread I ordered from the mercantile in town." Her fingers traced the pattern of the stitches. "I so wanted the matching dress to be finished before the baby was born. Then it was too late."

"I'm so sorry."

"We buried the child in her dress. An unfinished life in an unfinished dress. I wanted her buried in the bonnet, too, but . . ."

The woman shrugged her shoulders. "I was worn down and realized only after the coffin was sealed what was forgotten."

The woman sighed deeply and shoved the pieces back into the shadows of the basket.

"Perhaps for another grandchild," she said. "Someday, maybe someday."

Lainie reached for the woman's hand again. This time she held tight.

* * *

Miss Jayne surprised both her son and the girl when she announced supper should be held on the front porch.

"That cabin has stewed me up long enough," she proclaimed as she gathered cups and forks.

Some form of truce hovered over the evening meal. Jake watched the women tiptoe through conversation, both looking for points in common and giving a little, but not too much.

He watched his mother eat her meal—an actual meal—without flinging a single barb about Lainie's cooking.

Lainie, always quiet, always elusive, asked questions about the farm. "How many acres do you own? Do the cattle up on the ridge belong to you? Is it alright for horses to eat watermelon? Because O'Malley snitched a slice from me while I was eating next to the fence."

At one point of conversation, Jake saw Lainie's chapped lips curve upwards ever so slightly.

It was the first time he had ever witnessed her with a real smile.

After supper, as shade ventured across the yard, Jake and Lainie stacked firewood. Miss Jayne, seated beneath the alder tree, worked her knitting needles for the first time since her accident. Jake monitored her from afar and thought his mother ripped out more stitches than she seemed to put in. She renewed her efforts, time and again, and Jake let out a sigh of relief when at last the needles clacked with their accustomed cadence.

With the firewood stack nearly complete, Jake hazarded a personal question to Lainie.

"Mama mentioned something about you waiting tables and hauling travel bags," he said. "Did your grandparents own a hotel?"

"Of sorts," Lainie said. "They had a home station. We provided meals all hours of the day to travelers, and hay and grain for their stock. Anytime a stagecoach got within a mile or two of our place, the conductor would signal us with a bugle so we'd have enough time to finish preparing the food. We also offered lodging. We only had a couple of beds to offer, so most travelers slept on the dirt floor. We had muslin sheets hung up to create rooms and offer some form of privacy."

"Sounds like a busy life," Jake said.

"Busy days. Busy nights." Lainie shrugged. "Busy everything in between."

"How many people worked at the station?" Jake asked.

"Just my grandparents and me along with my grandmother's sister and a smithy," Lainie said. "Grandpa served as hostler and took care of the animals. Once he heard that bugle blow, he knew it was time to harness up the relay horses. While the stagecoach driver and the passengers freshened up and shared a meal, he'd trade out the horses, tighten up their cinches, then get to work watering and feeding the spent horses. The smithy, Lee Landers was his name, his job was to take care of wagon wheels and horseshoes and such. Leastwise when he wasn't too busy sucking down his drink."

"You didn't like this Landers man?"

"Moocher, swindler, and four-flusher, all rolled into one."

Jake considered the brand mark on Lainie's neck and wondered if Landers was the reason it existed.

"We had a lot of riders come in, as well, so Grandpa was always busy wiping down the horses, cleaning up after them, checking their hooves and whatnot. Grandpa always smelled like horse liniment and Beech-Nut. He swore the only reason he ever chewed on tobacco was to convince the horses to chew the plugs he gave them, you know, to keep their innards clean of gutworms. I'm pretty sure it was his way of getting around Grandma's rule of no tobacco spit on her dirt floors."

"Your grandfather sounds like an honorable man," Jake said.

"He was. Honorable to a fault, some would say." Jake noted the wistful quaver in her words.

"Grandpa also raised a garden that we mostly used for our own food, though plenty of it went to our customers. He kept a few cattle. Some for milk, some for beef. Whenever I could escape the house, I worked outside with him."

"You two were close?" Jake asked.

"He had my heart," Lainie said, and quickly turned away.

"Grandmother did all the cooking," she continued, her voice tight with unspent emotion. "Biscuits on even-numbered days, loaves of bread on all the rest. When cold weather set in, she made sure to keep her sourdough starter from freezing." Lainie yanked, then yanked again at a long strip of bark trapped within the layers of firewood. The bark finally broke free and Lainie was sent staggering. She caught her balance and threw the strip of bark to the ground. "The woman wouldn't offer a single human a hug or a handshake, but she'd crawl under the blankets each cold winter's night, arms wrapped around that bowl of sourdough starter like it was some frostbit child whose life needed saved."

Jake held quiet. It was the first time the girl had shared anything about her growing up years. What could he say to a statement like that?

"What about your aunt?" he finally asked. "I mean, your great-aunt. Were you two close?"

Lainie stared at Jake and wondered where all the questions were taking them. She couldn't see an upside or a downside to answering him, as long as she didn't get too specific, so she continued with her story.

"In some ways, yes, we were close. Noreen was what some might call feeble-minded. Never grew out of her doll-and-toy-horses stage. But she was a worker. And she doted on her sister, my grandmother, always trying to please her, always insisting on bringing her tea and combing her hair and rubbing her shoulders at night. Grandpa said Grandma saved Noreen from drowning when they were young and from that moment on Noreen swore she'd do anything she could to thank her sister for saving her. Their folks died when Grandma was sixteen and Noreen was ten. Since there wasn't much chance of Noreen ever becoming a wife, Grandma promised her a place by her side."

Jake and Lainie finished stacking the newly split logs. Once done, the duo leaned heavily on the stack of firewood and Jake used his shirt sleeve to wipe the sweat from his face. He nearly did the same for Lainie, then realized his actions and sheepishly pulled back.

That's when Jake spotted smile number two of the day.

Lainie kneeled on the ground and nibbled at a clover blossom. Jake plucked shoots of green from the stacked logs as he puzzled over what to speak of next.

"Nothing like awkward silence, is there?" Miss Jayne called from the distance.

"You listening to us, Ma?" Jake asked. "You know, you always scolded me and Paul if we homed in on your private conversations."

"Didn't know I was listening to a private conversation," Miss Jayne countered. "The two of you plopped me in this spot beneath the tree so I'd be close enough for you to babysit. It's not my fault if I can hear all of your prattlings."

Jake groaned. "Lainie, I suppose we should sit by her, so she doesn't wear out her hearing."

"I can hear you from a distance just fine, young man. But it would be gentlemanly of you to sit a spell with your mama. You too, miss. Might as well finish your story."

"There's not much story to finish," Lainie said, hoping to put an end to the topic and keep her past in the past.

"Come, child." Miss Jayne motioned Lainie and Jake forward with her hands. "We both want to hear more about your auntie."

"Mother," Jake warned, "Don't be nosy."

"It's fine, Jake," Lainie whispered. "One step forward, right?"

Lainie's mind flitted through the stories she could tell as she walked towards Miss Jayne. Memories of Noreen's doll collection that had filled a dozen or more shelves on a wall in the bedroom the two had shared while Lainie was given one shelf—just one—to house all that she owned. Details of how Noreen could recite each doll's name and birthday and which stagecoach driver had gifted her the doll, yet she couldn't read or write or move beyond her little girl ways. Descriptions of how Noreen's muscles would clench up tight and she'd become rigid as a board before convulsions swept through her body and how with each of her auntie's seizures, Lainie, too, was shaken to the core.

Then there were stories of how Auntie's laughter was too loud and her smile too large and how Lainie, even as a little girl, was reprimanded by her grandmother if she couldn't keep her auntie quiet when guests were about. How men snickered behind cupped hands and women blushed behind folded fans at Noreen's awkward ways. How Noreen won over the drivers and the riders who saw her often. How Noreen stumbled into a den of biting wolves whenever newcomers stopped by.

How out of place it had seemed to Lainie for someone to have such laughter, such happiness, with a life crowded with so much affliction.

Lainie sat on the ground a shadow's length from Miss Jayne and continued Noreen's story from its endpoint.

"Noreen passed away three days after I turned thirteen. On my birthday, I decided I was too old to play dolls with her anymore. After I broke the news to Noreen, she cried off and on all night long. It was one of the only times I ever saw Grandma divvy out any compassion. She kept hushing Noreen and promising her that I still loved her. But I really loused things up and Noreen wouldn't talk to me or stay in the same room as me, except when we had to work together. Then she was gone. No illness, no fever, no warning at all." Lainie stripped down a long blade of grass. "For me, it was proof that someone can die from a broken heart."

Jake sat down next to her, wanting to know the right words to say. Knowing from experience that no such words existed.

"Grandpa tried to convince me that my auntie's death wasn't my fault. He reminded me that Noreen had seizures off and on her whole life and that was most likely what caused her to die. Either way, her death has hung with me ever since."

"Are your grandparents still alive?" Jake asked.

"No, they're both gone. And the home station was barely making money with so many people relying on trains instead of coaches for travel. It didn't make sense for me to keep the business going, so I sold the station and used the money to . . ."

She tossed the remnant blade of grass on the ground. "Never mind. It's getting dark. I'll gather in the animals."

Antoine and Irene

"You're gonna have to meet people in this town someday," Jake told Lainie as they unloaded dozens of butternut and Hubbard squash into the root cellar. "Hiding in the bedroom, racing off to the woods—that's no way to live."

Lainie didn't respond. Jake broached the subject again but was interrupted by her question.

"Why did we cut the squash from their plants then leave them in the sun for so long?"

Jake groaned, knowing she wanted to turn the table of discussion.

"Leaving them in the sun hardens up the rinds so they'll last longer in storage," he explained. "The curing process also makes them taste better. A fresh-cut Hubbard doesn't taste so great, but give it a few weeks after it's cut off the vine and it sweetens up just fine."

"It's an ugly thing, this Hubbard squash." She held one up and studied it. "Looks like a phantom, all gray and scabby."

"Ugly on the outside, pretty on the inside," Jake said. "Once you cut it open, you'll see a deep sunset color."

"What does it taste like?"

"Sweet potatoes," Jake said. "Ma bakes custard pies with them. Sometimes she mashes them up and throws on some butter and cinnamon. Good chopped up in a stew, too."

"Does it taste as good as pumpkin pie? Because that's pretty much the only kind of pie I have an inkling of how to make. My grandfather used to get a wagon load of pumpkins every fall for me and grandma to make pies from. 'Course, they were mostly for the travelers stopping in for food, but we'd get to eat some, too, if there were any leftovers."

"Lainie."

"I always hated that you had to bake the pumpkins before you could bake the pumpkin pies. All that cutting and seed scraping. I near lost my finger once trying to slice through the thick pulp. We'd bake off the sections until they were soft, then have to pull off the skins before

173

mashing the pulp. Seemed unfair to have to do all that work for pies that disappeared so fast."

"Lainie, I know what you're doing. Stop trying to avoid talk about meeting our neighbors."

"And making all those pie crusts. Not my favorite thing to do in the world."

"Stop avoiding the subject, Lainie."

"What subject? I'm just learning more about what you grow on this farm."

Jake reached up and held her shoulder.

"Look, you can't keep on fearing people. Folks know you're in town. They're curious about you and want to meet you. If you keep on avoiding them, they might get suspicious of who you really are."

"That's just it, Jake. They should be suspicious. I'm not some girl from Pennsylvania. I can't talk like I'm from Pennsylvania and I can't act like I'm from Pennsylvania. I'm not even sure I know how to spell Pennsylvania."

"So, you talk around the subject," Jake said. "You tell folks that you've traveled some because of your father's medical practice. Better yet, ask whoever you're talking to about their own hometown and their own kinfolk. Most people are more than ready to talk about their own lives. Just keep them talking while you do the listening."

"And what about your mother? You made her promise not to tell anyone who I really am, but I'm sure she'd jump at the chance to make me muss up my own stories."

"You two are getting along better now. She wouldn't do that."

"You sure about that Jake? Things are getting better, but there are times she gets all fired up about something and I end up with sour milk poured all over my pillow."

"Mother poured sour milk all over your pillow? Criminy, I'll talk to her. But I know that she would never do anything to hurt you."

Lainie glowered at him.

"Alright, she has done all sorts of things to hurt your feelings. Look, beyond her asinine theatrics, I know deep down she'd never want you injured. And she'd never want to do anything to bring that McNally man back to town."

* * *

174

During the first leg of the journey to Irene and Anton Bauer's house, Lainie called out questions from her post in the bed of the wagon. She and Bristle were tucked between Jake's toolbox and a tower of bentwood bushel baskets stacked six-deep. The summer air was hot and muggy, and she pulled her skirts up to her knees, hoping Jake wouldn't look back and see her bare legs.

Dozens of questions floated through her mind pertinent to the place she was about to visit and the family she was about to meet. She did her best to keep to garden-variety inquiries. How far away does the Bauer family live? How long will it take us to get there? What types of fruit trees do they have in their orchard? How many children in the family?

Jake simplified the answer to the last question as best he could. "Twelve children, the oldest is sixteen, the youngest is almost two, Snow Owl was adopted into their family, and I suspect another baby's on the way."

Lainie attempted the math. "Are there twins somewhere in that number?" she asked.

"Nope," Jake replied.

"For goodness sake," Miss Jayne interrupted, "you are so nosy. Anton had four children with his wife, who passed away when the children were young. Irene had five children with her husband, who ran off to the gold fields and never came squirming back. After Irene and Anton married, they had two more children, and they took in Snow Owl when she was a youngster." She didn't mention the babies that Irene had lost. "If age wasn't beating them in the brow, they'd probably take on a dozen more."

"How long have Anton and Irene been married?" Lainie asked.

"Discussion over."

"I'm sorry, Miss Jayne, I just want to be prepared to meet them."

"Discussion. Over."

* * *

As Jake helped his mother step down from her seat in the wagon, Lainie watched a broad-shouldered woman bound towards them.

"As I live and breathe, I wasn't expecting such a wonderful sight," the woman called out.

Soon, Miss Jayne was wrapped in a bear hug. To everyone's surprise, the woman picked Miss Jayne up and the two twirled around like schoolgirls in the play yard.

"Oh, how I've worried about you. It's been so busy with our early harvest, I haven't had time to come back out and visit, dear friend."

Lainie had seen the woman at the house the day of Miss Jayne's accident, then twice again when she visited a few days after the accident. This was her first time seeing the woman up close. Could this really be Anton's wife? When she'd met Anton in the field the week before, she'd placed his age at thirty years old or so. This woman beat Anton's age by at least a dozen years.

"Come here, boy." Irene pointed at Jake. "You best give me a hug if you expect to take home any jars of that apple butter you like so much."

He walked into her open arms and the woman hugged him so hard, swaying back and forth, that Jake near lost his balance.

"Good to see you, Irene. Mama's been itching to get over here for a visit." Bristle barked from the bed of the wagon. "The dog's been wanting to visit, too."

"I'm so glad you're here." She held the side of Jake's face with one hand. "So very glad all of you are here."

"Where are the little ones, Irene?" Miss Jayne asked. "I was expecting a mess of squeals from them by now."

"I somehow convinced them both to take a nap. It's the first time they've taken a nap since New Year's Day when they tired themselves out from all the midnight whoopin' and hollerin'. I'm sure they'll be up soon, but we may be able to sneak in some grownup time."

"Somehow I doubt they'll want my attention anymore, Irene." Miss Jayne traced a scar on her face. "I'm not the auntie they remember."

"Nonsense. I already spelled it out to them. You've got a new look to your face, your eyes don't do no seeing no more, you can still find all their tickle spots, and you still bake the best mincemeat pies this side of the Mississippi. Once they spot you, they'll cover you with sticky hugs and kisses."

"But I can't—I don't—"

"No buts, can'ts, don'ts, or won'ts around here. You know the rules. Now, did you bring along that sampler I've been wanting to use as a pattern? Winter will be here all too soon and I want to make sure to have all my sit-down projects lined up and ready to go."

176

"It's in the basket," Miss Jayne replied. "We brought along some smoked trout and a huge bag of walnuts, too."

"Those nutshells will come in handy as kindling when the weather turns. And goodness knows that husband of mine loves walnut bread. I throw pieces of dried apple into the batter to make each bite moist and sweet."

"You throw dried apples into everything," Miss Jayne teased.

"And you love every bit of what I make." Irene took the package of smoked trout from Jake's hands. "Your mother especially likes my apple and rhubarb tea, though she still hasn't figured out its secret ingredient."

"I know there's lemon balm in there," Miss Jayne declared. "And cinnamon. There's definitely cinnamon in your tea. I just can't figure out that last hint of flavor."

Jake hefted the burlap bag of walnuts from the back of the wagon. "I'm sure you'll figure it out, Mother, either on your own or when you go snooping through Irene's recipe collection."

"Jake." A small voice came from the back of the wagon. Jake turned towards the voice to see Lainie's look of frustration. He mouthed the word, "What?" She pointed towards her eyes and Jake realized his mistake.

"Oh, Mama, I can't believe I said such a thing."

Miss Jayne reached for her eyes, then self-consciously pulled her hand away. "I forget myself sometimes. Waking up in the morning, expecting to see the sun ashining and the birds aflying, then remembering that milky darkness is the only thing that greets me anymore. No more recipe reading. No more ads from the Roebuck catalog. Newspapers are a thing of the past."

"Darkness may be clouding your eyes, darlin', but you've got sunshine beaming from within." Irene gave her friend a squeeze. "We've got some catching up to do. Frederick has befriended two more wild critters. He smuggled a badger into the boys' bedroom night before last. The next morning, I went in to make sure chores had been done when all at once the quilt on top of the bed started to move. I pulled the quilt back and discovered the badger had torn through the mattress tick and nestled himself in the chaff. And remember how we thought little Stephen would never start talking? He's certainly figured things out now. In the past month, that boy has turned into quite the chatterbox."

Irene paused, placed her hands on her hips, and stood on her tiptoes to get a better look at Lainie.

"Speaking of chattering on and on, I have forgotten my manners. Your guest is shying away in the back of your wagon."

Irene ambled to the wagon and stretched out her hand to Lainie who, half hidden by the stack of baskets, seemed a fawn peeking from the refuge of its grove.

"Constance Irene Singleton Wilson Bauer. I was born with three of those names, earned one of them the hard way, and proudly wear the last one on my heart. It's good to finally meet you."

Lainie pulled herself to her knees, then to her feet. She adjusted her skirts then put on her smile. "Ma'am, it's nice to meet you." She leaned over the wagon's side rails and accepted the woman's handshake. "I'm Lainie. Only one name for me. It's more than enough."

"Good firm grip. I like that in a woman. Now jump down from that wagon and all of you come inside. As mentioned, both of the little ones are taking a nap. The rest of the clan is harvesting peaches."

"If you don't mind, Irene, I'll head out to find Anton and the children. I brought along a ladder and some bushel baskets. Thought I could help pick fruit while you ladies visit."

"That's mighty kind of you, Jake. They're working down in the south corner of our property. We've got late-season peaches bursting off the trees."

* * *

Lanie helped Irene set the kitchen table for tea. A tablecloth the color of blue hydrangeas was topped with a lightly tarnished silver tea service, three mismatched teacups and saucers, and a wood tray piled high with different types of cookies. A mason jar filled with wildflowers captured the colors of the countryside outside Irene's window and Lainie realized that, until now, she'd been so absorbed in the mass of change and fear and frustration that she'd forgotten how to delight in the changing of the season.

"Now the brew I'm serving you is my latest recipe," Irene said as she placed a filled teacup into Miss Jayne's hands. "It's got rosehips, apple pomace, dried strawberries and elderberries, blackberry leaves, fresh-pressed black currant, and just a bit of lemon balm."

Miss Jayne blew gently over the steaming cup, then inhaled the scent. "It smells delightful."

"It tastes even better."

Lainie couldn't help but smile at the way Irene beamed as Miss Jayne took her first sip of the tea. And the change in Miss Jayne's attitude? What kind of magic did Irene hold over the woman?

Irene took a cookie from the tray and ever-so-gently cupped Miss Jayne's free hand around it.

"Now this is that spiced butter cookie recipe I told you about. Anton's mother, Marta, sent it to me recentlike. She lives in a German hamlet in Wisconsin after coming all the way from Austria when she was just about your age, Lainie. Austria is where her family landed after they fled Germany in the early 1800s."

Irene noticed that Lainie hadn't yet tried her tea or eaten a cookie. "Go ahead and try a cookie, missy. My girls and I just love making cookies. Go ahead, try one."

Lainie snatched a cookie and her hurried, graceless hand knocked three other cookies off the tray.

"Sorry," she whispered as she gathered the toppled cookies onto her napkin.

Irene waved away her apology and continued with her story. "Forty some-odd years ago, Marta's brother's best friend traveled from Austria to the States. Once he was settled, he sent a letter to Marta's family requesting her hand in marriage. He even sent passage money. Can you imagine? Sending passage money for a girl five years your junior who has no idea you want her to be your bride? Before she knew it, she was scuttled aboard a ship with one travel bag and a letter written in awkward English explaining who she was and where to send her once she landed on America's shore. I just can't imagine what Marta went through, traveling all on her own aboard a ship that was tossed and turned at sea, sickness and disease everywhere, and not a clue as to how her life would soon be. Can you imagine, Lainie? Can you imagine?"

"No, I can't imagine such a trip, ma'am." Lainie mumbled. She kept her eyes low as she tried to think of how to change the subject to one that didn't resemble the uncharted course of her own life.

It was Miss Jayne who came to the rescue.

"You mentioned that Marta sent you other recipes from her home country."

"Oh, my. The German cooking she's opened my eyes to is richer than Croesus and Solomon combined." Irene took a sip of her tea. "Of course, Anton had to dictate her recipes to me, them being written in German. I dare say I spent half the night cooking and the other half the night eating once I had those recipes in hand."

The women talked for several more minutes and Lainie marveled at the ease of conversation the two shared. She couldn't remember a time in her life where she'd held such fast-paced, authentic talk with anyone. She smiled from time to time when she thought a smile was appropriate for the words she wasn't really paying attention to. Mostly she wondered when Jake and Miss Jayne would be ready to leave so she could return to her life of hiding at the farm.

Lainie's stomach thudded when she heard Irene ask Miss Jayne to stay long enough for an early supper.

"We'll throw some potatoes in the fire, make up some milk gravy with the bacon drippings from breakfast, and have a fine meal," Irene said. "We had a nice harvest of yellow transparent apples this year. I'll have the little ones pack them in mud and we'll throw them in the fire, too, for a nice dessert."

"I haven't had mud apples in years, Irene. What a fine treat that will be."

"Now the butterhead lettuce has been a bit ornery this year, what with the heat and all. The most recent planting has bolted to seed twice now, but I cut it back a few days ago and there should be enough leaves for a nice salad. I've got plenty of honey and vinegar on hand. If my girls pick a few blackberries, will you promise to make your famous blackberry dressing?"

"Why, Irene, you trust a blind woman in your kitchen?"

"Darlin', I didn't say I'd be handing you the butcher knives."

Irene turned to Lainie. "This will give you a chance to meet some new friends in your own age range, missy. Our oldest, Peter, just turned sixteen and is ready to fly the coop. He's got his heart set on proving up some land of his own. Minna, she's fourteen and shy like you. Then there's Lilly."

Lainie didn't hear the rest of the family names that Irene listed off. She only heard the anxious rumble in her head that begged to go back to the farm.

"I was just starting a batch of salt bread for this evening," Irene said. "With this brood, bread making's a twice-a-day battle."

"Let the girl make the bread so you and I can keep on with our sitdown talk. It's the only bit of cooking the girl knows how to do."

"If'n you're up to it, missy, I always welcome a helpful hand in the kitchen."

Lainie slipped out of her chair and moved to the other side of the tiny kitchen. A batch of starter bubbled inside a huge wooden bowl. Lainie caught the fermented scent and it tugged her all the way back home to her grandmother's kitchen.

She mixed in the soft butter, salt, and half of the flour with a wooden spoon, then kneaded in the remainder of the flour as she half-listened to the women talk.

Lainie had just turned the dough out onto the bread board when she recognized the conversation had spun to her.

"See what I'm talking about?" Miss Jayne asked Irene. "The girl doesn't listen to half of what I'm saying, and she doesn't pay attention to the other half."

"She was probably just lost in thought, Jayne. After all, she's had a lot of changeabout in her life."

Irene poured herself some more tea.

"I was just commenting that you're the girl that's got the rumor mill a'turning."

Lainie blanched at Irene's words.

"Goodness, no need to go all pale on me. I'm joshing you. But folks have been wondering about this East Coast girl who's helping out at the Adamsen place. Personally, I was beginning to think you were a figment of Doc's imagination. But here you are, bright-eyed and keen on lending my dear friends a hand."

"Only for a few more days, Irene," Miss Jayne said. "Paul and Snow Owl will be arriving soon, then Lainie can be off to stay with Doc and Emmeline to receive her medical training."

Irene nodded her head. "Doc did mention that you've got your heart set on becoming a nurse. Your own pa is a traveling doctor, is he?"

Lainie gave a hesitant nod, never taking her eyes off the slab of dough she was kneading.

"Her pa was the drifting sort, never staying in one place for too long," Miss Jayne explained. "Isn't that right, Lainie?"

"Mm hmmm."

"He wasn't part of one of those medicine man shows, was he?" Irene asked. "Talk about the flim flam of the earth. One of those charlatans came through this area a few months ago and sold our oldest boy three bottles of some hocus elixir that was supposed to cure everything from a case of the rheumatoid to winter fever. The boy figured it would put hair on his pa's head, fix my gut pain, and uncurl his sister's spine. All it did was make us tipsy and give us the trots."

"He was just a regular doctor," Lainie replied. "Nothing more."

"That's good to hear. I'd hate to see your head filled with such nonsense. Wizard Oil. Magic Oil. Invigorating Bitters. Those medicine shows make you believe there's a cure for everything."

"Remember when Lucy Morteson bought those wafers?" Miss Jayne asked. "Goodness, what were they called?"

"Mormon Elders' Damiana Wafers. That's what they're called. 'The most powerful invigorant ever produced. Permanently restores those weakened by early indiscretions. Imparts youthful vigor, restores vitality, strengthens and invigorates the brain and nerves. A positive cure for impotency and nervous debility.'"

The two women howled with laughter. "I can't believe you can still recite that from memory," Miss Jayne said.

"'Tis easy to remember when you've been staring at the tin for the past four years of your life."

"No. You bought some of the wafers?"

"How do you think Anton and I were able to make those last two babies of ours? A dollar and two bits a box seemed quite the bargain."

Irene caught the girl's gape-mouthed stare. "Stop holdin' back the words, girl. It'll just give you heartburn. Go on. Tell us what you think."

"It's just that I've met a few Mormons, and I can't imagine any of them selling such a thing." Lainie fumbled the sentence as she realized she'd rather deal with the heartburn of unspoken words.

"Mormon folk didn't come up with the concoction," Irene explained. "The peddler told Anton that some druggist in New York came up with the name based on the notion that those Mormon elders—at least the ones practicing polygamy—have got more than their fair share of vitality. That drugstore man's making money hand over fist selling the stuff."

"Oh." Lainie said and turned her attention back to kneading the bread.

"Sounds like he sells the wafers in Mother England, too," Irene said.

"Certainly something to make the Londoners feel jolly," Miss Jayne added and the two women soared into another round of laughter.

Irene looked up to see Lainie, red-faced and shrunk in, still working on the evening meal.

"Goodness, if you keep kneading that bread dough, it'll turn to sludge." Irene walked to Lainie, grabbed a hunk of the dough, and shaped it into a loaf.

"Sorry, I guess I wasn't paying attention."

"She does that a lot," Miss Jayne chimed in. "The girl loses track of most anything she cooks. It's a wonder we haven't succumbed to fits of colic from her cooking."

"I'm sure she's doing just fine. Probably hasn't had much experience cooking, what with travel and all."

"Her grandmother barely taught her a lick of cooking," Miss Jayne said. "With no mama around, it was her grandmother's duty to teach Lainie at least a couple of domestic skills for her to get by in this world. Instead, all the girl knows how to do is fumble around the house and put together pasty meals that the dog will barely touch."

Lainie scraped at the white dough clinging to her fingers, humiliation furrowed and frozen on her face.

"I'm sure this fine girl has many other skills. Skills we've never even thought to have in our lives."

Lainie cowered into a corner, confused that Irene was defending her so.

"She has the skills of a garden snail hunkered down under a rock."

Irene bang bang banged a loaf pan against the bread board. "Jayne. That will do. I've never heard such words come from your mouth."

"I'm just speaking the truth. You don't know the half of what this girl is up to, so I'll thank you to tend to your own business while I tend to mine."

"Ich habe die Nase voll," Irene grumbled.

"What was that?" Miss Jayne asked.

"Nothing." Irene tossed off a few more German phrases and slammed a length of dough into a loaf pan before asking Lainie if she knew her letters.

"My letters, ma'am?"

"Yes, yes. Your letters. Do you read? Can you spell?"

"Yes, ma'am."

"Then fetch that recipe book from the shelf above the dry sink."

The book's tattered pages barely adhered to the binding. Snips of unrelated paper poked out at the edges and Lainie chased after a yellowed note after it slipped free and floated to the ground. She pushed the note back into the book and when she handed the book to Irene, the woman pushed it back toward the girl.

"You hold on to this book for now, Lainie. Let's find you a pencil, too. There are tidbits of paper inside the book that you can write on. Go outside and find yourself a nice patch of shade next to the corner of the barn. You look through the recipes inside and jot down the ones you think would make a good meal."

* * *

Irene waited until the girl was out of hearing distance before she hissed out her annoyance. "Jayne, what's got into you? I've never heard you swipe at anyone like that before."

"What are you talking about, Irene? I'm just telling you what's been going on over at our place."

"You haven't told me a thing of what's going on. All you've done is nitpick that poor girl."

"Poor girl? Poor girl? I'm the one who's injured. I'm the one who's been bested by life's misfortune. That girl's lucky to have four walls— my four walls, mind you—to live within." Miss Jayne threw her napkin on the table. "Heaven help us all," she mumbled, "that girl's been traipsing all over the countryside, spying on our neighbors, living hand to mouth, plotting who knows what while stealing away our lives."

"What are you talking about?"

"None of your nevermind."

"Jayne Adamsen, I swear you've turned brittle to the core. If flinging brickbats is in your nature now, then hell's bells, I don't want to know you anymore."

Irene cleared the tea service from the table. "Mourn all you want about missing your sight, but don't go flinging fire from your misfortune just to scorch someone else."

"That girl is taking over my life," Miss Jayne countered. "She's taken over my kitchen, my laundry, my egg money."

"I thought that was Hannah's egg money."

"It was, now it's back to being mine. I don't have a say in my life anymore, Irene. That girl tells me when to eat and when to sleep. She even tells me when it's time to use the privy, like I'm in the middle of diaper training." Miss Jayne reached for her cane, pulled herself from her seat, and attempted to thump tap her way to the door.

"Where are you going?"

"To find my son. He's the only one who cares about me anymore."

"And you're going to cane-walk two miles down the road to find him?"

At that, Miss Jayne broke. She dropped her cane, slumped to the ground, and blindstared in the general direction of the door.

Irene took off her apron and settled on the floor next to her.

"Darlin', you know I love you. We've been best friends for the good part of twenty years. Together, we've run all over hell's half acre taking care of moppets and mop-ups. When our menfolk's crops failed and cash didn't come in, it was us who funded groceries and winter shoes with pennies we earned, then saved, in a coffee can."

She used her apron to wipe away Miss Jayne's tears, then settled the apron into her friend's hands.

"I never had a sister exceptin' you. You've had to thump me on the head more than once when I was doing something foolish and you've had to step in and take over the reins when I was making poor choices. Like when you told me to give up on my moocher husband coming home. Like when you stayed with my children for five days straight while I searched the countryside for my man. Like when I realized I was expecting again, with no pa in sight, and was ready to farm out the kids to the orphan's home and, well, you know the rest. Now it's time for me to return the favor and thump you on the head to get you seeing straight."

"I don't need my eyes to see that the girl is trespassing on my life, trying to take my friends, my boy. She'll pigeonhole me into some asylum, you wait and see."

"Hush. Just hush. I know about Lainie. Meaning, I know more about Lainie than you think I know. Now I'm not gonna talk anymore on that, other than to say that girl isn't at your place to be a menace. She's not there to steal away your life and she doesn't deserve to be scourged by your words. Lord knows she's already raw from her own misfortunes. Seems to me that God dropped her off into your neck of the woods for a pretty good reason. Probably a few pretty good

185

reasons. So why not give her a chance? Why not see her presence on your farm as some sort of wild and wonderful grace?"

* * *

Jake perched himself halfway up the ladder. It felt good to be tucked inside this cocoon of leaves and branches with the scent of harvest, fresh and dauntless, settling over the land. His hands were sticky from the couple hundred or so peaches he'd already picked and tucked inside the harvest bag and his stomach panged with anticipation of lunchtime, when he'd eat some of the fresh fruit.

This year's harvest was beautiful. Spring's early blossoms, aided by bonfires tended round the clock to warm the air, had survived a week's worth of late frost. Small fruits had withstood heavy winds. Blight bypassed the orchard. The occasional summer rain had helped keep tree roots moist. Anton's skilled hands had thinned the fruit, so the remaining peaches received more sunlight and room to grow.

Many of the peaches had a small pock mark or two where a squash bug or a stink bug had bitten the fruit when it was young. The marks didn't change the way the fruit smelled or tasted, they simply served as scars that helped tell the stories of the land.

Jake leaned his back against a sturdy branch, wiped his hands against his trousers, and took in the sights around him. Lewis worked below him, quickly snapping peaches from the lower limbs, and setting them into baskets strewn across the ground. Jake occasionally reminded him to slow down, just a bit, to keep the peaches from bruising. The boy would take heed for a while, then need another reminder.

Just like his father, Jake thought. *Always the worker racing against time.*

Two of Irene's children, thirteen-year-old Lilly and eleven-year-old Frederick, kept a steady pace picking peaches from the mid to lower limbs of the trees. Hertha, Anton's oldest, was the daredevil of the group. She loved climbing anything—rickety ladders, spindly trees, rocky mountainsides—and she insisted on being the worker who picked fruit from the tallest part of each tree.

A few feet away, Anton herded younger children as he harvested the peach trees closest to the oldest part of the orchard, where dozens of apple trees were weighted down with fruit that would ripen in just a few days. Hyrum, nearly eight years old but small enough that he looked six, was focused enough to put some effort into helping with the harvest, and Anton patiently gave him guidance. Walter and Little Erich were near twins, them being born just eleven months apart. They both looked like Anton with their dark blond hair and pointed chins. At six years old, Walter definitely believed he was boss, and when he wasn't playing with Bristle or breaking twigs or chasing after grasshoppers, he was ordering his little brother to pick up dropped apples and put them into gunny sacks.

"This bag is for the giddyup horses and this bag is for the oink pigs," Walter instructed, and Little Erich laughed and made animal sounds and laughed some more. If the younger put an apple in what the older thought was the wrong bag, he'd get a reprimand. "Oh, no no no, this apple is for the giddyup horses, not the oink pigs. See how this apple has a stem? Only the giddyup horses get the apples with stems."

At the far end of the apple orchard, sixteen-year-old Peter worked alone picking crabapples that would be made into jars of apple butter and pickled crab apples to be sold in town. He enjoyed quiet hours and time to daydream. Of all the children, Peter was the one Jake felt most close to. He was Irene's oldest and Jake had known the boy ever since he was born. Peter had dreams of owning his own farm and looked to Jake for guidance. When the Bauers didn't need Peter working in the orchard, which was rare, he'd show up on Jake's doorstep looking to gain experience working the fields and managing animals.

Fourteen-year-old Minna, with her hunched back and fragile eyes, was like Irene, both in her features and in her pleasant disposition. Though shy around strangers, she eased in and out of conversations with each of the children as she went back and forth between picking crabapples at the north end of the orchard and peaches at the south. She, even more so than Anton, orchestrated the young crew's activities, making sure that each sibling was aware of their duties as well as their importance to the family business.

The orchard had certainly flourished from this family's hard work. Jake remembered a time when that first section of the orchard where Peter now worked stood in disarray. Irene and her first husband had planted those trees back in 1880, then doubled the size of the orchard a year later. Four years into the orcharding business, that husband decided the gold fields would serve him better than the fruit fields. That husband all but disappeared on a Tuesday morning. Over the next six months, that husband sent home just three letters, then was never heard from again.

$$* * *$$

Irene had near lost herself in the shuffle of duties she held on her own once that husband left. She had five children under the age of ten, another growing inside her, a flailing blueberry patch, half an acre or so filled with strawberry plants and raspberry canes, and the beginnings of an apple orchard with its first worthy harvest a year or two away.

A few miles north, Anton Bauer turned his four children over to St. Joseph's Mission to live with the Indian children, at least for a while. He returned to their home and camped out on their property where the blackened timbers of their house now stood encasing his wife inside. When he found the courage, he dug through the cinders, found her remains, and buried her beneath a stand of lodgepole pines.

He'd wanted to find a preacher man to pray over his wife's grave. A couple of them had been traveling through the area and had stopped at their home from time to time for meals and ministering. Neither of those preacher men came during his time of need, so he left the grave unprayed for and set out for a new way, a new life, a new home.

He hitched a ride with a freight driver traveling to Salt Lake. Neither had much to say, not that it mattered. Anton's English was limited and thick with a German accent. The freight driver was missing most of his teeth and Anton could barely understand the man's lisped out words. So, both stayed quiet until Anton spotted a man wearing a familiar suit in the distance.

"Halt, that's the preacher man I need."

"Five minush," the driver said. "Then I'sh back to the road."

Anton hopped down from the wagon. In broken English mixed with bits of German, he asked the preacher to stop by his place, pray over his wife's grave, and bless her with a safe journey.

He hurried back into the wagon, fearing his grief was about to spill over. The driver snapped the reins against the horses. The wagon began to move with the preacher man chasing after it, calling out, "Wait. Wait."

The driver stopped the horses.

"Anton, there's a woman over past Shield's Creek. Her husband's long gone, and she's got a brood of five with one on the way. She needs help with her orchard. Go on over, see if it's a fit. With all her children plus your little ones, the cabin will be overflowing, but that will be a long sight better than orphaning your children while you piecemeal a new life."

Anton and Irene struck up a business deal that included a wedding band. Neither could afford a ring and Anton didn't have time to carve one, so Irene slipped the one she had off her finger, washed it in a bucket of murky dishwater, and proclaimed it baptized and new.

* * *

Jake was lost in memories when Anton called out, "Essenszeit."

"That means it's time for chow," Lewis explained.

"Good thing," Jake said. "I was about to start gnawing on the tree limbs."

"Gnaw away, Jake. You fill up on leaves and bark, I'll fill up on Mama's corn fritters."

Jake hadn't experienced such a meal in weeks, not that Lainie didn't try her best to fix up a good supper. She really did try. But her hand at cooking turned out foods that were more suitable for a brickyard than a belly.

When everyone was filled up on fruit and boiled eggs and handpies dipped in mustard, the children asked Jake to play baseball in an open area near the orchard. He told them to go off and have fun on their own. The children had the upper hand. Pouting faces, pleas and persuasion, then two determined eleven-year-olds pulling him to his feet got both him and Anton out on the makeshift field, one adult on each team, both delegated the role of pitcher.

They had a couple of old pine slats to use as bats and work caps for bases. A baseball, on the other hand, was missing. They used dropped apples instead. Jake tossed the first pitch to Lilly and she hit the apple so hard that chunks of pulp split off in a dozen directions.

Lilly ran the bases. No one could tag her out for there was no apple left to tag her with. Peter grabbed her round the waist as she flew past home plate and spun her through the air.

"That's our Lilly-girl," Peter said. "Best baseball player around."

Each child had their chance at bat. Short, soft pitches to the little ones, bigger pitches to the older children. When the game was done and Anton called the children back to work, the children begged for just one more game.

This time, it would be Anton against Jake.

"You each get five apples," Peter explained. "Toss each into the air and hit it with the bat. Whoever creates the biggest mess wins."

Apples landed in Jake's hair, on his clothes, he even tried to catch pieces of apple in his mouth. Juice sprayed into the air and he laughed. He laughed for the first time since he'd lost Hannah and the baby. He laughed with such intensity that his sides hurt. He bent over, hands on knees, and was knocked to the ground by Lewis and his younger brothers, who piled on him and wrestled with him and tickled him just like Jackson used to do.

And it felt good. It felt so very, very good.

Mud Apples

Jake should have anticipated that Irene would serve an early meal. That was the tradition—two families working at the harvest, then sitting down in the late afternoon for food and conversation.

When he saw the makeshift table set atop old sawhorses, a fire burning in the fire pit, and Lainie bringing out stacks of dishes and platters of food, he knew tradition would go on. It would go on without Hannah. It would go on without Jackson. It would never be seen by their baby.

He supposed he should see this tradition as a guide and not a jailer, and near as quick as the thought formed, grief's shackles clinched hard and threatened to slam his earlier ease and frivolity behind prison doors.

He walked back to his wagon with Bristle by his side to unhitch the horses. He led them to a tall patch of grass where they could graze, tied their reins to a couple of tree branches, then leaned against the tree, suddenly tired from the day. All he wanted to do was head home and refocus his thoughts on the peculiar freedom he had felt working in the trees, tucked among sweetness, reaching for something new and tender and fresh, his feet far from the eroding bluffs he walked each day.

And the laughter. How much had he needed that laughter?

Maybe, just maybe, he could hold onto that freedom, that laughter, let them burrow in his mind and ambush his grievous thoughts.

God, those thoughts.

If today's freedom from guilt and grief and gutwrenched anger could just salt away, grow stronger, strangle the maligners running indignantly through his head, maybe he'd find some aspect of peace.

To be fenced in by peace. How would that feel? Was such an existence even possible? He'd thought so once, on an evening when Hannah was tucked beneath his arm, Jackson nestled on his lap, news of the baby was whispered in his ear. Peace. Tranquil, blissful peace.

Jake had thought he could fence that feeling in, protect it from outliers, wolfpacks, sins.

He was wrong.

Irene tapped him on his shoulder. He was lost to his own world.

"Those thoughts'll turn you inside out, then eat you from right to left, Jake."

"Yes, ma'am. I suppose they will."

"Your eyes tell so many stories. I'm hoping you see round the bend soon enough, to a place where your eyes have happy stories to speak. The stories your eyes are telling right now—well, they have me worried."

He didn't answer. She didn't expect him to. And she didn't expect that he'd want any advice or hemhawed platitudes. Instead, she gave him a hug and put him to work.

Jake carried out table chairs from the kitchen and found level landing spots for them near the vegetable garden. He shooed away the chickens and penned them up so they wouldn't flap onto the supper table as one had the year before.

When supper was ready, everyone gathered round the table for a word of prayer. Irene offered up words to her ever-abiding God and thanked Him for planted roots, bountiful harvests, and friendships old and new.

Jake surprised himself when he offered his own amen.

Did it almost seem like old times? The olders helped the youngers fill their plates with potatoes and vegetables and butter-slathered bread while the adults chatted about crops and weather and occasionally clicked their tongues when one of the children misbehaved. Bristle played his part. The dog licked his lips as he sat on his haunches and beckoned solemnly for snatches of food, which he received more than plenty of. Then the olders each took their turn at the food, taking too many slices of bread, not enough vegetables, and one spreading gravy over every speck of food that touched his plate.

Lainie hovered behind the children and apart from the adults. Jake was sure she didn't know which group she belonged to. Truth be told, he didn't know which group she should belong to. He was grateful that Irene nudged the girl towards the children and told her to eat up and be young.

The adults sat apart from the children as they ate, each group enjoying their own form of banter. Peter slipped from one group to

192

the other and back again. Jake supposed the boy felt ready to fit in with the adults, but the ease of childhood silliness and laughter was too much of a temptation, and the boy stayed by Jake's side only long enough to hear the latest troubles with crickets and potato blight before returning to the frolics of youth.

Miss Jayne nearly returned to her old self, and the crisscrossed frayed ribbons of red and white that painted her face pinched into laugh lines as she regaled the group with colorful stories about Jake's and Paul's childhood adventures. They'd all heard the stories before. How the boys pelted a robin with a slingshot, then decided to cook the bird over a fire and ended up burning down half an acre of wheat. How Paul tripped while carrying a bucket of milk to the house and, with half the milk slopped on the ground, made amends by adding water from the pig trough to what remained. For breakfast, Miss Jayne had hurriedly ladled out milk while she flipped flapjacks, then was shocked to find specks and straw floating in each mug.

Jake didn't hear the rest of her stories. He sat facing the children and was caught up in their antics. A smile tugged at his lips as he watched Margarete toddle over to Lainie and plunk down in her lap. On three occasions, Jake caught Peter side glancing towards Lainie. Lainie blushed each time she caught his smile.

He wasn't surprised that Peter was showing signs of sweetness for the girl. Lainie, despite her two-toned hair hidden beneath one of his mother's old scarves was a pretty, perhaps even charming girl. She had a soft spray of freckles across her nose, an intriguing scar just below her left temple that he'd recently noticed, and eyes a shade of green that melded the leaf colors of every plant he'd ever grown.

"Jake, would you like dessert?" Hertha offered him a tin plate topped with what smelled like apple pie. "Frederick and I made mud apples. Have you ever had them before?"

"Mud apples, huh. Can't say that I've ever heard of them."

"Mama used to make them all the time when she was a little girl. She says it's an old Indian recipe. You just pack each apple in mud about an inch thick and bury them in the hot coals of the fire."

Hertha beamed as Jake took his first bite.

"This is absolutely delicious," he said. "It's almost like apple pie."

"After they were all cooked, Mama and Minna helped us knock the dry mud from the apples. Then they scooped the apples from the skins. I was in charge of sprinkling the cinnamon on top."

"You did a mighty fine job, Hertha."

When the meal was finished and the dishes cleared, the children brought out instruments of various forms and gathered around the fire.

The younger children plopped on the ground with their cooking pots and wooden bowls, pounding at them with the drumsticks Peter had carved. Lainie accepted a wooden bowl and a drumstick with leather fringe at one end and padded leather at the other.

Anton adjusted the tuning pins on the mandolin for Lilly, then did the same for the scheitholt that he favored playing. He'd built both instruments from timbers found on their property.

"Put the land in your music and the music will lift your land," he'd once told Jake.

Hyrum beamed as he showed Jake the flute he'd made from elderberry wood, and Jake was impressed at the airy timbre the flute provided when the boy played a short song for him.

Irene trilled off notes from her recorder, an instrument she'd held onto from her childhood, while Frederick and Lewis argued over who got to play the larger of the two harmonicas. The boys decided to resolve their disagreement by seeing who could spit the farthest. When Irene realized what was going on, she took the harmonicas from the boys and gave them to Minna and Hertha.

"You two," Irene warned as she wagged her finger at the boys. "You bicker? You show bad manners? You play spoons."

"Ma," they both whined as their mother grabbed old metal spoons from the box of musical instruments and shoved a pair of them into each of their grips.

"Psht. No arguments." Irene wagged her finger again. "Benimm dich. Behave yourself or go to bed."

Minna grumbled something about little brothers as she settled a lap harp made from spruce into Miss Jayne's hands.

"You always play this so beautifully," Minna whispered in her ear.

Miss Jayne ran her hands over the smooth, hand-planed wood. Her fingers explored the strings, the hitch pins, the tuning pins. At last, she plucked her first tentative notes.

"No, I don't think so." Miss Jayne held the harp out, expecting Minna to take it.

Minna gently pushed the harp back towards Miss Jayne.

"You should play, Miss Jayne. Remember the girl with the hunched back? How you encouraged her to walk, to play, to run? Look how far she has come." Minna kissed her on the cheek, pulled fingerpicks from her skirt pocket, placed them in Miss Jayne's hands, and settled on the ground.

"I'll be right here in case you drop one of the picks," Minna said.

"You should've brought your fiddle, Jake." Peter offered him his banjo, which Jake declined.

"You and your family are the musicians tonight, son."

Anton called out the name of the first song. Irene played the introduction on her recorder and once Anton had cued each of the children in, he set the scheitholt in his lap and began to play.

Jake kept his eyes on his mother. He ached for her to join in as he watched a hundred emotions cross her face. At last, she plucked the strings slowly, awkwardly. With the next song, Miss Jayne built up courage and played bolder, louder, with near the same gusto she'd had before life's tempest blew her down.

Lainie, too, seemed to wear a different face. She was taking it all in, studying how each instrument was played. The pinch at the top of her nose had smoothed and she didn't hold back her smile.

Hertha pointed to the makeshift drum she'd given Lainie and called to her to join in. Lainie picked up the bowl and the drumstick and shrugged.

"Just drum in time with the music," Hertha called out. Lainie obliged.

Four songs in, Lilly made a special request.

"Papa, play *Suse, Lewe Suse* for us girls to sing."

"Das ist eine tolle Idee." Anton mussed the girl's hair. "Ich würde mich freuen, meine Liebe."

The girls gathered, including little Margarete, and Minna beckoned for Lainie to join them. Lainie, eyes wide and cheeks flushed, mouthed the word "no."

Big mistake, Jake thought, knowing that the Bauer family had a way of getting everyone involved.

Minna and Hertha didn't fail tradition. Each took one of Lainie's hands and dragged her to where the girls were ready to perform.

"But I don't know the words," Lainie protested.

"Just sing 'Suse, liebe Suse' whenever I point to you," Minna said.

Jake's thoughts faded back to when Hannah would stand with the girls to sing the German tune. How beautiful she'd been, swaying to the music, her high soprano voice tucked softly between the youthful tones of the girls.

The memories, moody and menacing, cracked Jake open and branded him with fire.

He walked away. He had to walk away.

* * *

Jake needed the escape. The music. The voices. There was too much life attached to it all. Too much impromptu-make-up-lyrics-dance-the-night-away-harmony-is-bullshit kind of life attached to every beat, every note, every mandolin string, every banjo strum.

He heard footsteps on the parched ground behind him. He assumed it would be Lainie, always suspicious whenever he disappeared.

Instead, it was Anton. The man who had known loss. And survived.

Anton stood quietly next to Jake for several minutes before speaking.

"I lost one. You lost all."

Jake nodded.

"Trauer kommt, es geht, es kommt zurück, es bleibt," Anton said. "Grief comes, it goes, it returns, it stays."

Jake gave a rueful laugh.

"It stays, alright." He picked up a handful of rocks from the trail and one by one threw them against a tree. "I've rubbed raw my emotions so many times, I'm surprised I have any left."

Jake picked up more rocks, then slowly dropped them back to the ground.

"I used to have a purpose in life. To Hannah, the children, to Mother, the land. Now this anger is the only thing I can give purpose to. If I don't feel anger beating inside my head, I feel nothing. And nothing is too shameful a word."

"When my Elsa died, I swallowed grief like whiskey. I nearly drowned in it. I nearly drowned my children in it. That was young grief, green-plucked from the tree and bitter to the core. Now, that grief has matured, mellowed. It hangs from the tree, ripe and ready and flavored with memories. Sometimes I pick a memory, sit down with it, taste it. Mostly I tip my hat to it, then move on to the rest of my orchard."

The men held quiet. Jake pondered Anton's words as they listened to the music in the distance.

"Alle Jahre wieder."

"What?" Jake asked.

"*Alle Jahre wieder. Every Year Again.* The song name just came into my head. Your Hannah, she sang this song often."

"She did. Especially at Christmas time."

"You know the English translation?"

Jake nodded. He knew it well.

The words, the melody, Hannah's voice—they were suddenly there. A song about the Christ child. Hannah was filling his head with a song about the Christ child.

Alle Jahre wieder kommt das Christuskind.

Jake didn't want to remember.

Walks on all paths.

She was so beautiful.

With us in and out.

She deserved more time on this earth.

Stands also at my side, quietly and unrecognized, to guide me loyally by the dear hand.

Jake squeezed his eyes shut against this sudden image of his wife and his children being guided by *His* dear hand. The dear hand of a cursed charlatan, guiding his family away from him. Guiding them far, far from him, from his love, from his failings, from his life.

He willed the lyrics to leave his head, but the words dangled and drifted, like autumn leaves skittering across the gravesites stranded in his mind.

Stands also at my side.

The words spun uncontrolled. The song was supposed to be about life, not death.

Loyally by the dear hand.

Loyalty. God showed no loyalty to me. Only disdain.

Stops with his blessing at every house, walks on all paths with us in and out.

Lies. This Christ-talk is all about lies.

Jake, those words are for you. In this life. In the here and now.

"Stop. Just stop."

Jake's breath stuttered. His eyes flashed open. God, he'd said the words out loud.

"Jake?"

Anton grabbed his friend's shoulder and gave it a quick shake. Jake locked in on Anton's eyes—eyes that pierced through Jake's darkness and grabbed at the question no one else had dare ask.

"Selbstmord. You think about taking your life."

Jake didn't respond.

"Have you tried to take your life?"

Still, no answer.

"Are you listening, Jake?"

"Yes."

"Are you listening?"

"Yes."

"Memories are strong. You are stronger."

Jake shook his head.

"I don't think so, Anton. I really don't think so."

The man's grip on Jake's shoulder tightened.

"There is nothing I can say to change your thoughts, but I say this anyway. Denken Sie an das Ende. Think of the end. Think of the end."

Jake huffed out his bitterness. Endings were all he ever thought of. Endings clawed through his days and stomped out the candle of night. What if I stay? What if I . . . ?

He could never actually say the words, though he could still taste the barrel of the rifle in his mouth.

For the past three weeks, that taste memory had crept into his mouth as he grappled with   conjured images of empty windows. He looks in, everything's empty. He looks out, everything's empty. How many times had he exhausted himself, his thoughts running in and out of the cabin to look through those empty windows? How many times had that emptiness hollowed out his gut and left him with this unkempt barrenness? How many times had those images left his mouth tasting of gunpowder and lead?

Twigs snapped in the distance. The men turned towards the sound and discovered their intruder—a young whitetail buck, its legs too long for its body, its left antler broken to a nub, its right antler intact. The men stared at the deer. The deer stared back, as if asking, how will this story end?

"Does it ever stop consuming you?" Jake asked as the deer turned and trotted into the woods.

"Consuming? That word—I do not know it."

"Consuming. Tearing at you, eating you from the inside out."

"Yes. And no. Time takes away grief's hunger for you. When it clamps its teeth again, you wonder why it still craves you. And why you crave it."

"Is that what has happened to me? I crave grief? I thirst anger?"

"Perhaps. But I think with you, there is more."

Jake eyed his friend warily.

"Say the words, Jake."

"I don't know what you're talking about."

"You're not the first to wish for it."

"I can't."

"Say the words, Jake."

Jake hunched over, hands on knees. His breath exploded with sobs.

"Say the words. Or I will say them for you."

"I can't." Jake's body quaked in anger, pain, duty, remorse.

Anton bent low, his face inches away from Jake's.

"I crave death and it craves me. Say it, Jake. Say it."

"I crave . . ." Sweat dripped from his forehead. "I can't."

"I crave death and it craves me. Say it, Jake. Just say it."

"I crave death." Jake choked on his sobs. "And death. Craves. Me."

"Do you want that?"

"No."

"Do you want that?"

"No!"

Anton grabbed Jake's face. "Memories are strong. You are stronger."

"Memories are strong. I am stronger." Jake gulped in air. Repeated the words. "Memories are strong. I am stronger."

He slumped to his knees.

"Memories are strong." Jake groaned with anguish.

Anton knelt beside him.

"And we, my friend, are stronger."

Wasp Nests

The cabin was nighttime quiet. The soft thup thup thup of moths flying into the window, the pop and creak of the cabin's timbers as they relaxed in the cool night air, the sound of animals as they settled beneath the moon—none of these sounds unnerved Miss Jayne on this night, for her mind was set on other things.

Bristle settled himself on the floor by the door, waiting for Jake and Lainie to come in from evening chores. Everyone was tired out from their day spent at the Bauer place, and Jayne was sure her son and the girl would rush through chores with plans of an early bedtime. Jayne figured she had a good ten, maybe fifteen minutes to sort through her thoughts before the two returned.

She used her cane to thump tap her way to her bedroom, shuffled past the bed to the wardrobe, and ran her hand along the wood until she found the doorknobs. As she opened the doors, the scent from the lavender wands she'd made nearly a year ago whispered reminders of happy times.

Happy times when Hannah, pregnant and laughing at how her newly pooched stomach got in her way as she helped Jayne pick lavender from plants scattered throughout the vegetable garden. Happy times of Jackson, tow-headed and intent on catching grasshoppers, pinching his nose and declaring the lavender stinkier than the stinkiest stink bug. Happy times of an afternoon beneath the shade tree with Jackson asleep on the grass, his tiny fingers wrapped around the corner of his favorite blanket, with Hannah and Jayne admiring his ability to fall asleep anywhere. Happy times of busy hands bending lavender stalks around purple blossoms, then weaving ribbon under and over each cage of stems to form scented wands to tuck on shelves, in drawers, in coat pockets.

Jayne handsearched the top shelf for the tintype of her husband taken a month before their wedding and five months before the accident that crushed his leg.

200

In the photo, he was eternally twenty-two. He had been her confidante, her partner in adventure, her rock through good times and bad. By the time he was thirty-two, he'd turned to drink to numb the pain in his leg.

She'd begged him to stop his drinking, or at least to slow it down.

It turned out numbness trumped marriage every time.

She needed her confidante now. She whispered her husband's name. Once. Twice. Then whispered her worries in earnest.

"I've got troubles, Martin. Troubles deeper than we've ever known. You know about Hannah, the babies. You know what Jake's thinking on. You know about my face, my eyes. All these heartaches are surely visible to you from heaven."

Jayne curled up on the bed and set the tintype on the pillow next to her. Martin's pillow.

"Remember that year we had yellowjackets all over this place? We couldn't take one step outside without dozens of them swarming us. And that sound. That monotonous haze of sound that filled the trees and followed us everywhere. We searched all over for nests. Sure, we found little ones here and there, and we snuffed them out good, all the while knowing there had to be at least one huge nest somewhere. We searched the trees, barn eaves, every corner of the farm, and found nothing. Nothing.

"You finally spotted one of their nests. You nearly stepped into it up on the hillside past the barn. Remember? You were tracking down a lost calf when you spotted dozens of yellowjackets sprouting from the ground. The nest was inside a fissure shaped like a lightning strike in the hard, dry earth. The wasps were flinging in and out of it like no sight you'd ever seen. You tried stomping out the nest and your foot broke through the ground and hundreds more of the vicious pests came flying out, swarming, furious with you for invading their peace."

She touched the scars on her cheeks, remembering the stings Martin had suffered to his own face as he escaped the swarm.

"The next day, before morning had a chance to say hello, you tried drowning out the rest of the nest with boiling water. That just made the yellowjackets madder. You dumped kerosene into the hole late that night. You said two or three of the wasps crawled out of the hole, took a few unsteady steps, then expired."

She sighed, remembering all the precious kerosene wasted that year.

"Little by little, you made progress. You figured out a dozen and one different ways to stamp out everything that stings."

Just outside her window, two owls began their duet of alternating calls. She closed her eyes and imagined one perched in the willow tree, the other perched on the barn, both waiting for complete nightfall when they would find their feast.

"Jake tells me I've got yellowjackets flying in my gut," she whispered to the picture. "I'm sure he's right. I feel them flying around, batting at my innards. They stay inside me just fine until that girl walks into the room. You know the girl I'm talking about. That trampchild who has Jake convinced she belongs here."

She cursed.

"See, there go those yellowjackets, biting down hard then plunging in their stingers. I'm not that person, am I? The one with the fiery bite, stingy in who I sting? Irene says I'm not, or at least I didn't used to be. Yet those wasp nests are knotted up inside me, ready to release at the sound of that girl's footsteps, the hint of her voice."

She tried to picture the girl's name in her mind. Lainie. She'd never heard such a name. Had no idea how to spell it. Stupid name. Stupid girl. Stupid tears staining her pillow.

"I've been stomping at those yellowjackets, dearest Martin. I stomp at them and I stomp at them and they become angrier and angrier. I don't want that anymore."

She realized her right hand was clenched so tightly around a piece of her bedquilt that her fingers were numb. She dropped the fabric, smoothed its creasemarks.

"I'm tired, Martin. I'm tired of this green-edged bitterness, this menace that's built its kingdom inside me. Rain down kerosene on me, dearest husband. At least on the part of me filled with this fiery bite. If you've got that ability to drown my yellowjackets out with kerosene, do it now before the swarm grows bigger and my words sting harder."

* * *

Neither Miss Jayne nor Lainie could find sleep that night. They listened to each other's frilled sighs, neither wanting to admit she was awake, neither wanting to acknowledge the other was awake.

It was Miss Jayne who finally broke the silence.

"It was a good day today."

"Yes."

"The Bauer family, they have some sort of magic in them."

"Seems so."

"You enjoyed yourself?"

Lainie didn't respond.

"I hope you did. Enjoy yourself, that is."

"Irene's family was very kind to me."

"They're the reason Snow Owl came into our lives."

"Oh?"

"After Anton's house burned and his wife died in the fire, he left his children at the Catholic mission over in Slickpoo. Just for a short time, you know. His oldest was only six and the youngest was just a babe, so he took them to the mission to stay with the nuns until he had a new home and could take care of them properlike."

"You never mentioned a fire."

"It's hard to think on. Even harder to talk about."

Lainie bunched the quilt under her chin. Loss was something they were all tired of thinking on.

"Over at the mission, the sisters had taken in several Indian children. Mostly Nimiipuu, I believe. They took in Snow Owl after she'd weathered some pretty harsh abuses.

"Snow Owl had a difficult time settling in at the mission. She refused to learn English. She rarely said anything in her native tongue. She was rawboned when she arrived and became scraggier because she refused to eat the food the nuns served.

"Things changed when Anton dropped off his children. Four little ragamuffins covered in soot and grief. Snow Owl spotted them, stomped past the nuns who were greeting them, grabbed little Hertha by the hand, and led the train of children to her bed in the dormitory. She tucked them underneath her blankets, sat on the floor to guard them, and sang them her Indian lullabies."

Miss Jayne imagined the scene and felt a hint of the heartbreak Anton must have felt as he watched his children being led off to their new world.

"The nuns had never seen anything like it. This Indian child, so remote, took the Bauer children underwing and mothered them like a swan with her hatchlings. The day Anton retrieved his children to move to their new home, Snow Owl chased after his departing wagon while his children howled out Snow Owl's name from the wagon bed.

Next thing you know, Snow Owl is up in that wagon and headed to her new life with Anton, Irene, and their flock of children."

Miss Jayne turned over in her bed and scowled at the question that kept floating to her thoughts. It was similar to the question that had floated to her thoughts when she first heard about Snow Owl and the abuses she'd survived.

"What else happened with your great aunt that day?" Miss Jayne asked.

"How did we get from a story about Snow Owl to questions about my aunt?"

"I know there was more to your aunt's death than a broken heart. I could hear it in your voice."

Miss Jayne felt time slow as she waited for Lainie's response. Each second matched the low, repetitious drone of a bullfrog in the distance.

"Did her death have anything to do with that man? That smithy who worked for your grandparents?"

"It's late. We should both get some sleep."

"Lainie, did that man hurt your auntie somehow?"

Miss Jayne heard the girl gulp and determined that memories must be slingshotting through the girl's mind.

"Lainie?"

"We had a vegetable garden out back of the livery. It was the perfect spot. Plenty of sunshine, not too far from the well so we could easily haul water to the plants. Grandfather grew the sweetest tomatoes back there. He'd plant them right up close to the building, so the heat of the sun reflected back on the leaves and the fruits. Some of those plants'd grow ten, twelve feet high and he'd built these tall trellises from broken down wagon parts for the plants to climb.

"One day, I was tying the plants to the trellises with strands of fabric torn from worn out washrags. Mr. Landers came around the corner. Startled me something fierce. He said he'd known my daddy. That he used to beat up my daddy because my daddy couldn't talk right. He knew my daddy had never told his parents about who'd been beating him. If they'd known, they never would have hired him to work for them. He talked about how I was looking all grown up, how I was tall and curvy, not like other girls my age. I called out for my grandfather and Mr. Landers just laughed. He said my grandfather had headed off down the road, chasing after one of the pigs that had slipped through the gate. I started walking back to the house. He snatched my arm and pulled me to him, started grabbing me—well, that don't need repeating. I fought hard as I could. He was so strong. So strong. I kicked and squirmed and screamed as best I could. Finally, I kneed him in the groin, then I kneed him again. His grip on me loosened and I spit in his face and I ran and ran until I was tucked away inside a thicket of bushes where I prayed he wouldn't find me."

Miss Jayne reached down and settled her hand on the girl's shoulder.

"A couple of days later, grandmother and grandfather took the rare chance for a trip to town. Grandmother had stayed up most of the night getting much of the day's food ready so she and grandfather could have some time alone together, a chance to pick up necessaries from the store.

"Noreen and I stayed behind to work on our own chores. Noreen had taken her pail and her watering ladle out back to water the vegetable garden. She used to sing the entire time she'd be out there, and we always kept our kitchen window open so we could hear where she was at and know that she was safe.

"I don't know how long it took for me to realize she wasn't singing. I looked out the window, called her name. She didn't answer. I went in search of her. No Noreen. Not at the well, not at the garden, not at the tree swing. I headed back to the vegetable garden. The pail, the ladle, they were both there on the ground. That's when I saw the drag marks. I followed those marks and found one of her shoes. Then I heard muffled sobs coming from the bunkhouse. Mr. Landers had left the door cracked open.

"I opened the door real slow, and when he spotted me, he called out, 'Look who's in my bed instead of you.'"

Lainie choked back a sob.

"I lunged at him. Noreen scrambled away, fell out of the bed and onto the floor. I yelled at her to run. She pulled herself up and ran outside. I kept fighting, kicking and biting and getting slapped and punched. Noreen, she found a bucket of old nails and scraps of metal inside the smithy house. She dumped the bucket all over us. It was enough to startle Mr. Landers and I was able to break free. I grabbed Noreen's hand and we raced back to our house. We bolted the door shut and hid and prayed. When we heard horse hooves, I peeked out the window and saw the dirty letch ride away in the opposite direction of town."

"Dear Lord in heaven," Miss Jayne whispered.

"Noreen's clothes were torn. Nearly all the buttons on her blouse had been ripped off. There was blood all over her skirt. I cleaned her up best I could. I could get the blood stains from her legs, but I couldn't wipe away the scrapes or the bruises. Or the loss. I tried to wash all the blood from her skirt before my grandparents got home. I didn't want them to see, to know. Grandma caught me, elbow deep in pink-tinged water. She suspected. Then she knew. She ran to Noreen's room and for the first time in my life I heard my grandmother cry. Huge wailing cries. 'I shouldn't have left. I should have protected you.' Grandmother cried out those words again and again. And those words caved in on her, they weighted her down with a quarry of stone. A quarry of guilt-ridden stone."

Lainie bit the base of her thumb in a feeble attempt to ward off the pain.

"To this day, my thoughts have tried to convince my grandmother that it wasn't her fault that Noreen was forced. The fault was all mine. The fault was all mine. Too bad I never couraged up to say the words out loud."

"The fault was neither yours nor your grandmother's," Miss Jayne whispered. "And it certainly wasn't your great aunt's fault that this man violated her. Why do we women feel the need to take on the fault of someone else's wrongs?"

When Lainie didn't respond, Miss Jayne asked, "How long after did your aunt die?"

"A few weeks. On my thirteenth birthday, I decided that I needed to be an adult so I could protect her from men like Landers. If I was going to be a grownup, I needed to give up childish things. That's why I told her I couldn't play with dolls anymore. Three days later, she died."

"Did you ever tell your grandparents how that awful man first tried to—how to put it?—lure you?"

"No. I knew Grandmother would say I'd teased him, flirted with him, somehow led him to believe I wanted his attention."

"You were only a child. It wasn't your fault."

"Sure, it was my fault. I don't mean that I flirted with the man in any way. I wanted nothing to do with that man, ever. But it is my fault that I didn't protect Noreen. I didn't even think to protect her. Maybe if I had let him touch me, if I had given in to his ways, he wouldn't have hurt Noreen. I was already a throwaway, so it wouldn't have made much difference if he'd hurt me, forced me. Right? I was twelve, yes, but Noreen was nowhere near my age. Her body may have been fifty-two and all grown up, but in her mind, in her thoughts and actions and abilities, she was only five, maybe six years old. I could have understood what he did, that it was wrong. For Noreen, that nightmare was too beastly to survive."

Two Dresses

Lainie was down to two dresses that fit. The one now covered in coffee and the pink frock stashed in the laundry basket. She assumed these dresses had been part of Hannah's maternity wear, for each was roomier and had a long cinch belt above the waist.

It wasn't the waist that was the problem for Lainie. It was the bodice. When she'd arrived at the farm, she was rail thin and the clothing Jake provided hung loose on her lack of curves.

The same held true of the two outfits purchased with Doc and Emmeline's money. They fit a half-starved girl. Now, with a steady diet and chores that built up muscle, Lainie's shoulders all but burst from the seams. And she dared not think about the bustline that was about to explode.

She retrieved the pink dress. Gave it a smell. Decided its stench would curdle milk.

She tossed it back in the laundry and changed into the only other dress she could still move her arms in. Somehow, she'd cover up the gapes between the bodice buttons.

Lainie grabbed an empty flour sack from the larder, pulled Jake's Barlow knife from her pocket, and sliced off a large square of the material. She raced to pin the square of fabric to the front of her waist apron. She slipped the apron on, then stood before the front room's window, using its reflection to adjust and pin the top of fabric to her bodice.

The hurried effort was pitiful poor, so she worked the pins again.

"What's with the new getup?" Jake asked as he and Bristle walked through the front door.

"Oh, nothing," she stammered. "I was just tired of staining all the beautiful clothes you gave me to wear."

Jake grinned at Lainie's red cheeks and hasty retreat from the window.

"I thought you were wearing a blue dress earlier."

"Spilled coffee all over it. I'll have to fit in a load of laundry this afternoon." Lainie filled a mug with freshly brewed coffee, handed it to Jake, and hurried back to the stove. "I'll have breakfast served in a few minutes."

She returned to pouring flapjacks and cooking bacon.

"I'll head back out and gather the eggs," Jake said.

"Already done."

"The chickens are fed?"

"Done."

"Alright. After breakfast I'll take care of the milking."

Lainie nodded toward the bucket, already filled with milk, the cream rising to the top.

"Have you left me any chores at all?"

"There are a thousand chores to do on this farm, Jake. I'm sure you'll find a couple."

"Snippy, snippy. Someone woke up on the wrong side of the bed."

"Snippy, snippy," Lainie mimicked. "You just earned the honor of setting out plates for breakfast."

Jake retrieved plates and cups from the shelf and set them precariously on the edge of the dry sink where two buckets of dishwater already took up most of the workspace. Catacorner to it, the small slab of counterspace was filled with a pitcher of milk, a bowl of sliced tomatoes, a butter dish, honey jar, and enough space to overlap the serving plates Lainie was preparing.

He noticed Lainie had perfected her ability to hold three serving plates on one arm as she loaded them with flapjacks, eggs, bacon, and fried potatoes, and he felt a jab of regret that there was no table to eat breakfast at.

"You've got some skills there." Jake nodded toward her balancing act.

"That's nothing. Back at the home station, Grandmother could balance seven plates of food on her arms, a tray filled with biscuits on her shoulder, and a hot pot of coffee perched atop her head—all at the same time, mind you—while she served her guests."

"You're kidding."

"I never kid, Jake. You should know that by now."

"So that little dimple that just showed up on your face is an indication that you are being completely serious?"

"As serious as a porcupine dancing a polka."

Jake laughed and helped carry the serving plates to the counter.

"Do you miss your grandmother?"

"You should probably holler for your mother to come in. The food's getting cold."

"Alrighty. Nice sidestep of my question. I'll get Mother, but she'd probably be perfectly content if we leave her out with her new babies. I couldn't believe the look on her face when Mr. Fletcher offered her those two bum lambs."

That image of Miss Jayne gathering each lamb into her arms, watching them suckle her fingers and lick her face, was the first happy memory Lainie had experienced on the farm.

"Change of plan, Jake. We'll take breakfast out to your mother."

* * *

Two days previous, a man by the name of Howard Fletcher stopped by the Adamsen place with a baby lamb tucked under each arm. He'd heard Miss Jayne had a way with animals and a gift for healing. After he proclaimed Miss Jayne would be the ideal person to nurse the bum lambs back to health, he set the lambs on the front porch, tipped his hat, and marched back to his wagon where a hullabaloo of sound was coming from.

Hitched to the back of the wagon were two milk cows, one calf, half a dozen goats, and a mule. Within the wagon bed, several chickens, ducks with ducklings, and one sorry-looking turkey commiserated inside pens. A black and white hog squealed its protest at being tied in place next to the feathered cacophony, and Jake was sure that he heard soft mewls coming from a tied-up gunny sack.

"Gotta find homes for them all," Mr. Fletcher told Jake.

He explained that he and his missus had tried their best at homesteading and were coming up on their two-year anniversary of working the land. Though he found farm life quite exhilarating, the missus was lonely for family, friends, and finesse.

"We're headed back to Massachusetts, where I'll grow fat and lazy working in her father's bank," Mr. Fletcher said. "I've got a worthless world ahead of me. The least I can do is find proper homes for each of my animal friends."

"You got homes for those kittens yet?" Jake asked, pointing to the gunny sack.

"I have a couple of people in mind. The mother cat is a mighty fine barn cat. I'm sure the babies will grow to be just like her. The whole lot is yours if you'd like them."

Jake settled on two, both with green eyes. When he handed them to Lainie, said they were a gift, she backed away as if a wailing banshee stood before her.

"You don't like cats?" Jake asked, confused by her response.

"Don't hand me any commitments, Jake. Remember. No commitments, no connections, no reasons to stay. As soon as Paul and Snow Owl arrive, I'm hightailing me and my curse out of your lives for good."

* * *

After breakfast, Jake hitched the horses to the wagon and made an unplanned trip to town. He didn't have time to walk away from his harvest, but he also didn't have time to deal with the guilt that was crushing in around him.

The guilt had begun with Lainie's dress.

From the start, the dresses he'd provided Lainie hadn't fit right. They were at least four inches too short and hung on Lainie like those reform dresses he'd heard about, with the skirt showing too much ankle for modesty's sake. Sleeves that had reached Hannah's wrists hung just past Lainie's elbows. Beyond that, the dresses seemed to fit fine. At least when Lainie had first arrived at the farm.

Then there was this morning's conversation when he realized exactly how much work Lainie did each day, without as much as a thank you from him.

And there was his mother. Jake could barely keep up with her moods. He was rarely at the house, so clambering through his mother's whirlpool of emotions was left up to Lainie. How was the girl coping with it all?

He supposed he should throw one other layer of guilt into the mingle. For the past few days, he'd been comparing Lainie to Hannah, Hannah to Lainie.

There were nuances that caught his attention. How each pushed wisps of hair from her face as she prepared meals. How each stretched, back arched and arms raised to the sun, after working in the garden.

How each pursed her lips when there was something on her mind, but she wasn't yet willing to give it words.

At first, those nuances troubled him, frustrated him. How dare he see hints of Hannah's traits in another woman? How dare he think of anyone other than his wife?

Now, he wasn't sure how to feel.

Hannah. His childhood sweetheart. The girl, and then the woman, who'd put up with his practical jokes and horseplay and oversized dreams. He missed being with Hannah. He missed lying in bed with her, nuzzling her neck, sharing visions of what their future could be. He missed picnics in the field with their son chasing butterflies. He missed placing his hands on her belly and feeling the tiny movements—so small, so cherished—of their unborn child. He missed arguing with her and laughing with her and rushing home from a hard day's work to catch a glimpse of that smile. That smile.

Lainie. She landed on the farm crumpled and torn. And Jake, ragged and furrowed from his own weeks of endless strife, saw her as nothing more than a substitute for him for the parts of life he wasn't prepared to handle. At first, she was this clunky, awkward presence that he'd avoided. Work all day, disappear into the night, avoid his life as best he could. But the other day, as he'd watched Lainie play with little Margarete, he'd felt pangs of regret mixed with peace. What an awkward combination of emotions. This morning, he'd actually wanted to make Lainie smile, had purposefully brushed her hand with his, had lingered over breakfast to watch her play with the new lambs.

As time smoothed creases, this stranger, this beautiful intruder softly trespassed his thoughts as quietly as stars enter the night sky.

No commitments, no connections, no reasons to stay.

Shit. Lainie was right. Neither of them stood worthy of commitments, connections. He had to hold on to his young grief, the mad words, the bitter resentment. He wouldn't let his grief grow old. He wouldn't let it cave in, coil up, collapse on itself. He wouldn't concede to greying images and blurred lines, stone deaf to Hannah's voice, Hannah's words, Hannah's whispered I love yous. He wanted, needed, beckoned young grief to stay.

And yet, he realized that he missed having someone to share things with.

No commitments, no connections, no reasons to stay.

Lainie was escaping her own troubles. She didn't need to fall into the depths of his own.

Lainie.

The buttons tugging just a bit below her neckline.

Jake near bolted from the wagon once he landed in town.

He rushed into the mercantile, headed straight for the counter, and snapped the bell for service.

"Yes, sir, how may I help you."

"Two bolts of dress fabric."

"Any particular color or design? I'd be happy to show you a lovely sampling of summer colors."

"Any damn color will do."

The woman came back with five bolts of fabric. "These came in last week. The green shade would look lovely on your mother. And the pink shade is quite flattering."

"No pink." Jake realized the gruffness in his voice caused by the image of Hannah, always so lovely in pink. He softened his tone. "A color that light would just get stained out there on the farm."

"Of course. Perhaps these deeper tones?"

Jake grimaced over the options of dainty flowers and leaves and dots. He was ready to demand that the clerk make the choice for him when his eyes wandered to the fabric display a few feet away.

"Um, yeah, the green one and the dark red one." He pointed to the display. "The blue fabric over there, I'm buying that one, too."

"Ah, yes, cornflower blue. It's one of my favorite colors. I'll be right back with it."

Cornflower blue. That's the color he wanted to see Lainie in. Cornflower blue.

* * *

Lainie heard screams coming from inside the house. She ran in to find Miss Jayne standing in her rocker, one hand against the wall to steady herself against its sway.

"What's going on?"

"Stop right there, Lainie!"

Miss Jayne didn't have a chance to finish her warning before Lainie spotted the trouble slithering along the floorboards just inside the door.

213

"Is that a rattlesnake?"

"Of course, it's a rattlesnake. Now do something about it. But don't move fast or get too close. It'll strike."

"How do I get it out of here?"

"You don't get it out of here. You kill it."

"Maybe I should get Jake."

"Jake's gone to town. It's either kill the snake now or wonder where it's slunk off to and chance getting bit."

"What happens if it does bite?"

"You don't want to know."

Lainie thought about running to the barn to find a shovel or a hoe to kill the snake with. If she left and the snake disappeared, then what? There was nothing on the front porch of any use. She only had about two feet of walking space to get around the snake, with its nasty eyes and its even nastier fangs. She backwalked the slim trail into the room and eyed her snake-slaying options. The snake was in the path to Jake's rifle that she had foolishly left tucked in the corner next to the door. Miss Jayne's knitting needles lay on the floor and seemed little defense against the slithering monster. She had Jake's pocketknife with her, but its small blade seemed of little use against something so long and thin. She could throw a chair against the snake, but that would probably just rile it.

The kitchen seemed the most likely place to find any armament for the enemy at hand. Lainie hefted the butcher knife from the butcher block, raised her arm to the ready, braved forward a few small steps, and hurled the knife at the snake. She missed her target. The snake was now defensive.

Lainie backed up. The snake flew forward.

"Oh, shit. Oh, shit."

"Lainie? What's going on?" Miss Jayne shrieked.

"The snake's fangs are caught in my skirt."

"Are you hurt?"

"I don't think so. Shit, what should I do?"

"Very slowly, take your dress off. Try to keep the snake's fangs hooked in the fabric. Then let you dress drop onto the snake."

"Are you joking me?"

"Just do it. While the snake is tangled up in the fabric, clobber it hard."

Lainie untied the apron at her waist, undid the pins to the scrap of flour sack she'd earlier attached to her dress bodice, and tossed both aside. Her hands faltered as she unfastened the collar button, then the next and the third until she realized it was much faster to rip the dress front open. Buttons flung across the room.

All the while, the snake arched itself back and forth, trying to free its fangs.

Lainie peeled off the bodice and sleeves, pushed the dress past her hips then high stepped from the dress, angling the skirt, with the attached snake, away from her body.

Once freed, Lainie flung the bulk of the dress onto the snake, snatched a chair from against the wall, and set it next to the squirming bundle of clothes. She climbed onto the chair and reached across the counter, nearly losing her balance as she did so. Her fingertips barely reached the cast iron skillet hanging on the wall. She fumbled with it until it clattered to the counter. Both she and the snake jumped. Miss Jayne let out another shriek.

"It's alright. It's gonna be alright," Lainie kept murmuring.

She leaned down and grabbed the skillet. She cinched her hand up the handle to balance its weight. She raised her arm, took aim, and pitched the skillet hard, clobbering the snake's head just as it peered from the fabric.

"Is it dead?" Miss Jayne hollered.

"No, just dazed. Shit."

Though it still moved, the snake had lost its vigor. Lainie jumped from the chair and yanked at the butcher knife firmly embedded in the floorboards. The snake was slowly coming to its senses and inching out from underneath the dress. Lainie attacked from its tail end, slicing the snake in half then slicing it again and again until its body fell limp within the dress and its head fell in defeat.

Bristle beat Jake through the door. The dog saw the snake and the dress and, deciding they were both play toys, grabbed them with his teeth and flung them back and forth.

Jake spotted his mother standing in her rocking chair, Lainie standing in her skivvies, and his dog tossing around what was left of Lainie's dress.

"Anything I should know about?" he asked.

Lainie cringed, dropped the bloodied knife, and pointed to the dress.

Jake pulled the fabric from Bristle's grasp and spotted what was left of the snake.

"You ladies certainly know how to entertain yourselves."

He held up the dress and stuck his fingers through one of the slash marks.

"Good thing I made that trip to town. Looks like you'll be needing some new clothes."

The Corncrib

Jake slumped against the door frame of the corncrib. Half full. The scrawny building was only half full of dent corn, still on the cob. Between what they'd need to feed the chickens and two pigs, he doubted they'd have enough feed to make it to spring.

It was going to be a long, lean year.

He'd been a fool not to plant those last acres with corn, with wheat. A fool to wallow in grief rather than forge ahead and work his fields and honor his duty to the land.

And now, this fool's reality stood before him. Four feet wide, ten feet long, not enough food for a year.

When Jake was fifteen, he and his father had spent backbreaking hours cutting timbers, chiseling out mortise holes, and forcing tenons into place for this one small building. They'd stacked stones to support its base. They'd made sure the walls tapered outward at the roofline and the outer planks were spaced an inch apart, all to circulate the air to completely dry the corn. They'd secured braces and cross ties so the crib walls would be strong enough not to bulge from the outward pressure of the corn and to prevent the crib, when it was near empty, from rocking when strong winds came. They'd dreamed and schemed as they'd worked. Someday they'd raise a huge herd of cattle. Someday they'd have a bigger barn. Someday they'd build a crib triple—no, quadruple—the size of this one and there would be bins for all sorts of grain and a center drive where they could park their wagon and unload hundreds of bushels of field corn that they'd harvested using that newfangled machine they'd overheard the Flersching brothers talk about.

Big dreams.

He'd let his father down.

He set his shingle hatchet and box of nails into the back of the wagon, then fetched the ladder he'd left leaning against the building. At least the corn was in, at least the roof was patched.

Bristle was off traipsing through the tall, dry grass, barking like mad at something in the distance. "What's gotten into that dog?" Jake muttered. "Bristle, get back here," he hollered. "Don't need you getting swallowed up by some bear."

The dog didn't return. Jake grabbed his shotgun from the wagon and set off to find Bristle and take care of whatever trouble he might have found.

He expected to see a raccoon or maybe a cougar. Bristle was famous for warning off wildlife. Instead, he spotted two riders in the distance. One of their horses was a chestnut that could belong to anyone in these parts. The second horse had him worried. It was a grey, like the one Niall McNally rode.

Jake slipped behind a tree and readied his gun. He didn't think he'd been spotted yet. The pair's attention was too focused on the dog and his never-ending bark. Jake studied the scene. As the riders neared, he listened closely for voices.

He kept his gun aimed at the rider on the left. If it was McNally, he'd take him down first.

Could he do this? Could he take down a man who wasn't drawing a bead on him? Jake's wavering breath said no. His sweaty palms said no. His jumping heart said no. But some innate tenet seated deep in his core barked out, "Kill the monster."

And so, he waited. Fear spiderwebbed over him. He wanted to itch at it, grab at it, smash it against the rocks. He mouthbreathed haggard, quavering breaths. He couldn't swallow. His mouth was a desert.

Something about the scene didn't make sense. The dog's bark had changed. Bristle's bark was no longer a warning. Had the riders thrown his dog a scrap of food? Convinced him to calm down to keep him from alerting anyone inside the house? Or maybe Jake's sense of foreboding was playing tricks on his mind.

No matter. He kept the shotgun aimed. He wouldn't fail at protecting his family this time.

A trail of sweat ran down his back. Jake was tempted to wipe away the sweat trickling into his eyes. *Stop. Steady.* He scolded himself. *Think of Mother. Think of the girl.*

Voices. A deep baritone. And a woman's voice? Jake couldn't be sure. Then laughter as one of the riders pointed to the dog and called out his name.

Jake lowered the gun and slumped against the tree.

"Criminy sakes, Paul Adamsen, you near got a bullet through your head."

"Is that you, Jake?" the rider called out.

Jake stepped out from behind the tree. "It's me. And I should put some buckshot in your butt for sneaking up on me like that."

"T'weren't no one sneaking up on anyone, though I'd laugh my head off if I left you with your britches in a puddle."

Paul dismounted his horse and the two men faced off, two scrappers toeing the line.

"'Bout time you came sashaying back to town, Paul. The world don't know how to turn without your saddlegoose expertise."

"It's pity poor that I can't astound the entire country with my savvy and my charms."

"Pity poor."

"That's right. Pity poor."

Paul wrapped his arm around Jake's neck and tousled his hair.

"Tarnation, boy, you look like you haven't slept in a month."

"Change that to a few months and you'd be close to right," Jake said.

"Is that pretty lady of yours at the house? And my little guy? I brought my nephew a stick horse and Snow Owl's been working on a papoose for the baby."

"You didn't get my telegrams."

"Telegrams? You know how hard it is to get a telegram when you're moving from job to job."

"I tried. I really tried to let you know."

Paul stared at his cousin's pained expression. "Dear Lord, say it isn't so."

"They're gone, Paul. Hannah. The children. They're gone."

* * *

The trio sat on the trunk of a fallen pine tree as Jake shared the news with Paul and Snow Owl. He noticed that Snow Owl's hands covered her stomach as he explained how Hannah and the baby had died.

"You're expecting a child, aren't you?"

Snow Owl nodded.

"I'm happy for you. Real happy."

"Qe'ci'yew'yew', dear brother," Snow Owl said. "Your words mean much to me."

"And you're feeling well?"

"Much better now."

Jake raised his eyebrows in question.

"I was quite ill. Pains. Bleeding. But better now."

"That's why we came in so late," Paul explained. "This midwife, well, once she saw how sick Snow Owl was feeling, she kicked me in the keister and told me to give up the trail for a while so Snow and the baby could rest. We stayed on with a family down south for a time. I helped build their herd and did a bunch of work on their farm. They paid me with a place to live and four head of cattle."

"I'm glad things turned out well for both of you and the baby." Jake reached out to Paul and the two clasped hands in celebration. "Land's sake, cousin, you're gonna be a pappy."

"Yeah, I am, though I'm not sure I want to be called pappy. And Jake, if I'd known about—you know—we would have come back sooner."

"I know. You're here now. Mother will be thrilled that you're back."

"Is she at the cabin? I'm ready to take that girl for a spin on the dance floor."

"Paul, all is not well with Mother."

"What do you mean?"

"She's lost her sight."

Jake detailed the accident, Miss Jayne's stay at Doc's, the frustrations she'd had since coming home.

"Criminy, Jake, it's been a regular shitstorm around here."

"You could say that. Mother's probably in the house. I imagine once she hears your booming voice, she'll want to get gussied up. Lainie's at the house, too."

"Lainie?"

"She's part of what the shitstorm blew in."

* * *

Lainie saw it all. The joyful embraces. The laughter. The announcement of a baby. The reverence of loss. The celebration of possibility.

She saw it all and knew she didn't belong. Throwaway. She was a throwaway.

They didn't see her standing in the doorway. They didn't see the tremor of her chin or the sadness in her eyes. They didn't see her leave.

They didn't see her walk to the graves of Hannah and the children to say her goodbyes.

* * *

"Who knew on this last cattle run that I'd turn into a full blown salesman." Paul poured himself a third mug of coffee from the kettle on the woodstove. "Two years ago, this company out in Illinois sold forty-five of their steel windmills. Since then, they've had so much interest in the machine that they've built a big ol' factory and are talking about adding on another building. Lucky for us, I hit the right-place right-time windfall. I sweettalked the boys at the factory into letting me plant their windmills for some top-notch ranchers to drive up business and make a small bundle for them. Not that they need any help bringing in business. Western Union can't deliver orders fast enough to their office."

"Wait, I thought you were helping herd cattle between Texas and Montana," Jake said.

"You never mentioned in any of your letters that you were doing something different," Miss Jayne added.

Snow Owl explained. "There is much change to the cattle trail. Many cowboys, few herds to move by trail. Railroads now cross the land. Railroads carry the cattle. Many cowboys no longer needed. Paul no longer needed. We find another way to earn money."

"Snow is the one who came up with the idea," Paul said. "She'd heard a couple of ranchers talking about this steel wind wheel that served up more muscle than any wood wheels around. We learned what we could, considered our options, and next thing you know, we're on an eastbound locomotive headed for the big city of Chicago."

"So, you're no longer riding the trail? You'll be a windmill salesman instead?" Jake mulled through the impact this would have on their plans for the cattle ranch.

"For a time. I'll head back east after the baby's born. I'll be a freelance windmiller. You know, a windmill boss with a team of windmill men and well diggers. We'll migrate across the plains, from the Dakotas to the Pecos, following our trade."

Jake echoed Paul's words. "A freelance windmiller."

"When you get down to brass tacks, millions of dollars have been put into the manufacture and purchase of mills." Paul looked Jake directly in the eyes. "Over the next year or two, I aim to make a small bundle off this Aërmotor enterprise so we can have a tidy sum of money for our cattle operation."

"Sounds like a fool's errand to me," Jake said. "There are plenty of steel windmills taking over the horizon."

"But nothing like the Aërmotor," Paul interrupted. "This guy, last name of Perry, he's some math genius who's figured out how to build a windmill that won't be harmed by changing winds. He's tested his machines in this huge room—thirty-six feet wide, forty-eight feet long, with a ceiling almost twenty feet above the ground. He created his own wind power using an eighty-horsepower steam engine to test the wheels out. On top of that, he's made over five thousand measurements and tested sixty-one different wheel forms. Perry's wind wheel is faster in the wind, it starts up in a light breeze, and it's got a back-gearing system to keep big winds from damaging the pump rod."

"Paul, I understand Jake's concern," Miss Jayne said. "It's much too risky to put your trust and livelihood in a company that only sold forty-five windmills."

Paul pulled a folded newspaper advertisement from his pocket. He smoothed it out for Jake to see. "Two years ago, they sold forty-five windmills. Last year, that number jumped to over two thousand. Do you know how many windmills they expect to sell this year? Over six thousand. They've moved to a factory right next to the railway and they're set on building over twenty thousand windmills in 1891. You might see it as folly. I see it as a business opportunity. When you think about drought years, irrigating acres of crops, the need to run machinery, there ain't nothing going to dent Aërmotor's success."

* * *

Paul slammed the cabin's door as he followed Jake out of the house. "Since when did you become such a fussbudge, Jake?"

"Since when did you begin spending our hard-earned money on some flight of fancy?"

"You didn't let me finish my story."

"It's a mighty longwinded story, Paul. What it comes down to is you spent your time galivanting around, pitching windmills, and throwing our money away on train fare. You totally forgot our plans to raise cattle. You threw away our dream to turn this place into a full-fledged cattle operation. We pooled our money so you could buy cattle for our ranch. Our ranch, Paul. Now we've got nothing except your big stories and cockamamie plans to head back east when we need you here. Here with our family. Here with our land."

"I didn't throw away our dream, Jake. I've got thirty-five head of cattle grazing downriver inside the corral at Kay Morren's place. My crew is there—a crew that includes her brother, who has been working with me for the past three months." Paul lowered his voice. "You know as much as I do, we'll both be working more than one job just to live on this land, let alone build up a herd. Putting up windmills will earn us some well-needed dollars. Snow Owl and I have talked this over and both agree this is the course we need to take."

Jake took off his hat and slapped it against his leg. "I know you're right. You're always bullheadedly right. That doesn't mean I want you to be right. I just thought you'd be working close to home, especially now that Mother's sight is gone."

"We'll figure out something, Jake. Our place ain't far from yours. Maybe Mother can live with Snow Owl when I'm away. Besides, you've got that Lainie gal here to help."

"She's not permanent."

"Oh?"

"And there's no way any of us want her to be permanent."

"Why's that?" Paul asked.

"That girl's got trouble nipping at her heels."

The Request

Jake had made a promise. And he was about to break it.

"Lainie, we need to talk."

"I know, Jake." A dark cloud shoved its way across the sun and Lainie shivered at the quick dip in temperature. "It won't take but a few minutes to gather my things to leave. Though I would appreciate it if I could wash my clothes before I go. Unless you want me to leave the dresses? After all, you paid for the fabric. I'm afraid the original dresses you gave me are worse for wear. I tried to keep them nice, but they took quite a beating from all the farm chores."

"Lainie." Jake tried to edge into her monologue.

"If you're alright with me washing my clothes, I mean the clothes you provided me, I can launder them this evening and maybe they'll be dry by tomorrow. Mostly dry, at least. I'll also wash your clothes and Miss Jayne's, of course. And if your cousin and his wife need their clothes washed, I can do that. I'm also hoping that Mrs. Fischer will drop by early enough in the day to purchase more eggs. That extra money would sure come in handy. Unless you've changed your mind on that? The egg money, that is. I will understand if you do change your mind. After all, you've provided me with plenty. You can drop me off at the train station any time you want. I don't have plans to travel any specific direction, so I suppose it doesn't matter much what the train schedule looks like. I'll just board whichever train feels right."

Jake tried to interrupt her again.

She continued.

"I know Doc and Emmeline invited me to stay on at their place." She sniffed and wiped her eyes. "I can't keep counting on other people to help me. So, if you'll please tell them I appreciate the offer and all their kindness, I'd be ever grateful."

Jake placed his hands on the girl's shoulders. "Lainie, I'm asking you to stay a while longer."

Lainie felt queasy.

"I promised to pay your train fare to anywhere you like, and I'll still hold to that promise if you don't want to stay. I'll still hold to that promise if you stay on for a few more days, better yet, a few weeks."

Lainie pulled away from Jake. "I don't understand. Your family is here. They are finally here, and I shouldn't be. You know I shouldn't be. Why would you put more of your family in harm's way?"

"It's been weeks since that man came for you."

"And you think a madman gives up his hunt after a few weeks?"

"I think that madman doesn't have much of a chance of finding you in the middle of a cursed wilderness."

"He found me once. He just doesn't know it."

"He won't be back. Besides, why do you think he's still looking for you?"

"Because I'm the reason his son is dead."

McNally and His Mine
Thurmond, Montana — October 1890

"Welcome back to your office, Mr. McNally. I trust that you'll find business has been well-managed and that delivery of orders are on target for our fourth quarter."

"Who the hell shut down the Redhawk, Peterson?" McNally stubbed out his cigar on the ledger book his manager carried like a tray. "Ore from that mine had the best assay yields we've ever seen. I've spent a fortune on a twenty-horsepower hoist, two boilers, and the best steam engine available for that operation."

Peterson tamped out the sparks left by the cigar on the ledger's leather cover. "As you know, sir, that mine began as two shafts connected on the one-hundred-foot level. Both shafts produced well, with ore trammed through an adit on a consistent basis until . . ."

"Quit the history lesson and tell me why you closed my damn mine." McNally tossed the spent cigar on the floor and crushed it with his boot.

"This past year, the main shaft was brought down to two hundred feet, opening onto two levels."

"I'm still waiting for my answer."

"Sir, the lower areas produced very little ore of any value." Peterson cleared his throat. "We thought it best to close the Redhawk and move our investment of machinery to another location."

"We? Who exactly do you regard as *we* in this decision?"

"Myself. And Mrs. McNally, of course."

"My wife played a part in this decision?"

"You *have* been out of town for quite some time, sir. Your wife assured me that she had your blessing in making business decisions while you attended to family matters."

"Did she." McNally moved to the window and considered his options as he looked towards the construction area of his new forty-two-ton smelter. "Where is she now?"

"I believe she returned to her residence, sir. It is quite late in the day."

"Go to my house and drag my wife back to this office. Now."

"I'm sorry, sir, she isn't at your home."

McNally stormed towards Peterson.

"What?"

"She continues to live at the hotel, as she has since your son's death."

"Peterson, inform my wife that she'll be moving out of the hotel immediately. I expect that she and all of her things will be back at our home tonight."

"Sir, she insists that she stay at the hotel due to the memories of your son's untimely demise. Witnessing the murder of her son within her home was quite traumatic, after all."

"We both watched as our son was butchered."

"Yes, sir, but the female persuasion is perhaps less adept at surmounting such atrocities."

McNally marched past Peterson and took a seat at his desk. "I've had enough of her hysterics. Either she returns to our home at once or else."

"Or else what, sir?"

"Just remind her that the insane asylum in Warm Springs is quite hospitable."

* * *

Shortly after Peterson was sent on his coarse mission, a secretary tapped on McNally's office door.

"So sorry to intrude, Mr. McNally. You have a guest who claims to be here on quite urgent business."

Before McNally had a chance to respond, a filthy man burst into the room.

"You still bayin' for blood, Mick?"

The intruder rudely gestured for the secretary to leave, then pushed aside papers to take a seat on the corner of McNally's desk.

McNally rubbed his hand across the stubble of his chin. "You one of Bogger's boys?"

The man smirked.

"I recognize you from Whitepine Canyon. You bringing news from Bogger?"

"Hell, no. He ain't interested in your money. But I am."

The man tossed a tattered copy of Stut's wanted poster on the desk.

"Double the amount on that poster, and I'll bring Stut to you with a bullet hole between his eyes."

McNally studied the man. "Bring Stut back to me alive and I'll triple the price."

Cattle Drive
Leeds, Idaho — October 1890

The men set out for the Morren place on a morning Jake proclaimed too windy to load rocks. Paul and Snow Owl had only been home a few hours, and both would have appreciated a day or two spent together recovering from their long travels, but October's race-against-the-weather temperament weighed heavy in everyone's thoughts and it was decided Jake and Paul would trudge out at dawn with the aim of beating worse storms.

As Miss Jayne washed the breakfast dishes, she reminisced October days when it was hot and balmy and October days when you had to bundle up just to go to the privy. While Lainie laced clothesline across the front room, Miss Jayne rambled on about an early October day during which she watched a flock of geese bask in the daytime sun, then woke the next morning to see those same geese sitting out in the field, their tailfeathers pinned to ice.

Snow Owl pulled the few clothes she and Paul had carried with them from their packs and set them in the tub of hot, soapy water. Miss Jayne heard the sound of homespun being scrubbed against the washboard and quickly shooed Snow Owl away.

"I'll take care of that. You and that baby should sit still for a spell. If you're heading to see your family tomorrow, I want you rested up. The ride out to the Bauer place will be short compared to what you're accustomed to, but it's still quite a trek when you've not been feeling well."

"Thank you. It is nice to rest. But please give me small chores to keep me busy so I will sleep well tonight. My head is already filled with worry for Paul." She looked to Lainie. "And Jake."

Lainie wasn't sure why she blushed at Snow Owl's words. She saw Snow Owl flash an I-know-your-secret grin and blushed even more. It was the kind of grin the servers at Lady Gretchen's teased with when

229

one of their coworkers had her chance to serve food and drinks to a miner she'd set her sights on.

Miss Jayne, oblivious to the silent banter the girls shared across the clothesline, tried to calm all their nerves. "I'm sure Paul and Jake will be safe," she said. "The storm's bound to settle down soon."

* * *

Mid-day, the wind was outperformed by unseasonable rain, and Bristle, unexpectedly caught in the cloudburst, pawed at the front door begging for shelter.

Lainie dried the dog with a towel as she watched Snow Owl retrieve a pouch from her saddle bag. Inside the pouch were long strands of dried grass which she layered in a bowl of water.

Once the grass was supple, Snow Owl pulled out a few strands and began twisting and weaving them into a small coil. From there, she curved up her design and seemingly narrated her project's heritage.

"When you pick the grass, you sing to it. When you dry the grass, you sing to it. When you soak the grass, you sing to it. When you weave the grass, you sing to it."

The basket was ever so tiny and Lainie marveled at how Snow Owl delicately twined the edge of her creation. Snow Owl pulled something from her skirt pocket, nestled it inside the basket, and closed its lid. She beckoned Lainie to her.

Snow Owl squeezed water from the remaining grass in the bowl and placed the small, damp bundle in Lainie's left hand. "I have collected this sweetgrass from each town Paul and I visited, each farm we worked on," she said. "Close your eyes and take in its scent. It is the scent of sweet earth. The spice of changing seasons. The spirit of each tomorrow. Sweetgrass keeps each basket strong, alive."

Lainie closed her eyes and took in the freshness, the earthiness, the promise and weight nature's perfume brings.

Snow Owl reached out and settled the tiny basket within the cup of Lainie's right hand.

Surprised, Lainie opened her eyes. She squinted and studied the basket's lines, traced the intricate texture with her finger, carefully opened the lid. A silver thimble was held inside.

Snow Owl smiled. "Do you see? A basket is a song made visible."

The rain piled up like laundry. After weeks of absolute dry, the sky plunged to the earth and channeled out the ground. Rivulets streamed past the barn, past the henhouse, until small lakes twinkled under each drop of rain.

"Do you think Snow Owl had any difficulties getting to Irene and Anton's place?" Lainie asked Miss Jayne, who'd spent the past hour sitting in her rocker as she worked on her knitting.

"That break in the weather should have been long enough for her to get there safely," Miss Jayne said. Her voice didn't convince. "I sure pray folks living in the lowlands don't end up getting flooded. Rain falling this fast onto hardpan is bound to cause troubles."

"Are Jake and Paul riding through lowlands that might get flooded?"

Miss Jayne didn't answer.

"You don't think the boys would ride in this kind of weather, do you? Especially if they're moving a herd of cattle."

Again, Miss Jayne didn't answer.

"I suppose it might not be raining this bad where they're at. But if it is, will they still travel in it?"

"Child, my nerves are near frazzled from all your questions." Miss Jayne threw back her head and thumped her feet against the floor in rapid succession until the knickknacks on the shelves clattered about. "Sorry. The sound of this rain, not knowing how things look outside— it's all quite overwhelming. Noise everywhere, and no eyes to see it."

"I'll keep quiet," Lainie murmured.

Time clicked on. Bristle whimpered in his sleep. Miss Jayne threw her knitting to the ground.

"Yes, they're probably moving the cattle in the middle of the storm. Worse weather is for sure on its way and there's still work to be done before winter sets in."

"Oh." Lainie shrunk away from Miss Jayne's abrupt declaration.

"The boys are both experienced in dealing with whatever Mother Nature throws at them. Especially Paul. Drovers are a nervy bunch and Paul's told stories of driving cattle in weather ranging from boiling heat to driving rain. One summer, when the sun sweltered down and there was no water for man or beast, he and his riders rode through a dried-up riverbed and watched for muddy water beneath hoof prints to drink. He even had a time when the trail cook had no salt, so he resorted to licking horse sweat from his saddle to help keep himself from drying out."

A burst of rain pelted the window. Both women flinched at the sound.

Miss Jayne closed her eyes and slowly whispered one, two, three, then continued her story.

"Paul told me that once, during a hailstorm, he and his riders were getting cannonballed so bad they had to hold saddles over their heads to protect themselves. Another time, a lightning storm brewed up quicklike and one of the riders got zinged by a bolt. After that, whenever a lightning storm came about, the riders all stashed their pistols and belt buckles away from themselves and the herd. Goodness knows a steel pistol serves as a natural path for a lightning strike."

"Well, that's comforting," Lainie moaned.

"Yes. Looks like I comforted us both into a boatload of misery."

* * *

After three days of pounding rain followed by three days of cool temperatures, Lainie and Miss Jayne were more than ready to escape the confines of the cabin to embrace warmer weather. Though the ground still gummed at their shoes, rays of sunshine set a fine pace for choring and the women scrubbed clothes and sheets and aprons, then pinned them on the line to dry.

Late afternoon, the two were set on hanging bed sheets. Miss Jayne worked her way along the lengths of clothesline, one hand wrapped around the line for each footstep she took, while Bristle napped in a patch of sunlight near the corner of the cabin.

Lainie winced at the sliver she'd gained from one of the old wooden clothespins. Removing it would have to wait until late in the evening when needlework finished out the day. In the meantime, the good strong sun and a fitful breeze would easily dry most of the clothes by day's end.

"Did you hear that?" Miss Jayne asked. "I swear I hear the herd coming in."

Lainie heard nothing beyond the wind's hushed tones and the rush of rivertalk in the distance.

"Listen. There's a bit of a rumble. It's faint, but it's there."

The girl tried to tune in to what Miss Jayne was hearing. Maybe. Maybe there was a rumble in the distance. She looked in the direction she expected the boys would come, hoping to see dust kicked up by the herd's movement, then realized that the ground was so wet and boggy that a sighting of dust would be an impossibility.

Suddenly the sound was there. Bellowing. Rumbling. Faint, yet distinct.

"That's them. That's definitely them," Miss Jayne proclaimed, and Lainie thrilled at the sight of relief washing over the woman's rippled face.

"I'll go inside and put the kettle on so my boys can have hot coffee when they get here. They'll be hungry, too, so I'll fix up a meal. Do you mind hanging the rest of the sheets on your own?"

"A few more minutes and I'll be all done," Lainie reassured. "Go on in. Jake and Paul will be ready for some down time once they get the cattle in the corral."

Lainie finished with the sheets. The sound of the herd was louder. Curiosity itched inside her and she gave in to the urge to climb her favorite cottonwood that overlooked the valley below.

From the lowest branch of the tree, she could see animals moving forward, all minuscule in the distance. She sat down on the tree limb and let her legs dangle to the music of the river. Her heart raced as she watched six, maybe seven riders guide their horses to and fro to keep the herd intact.

Bristle, who'd followed Lainie to the cottonwood, barked at the sight.

"You'll be a cattle dog soon, Bristle. You'll teach those cows the lay of the land in no time."

As the group edged closer, Lainie waved her hat in greeting not knowing if the riders would see her from such a distance. One rider returned the greeting, waving his own hat then turning his horse to head off a cow.

Lainie spotted Jake on his Palouse. The horse, mostly chestnut in color, had a midsection and hindquarters blanketed in white. Chestnut spots dappled the blanket, and the horse's hooves each had a vertical striping pattern that alternated between dark and light. The horse had fascinated her the first time she'd spotted it at the farm. Now, watching it instinctively stop and turn and respond to the herd's movement, she was even more impressed with the animal.

And its rider.

The other horses, the other riders, the herd of cattle—they melded into a backdrop that Lainie forgot to pay attention to. Her focus was on the man riding the Palouse.

Jake eased his horse around the herd, heading the cattle towards a wide span of the swift-moving river. She watched him twist in his saddle, then turn his horse towards a stand of riverside cottonwoods. It appeared that an obstinate cow had led her baby to feed on the grass beneath the trees. Lainie immediately nicknamed the cow Miss Priss and pondered on a name for the calf as she watched Jake drive them forward to catch up with the rest of the herd.

Lainie savored the moment. Watching Jake maneuver his horse had been—what? Exciting? Reassuring? She tried to define the emotion as she watched the herd move lazily along. There were occasional quickening of hooves, and the mingling of gruff snorts and prolonged bawls the cattle made was like nothing Lainie had ever heard. Slowly and smoothly, the animals crossed the river. Jake would be happy with that.

She stayed in the tree as the herd moved towards the gradual hill. Mesmerized by the scene before her, she didn't notice that Bristle had raced off towards the herd until it was too late.

"Bristle!" Lainie called out the dog's name several times, her voice lost in the maelstrom of sound.

She cursed her stupidity. Her foolish curiosity had put Jake's dog in jeopardy. She searched the scene before her, trying to find Bristle, willing him to not get kicked or trampled by one of the cattle.

There. On the left. Bristle was safe, at least for the moment, and he was turning away from the herd, but moving closer to an escapee cow and her calf.

"No! Bristle, no!" Lainie shouted the words, knowing they were of no use as Bristle chased a mother and her baby back towards the river.

Was it the same pair she'd watched Jake gather from the water's edge? Yes? Maybe?

The mother trotted towards a section of the river that was narrow, its water choppy and swift. Her calf followed, with Bristle nipping at its hooves. The cow plunged down the embankment and into the rushing water. She bellowed for her calf to follow. The calf stopped shy of the water. Bristle pounced at the calf again and the calf shifted and sidestepped and let loose a mournful cry.

From her perch in the tree, Lainie willed Bristle to stop barking. Please, please stop barking. The frantic calf twisted and turned as Bristle persisted with his herding, until it slipped on the muddy soil and fell awkwardly into the river.

"Jake! Paul! A calf is in the water!"

Again, Lainie's words were lost within the sounds of the herd.

The mother cow, too, seemed to call for help. She'd made it to the opposite riverbank and bellowed to her calf.

The calf had regained its footing and awkwardly moved through the water. Midway across the river, the water reached its ears and the calf bawled with fear. He lost his footing and his head slipped below the water.

Lainie had climbed down from the tree and shouted for help the entire time she ran towards the river. She raced down the hill with an aim to intersect the river where she thought the current may have carried the calf.

It was Paul who caught sight of Lainie's skirt as she darted to an outcropping of rocks and searched the water. He turned his horse and sped to her position.

Lainie searched frantically for the calf. She spotted him, its legs flailing in the air. She tried to find a way to reach him and pull him to safety. Ahead, long lines of tree roots bled out into the river. If she could hold onto a strong, sturdy root with one hand, maybe she could snag the calf's leg with her other.

Jake spotted Paul and his horse working their way downstream. *Must have had a cow break free,* he thought. But Paul was racing at breakneck speed. Jake turned his horse and followed. A hard knot filled his gut—a knot that told him there was trouble.

Lainie splashed into the water, moving as fast as she could against the sharp, mossy rocks, finally able to half walk, half swim to the jumble of roots. The water was bitter cold, and she felt her movements tighten as the strength of the river pushed against her. She fought back, gripping a hefty root with both hands, then both arms, to stabilize herself. Lainie searched for the calf and spotted it floundering in the churning river, its hooves flailing, its head dipping below the onslaught of current. She wrapped two roots multiple times around her left hand, held them tight, and planted her feet as best she could amongst the slippery rocks.

"Lord, if you're out there, give me strength and send that animal within my reach."

* * *

As soon as Jake saw Paul position his horse along the riverbank and ready his lasso, he knew what had happened. A cow had strayed off and was caught in the current. He pulled up just short of Paul's mount and readied his own lasso to help retrieve the stray.

His search for the animal halted when his eyes landed on Lainie, chin deep in the frigid water, her skirt billowing behind her, and her arm wrapped around a calf's neck.

Paul's lasso landed short of its target. He pulled the rope back and tried again, this time landing the lasso atop the calf's head, but it wouldn't fall over its muzzle.

One of Lainie's arms was stretched taut. The roots, wrapped tight around her hand, bit into her skin. Her fingers were numb. She didn't know how much longer the roots would hold her weight combined with that of the calf or if the roots would suddenly slip across her hand.

The calf flailed its legs against the rapid moving water, twisting and straining its head in fear. Twice, its hoof kicked Lainie so hard that she grunted from pain.

Jake rode a short distance upstream and edged his horse towards the water. He spotted a sturdy tree, dismounted his horse, and tied a rope around the tree trunk. Back on his horse, Jake coaxed the animal along the muddy riverbank until they were a few feet downstream of Lainie and the calf. He eased the horse into the water and the two slowly moved against the current towards the frightened pair.

He positioned his horse next to the calf, near the head and away from the calf's legs where it might kick the horse.

"Toss me your rope," he hollered to Paul. Paul pulled back and threw the lasso again. Jake caught it in his hand, leaned down, and dangled the lasso until it slipped around the calf's neck.

"Alright, pull back." Jake held the rope until the slack tightened, then released it.

"Okay, Lainie, keep hold of the calf and let go of the roots so I can slip a rope around you and get you back to shore."

"I can't, Jake, the roots are twisted tight around my hand."

"You've gotta let them go, honey. You've gotta get yourself loose so I can keep you safe and Paul can pull the calf to shore."

She struggled her hand, twisting and turning, the raw edges of the roots biting deep into her flesh.

"Come on, Lainie, you've gotta get loose." Jake had a knife with him that he could cut the roots with, but he couldn't reach them from atop the horse. Certainly, he could slip down into the water to tie the rope around Lainie's waist, but if he got off the horse, he might become another captive of the river's current and, in turn, useless to Lainie. He considered slipping a lasso around her neck as a drastic means of saving her life, but the word *strangulation* boomed inside his head with such ferocity, that he abandoned the idea completely.

If Lainie let go of the calf, would the sudden release of its weight send her spiraling in the current enough so that the roots would loosen their grip around her hand, and she would be left untethered, unanchored, adrift in the rapid, dangerous waters? Or would the roots continue to support her weight and she would have one hand free to slip the lasso across her left shoulder and underneath her right arm?

"Paul, hold steady with the calf. You're going to have Lainie's weight added to it in a minute."

"What?" Lainie gasped.

"Listen, Lainie, I'm going to slip my lasso around the calf's neck, then pull you both closer to the embankment. This should produce some slack around your hand. Once you feel that slack, I need you to loosen yourself from the tree roots then wrap yourself around the calf's neck."

She started to protest.

"Once you're steady, Paul will pull you both to shore."

She looked up, then down the river, frantically looking for another option.

"The rope is strong enough to hold the weight of both of you. Paul's horse is strong enough to pull you both against the current. I promise."

Jake was sure of neither of the promises that came from his mouth, but he saw no other option. He was placing Lainie's safety, her very life, into a risky plan.

"When it's time, take a couple of deep breaths, then hold your breath so you don't swallow any water. You can do this, Lainie."

She gave a slight nod and raggedly gasped in air as Jake dangled the second rope around the calf's neck.

Jake edged his horse as far as he could towards the embankment, then slipped off the animal and clambered up the slippery slope of roots and rocks and mud to where he could get a foothold on some brush. He pulled the rope with all his might, moving the river's victims closer to him, closer to freedom.

Once the roots felt looser on her hand, Lainie took a huge gulp of air, twisted her hand free of the roots, and flung herself forward, flailing until she had both arms wrapped around the calf's sturdy neck.

"Hold on tight," Jake reassured as Paul encouraged his mount backwards. Lainie closed her eyes tight and pressed her mouth and one side of her nose shut with her forearm as she clung to the calf. Bits of debris pelted her bare legs as the two were dragged through the water.

The calf was exhausted. It had stopped kicking and its eyes were glazed.

"You're okay, baby," Lainie whispered. "You're going to be okay."

The scraping of rocks against the back of her legs was welcome. As the rope continued to haul them ashore, she clung to the calf. "Almost there, little one. Almost there."

When her head and shoulders were safely above water, Paul stopped pulling on the rope. Lainie sent a wavering look around her surroundings and instinctively used her left arm, pinned beneath the calf's head, to lift its muzzle towards the air. The calf's hindquarters were stretched across her legs and she was left paralyzed from both its weight and the cold.

Jake scrambled towards Lainie, pulled the calf off her legs, and hauled it slightly upshore. In mere moments, he was back at her side, gently lifting her from the mud and water. He settled her on level ground, pulled off his shirt, and tucked it around her.

She was still. Pale. Bluelipped. He watched for life, felt for a heartbeat.

Slowly, she placed her right hand atop his, atop her heart.

With a trembling voice she asked, "Is the calf alright?"

Jake let out a sigh of relief. "Yeah, the calf is alright."

She smiled back. "How about you?"

* * *

Jake was not alright. He had wanted to yell that to Lainie there on the riverbank. He had wanted to shake her and scream at her and make her understand the danger she had put herself in. The danger she had put all of them in. At the same time, he'd wanted to hold her, to rock her back and forth, to comfort her. The mixed emotions were a chokehold on his thoughts as he carried her into the cabin.

Miss Jayne helped Lainie into warm, dry clothes while Jake sat on the front room floor and rubbed down the calf that Paul had revived some life into. Once the calf started moving and lifting its head for attention, Jake settled him into a pile of blankets next to the fireplace.

He built a fire then stepped outside to check on Paul's progress with the rest of the stock. The cattle were in the corral, calling out and getting their fill of the dried grass the ground had to offer. It would take a few hours for them to settle down.

"Blast it all, those cows will settle down before my nerves do," he muttered to himself.

Paul spotted him and explained that one of his workers would unsaddle and feed Jake's horse.

"What about the cow that crossed to the other side of the river?" Jake asked, relieved to see Bristle following his cousin around.

"She'll find her way home. Calf ain't full-weaned yet, so she'll be hurting to feed him soon."

Sure enough, as the light began to fade the mother cow made her appearance, bawling so loud that no one could find peace.

Jake worried the calf was still on shaky ground. It still shivered and hadn't tried to walk around yet. Miss Jayne had tried to feed it some milk, first from a bowl, then from the cup of her hand.

"Maybe he's too tired out and just needs to rest," Miss Jayne offered.

"He needs a good meal, or he won't have the strength to recover. It's getting mighty cold outside. I'll go fetch his ma."

"Jake Adamsen, you are not bringing that filthy animal inside my home. A calf is one thing, but a full-sized cow will leave this place a disaster."

What's one more disaster? Jake thought.

"I don't want the calf out in the cold just yet. If the calf gets some dinner, the cow will settle down and maybe we can have a bit of quiet around here. I'll put the cow in the barn once junior gets his fill, but if we keep them apart much longer, that cow's going to plow through the window."

"Miss Priss already took over a good part of this day," Miss Jayne complained as she scurried around, hands out, looking for knickknacks to keep safe from the ornery cow's switching tail. "Once she's inside the house, she'll want to choose new curtains and rearrange the furniture."

"Miss Priss?" Jake asked.

"That's the name Lainie gave her. Said she was this prissy cow that kept straying from the herd in search of private dining."

"Sounds about right. Once we got her back with the herd, Bristle spooked her across the river. This little guy tried to tag along."

Miss Jayne reached out for Jake.

"Son." Her voice was hoarse with emotion.

He took her hand and squeezed it.

"Son, thank you for saving my girl."

* * *

Jake had no problem leading the cow into the cabin, who immediately nipped at the curtains as she walked through the front door.

"You're right, Mama, this cow does want to redecorate."

"Son, if that cow ruins one thing in this house, she'll be pot roast by dawn."

The calf greedily guzzled his dinner. Afterward, as Jake watched the cow bathe her calf, he nearly forgave her day's-worth of trespasses.

* * *

Paul spotted lamplight in the barn. Inside, he found Jake pitching forkfuls of hay to the rebel cow inside the stall.

"You keep quiet for the night, you hear?" Jake scolded Miss Priss. "We humans and all your bovine neighbors could use a good night's rest."

"That cow's got an ornery streak," Paul teased from the doorway. "I'm not sure she's going to abide by your rules."

"I'd be shocked if she did," Jake muttered. "I don't have much say in what goes on around here anyway."

Paul leaned against the stall gate and studied Jake as he finished his chores. He wasn't sure what to make of the version of Jake he'd come home to. The Jake he'd grown up with and gotten into mischief with and made big plans with had fire in his belly and swagger in his dreams. The old Jake put muscle and grit and zest into work, life, laughter, love.

This new Jake was a wrung-out rag.

This new Jake was raw and wry.

This new Jake worried him.

"I figured your drovers would bed down here in the barn," Jake said.

"Nah, they're accustomed to sleeping underneath the stars."

"Awful cold out for that."

"They'll survive. In the morning when they wake up with beards filled with frost, I'll remind them that the barn has outstanding hotel accommodations."

"Accoutrements aplenty, right?"

Paul grinned at the familiar phrase. "Boy, talk about a trip down memory lane," he said. "That was one of Hannah's best phrases. I swear for six months straight, any time she walked into a room she'd say, 'accoutrements aplenty.' We walked into the store for some penny candy one day, and she announced that 'Master Hamilton's Mercantile has accoutrements aplenty.' First day of school, she said the same thing. 'Ms. Winthrop's classroom has accoutrements aplenty.' To this day, I have no idea what an accoutrement is."

"Me neither." Jake's voice was sullen.

"Where'd she even come up with such words?" Paul asked.

"Some book, I suppose. Hannah always had her nose in a book."

Paul watched his cousin move feed sacks of grain for seemingly no better reason than it kept the two from keeping up conversation. Where was the cousin Paul once knew? Where was that unbound energy, that teasing banter, that mischievous stride?

Maybe Paul was measuring Jake all wrong. His cousin's losses were stacked high as a mountain and the past week's cattle drive, ambushed by seething winds and piercing rain, was enough to wear any man down.

Yet, based on the hushed conversation he'd had with Miss Jayne, it was obvious that Jake's loss had tethered him to a misery that tugged towards a final escape.

This new Jake, all etched out and forlorn, seemed a minstrel ghost without a song and Paul wondered, with Hannah's and the children's deaths, had Jake's very soul been ripped right out of him?

Grief was miserly that way.

Since returning home, the only times Paul had witnessed any fire in Jake's eyes was when he talked about Lainie. Or dealt with her antics.

"You gonna marry her?" Paul ran his hand over his stubbled chin, hoping—no, knowing—his question would whirl up a new kind of storm inside his cousin.

"Miss Priss?" Jake mumbled, pointing at the cow. "I don't think she's the marrying kind."

"Well, I'd say Miss Priss is smart enough not to marry a bull-headed man like you." Paul held the lantern high enough to catch Jake's reaction to his next statement. "Lainie, on the other hand, is just looking for trouble. You two would fit together quite well."

"Lainie? Hell, no, Paul, she's just a kid."

"That ain't no kid, Jake. That's a full-fledged beauty of a woman you've got there, in spite of that crazy hair of hers. Maybe she's green to farm life, but she's got grit and she's got fire."

Jake looked away. Remembered pain creased his brow.

"I'm not plannin' on marrying her or anyone else, Paul. Hannah, she's the only one I'll ever love. The only one I ever wanted to be with."

"Whatever you say, cousin. But that girl fits here on the farm. And whether you see it or not, she fits with you."

* * *

Back inside the cabin, Jake checked on the calf again. Its shivering had finally stopped, but Jake would keep the animal indoors overnight for safety's sake.

Miss Jayne sat in her chair, clacking together knitting needles and staring at her work as if her eyes could see.

Lainie hovered in the corner of the kitchen, not sure what to do with herself. She still had the blanket wrapped around her, unable to shed the cold running through her veins. The shiver she felt came from the time spent in frigid waters and from the apology she needed to make.

She walked over to Jake where he sat on the floor by the fireplace, rubbing the calf with his hand. Bristle was nestled on the opposite side of the calf, happy to have some four-legged companionship inside the cabin.

"How's he doing," she asked softly.

"He'll be fine as long as his crazy mother doesn't lead him into any more mishaps."

Lainie sat on the floor just behind Jake. She leaned against the wall, pulled her knees to her chin, and shrouded her cuts and scrapes and bruises with the blanket.

Nightsounds crept over them as Miss Jayne laid down her needlework, said goodnight, and headed to bed.

Jake continued to stroke the calf, lulling it to sleep.

Lainie kept her eyes on Jake's back. She knew she was the culprit of the tension in his shoulders, the clench of his jaw. She wanted to make things right between them but wasn't sure how.

"I'm sorry," she whispered.

He ran his hand through his hair. She needed a response, but he didn't know what words to give.

"It's my fault Miss Priss and her baby landed in the water," Lainie continued. "I shouldn't have been in the tree. I shouldn't have let Bristle follow me. Before I knew it, Bristle started chasing the cows and I couldn't stop him, then the animals were in the water and the calf couldn't make it across the river and it's all my fault because I should have just stayed away from everyone and everything." She balled a corner of the blanket up in her hand. "I didn't realize the water would be so swift, Jake. I shouldn't have jumped in. I just couldn't stand watching that calf all wild-eyed and scared, losing himself to the current. He would've died if somebody didn't help."

Jake rose, paced back and forth until Lainie was sure he'd explode, then settled back on the floor next to her, his back against the wall.

"It's a calf. Soon enough he'll end up as dinner on somebody's plate. That's the way of farm life, Lainie."

"I know, Jake. I know all about farm life and sacrificing animals. And I know about babies losing parents and parents losing babies. And it's not fair, it's not fair that . . ."

He grabbed her hand. "Don't. Not now. Neither of us can take it."

She nodded her understanding. It was several seconds before she realized his hand remained wrapped around hers. She pulled her hand back and tucked it within the blanket's security.

They sat quiet for a while, neither knowing where conversation should flow. Neither willing to let free the scenes of the day. Lainie closed her eyes. Eventually, her head landed on Jake's shoulder. The motion took him back in time to Hannah.

Beautiful Hannah, head propped on his shoulder, blond hair brushing his arm, softly parted lips sighing out whispers of sleep.

A yearning and total saturation of love scraped at the hardened edges of Jake's heart, knifing out her name. Hannah. Hannah. Hannah.

He looked towards the girl and immediately the knife fumbled. Gooseflesh pricked his skin as he realized that Lainie was softening his heart.

Just the way Hannah used to.

The Windmill

"Can't believe how many people just started showing up yesterday to see the windmill," Lainie said as she sliced apples for pies.

"Word travels fast," Irene said. "Folks'll walk a dozen miles just to flap their gums to share some gossip." The woman snugged a ham hock into the huge pot of beans. "Pass me those onions, girly-girl. If I don't get this pot of beans on the fire soon, we won't have enough food to feed the masses."

"Who was the family that showed up in the shiny black carriage?" Lainie asked. "They were sure dressed fine."

"That's the Hervey family," Irene said. "Claim to be descendants of some duchess in England. They always have their noses in the air while they spread high-falutin' ideas on how to gussy up this town and bring the railroad through."

"That family won't survive farming lest Mrs. Shines-Her-Shoes and her girls bust out of their city selves and start working outside the family," Miss Jayne said as she mixed bread ingredients together with her hands. "Right now, they won't milk a cow, they won't raise chickens, they won't do anysuch work like that to raise good money."

She dumped the mixture onto the countertop and put her might into kneading the dough.

"Can't just be a wife, a mama, and a cook," Miss Jayne continued. "Us women, we're the linchpins of the land. Those city folks who think farm success hinges on the menfolk need to strap on our aprons for a while and tackle just a handful of our days. Us women supply the family's income by raising fowl, pigs, milk cows, and vegetables for gain."

Miss Jayne inched her hand to the grain bin and grabbed a handful of flour to spread over the sticky dough.

"Laura Stephenson, why she decided that instead of hauling a skimpy wheat crop to Lewiston, she would feed it to her chickens. She soon doubled her flock of birds and sold eggs in nearby Asotin.

Further on, she and her kinfolk butchered and dressed the chickens forty at a time, then peddled them out to townspeople. If it hadn't been for the chickens, her family would have lost their farm."

Irene added, "When wheat prices were low, the Fletcher women sold muskmelons, potatoes, beets, and onions to pay their taxes. Back in Wisconsin, my cousin Eileen ended up selling tomatoes to Italian families over in Vernon County, and my neighbor, Janet Zanto, raised navy beans, once selling four hundred pounds of them in Westford's Township."

"I know for me and Mr. Adamsen, the cream check covered everything the egg money didn't buy. That was the bank account right there. Sure, you could raise cows and come home with a paycheck once a year, but the cream check gives you cash year-round."

"So why do Jake and Paul want to raise cattle?" Lainie asked. "If they only get paid once a year, how will they have money for the rest of the year?"

Miss Jayne hefted the dough back into its bowl and walked away.

"What did I say wrong?" Lainie asked.

"Nothing, child," Irene said. "The cattle business is a sore spot between Jake and his ma. Jake's always dreamed of being a cattleman, mostly because it was his pa's dream. But Miss Jayne thinks it's a fool's errand to run cattle on their land."

"Why?"

"The economics of it, mostly. Cattle are expensive to buy, expensive to raise. Just one cow drinks a bathtub full of water a day," Irene said. "Sheep only need a gallon of water, maybe two for the day, and they'll eat pretty much anything that cows just outright avoid. Got a problem area of weeds? Introduce some sheep to the area. Those wooly range maggots will clean up the place in no time, then snack on grass for dessert. And pigs? You can raise them in the woods without much bother at all."

Irene set a towel across the bowl of dough and set it in the early morning patch of sun streaming through the window.

"Cows, on the other hand, need more than just forbs and weeds."

"Forbs?" Lainie asked.

"Milkweeds, sunflowers, pretty much any wildflower that grows on this land, and the good Lord knows we have plenty of them. But cows, they need grassland, and lots of it. Come wintertime, they'll need a

246

hefty amount of silage from alfalfa, grass, and corn, which means more work, more property, and more money."

"Seems like Jake and his ma have plenty enough land for cows or sheep."

"Land, yes. Time and resources, not so much. The boys will work it out, but I suppose Miss Jayne will always hold a grudge against her husband for influencing the boys away from sheep farming. It's the life she grew up in—her daddy, her daddy's daddy—they were all in the business of tending to flocks, selling off wool. She misses that life, the stability wool provided. Out here in the rocks of Idaho, money is a fragile thing."

Lainie thought back to Miss Jayne's mention of egg money—the money she was now pocketing for train fare.

"The boys will work it out," Irene assured. "That windmill, if it works like Paul says it will, is going to be a big help. If they can keep the herd watered while keeping the river clean, Miss Jayne will perk up some."

* * *

At his wife's request, Anton loaded Miss Jayne's rocking chair into their wagon and hauled it to the windmill site. He found a level patch of ground and placed the rocking chair on it, just outside the work area where Jake, Paul, and Paul's recruits had pulled out pail after pail of earth for the water well.

Paul and his crew had spent hours hollowing out the ground, with one man digging a tight vertical tunnel and another cranking up each bucket of dirt with a windlass, then lowering an empty bucket back down. Lengths of timber had also been lowered into the hole to brace the walls and prevent the ground from collapsing. The man up top was always on the lookout, making sure the person in the well was safe.

When the rest of the crew wasn't digging or emptying buckets, they were hauling stone to the site to replace the timbers and permanently line the well. Once the well was lined, more stone would be needed for the three-foot walls that would create a reservoir.

At the one hundred twenty-foot mark, the man they called The Human Badger had used a crowbar to punch through a layer of bedrock. Within seconds, cool water had risen to his armpits.

With that massive project complete, Paul and his crew members set off for the train station to pick up the windmill. That's where the hubbub of excitement began.

Paul proudly paraded his shipment around Lewiston, then around Leeds. Word spread and the next morning, a dozen men showed up to see the Aërmotor steel tower take shape. By noon, that number had doubled and by the suppertime hour, most of the crowd claimed they would be back the next day with family in tow.

Miss Jayne underestimated how many families would show up to see the windmill Paul was so proud of. By the time she and the Bauers arrived with the food, the pasture was filled with onlookers curious to see if the rumors about the Adamsens' steel tower were true.

Debate about the project was strong.

"A tower of steel on the horizon? Those Adamsen boys have gone barmy," she overheard someone say.

"Don't make no sense using steel when we got plenty of good Idaho timber to build with," another said. "Just ain't right. No, sir, just ain't right."

"That thing will never outdo the wooden windmill we put up. The wheel on our windmill is twelve foot across. That pile of metal won't amount to anything." That comment came from Cashton Cooper, Miss Jayne knew, by the gravel in his voice and the stench of his cigar.

"When will we see the windmill go up? All they're doing right now is gabbing," a little girl said to her mother. The mother shushed her child and waved her off to go play with the other children.

It felt good to be outside, huddled among friends. Miss Jayne assumed the sky to be blue and as the day wore on, she felt the play of clouds against the sun in the temperature on her skin.

The workers and the windmill were the center of attention, though Miss Jayne's resting place became the polestar for conversation. Thankfully, the excitement over Paul's windmill kept the focus off Miss Jayne's scars, though there was the occasional comment.

There were also inquiries about Lainie.

"We hear Doc brought in a young woman to help you out for a spell," Sally Jansen said. "I was hoping to meet her today."

"I'm sure she's flitting around here somewhere," Miss Jayne replied, sure that Lainie had raced towards her hiding spot among the trees as soon as the last pie was pulled from the stove.

"Well, word has it she's got a twin traipsing through these parts."

"A twin?" Miss Jayne could picture the smug look on Sally's face.

"Why, yes, a twin. Of course, I only saw your helper that one time. She was walking towards Doc's place when she first arrived in town. But I'm sure she holds resemblance to a girl my brother mentioned. You know my brother Klein drives a stagecoach, right? He mentioned a few weeks ago that a young woman, a murderer, is on the run through these parts. He described her aptly and warned me to be on the lookout. He's warning other folk, too."

A shiver crossed Miss Jaye's skin as Sally leaned in close and grazed her with an ominous declaration: "My, oh my, how word travels between stagecoach stops."

* * *

Paul was indeed a salesman. He stirred the crowd's interest with the sales pitch Snow Owl had listened to dozens of times over the past several weeks.

"Have you got cattle? Sheep? Horses? A brood of kids like the Bauer clan?" Paul received whoops of laughter from the Bauer children. "On a hot weather day, a steer needs at least ten to fifteen gallons of water. A cow that's nursing a calf is gonna need twenty gallons or more. These windmills can pull up sixteen barrels of water in ten minutes. That's almost five hundred gallons of water in just a few minutes. Think long-term into your future, folks. When the creek dries up in the summertime, you'll still have water for your herd—or your brood—because an Aërmotor windmill will pump water from deep inside the ground. Plus, you'll have water in the winter when the world is froze over."

"How much noise does it make?" someone in the crowd hollered.

"I'll tell you what, when the wind is whipping through our valley, the sound of those blades a-whirring will be the most beautiful sound you ever heard, because you know your family's livelihood depends on that windmill." He turned to Snow Owl and pulled her close to him. "And ladies, if you're like my beautiful wife, the gentle purring of the rotary wheel will keep you company during the day and softly lull you to sleep at night."

* * *

Paul finished tying the guide ropes to the top section of the windmill. The forty-foot tower was built, the blades and tail vane were attached, the gearings were oiled. They were now at the mercy of strong rope, a sturdy gin pole, and solid horsepower.

Three of Paul's men were set up several yards north of the windmill. Their wagon, fitted with guide ropes attached to the gin pole, would ease the windmill from the ground to a standing position.

Jake and The Human Badger were teamed up south of the windmill. Their wagon, with its guide ropes attached to the upper portion of the windmill, would serve as the counter pull.

"Steady as she goes, boys," Paul hollered to his men as he inspected the rope lines between the gin pole and the tower. "We've got a few hundred pounds to lift into place."

A man who went by the name of Gravel Joe hawed his team into motion. The horses easily moved forward until the ropes grew taut and the weight of the windmill set in. Gravel Joe clicked his tongue, encouraging his team forward.

The crowd, who'd been cautioned back a safe distance away from the work, held a collective breath as they watched the top of the steel tower slowly rise from the ground.

Jake took his cues from The Human Badger on the speed he should move his team forward. Move too slow and you impede progress. Move too fast and the windmill might upend itself.

Inch by aching inch, the tower was pulled vertical until it stood sentry over its new land.

Suspicion

Miss Jayne couldn't get Sally Jansen's words out of her head. Murderer? Lainie? It couldn't be.

Yet the story fit. Lainie had been traipsing through their town. She had been on the run. She was disguising herself by blackening her hair and always wearing it covered.

Lainie is a murderer. Lainie is a murderer. Lainie is a murderer.
Lainie is asleep. In the bed just below mine.

* * *

"Something's troubling your ma."

"What do you mean?" Jake asked as he helped Lainie heft a heavy braided rug over the clothesline. "She was in perfect spirits yesterday at the windmill raising."

"She was in terrible spirits when she got home. Barely said a word to me or Snow Owl. You left the house too early to see her at breakfast. She didn't eat a thing."

"Maybe she's worn out from all the activity. You ladies put on a mighty big meal yesterday. Plus, the crowd and all the people visiting with her must have tired her out."

"Do you think anyone said something cruel to her?" Lainie asked. "She's come so far in gaining confidence since the accident."

"Listen, Lainie, I've got to get back to the field. If there's anything about Mother that I should know, you'll be sure to tell me, right?"

"Of course. Things will be fine. I'll make sure that everything is fine."

* * *

Miss Jayne certainly hadn't volunteered to beat out the floor rug. All things considered, she was glad for the exertive task, for an anxious night had plunged her into another wasp nest of fear.

She whacked the carpet beater against the rug as she replayed Sally Jansen's words about a murderer—no, a murderess. A murdereress Sally claimed resembled Lainie.

What a baseless assumption. Sally had never viewed Lainie up close, and she was relying on a description from her brother to make the comparison.

Still, the claim held some merit. After all, the timing of Lainie's arrival at the farm coincided with suspected sightings of the killer. And the girl's life was swarmed in secrets. Yes, her few divulgements swooped on the wingbeats of woe, but Miss Jayne now suspected venom in Lainie's untold truths.

She considered how the girl had systematically entrenched herself in their lives. How susceptible a lonely widower might be to the deceptive charms of this girl. How a blind woman would seem feeble in her ability to detect a swindler.

Had Lainie blinded her? Had she and Jake walked into some nest of deceit? She had begun to trust the girl, to envision the girl staying on at the farm. Could Sally's account of a murderess—an account that was being spread from the Montana mining district to the lands around the Great Salt Lake—be Lainie's hidden truth? Did Niall McNally have legitimate reason to find the girl? To make her pay for her crime?

Barbed stings continued to attack Miss Jayne's thoughts. A hum, menacing and low, filled her mind. Were these waspish actions of her own nature? Or warnings that a murderess was in her midst?

The rebounds of the carpet beater against the rug jounced through Miss Jayne's body. Soon, words tumbled from the beat: *Lai-nie-is-a-mur-der-er. Lai-nie-is-a-mur-der-er.*

The cadence and its words stumbled when the carpet beater's handle broke in two.

Embittered by her suspicions against Lainie, Miss Jayne pitched the handle. It hit hard against the kitchen window.

Lainie ran outside and discovered what had happened.

"Wait. Stay right there," Lainie hollered. "I'll be back with something else to use."

Lainie ran into the kitchen and grabbed the cast iron skillet from the nail on the wall. She was determined that Miss Jayne would pound out her frustrations on that rug.

She hurried back to the woman, now seated on the grass. "Come on, Miss Jayne, off the ground."

"Nope."

"No sense sitting and moping. Besides, I brought you something that could beat turpentine out of stone."

She grabbed the woman's wrists and pulled her to a standing position and pressed the handle of the skillet into her hands.

Miss Jayne explored her new tool, all weight and roughcast in her grip, then dropped the skillet to the ground. It bounced, barely missing her foot.

Lainie picked up the skillet and returned it to the woman's hands. Miss Jayne wouldn't take hold. Lainie tried to force the woman's fingers around the handle. "What is going on with you, Miss Jayne?"

"Don't yell at me. Don't you dare yell at me. And I'm not a baby, so stop pushing things into my hands."

"I wasn't yelling at you. Where is all this feistiness coming from?"

"Give me that." Miss Jayne aimlessly reached for the skillet. "I'll show you what feisty can do."

With the skillet in hand, Miss Jayne lashed out her anger and fear on the rug.

Lainie swiftly stepped back and watched as the woman continued the heated motion of slamming the skillet against the spiral of braided wool and cotton and burlap. Suddenly, heated words flung through the air. "I hate this! I hate this! I hate this!"

Miss Jayne stopped, growled out a scream, then continued her bitter foray.

Finally, energy spent, Miss Jayne lowered her arms to her sides. The skillet dropped to the ground. Her body followed its course.

"I hate this so much." The woman trembled. She balled herself up with her arms wrapped around her legs.

Lainie dropped to her knees and held Miss Jayne and was shocked when the woman seemed to freeze at her touch. She wanted to envelope Miss Jayne in a blanket of protection, to hush her worries with words of reason. At the same time, she knew words of reason had no soul.

The woman at last whispered. "I can't see my son. I can't see my reflection. I can't see truth from lie. And I have never. Seen. You."

Those last words sent a chill through Lainie. Was there accusation in the woman's voice?

Lainie scrambled for words to say.

"Oh, Miss Jayne, I'm so sorry. Your world disappeared from sight, and we never thought . . . we don't know how to . . ." She released the woman from her arms and gave an exasperated groan. "Blindness is new to us, too."

Lainie positioned herself in front of Miss Jayne and used gentle fingers to lift the woman's trembling chin.

"Miss Jayne, tell me how to help you."

The woman recoiled from this pretensive, caring gesture, then realized an opportunity to expose Lainie's true past, to identify her sly intentions for Jake.

"Remind me what my son looks like. His image is fading too quickly from my mind."

"Oh, Miss Jayne, he's still your handsome son."

"Remind me."

"Alright. Well, you know how Jake has wavy dark hair with a cowlick in the back? I didn't realize how thick his hair is until you asked me to cut it. And I suppose it's confession time, because I did such a poor job at cutting his hair that when he went to town, he had the barber fix my mistakes." There was no response from the woman. Lainie continued. "I've never been able to decide if Jake's eyes are blue or grey, but the other day a spark of happiness hit him and he started to grin and his eyes suddenly turned the same shade as a springtime pond on a cloudless day. The other night at supper, I noticed he has two mismatched dimples. The one to the right of his mouth looks properly placed, but the one on the left seems an inch or so off."

Lainie paused, hoping the woman would recapture Jake's features, continue Jake's description. But the woman held quiet as the devil's blues painted her face.

Lainie continued. "On Tuesday Jake came in, all sweat and dirt from plowing, and when he pulled off his hat, I noticed he has a widow's peak starting. Don't tell Jake, but I almost laughed because it reminded me of how my grandfather looked. Anyway, low and behold, at the front of your son's wavy dark hair, two high lines are starting to form."

Miss Jayne's ghostly glare began to frighten Lainie. Somehow, somehow, she had to help this woman get past whatever dreadful thoughts besieged her.

"But that widow's peak is a handsome sight, Miss Jayne. Something masculine, yet tender. A mark of distinction that comes with age. It's like the crinkle lines you get from laughing in the sun."

"It's so obvious. So obvious," Miss Jayne murmured.

"What's so obvious, Miss Jayne?"

The woman wouldn't let the girl know that she'd latched on to her secret. That this girl paid too much heed to her son. That this girl intended to break the bond between Jake and his family in order to claim him as her own.

Lainie cringed at the shadows that darkened Miss Jayne's face. She had to get through to this woman, to reinforce trust. They had made so much headway. Their delicate friendship couldn't break now.

"What do you look like?" Miss Jayne asked harshly.

"Pardon me?"

"You aptly described my son. Now describe yourself."

"Surely, Jake has told you what I look like."

"I want to hear it from you. Let's start with your eyes. What color of green are your eyes?" Miss Jayne wondered if Lainie's description would match the one Sally provided for the killer.

"I . . . I really don't know how to describe my eyes," Lainie stammered, then took time to deliver her answer. "Darker than cat's eye green, I suppose, but not as dark as the forest. And my eyes have small flecks of gold that worried my grandmother some. She concocted some strange superstitions about my eyes."

"And your hair?"

"That's an easier question to answer," Lainie said with a laugh. "Once, a lady called my hair dramatic. Can you imagine? Grandmother called my hair irreverent since it would never settle into one style or another. And Grandfather, well, I won't tell you how he described my hair since there's a curse word involved. Let's just say his description was based on my hair's fiery red color."

Lainie watched Miss Jayne's eyes. They were vacant, yes, but the rest of her face concentrated on discovery.

"I guess I shouldn't say my hair is fiery red anymore. Once I turned thirteen, my hair began to look like old rust on a burn barrel. These days I keep it dyed dark, for obvious reasons."

255

Miss Jayne flinched at the reminder of Lainie's runaway status, and Lainie puzzled over her reaction.

"You'd think my hair should turn out black when I use the fabric dye. Instead, the color turns out more blackish grey. It only takes a few days for my roots to show through, red as cockscomb. I keep the scarf on so poor Jake doesn't have to view the mess. Besides, my hair looks and feels like hemp rope gone unspun, so it's not much to look at in the first place. Grandmother used to slick tallow through my hair to try to soften it, and I kept the practice up after she died, but since I left home, well, it just isn't a priority."

"What about your hands?" Miss Jayne asked.

Lainie placed her hands in Miss Jayne's and watched as the woman explored the landscape of hills and dales, the topography of cracked crevices and hardened blisters and stubby nails. Then the woman snatched the girl's hands between her own and squeezed hard.

"Tell me, child, are yours the hands of a killer?"

Discovery
Thurmond, Montana — May 1890

Stone-faced courage. That's what she needed as she stepped off the railcar. Stone-faced courage and a windfall of luck.

She tucked a sweatdamp strand of her red hair behind her ear, hefted her travelcase with both hands, and took her first steps on unfamiliar soil. The crowd moving about was as frenzied as the nerves and excitement jostling through her veins.

At the age of seventeen, she was finally going to meet her father. At the age of seventeen, her new life was about to begin.

The clue to find her father was discovered in her deceased grandparents' belongings: a stack of banker's bags imprinted with the words "Thurmond Bank and Trust."

These bags were part of her story, a story she had heard dozens of times. Her grandfather had always spun more magic into her story than it probably deserved, she was sure, but she had always loved to hear it.

"Your father, Nicholas Ian Edwards, rode his horse through the pouring rain to bring us the most beautiful gift ever," Grandfather would say, tweaking her nose. "The night he dropped you off on our front door stoop, magic returned to my life."

Grandmother would always snarl at that statement and tell her husband to stop filling the little girl's ears with such nonsense, to which he'd shush her with his hands, then tuck his little girl closer to him to spin more of the story.

"But why did he bring me here?" she would ask. "Why didn't he keep me?"

Her grandfather always gave the same answer. "We may never know the reason. We can only be confident in the love."

She felt her father's love. Her grandfather's, too. But no amount of love ever seemed to break through the barrier she had with her grandmother, even when the nighttime gifts came.

257

One late evening every year, near the anniversary of the baby arriving at the Edwards home, a bag of coins would land on their home's front stoop with a note filled with three short words, "For the child."

Whenever her grandparents discovered the money had been soundlessly delivered, they would search the dark distance, hoping to catch sight of their son. On two occasions, they spotted him. Their son waved, then disappeared before either of his parents had a chance to run after him.

Each giving season, when the coins were delivered and the little girl was old enough to realize what was going on, she'd stand on the front stoop and wave and blow kisses, hoping her father was near enough to see.

In time, the railway's evolution stunted stagecoach travel. At the Edwards' home station, visitors were few, boarders were rare, money was scant. Age caught up to her grandparents. After their deaths, the seventeen-year-old was left with desolation, a crumbling building, and enough money for train fare.

She sold the home station, the land, and tucked money from the sale into a single banker's bag that now held her grandfather's bible and her uncharted destiny.

On the train ride to Montana, she carried the tintype of her father in her dress pocket and occasionally pulled it out to study his mop of blond hair, his lopsided grin, his hint of a mustache. Would she recognize him? The picture of the manboy was over twenty years old. Would he resemble his mother? His father? Would he want to be recognized?

Perhaps she was on an absurd mission.

Upon arrival in Thurmond, the girl asked the ticket agent if he knew anyone by the name of Nicholas Edwards. The answer was no. She pulled out the tintype and he studied it some, then came the surprised realization.

"Oh, that's Stut. You'll find him at the jailhouse."

"Is he a prisoner there?" she asked, afraid of the answer.

"No, no, Stut couldn't hurt a flea. He's our local jailer."

She gathered directions to the jailhouse and asked a recommendation for lodging. After paying for a hotel room and dropping off her travelcase in the small room, she walked to the jailhouse and hesitantly set foot inside.

"I'm looking for Mr. Edwards—I mean, Stut," she said to a man whose thin hair was combed over his head, from left to right, and hung at greasy angles.

The man peered over his blued steel spectacles.

"Stut? Nobody around here ever looks for Stut."

"Is he here?"

"No, ma'am, Stut ain't here for the now. Mr. McNally has him running errands today. Best place to find him would be at the McNally's house. He'll be delivering a new surrey for the missus. The boss man ordered it all the way from South Bend, Indiana. Paid for it to be put on a train and delivered out west. Traveled all the way to Helena to pick it up, Stut did. Supposed to be a fancy thing, a Studebaker all decked out with red leather and showy paint."

"That sounds very nice. Where shall I find the McNally home?"

The girl did her best to retain the man's long-winded directions. As she made her way to her destination, she ended up asking for directions two more times and puzzled over the prolonged side glances she received from those passing by.

It was late afternoon when she walked up the grand set of stairs of the three-story McNally home.

A ruddied woman wearing a long navy dress and a starched white apron opened the door.

"Good afternoon, I'm looking for a Mr. Nicholas Edwards. I was told I might find him here."

"Mr. Edwards hasn't arrived yet. And if he did, he certainly wouldn't be greeted at the front door."

"Who is it, Marta?" A woman's voice came from the background.

The woman pushed past Marta and filled the doorway with her satin bustle skirt and high couture hair.

"I'm Agrippina McNally. And who might you be?"

The girl made her introduction as Mrs. McNally studied her travelweary dress and beseeching green eyes.

"And how do you know Mr. Edwards?"

"I am a relative of Mr. Edwards. I'm happy to return at a later time. Or perhaps you could provide a message to Mr. Edwards? Let him know that I am staying at the Hilltop Hotel in town?"

"Nonsense." The woman's voice sweetened. "There is absolutely no need for you to waste your money on that ramshackle hotel when I have plenty of rooms to spare. After all, Mr. Edwards is like a member of our family. My husband and I would be delighted to have you as our guest."

"Thank you, but that isn't necessary. I've already delivered my luggage to the hotel."

"Then you must stay for tea. Surely you must be famished after your travels. Please, come in, sit, rest, enjoy some refreshments."

Mrs. McNally ushered the girl into the entryway.

"Marta, please show our guest to my sitting room." Mrs. McNally turned to the girl. "I'll join you shortly after I change into a dress much more suitable for afternoon tea."

* * *

The girl dared not sit on the blue velvet settee Marta led her to. Instead, she stood awkwardly in the middle of the room, transfixed by the ornate chandelier, the wall sconces dripping in crystals, candelabras of gold. All around her, intricately carved woodwork framed a world she could never imagine. A wall of leather-bound books, a solid stone fireplace, brocade draperies tied back with tassels fatter than her fist.

She stood on a thick rug woven with images of flora and fauna, its textures and colors lush, vibrant. Above, a medallion of cherubs and rosettes centered each panel of the coffered ceiling. And all around—all around—paintings of women jolted from walls and easels, and their fiery colors, it seemed, nearly blistered her skin.

Mrs. McNally joined her.

"How do you like my paintings?" she asked.

Before the girl could answer, Marta carried in a tray filled with tea and fancy cakes.

"Leave the tray on the sideboard, Marta. I'll serve the tea myself."

Mrs. McNally and her guest settled into small talk as they enjoyed refreshments. As the weariness of travel set in, the girl fought to keep her thoughts on the conversation and found herself nodding off as the elder discussed her affection for opera and her plans to build an opera house to attract roving performers who used the railroad to move about the country.

* * *

The girl pushed past the bondage of sleep. She stretched her neck to the left, then the right. When she lifted her shoulders to loosen the strain at the tip of her spine, she discovered ropes bound her to a dining chair.

She pulled against the ropes and grimaced as the bristly twists burned against her arms and legs. Her waist was cinched tight against the back spindles of the chair. Each gasp for air was bound in place, her ribs ready to explode from the fear welling inside her. Panic scourged the girl's thoughts as waves of nausea pushed dry heaves of sour bile through the girl's mouth and nose.

Twisting, contorting, arching her body in any manner possible, the girl tried to escape. The chair legs lifted with each movement, keeping time to her frenetic pace, drumming out their amusement at her foolhardy efforts. Another wave of nausea burst forth and she vomited more bile on her skirt, her shoes, the floor. Exhausted, she looked up, bile dripping from her chin, to see a painting positioned a few feet in front of her.

With wide, wild eyes, the girl took in the change to her surroundings. Clustered all around her, paintings of a woman with a baby or a small boy or a young man stood on easels or were stacked against easel legs.

"I wondered when you'd notice my work," Mrs. McNally called out, gesturing towards the newly gathered paintings. "Quite striking, aren't they?"

The woman stood at the far corner of the room, a canvas atop an easel in front of her, an artist's brush in her hand. She dipped the brush into the painter's palette atop a small table filled with supplies, leaned forward, and added brushstrokes to the canvas. "I call the one in front of you 'Dante's Mistrust.' The one to its left is 'Son of the Deified.' To its right is 'Empress Conquistador.'"

The girl's pulse thrashed through her skin as the woman walked towards her, the artist's brush still in her hand. She stopped at the first painting and used her finger to trace the cheekline of a boy's depiction.

"I've painted at least a hundred portraits of me with my son, my one and only heir. They've been stored in my private chamber, away from my husband's resentful stares." The woman walked from painting to painting, running her fingers across the gildwork of each frame as the girl strained to keep her in view. "Now, our portraits surround you."

The woman ambled towards the girl. "The paintings you saw earlier are of Agrippina Minor, one of the greatest minds of the Julio-Claudian dynasty. And, yes, I bear her name. My mother adored her, for this woman of Imperial Rome was immensely powerful, politically adept, persuasive, shrewd. My mother knew I'd turn out like her. Sadly, Agrippina Minor held one fatal flaw." The woman leaned over and traced the girl's cheek as she had traced the boy in the painting, then clutched her hand around the girl's jaw. "Agrippina Minor turned her son into a monster—a monster who would become her murderer. It is not a flaw I will paint into my life as I nurture my son's ascent to the throne."

The girl's chin quivered from pain, from fear. The woman finally loosed her grip.

"Oh, my. I've left a smear of crimson paint on your beautiful face." The woman pulled a handkerchief from her pocket. "Just let me clean. That. Up."

The woman dabbed at the girl's chin, her cheek.

"Now, now, no tears. No tears, darling girl. Let me wipe those tears away." The girl flinched as the woman smoothed damp paint bristles across her skin. The downward streaks of black paint mixed with the girl's tears and slid down her jawline and onto her dress.

"Where was I with my story?" The woman returned to her paint palette, her canvas, and added a few more brushstrokes. "Ah, yes. Soon, portraits of me with my son will line these walls. Soon, he will take over my business, my mountain, my land of silver. Oh, you may have heard that Mr. McNally is king of this land, but that would be wrong. He only thinks he is king. Twenty years ago, he conspired his way into my father's favor then cheated his way to a winning hand of cards."

The woman stood back and admired her work as she continued her story.

"My brainless father used our family's mine as the ante. It was up to me to save our land and the Alger family honor after my father's five-card straight was mowed down by McNally's hand of spades. When I should have been painting in Venice and Rome, I instead martyred myself to become Mrs. Niall McNally to return this land of fortune to the Alger name."

The woman picked up the wet painting, carried it to the easel in front of the girl, and set it in place.

"My so-called husband has the intellectual wherewithal of a spittoon, the strategic capacity of a toadstool. Without me, this mountain would be a ghost town of gravel."

She turned to her prisoner.

"Look at the painting, child." The girl kept her eyes on the ground. "Look at the painting!" The girl squeezed her eyes shut, then gave in to the woman's demand.

"What do you think of my newest work? What do you see before you?" The woman walked behind the girl and began stroking the girl's hair. "My son looks so much like you. Same flaming hair, though his is fine and straight. Same cheekbones, same nose. And those eyes. Yes, those eyes. You each share the same eye color as your father."

The woman waited for the girl to comprehend, then whispered into her ear.

"Stut is not your father. I believe I hear your true father walking through the front door."

* * *

"What have you done to her?" Niall McNally asked of his wife as he studied the red-headed girl in front of him.

"We've simply enjoyed refreshments, small talk, a tour of my art collection." Agrippina replied.

He circled the girl, eyeing her as if she were some curiosity inside a circus tent.

"She's covered in stench," he said, revulsion dripping from his words.

"She vomited from the sleep aid I slipped into her tea."

"Remarkable," Niall whispered as he twisted a curl of the girl's hair around his finger. "Remarkable."

Agrippina marched to her husband and slapped him in the face.

"Tell me, Niall, how is it that this girl is here, alive and well and reeking of your bloodline?" Agrippina demanded. "I recall the mongrel child fell several feet from her mother's arms to the ground below the gallows. At least that's what you reported."

"The baby did fall," Niall blustered. "She fell from her mother's arms, through the floor opening and past the boulders dangling from the dead woman's legs. I witnessed it myself. You know I witnessed it,

Aggie. I saw that baby lying broken on the ground. That baby did not move or cry. She was dead, Aggie. I swear it."

A crashing sound interrupted the argument. The two turned to find the girl had toppled the chair in her attempt to escape bondage and fate.

Agrippina hurried to the girl who squirmed within the overturned chair and its bindings. The woman's skirts billowed as she lowered herself to the marble tile to nestle the girl and console her with whispered words.

"Dear child, how sad that you weren't aware of how your mother died." Agrippina stroked the girl's hair. "You see, I was unable to have a baby of my own, so I found a woman who looked like me for Niall to, well, have relations with in order to provide me a child. You, dearest one, were meant to be my child." The girl sobbed uncontrollably. "Don't be sad, don't be sad," Agrippina continued. "I'm sorry I didn't end up your mother. Alas, life has its turnabouts. After two years of trying, I found myself with child at the same time Niall's mistress was due to whelp. You and your mother were allowed to live until my son was born, in case I required you instead. I needed to be sure my son was healthy, that he would thrive. Once I saw his vigor, you were of no use to me."

The woman kissed the girl's forehead, then stood up and walked to the fireplace where a fire blazed, adding fever to the sweltering day. Agrippina continued her story. "We hadn't enjoyed a proper gallows hanging in our town for years, so we treated our silver haven to a spectacle. Your mother atop the platform, a noose around her pretty neck, a baby in her arms. People reminisced that image for years."

The woman picked up a length of iron from the fireplace hearth and used one end of it to stir up the flames. "The boulders attached by rope to your mother's ankles were added at my request," she said. "Without them, your poor mother would have dangled for much too long before the noose fully strangled out her life. Thanks to my thoughtfulness, the weight of the stones dropping through the floor opening helped to snap your mother's neck. She hardly suffered at all, or so I was told."

"Enough of the dramatics, Aggie." The man walked towards her as he bellowed. "What are we to do with the girl?"

"I've already called for Arthur Napier," the woman replied. "He is quite adept with a bludgeoning stick."

Her husband concurred.

"In the meantime, I say we give this child a proper, meaningful welcome to the McNally name." She handed him the red-hot iron, its branding head shaped with the letters N and M. "I'm sure you will enjoy the honor, dear husband."

McNally smiled at his wife, and then the girl. "Yes, Aggie. I quite certainly will enjoy this honor."

* * *

"Where shall I dispose of the body," Napier asked, his arm wrapped tightly around the writhing girl's neck. The girl shrieked in pain as the man's shirtsleeve raked against the cattle brand singed into her skin.

"Cripple Creek's east trench is spent out. Shove her into some corner and dump a load of rocks on top of her," McNally said. "Once you've taken care of the girl, find Stut and haul his ass to my office. Be sure to stick around. You'll have a chance to use that fancy .38 you carry."

"My pleasure," Napier said as he dragged the screaming girl from the sitting room to the hallway.

McNally turned to his wife. "Do you want to be there? For Stut, that is?"

Agrippina brushed his question aside with her hand. "I'm exhausted. I will have Marta draw me a bath."

* * *

Marta flinched at the mention of her name. From her hiding place in the butler's pantry, she could hear nearly all the heinous conversation going on across the hallway. "Mr. Edwards, you must save that girl." She feared Stut couldn't hear her whispers and leaned in closer to his ear. "They have had the girl tied up for hours and now they are going to have that nasty man kill her."

Stut nodded his understanding, grateful that Marta had sneaked to the carriage house to find him.

He had his gun with him, but what good would it do to shoot and hit the wrong person?

Brute force was what he'd need to save his girl one more time.

Napier dragged the hand-bound girl from the sitting room and headed through the wide hallway towards the servant entrance.

Stut slipped out of the butler's pantry, grateful to see the door to the sitting room was closed.

He gauged the distance to cover, the angle of impact, the speed he'd need to flatten Napier, giving his girl a chance for escape.

He ignored the pain in his spine and bolted down the hallway and plunged into Napier with the force of a cannon shot, knocking the assassin into the opposite wall and loosing the man's grip from the girl, who stumbled into a hall table, knocking over a crystal vase that shattered when it hit the ground.

Napier dropped to the ground as Stut stumbled backwards. Stut kept on his feet, however, and swiftly grabbed the girl's upper arm. Together, they staggered to the front door.

Hearing the commotion, Niall and Agrippina hastened from the sitting room to the hallway in time to watch Napier pull himself to his feet. Blood gushed from the assassin's nose as he steadied himself and drew his pistol from its holster.

The front door opened unexpectedly and slammed into Stut as he and his girl tried to make their escape. Napier's gun fired once, twice, and the young man walking through the front door toppled onto the marble floor.

Stut didn't give his girl a chance to survey the scene. He grabbed her hand, stepped over the man's body, and dragged her with him.

Stut was sure the man with two bullets to his chest was August McNally, heir-apparent to the town of Thurmond in its entirety. The death-scene screams from Agrippina McNally confirmed his suspicion.

Convincing Herself
Leeds, Idaho — October 1890

I am not a killer. I am not a killer. Lainie chanted the words to herself, fearing she hadn't convinced Miss Jayne of the fact. Fearing she wouldn't convince Jake when he came home.

She had told Miss Jayne her story in entirety, including her connection to the death of August McNally. When her admission was made, her confession complete, all she could see was absolute distrust in the woman's bleached out eyes.

I am not a killer. The son didn't die because of me. I am not a killer. I am not a throwaway.

She bit into her wrist as despair crushed down on her.

Throwaway go away. Throwaway go away.

"Stop thinking these things. Stop thinking these things."

Go back to Wallace. That's where throwaways go.

"No. No. I will never go back to Wallace. Somehow, I will prove my worth."

The Ache of Never

Lainie was nearly finished restocking the firewood on the front porch when she heard an approaching wagon. She slipped into the house, wrapped a scarf around her hair, and peered through the window to learn who approached.

Relief slowed her pounding heartbeat when she saw the bright sign on the side of the wagon that announced the arrival of Halifax Timberman's Notions, Sundries and Exotic Junk.

Halifax let out an interminably audible blast of a horn to proclaim to the Adamsen family that he was open for business.

Lainie stepped out, fingers crossed that the salesman hadn't discovered her former identity.

"Hello, Mr. Timberman. How are you this fine day?"

"Why, Miss Lainie, I'm a bit nipped by the frost, plump round the middle, and drained of good booze. Other than that, I'm feeling quite spry."

"In other words, life on the trail has treated you well."

"Yes, and it should until the snow flies. That's why I'm here, little lass. It's my last trip of the season to these parts and have I got some deals for you."

"I'm afraid Miss Jayne is in town with friends and Jake is off hunting."

"Do you know if Jake needs any more of those notebooks he likes so well?" At the look of her confusion, he moved the conversation on. "Well, maybe we can find something to suit yourself, little lass. How about a wash set? I've got a beautiful set right here." He retrieved a wooden crate from his stash of this, that's and th'others, as he put it, and pulled out an item wrapped in crinkled newsprint.

"We've got a pitcher and bowl, a vase, and a soap dish as well. All white enamel with a gilt trim and blue roses." He handed the vase to Lainie. "T'would look quite regal in this fine home, don't you think?"

She admired the elegant roses and turned the vase to see it from all angles. "It is beautiful, Mr. Timberman, but I'm afraid it's out of my price range."

"But I haven't even mentioned a price, my dear. Never you mind. Winter's coming on, so let's consider your wardrobe."

He set aside the wash set and rummaged through another box.

"Ah, yes, this is it. This is it." He pulled out a plush cape trimmed with bear fur and beads.

"A cape such as this will be mighty cozy to wear come wintertime."

Lainie wrinkled her nose. "I don't think so."

"Indeed. Indeed. I am determined to find a trinket that will truly steal your heart."

He unbuttoned his overcoat to show off an array of watches, jewelry, and fishing lures attached to the coat's inside panels.

"I've got a watch here that would rival any sold by the Sears Watch Company. 'Twould make a debonair gift for the handsome gent in your life."

He dangled the pocket watch into her hand. She opened its case and listened to its tick tick tick. She could imagine Jake priding ownership in a piece such as this. If she had the funds, it would make a right fine thank you for the food and home he'd provided.

Lainie passed the watch back to Mr. Timberman's hands.

"I'm sorry. I simply haven't the money for such a beautiful piece. Perhaps I could thank you for your time with a slice of pie?"

"Of course, little lass," he replied. "By the way, did Jake find a use for those old, framed windows he bought?"

"He certainly did. Would you like to see?"

Lainie led the salesman to the side of the house where she and Miss Jayne had planted a cold weather garden inside framework boxes filled high with soil and worm castings.

"Well, I'll be," Mr. Timberman exclaimed as he admired the peaked garden cover Jake had built from the windows and a few lengths of timber.

"Jake hinged the windows to open and shut so we can easily reach the plants," Lainie said. "Plenty of sunlight reaches this side of the house, so the boxed-in garden should stay warm enough to beat the cold and give us fresh vegetables throughout the winter and in early spring. We'll surround the plants with straw to help keep them warm. I guess we'll learn through trial and error what will survive the winter."

"Well, give my compliments to the craftsman. That is some sight. And you've already got peas, collards, and cabbages growing quite nicely. What else have you planted?"

"Miss Jayne and I transplanted beets, cauliflower, parsnips, and onions. We also planted some radish seed and lettuce. Maybe they'll get a good start before the weather turns especially cold. I read that fava beans would do quite well in cold weather for spring harvesting, but Jake didn't find any seeds."

"Fava beans, you say. A native to North Africa and Southwest Asia and quite delicious in pork stew. Well, little lass, I believe I can help."

They walked back to the wagon. Mr. Timberman climbed in, searched through a few bins, and pulled out a small packet. "This certainly isn't junk, but it should be considered exotic. Hold out your hands."

Lainie opened her hands and thrilled at the sight of the seeds Mr. Timberman poured from the packet.

"Mr. Timberman, are these fava beans? Where on earth did you get them?"

"Never you mind. A salesman always has a few tricks up his sleeve." He gave her a wink. "Besides, Jack and the giant could get mighty upset with me if I shared the source of their magic beans with too many people."

"Still, I don't have money to make a purchase." She held out the seeds for the salesman to take back.

"The only payment I ask is that piece of pie you mentioned earlier. In fact, I have a tin here that you can set it on."

"Of course. I'll be right back with the pie."

Lainie rushed inside and set the beans in a bowl. She cut two large hunks of pie and placed them in the tin, followed by a scoop of fresh whipped cream.

Back outside, she found Mr. Timberman resecuring the load tied to the far side of the wagon.

"I can't thank you enough for the bean seed, Mr. Timberman. Miss Jayne will be right pleased to add them to her garden."

"Please tell Miss Jayne that I truly missed visiting with her."

"Mr. Timberman, what, may I ask, do you have underneath that tarp?"

Lainie pointed to a long rectangular shape roped tight to the wagon's frame.

"That's a table I picked up in Worley. Family was moving on to Spokane to find work. They wanted to lighten their load, so I traded some winter blankets for it."

"May I see what it looks like? Just a peak underneath the cover?" Lainie asked, knowing she was requesting much as a customer with no money.

"Of course." He tugged at a corner of the tarp. "The table is in a dismal state, I'm sorry to say. The family had half a dozen rapscallion kids mistreating it. Never saw such a sight of unruliness before. But Lord knows they needed those blankets, unruliness or no, more than they needed a table."

Lainie peered under the tarp and nearly gasped with joy. The table was solid. It was mournfully scraped and scarred, but it was solid.

"Mr. Timberman, do you think this table could be salvaged? I mean, do you think, with a bit of work, it could be sanded down and oiled to a welcome state?"

"It certainly would take some work, but the table is well built. If memory serves, the legs seemed fairly steady. Probably will need a bit of effort to take out any wobble, but yes, I believe the table would turn out fine. Why do you ask?"

Throwaway go away. Throwaway go away. The mindchant thrummed. *Because I'm a supposed killer and I need to prove my worth.*

The mindchant cinched her eyes shut until the kindly peddler touched her arm and asked if she felt faint.

She forced her eyes open and smiled.

"May I purchase the table with a few coins and a fruitcake soaked in brandywine?"

* * *

Paul helped Lainie move the finished table pieces into the kitchen while Miss Jayne and Snow Owl went for a walk.

Lainie had wanted to keep the table a secret from the entire family but ended up conspiring with Paul and Snow Owl when she realized she'd need some help.

For the past week, she'd kept the tabletop and its square tapered legs hidden under an old canvas sheet behind the hen house. Each day, she'd eked out time to sand the pieces, to coax mars into beauty. The finish would never be smooth, but the pock marks wouldn't snag their

271

skin or their clothes. She didn't have any varnish or shellac, so she broke up some beeswax she'd found from an abandoned hive, mixed it with a bit of turpentine, and rubbed the mixture into the surface. She buffed out each of the three coats of beeswax and was quite happy with the results.

Within the kitchen, Paul helped her attach the legs to the tabletop. Once the table was upright and in place, Lainie topped it with an old banged up copper kettle that she'd filled with dirt and wildflower seeds.

"Will they like it, Paul?"

"Don't see why not. You said they got rid of their old table because it was rickety."

"That one was made by Jake's pa. There's no way this one will ever compete."

Lainie's nerves twisted into a snarl of prickly vine as she watched Snow Owl and Miss Jayne return. Before the girls had a chance to lead Miss Jayne to the table to discover the surprise, the woman commented on the scent of turpentine in the air.

When the girls placed Miss Jayne's hands on the table, the woman smoothed her fingers across the wood's grainy surface. She tapped the tabletop twice, then handsearched the edge until her wrist bumped into a chair nestled into its new home.

"What is this? How did this get in here?" Miss Jayne backstepped, her hand at her mouth.

"It's a kitchen table." Paul gave Lainie and Snow Owl a perplexed look. "Lainie fixed it up for you."

"No, you shouldn't have done that. He's going to throw a fit. Paul, keep Jake out in the barn. Girls, haul this table out of here and hide it in the woods. Don't let Jake see you."

"Miss Jayne, what are you talking about?" Lainie asked.

"He can't see it. Don't let Jake see it."

Lainie took the woman's hand.

"Miss Jayne, you're not making any sense."

"Who's not making sense?" Jake asked as he strode through the doorway.

The room went silent.

"We were just talking about how exciting it will be to play card games at the table that we got for Ma," Paul said.

Jake spotted the table. His face paled and the clench of his jaw hollowed out his cheeks.

"And whose idea was it to get this table?" Jake's voice was low.

"It's a gift. From all of us." Paul pulled back his shoulders as he walked towards Jake. "A gift. You got that?"

"You have no right, Paul. None of you have any right to bring that thing in here."

"Calm down, cousin. It's just a table."

Toe to toe, Jake confronted Paul. "Get that table out of my home."

Paul didn't move.

"Now."

"Don't you dare yell in front of our mother, Jake."

"Stop. Both of you stop." Lainie pushed her way between the men.

"You're not part of this family," Jake growled. "Leave us be while we sort this out."

"No, I will not leave you be. It was my idea to get the table. Not Paul's. Not Snow Owl's. Not your mother's. It was my idea. Don't you dare go starting some brawl with your kin, Jake Adamsen."

"And don't you start ordering me around, little miss no-name."

Paul pulled Lainie back to move between her and Jake.

"No. No. I am talking to the girl. I want to know where in tarnation she got a table?"

Lainie pushed past Paul. "From the peddler, Jake. I saw it strapped to the side of his wagon and I bought it."

"Bought it?" Jake snapped. "Where'd you get money to buy anything? Or did you steal money from the flour tin? Is that how you paid for this so-called gift?"

"I didn't steal any money. I used my egg money. *My* egg money. Remember Jake? You're the one who said I could raise money for my trip onward by gathering and selling eggs. Or do you want to break that deal?"

"Well, wasn't that a smart decision. You spent your trip money on a piece of junk. Good for you." Jake pointed his finger first to Lainie, then to Paul. "If that thing isn't out of my house when I get back, I'll destroy it where it stands."

* * *

"Jake Adamsen, don't you dare walk away from me."

"Get back in the cabin, Lainie."

She tried to keep up with Jake's long strides.

273

"You are one callous, mule-brained, contemptuous doom marshall."

"I told you to get back to the cabin," Jake hollered over his shoulder.

Lainie picked up her skirts, ran in front of him, and blocked his path.

"Why are you fuming about a table? Is it because of your family? Because they aren't here to sit around it anymore?"

"Out of my way, Lainie."

Each time Jake tried to sidestep her, she darted in front of him.

"Why don't you talk about your wife? About your children?" she demanded. "Why don't you ever sit with your mother and ask her how she's doing? Or spend a few minutes of time with her beyond mealtime? You might as well live in the barn and take your meals from a nosebag. Maybe then your mother would stop pining away, hoping her son will take notice of her."

"You want to talk about my wife? My children? Fine. Let's start by talking about my son who died on the kitchen table. Yes, Lainie, you heard right. Doc amputated my son's arm on our kitchen table. I watched my son gasp his last breath on our kitchen table. I scrubbed my boy's blood and flesh and bone from our kitchen table. And when I couldn't bare the pain of seeing that table every day, taunting me with its stains so easily covered by a tablecloth, I took an axe to it and I tore it apart and I set it afire. And I was glad to watch it burn. I was glad the demon stains and the guise of life were devoured by flames. Now out of my way."

"No."

He shoved past her.

Lainie hollered after him. "You're not holding on to their memories, Jake. You're strangling yourself with them. And you can't hoe a weed or take a piss without cinching the noose a bit tighter."

Jake barreled towards her, his fists clenched.

"Don't you dare talk that way about my family."

"Grief's got a stranglehold on you, Jake. Somehow you've got to knife your way out of it."

"You're wrong. So, hush up, Lainie. Just hush up."

"Am I wrong? Am I?" Lainie lowered her voice. "It's as if grief gives you purpose, some sort of cruel satisfaction. How can Hannah, Jackson, and your sweet baby find peace in heaven when they're watching you traipse around this farm like a demon set on dying a long, slow death?"

"Purpose? Satisfaction?" He snorted his derision. "Let me know how it feels when never comes knocking at your door."

* * *

Jake had no idea of the nevers in her life.

"How dare he? How dare he?" She kicked at a rut of soil and stones, sending up a plume of dirt that put a haze between her and the man walking away from her.

That man—that man who'd found her half-starved in the woods—had no idea that her nevers were stacked so high that sometimes she couldn't see past them.

Memories of her mother's cradlesongs.

Never.

Lessons in braiding hair and blushing lips with berries.

Never.

A father's goodnight kiss.

Never.

A childhood free of boiling sheets and fighting lice and making beds before cleaning dirt floors slopped with tobacco spit and stenched manure.

A life beyond serving breakfast and supper to men whose bodies and language flowed with filth and fowl, men who never paid her any mind until puberty took control of her growth spurts and she quicklearned to slap grabbing hands every time one neared her bosom or her ass.

A youth free of granddaughter do this, granddaughter get that, granddaughter move faster there are rooms to be cleaned and chamber pots to be dumped.

An education past the fifth grade. A beau to bring her pretty ribbons. An occasion to attend church. To find grace. To find absolution. To find God.

Never. Never. Never. Never.

Never was a callous dungeon for hope, comfort, kinship, support, all defeated before they were dreamed.

Lainie needed to escape never.

275

She ran. She raced past work to be done and plans to be made, the nevers in her life spurring her on to whatever freedoms she could muster.

But never could only run so far. Lainie stopped along the riverbank, bent over to catch her breath, then sunk to the earth and wept.

Regret

Jake balanced a grease bucket in his hand as he climbed the windmill tower. He wasn't keen on climbing ladders or standing on rooftops—he wasn't quite the daredevil Paul made him out to be—yet there was some spark of adventure, even thrill, at looking over one's land from forty some-odd feet above the ground.

Perched on the windmill's small, precarious platform, he dipped a ladle into the grease bucket, then poured the grease over the wheel gears. He spotted the fringe of a wasp nest too late and was pelted by angry wasps as they defended their home.

He lowered himself to his belly with his shoulders hanging over the edge of the platform, reached underside, and mashed the nest with his gloved hand.

Paul had forewarned him that wasps were known to use the platforms for nest building, and to use caution for fear of falling from the tower should he be swarmed. The notion of toppling off the windmill was made worse by memories of the last time Jake was stung by a wasp and the left half of his face swelled up so bad that his upper eyelid split open and his ma feared he would lose sight in that eye.

He brought himself to his knees, then upright, in time to see a figure walking past the grazing cattle.

Lainie.

It had been three days since their clash, three days since either had attempted conversation with the other.

Her words had pummeled him.

Had his words to her done the same?

He finished greasing the gear box then made the long climb down the steel tower. Back on the ground, Jake left the bucket on the ground and raced to catch up with Lainie.

"We need to talk," he said. The whirring of the windmill masked his short-winded words.

Lainie quickened her pace as she balanced a shovel across her shoulder.

"There's tansy weed growing in the upper field," she said, refusing to look at him. "I pulled some of it yesterday, piled it at the edge of the field. I'm headed up there now to finish up. I'll be back in a couple of hours."

"Lainie, forget the stupid weeds. They can wait."

"You said it yourself, Jake. The tansy weed will kill the cows if they eat it. Horses, too. We've got to get it out of your pastureland before the seeds drop and more plants grow. Invasive. You said it yourself. That weed is invasive."

He stepped in front of her. "You're avoiding the issue."

"Yes, Jake, I'm avoiding the issue. More importantly, I'm avoiding you. I can't stop you from being a muckbrained, horn-mad pain in the ass, but I can certainly avoid having you sucker punch my day."

"Sucker punch? How in the world do you even know such a term?"

"Seriously, Jake? I grew up around miners and loggers who didn't care if they brawled with a chimney pipe or a grizzly bear. Bunch of fool men trying to cause problems. I learned to throw a left uppercut by the time I was twelve. Now, I suggest you get out of my way."

He stepped back, thumbs tucked in his pant pockets. "I'm officially out of your way."

She hurried past him.

"But if you were to give me just three minutes of your time, you'd hear a very sincere apology about the way I acted the other day."

His words piled up in his throat as he watched her stop, turn around, and walk towards him. Why was it so hard to read her face?

She jabbed the shovel into the ground, then pulled off her oversized leather work gloves and let them fall to the earth. He took a step towards her. She held up her hands to ward him off.

"You don't owe me an apology, Jake. I overstepped. Your life is not my business and I have no right to judge your actions. You're handling your grief in a way that keeps you from going too far insane. I see that now." She pushed a strand of hair from her face. "Grief soars, it scrambles, it shies away, it shoves. I see that now, too."

Jake stumbled for words. He had expected a litany of unwanted advice, another verbal scourge.

"You asked me why I don't talk about Hannah and the baby." He stopped, swallowed hard. "Or my little guy."

Lainie moved forward and touched his arm.

"Hannah, the children—they were my compass, my destination. Since their deaths, I walk the same paths, I travel the same roads, and there's always some landslide blocking them from me. I try to dig my way through. I heft away boulders and claw through swirling mud and muck until my fingers bleed, and I can hear their voices calling from the distance, but the mud sucks at my boots and I'm pulled deeper into the earthfall until I'm too damn tired to crawl over one more memory, past one more grave."

Jake pulled away from her touch.

"If I turn my senses back on, if I put their reality into words, I have to rewrite what my life is going to be. I'm not ready for that. I don't think I'll ever be ready for that."

Storm Clouds Brewing

"Either one of you planning to mention those storm clouds brewing?"

Lainie and Snow Owl smiled at each other and rolled their eyes.

"Yes, Mother, we planned to mention them," Snow Owl said, trying not to giggle as she set another bushel of beets on the hardpan ground next to her chair.

"We figured with that almighty sniffer of yours, you'd smell the rain in the clouds long before it had a chance to decide where to fall," Lainie added.

"You two laugh all you want about my keen nose and ears," Miss Jayne said. "My grandmother used to say that I could smell lilacs in a snowstorm, and I could hear a ladybug sigh."

Lainie and Snow Owl let out deep, dramatic sighs.

"Oh, bosh. The two of you are silly as schoolgirls."

The girls let out two more big, even more playful sighs, to which Miss Jayne stuck out her tongue.

"Time to get back to serious, girls. No sense starting that last bushel. Storm will be here before you've got the beets peeled. Let's get all the filled jars inside the house to finish cooling."

"Why not just leave the jars here?" Lainie asked. "A little rain won't hurt them."

"It isn't the rain I'm worried about. This storm's going to be a brick spitter. Anything that's not tied down will land in the next farm."

"Wouldn't it be better to store the jars on the shelves in the fruit cellar?" Lainie asked.

"The jars are warm still," Snow Owl explained. "They need space to cool so they seal proper."

"That's right, Snow Owl. No sense throwing away our labors by pinching time. There's plenty of floor space inside. Just start lining the jars up, leaving paths where we need them. Let's get moving. I just heard the first growl of thunder."

The air turned heavy and tempest dark as the women scrambled to move the dozens of jars of pickled vegetables inside. The smell of the food's spicy brine that lingered on the jars and on the women's clothes soon competed with the earthy scent of rain tumbling to the ground.

The cabin shielded the women from the rain, then from hail, but not from the percussive uproar slamming against the roof, pelting the windows, pulsating the house.

Within minutes, lightning and thunder spiked scorn like swordsmen on the battlefield. Miss Jayne held her hands tight over her ears to muffle the torrent of sounds. But each smack of thunder sent her body tight and quickened her whisper of plainsongs and bible verse.

Lainie and Snow Owl flanked Miss Jayne, cocooning, shielding, lending courage in earnest. Facing the storm eyes-wide-open was frightening enough. What should they expect of one so new to eternal dark?

So, they hushed and soothed and consoled and tracked time on the drop dial clock hanging on the wall, its face brightening and dulling with each prolonged flash of light.

At the twelve-minute mark, the storm screamed louder, and a particular lightning strike rocked the house enough to make the china dishes clatter.

"What did that hit?" Lainie asked.

Snow Owl cringed, afraid to imagine the possibilities.

"Do you think our men are safe?" Snow Owl asked.

"They have to be," Lainie said. "They just have to be."

* * *

Stillness finally came. Pearls of water slipped from the roof, audible but reverent, and the girls knew to take Miss Jayne's hands in their own, indicating the shield from sound was no longer needed.

"I've gotta find Jake and the Bauer boys," Lainie said.

Snow Owl nodded her agreement and Lainie ran from the house into the heavy air, still tempest dark, shouting out Jake's and the boys' names as she skittered along the slippery path.

"Over here." The small voice came from the corncrib. Lainie opened the door and found the youngest boy and Bristle standing on top of corn cobs stacked three feet deep. She reached up to Lewis and he leaped into her arms while Bristle jumped out and took off running.

"Are you alright, Lewis? Where are Peter and Jake?"

Lewis wiped at his eyes. "They were both here. When the storm died down, Jake told us both to stay in the corncrib while he checked the cows. But my brother took off after him."

The boy cried harder and Lainie set him on the ground and did her best to console him.

"Let me take you back to the house. Miss Jayne will fix you some bread with sugar and cinnamon on top."

"No, I wanna find my brother."

"He'll be back at the house soon, too."

"No, I want my brother now."

Lewis shot off in the direction of the windmill, and Lainie took off after him, her speed no match for his as her footsteps sunk deep in the sloppy ground and her dress hem grew heavy with mud.

The boy crested the small hill a few footsteps ahead of Lainie and came to an immediate stop. Lainie understood why when she caught sight of the image before her.

Devastation.

Surrounding the windmill, at least two dozen cattle lay on their sides. Lifeless.

"Lainie?" Lewis called out. His voice was thin with fear as his eyes affixed on the horror before him.

She gathered the boy to her, unsure whether to force his eyes from the scene or to let him comprehend the image he'd already faced.

The boy hid his face in her skirt, then returned his eyes to the horizon. Mounds of black and white cowflesh, hooves midair, jaws agape. Jake and Peter throwing rocks at each cow's body to differentiate the lifeless from the near dead.

"Perhaps we should go back to the house," Lainie said.

"I'm alright. I've seen worse."

Lainie knew the boy hadn't seen worse. She doubted that many in the world had seen worse.

She pulled him close and whispered in his ear, "Lewis, I don't think your ma or pa would want you to see the cows up close."

The boy sniffled and wiped his eyes with his fists, then with Lainie's apron.

"When Baby Becca died, each of us brothers and sisters got to hold her in our arms." The boy's voice held a quiver. "We got to say goodbye."

Closure. The boy was asking for closure.

Lainie wasn't sure if the site ahead held a future of closure or terrors for the night.

Probably both.

She gritted her teeth. Shut her eyes. Felt the answer in her gut.

"Stay near me. And will you hold my hand? In case I get scared?"

The boy nodded his head, took her hand tight, and shuffled forward.

Nearing the scene, the air grew acrid with the smell of singed flesh. Lainie removed her apron and folded it into long layers to cover the boy's mouth and nose. She tied the cover off at the back of his head then let him continue leading her to the scene.

The first cow they came upon had unusual dark spots on its belly and Lainie wondered if the spots were natural to this cow. As she and the boy continued their inspection, they discovered similar dark spots singed on all the cattle and Lewis questioned if the animals had experienced much pain.

Lainie didn't have an answer.

They walked towards Peter, who had discovered a cow with some life still in it.

"Is she suffering?" Lewis asked.

"Yes," Peter answered. "Jake thinks the others died quick-like. Probably suffered a heart attack from the lightning rushing through the ground."

"Will you have to shoot the cow, Peter?" Lewis looked at his brother with huge eyes. "I don't want you to have to shoot the cow."

"Grow up, Lewis. Of course, I'll have to shoot the cow." The manboy turned away from his little brother. "That's what a man does to keep his animals from suffering."

Peter walked to the windmill and kicked at its base.

"Should have never brought this piece of contraption to the farm," he shouted, kicking at the base with vengeance. "Ain't natural to have metal popping out of the earth."

Jake ran over and pulled Peter from his tirade.

"Hold on, son. You'll break your foot before you make a single dent in that steel."

Jake put his arm around Peter's shoulders and led him a distance away from the carnage.

"I want you and your brother to run on home now. Check on your family. Your farm. Make sure everything is alright."

Peter nodded.

"Tell your folks what happened, that we've got plenty of beef to harvest. If they're able, tell them to bring their tools out and take as much beef as they want. You understand?"

"Yes, sir."

"Now, if everything's calm at your farm, if your ma and pa give you permission, I want you to ride on into town and ring the church bell long and hard. People will know to come to the church. Tell everyone you can that we've got beef to harvest. We've got a lot to do before dark. Can you do this for me, Peter?"

"Of course, I'll do this for you, Jake."

"Good, good. I appreciate your hard work. You're a strong young man. I'm proud of that. Your ma and pa are proud of that. Now go and get your brother. There's no time to waste."

Peter wiped his ragged sleeve against his face.

"One more thing, son. Sometimes tears are good for a man. Don't ever forget that."

* * *

"Jake, there are still animals suffering." Lainie hated to probe the dilemma, but the sound of Jake's silence was almost as unnerving as the sight before them.

"I'll handle things once the boys are farther away."

Lainie nodded her understanding. She dared not reach out to him with words, with touch. She knew he'd push them away.

Instead, she settled on the ground next to the dying cow Peter had discovered. She stroked the cow's neck and whispered a bedtime story to soothe. Jake watched for a moment then turned his eyes to the rest of the quiet herd.

"The rain came on fast. We holed up in the corncrib. We could see the whole lightning storm through the cribslats," Jake said, his voice solemn. "There were huge sparks in the air just south of us. Nothing else in the area to create such sparks, excepting that hunk of metal."

Jake walked to the windmill and ran his hand along the spire of grey. He punched it. Once. Twice. Then he thrashed the tower with his fists and his tirade became bloody and spatters of red painted the metal, Jake's hands, his clothes.

"Stupid thing," he yelled. "You were supposed to save the farm, not ruin it."

Lainie ran to him and pulled him back.

"Stop," she pleaded. "Please, Jake, stop."

She pulled Jake to her and he strained to pull away. She pulled him in harder until her arms ached from the effort. His shoulders, at last, slumped in exhaustion. He buried his eyes on her shoulder.

Several heartbeats later, he whispered, "I can't do this anymore, Lainie."

"I know, Jake, I know," she whispered back. "You can't do this anymore. But *we* can."

* * *

The cow took in, then let loose, one last breath.

"This one's gone now, Jake, I think it's time we help out the rest."

He nodded his agreement. He bit his lip and swallowed hard. "Lainie, there's something you need to know."

"What?" Realization hit hard. "Junior and Miss Priss were out with the herd."

Jake nodded his head.

"I put them out with the herd this morning. I figured with the fence finally complete that she wouldn't be able to wander off."

"Where are they?"

Jake nodded to the backside of the windmill.

Lainie trudged to the spot indicated by Jake, switchbacking past lifeless forms of cowstock. Miss Priss lay still. The rise and fall of her rib cage was labored. Her eyes were glazed over.

The calf stood up and nudged his mother, tried to coax her to move. With each awkward attempt, Junior mewed and snorted. Lainie hugged the calf around its neck and cried into its bristly hide.

Jake removed his suspenders and wrapped them around the calf's neck. He led the calf to a stand of trees off in the distance and tied the makeshift halter to a limb.

When Jake returned to Lainie's side, she was on her knees upon the scorched grass, smoothing her fingers across the bridge of the dying cow's nose.

"We need to do this," he said.

"I know," she replied.

Lainie said her goodbyes and took her place by Jake.

Jake lifted his shotgun and tried to hold it steady as he took aim.

Lainie recognized the tremor in his hands. She placed her hand on his shoulder.

"I'll do this, Jake. You go on back to the house, pick up the supplies we need. I can handle this."

Jake shook his head, shotgun still at the ready. He tried to pull back on the trigger, tried to set the firing pin into action. It wasn't in him. For God's sake, it just wasn't in him. He dropped the gun to his side.

He trembled out words. "Keep the gun loaded. Make sure Bristle stays nearby to warn of danger. Blood is in the air. Who knows what predators loom."

* * *

The townsfolk were grateful for the meat. Menfolk, and in some cases whole families, came out to provide consolation and to accept Jake's offer of bounty from misfortune. The experienced butchered out meat for their own needs, then helped the inexperienced to incise, skin, and portion off the beef.

The work was long, exhausting. The already sloppy field was further muddied with blood and the occasional display of vomit from those less stouthearted to the stench of fresh meat.

Some handed over a small amount of cash to Jake, others promised batches of jam and pickles and corn seed in trade. Jake told them all it wasn't necessary, but knew they'd live up to their word and travel out to the farm for the next few days to repay their unanticipated debt.

The town butcher wrote out an IOU to Jake, offered his thanks, and apologized for his hasty retreat. He needed to hurry back to town. Some folks would end up storing their meat at his butcher shop—his was the only place in town with suspending hooks and ice—or hiring him to smoke the meat. He needed to be ready for the influx of business he was about to receive.

Gawkers and gossips avidly scoured the scene for a tale to spin at the next church picnic. It would have been one thing for them to stand on the fringes of the field, pointing their fingers at episodes of disgust and intrigue, but the worst of the busybodies and newsmongers trounced through the bloodied landscape in gruesome fashion. Two women purposely splashed their skirts with bloodied mud as proof for their fabled stories of animals still alive and kicking. One mother actually swooped up her toddler, set him atop a carcass, and proclaimed she wished a photographer was on hand to capture a tintype.

Then there were the transplants from the city—the Hervey brothers—who plunked their manicured hands into steaming cavities just long enough to touch an intestine and conjure a few beats from a lifeless heart.

That day, of the thirty-five cattle Paul and Snow Owl had purchased during their travels and the dozen cattle the family already owned, forty-one animals were lost. Seven hosted buckshot to the head. Only three ended up in the Adamsen wagon, to be taken home, further butchered out, then smoked or salted or cooked up fresh.

One of them was Miss Priss.

"Lainie," Jake said, "if anybody tries to explain this away, tries to tell you that God works in mysterious ways, you tell them they're full of shit. If God's gonna make something good happen through suffering, it doesn't need to be through blameless animals."

* * *

The remains of carcasses were piled, then burned. The stench of blood and smoke blighted the Adamsen's land for days.

Those days were further blighted by the absence of Paul. Snow Owl didn't know the fate of her husband until three days past the storm.

When Paul walked through the door, long past dusk, Snow Owl flung herself into his arms and cried out, "We are one. We are one."

Jake slipped out the door, not wanting to intrude on the couple's reunion. He held back on shutting the door completely when he saw his cousin place his hand on Snow Owl's belly.

And Jake surprised himself when he realized the smile on his own face.

Jake Adamsen. Smiling. Feeling a hint of gratitude after too many seasons of loss.

* * *

287

"Thought you'd be celebrating your return with a little moonlight serenade," Jake said as Paul joined him on the log bench by the campfire.

"Trust me, Cuz, Snow Owl and I will be serenading the moonlight in the very near future."

"Soon enough that stomach of hers is going to get in the way."

"She and I will have to get creative then."

"I suppose you will."

Jake set aside the whetstone he'd been using and pulled a second one from a bucket of water. He continued sharpening his knife against the finer grit of the second stone. Each raspy stroke trailed into the night's song.

"Snow Owl told me about the lightning storm and the cattle."

"I figured she would."

"Over in Asotin, Tim Wessman's sheep got spooked by thunder and broke through the corral. The whole herd ran in the storm and fell off an embankment to their deaths. Coming into Leeds, I saw that Harriet and Lawrence Thompson's barn went up in flames. They lost their entire crop of hay."

"This certainly has been the year of storms," Jake replied.

"The year of storms," Paul repeated, knowing Jake was meaning more than weather.

"Jake, as far as the windmill goes, I've never heard of such happening before. You've got to know that. Steel windmills are popping up all over Texas, and I've . . ."

"Steel windmill, wooden windmill, it doesn't matter what kind of windmill was in that field, Paul. It could have been an apple tree with all the cows tucked underneath. That lightning strike was bound and determined to hit something. It did its job and then some. So, don't take on any blame. There's nothing we can do about it, there's no way we could have prevented it, end of story."

"Is it the end of the story, Jake? Are we done trying to get into the cattle business?"

"I don't see that we can stay in it."

"And I don't see that we can't stay in it, Jake. We've worked at it too long. Too long and too hard." Paul pounded his fist against his leg. "I've got Snow Owl to think about, a baby on the way. Somehow I've got to make this cattle business happen."

"How, Paul? We've got six cows left, and one of them's a barely-weaned calf with a huge zigzag mark burned across its side. We lost the bull in the lightning storm, our funds are dried up, and I'm tired of . . ."

Jake hesitated, not wanting to form the words.

"Just spill it out. You're tired of what?"

"Nothing. You're right. We've got to make this work for Snow Owl, for your baby, for Mother, for . . ."

"You can say her name, Jake. It's obvious she's part of this family now."

"She'll be leaving in the spring. I promised to pay her way back east." Jake said. "We have to make this farm and our cattle business work so I can keep my promise to Lainie."

Hidden Treasure
Leeds, Idaho — February 1891

Jake rode his Palouse to the edge of the garden where Lainie pulled at winter weeds.

"You're not taking part in the monthly Scuttlebutt Seamstress Society?" he asked.

She stood, straightened her back, and stretched. "So that's the latest name for your mother's quilting group. I wondered when you'd tire of calling them The Fabulous Flibbertigibbets."

"It's a new year. I figure a new name is in order."

"Your smart-alecking is going to land you in a heap of trouble, Jake Adamsen. You know that, right?"

"A man's gotta have a hobby. So, what led you on this chilly exodus to the far corner of the weed patch?"

"Better to pull this garden's weeds than to shovel that group's pile of you know what."

"So true. So true."

Lainie walked to the mare and rubbed its ears. The horse snorted and nudged its nose at Lainie's skirt pocket where she expected to find an apple or two.

"Sorry, Iya, no apples today. My apologies. I didn't know I'd be seeing you."

"I don't think she believes you," Jake said with a laugh as the horse checked out a second skirt pocket.

"Hey," Lainie exclaimed, twisting away from the horse. She grabbed a handful of dandelion leaves from the ground and offered the snack to Iya.

"How did you come up with your horse's name?" Lainie asked.

"Snow Owl came up with her name. When she saw the horse speed across the field, she called her Iyalásasa, which in Nimiipuu means to soar like a bird." The horse whinnied, as if in approval of her name.

"We shortened it to Iya when little Jackson pretended to be the horse and kept calling out, 'Iya horsie. Iya horsie.'"

"That's adorable," Lainie said, surprised at Jake's openness in sharing the story about his son, then disappointed when he quickly moved on to a new topic.

"The windowed-in garden frames seem to be working out well," he said.

Lainie nodded. "Some plants have done better than others. Some failed miserably. It's surprising how much warmer the soil is within the frames. I planted pea seeds a few days ago. I'm not sure how they'll do with the weather so cold, but there's a chance your family will have fresh peas for Easter dinner."

Jake noticed the reference. *Your family*. He supposed leaving was on her mind with a long-craved stretch of springtime just a few weeks in the distance.

Lainie cringed at the strained silence that had once again settled between her and Jake. They could quip, joke, and banter. They could argue like bobcats. But the two of them still couldn't hold a simple conversation. In truth, conversation had become so difficult between them that a few weeks earlier Jake had moved out of the house and into a tiny, cold building that Miss Jayne and her husband had lived in when they first settled the land. Jake's sudden departure from the house confirmed her need to soon be moving on.

She kept her eyes focused on the horse, hoping Jake would say something to fill the void. His words never came.

"Guess I'd better get back to weeding then," Lainie finally mumbled and walked back to her shovel and hoe.

"Come with me?" Jake blurted. "I mean, if you want to take a break, you could come with me. I just finished checking the cows. Thought I'd take a ride up the canyon. Come with me."

"I don't know," Lainie said as she scrutinized Jake's sheepish grin. "There's so much to do, and this is the first lasting sunshine we've had in a few days."

"Precisely why we should take some time to actually enjoy it." Jake held out his hand. "Come on, we won't be gone long."

Lainie looked at all the work around her. Snow had stopped weeds from growing for a time, but since the weather had warmed and the snow had disappeared, the garden was filling in with chickweed and catchweed and at least half a dozen other weeds she couldn't put a name to. She really needed to get the gardening under control. But a horseback ride in the sunshine away from the house, from work, from worries—the invitation was too good to pass up. She grabbed her heavy coat from where she'd draped it across the fence, slipped it on over her sweater, and took Jake's hand.

He hoisted her up onto the horse. Seated behind him, the best way to anchor herself was to hold Jake around his waist. She was shocked to realize she was both glad and frustrated that two heavy coats separated them.

* * *

The sun lazily arced out its rays and the softening snowline left miniature, majestic lakes on the meadow. A solitary blue heron ever so slowly stalked one stretch of water. More birds welcomed the spring-like day. Swans glided past the high skim of clouds, their bugled calls resonating across the expanse of blue sky. Red-breasted nuthatches and black-capped chickadees flitted about, piping their songs as they searched plants for last summer's seeds. Once Jake and Lainie reached the wide canyon, Jake pointed out an owl, seemingly unperturbed by daytime's light, watching them from a huge cottonwood tree.

"It's beautiful," Lainie whispered, allowing her head to rest against Jake's back.

A few minutes later Lainie realized she was dozing. The gentle sway of the horse, the warmth of being nestled against Jake, it all felt so good.

Foolish girl, she silently reprimanded herself. *Snap out of it. This is Jake. This is momentary. This isn't real.*

"Does this canyon have a name?" she asked, trying to change her course of thinking.

"Depends on who you talk to. Back before white settlers came to this land, the Nimiipuu called the area Mitáu mimiógat, The Three Kings, in honor of the three hills you see in the distance. When settlers started buying up the land, they claimed its name was Whitetail Canyon due to the numerous whitetail deer in the area, and that's what most folks call it today."

"What do you call it?"

"I know it as Kuléuit Canyon. That's the name Hannah came up with. Kuléuit."

292

Jake fell silent. Lainie understood why. She was sure this was a place Hannah had loved.

"Kuléuit is the Nimiipuu word for evening," Jake continued. "That was my wife's favorite time of day to wander through this area, when the sun exaggerates the shadows of the trees. And over there," he pointed westward, "just beyond that ridgeline, the changing sky puts on one hell of a show."

They continued their travel silently until they approached a two-story cabin still in the process of being built.

"Whose cabin is this?" Lainie asked.

Jake helped Lainie slip off the horse. He dismounted and tied the reins to a tree branch.

"It's mine." He shrugged. "The cabin is mine."

"But you already have a cabin."

"Hannah and I stayed on with my mother after my father passed away. We were newly married, had little money of our own, and found ourselves expecting a baby due just ten months after our wedding day. It made sense to stay on the farm, work the land, help Mother out." He led the way to the front porch. "In time, we earned enough money to buy this land and build this cabin, bit by bit. We built the cabin big enough that Mother would have her own room. The plan was to move in, then use her cabin as a bunk house for hired hands. Once our cattle operation got big enough to need hired hands, that is."

Lainie judged the cabin to be large enough for a growing family, but not so large that space was frivolous. There was a covered front porch with a windowed loft that centered two-thirds of the building. From the front porch, a wide, arched entry was flanked by six-pane windows. There was room underneath the porch to store firewood, and Jake—or perhaps his wife—had dressed the porch with a fine-looking rocker.

They walked up the steps. From the front porch, Jake pointed to a section of land completely cleared of trees.

"That southwest portion of the property will be for a vegetable garden. We clear cut the area and used a good portion of the timber for the porch and entryway," he explained.

Inside, the cabin felt colder than the outdoors and Lainie shivered from the unexpected change in temperature.

Jake noticed Lainie pull her coat sleeves past her fingertips. He took off his gloves and slipped them onto her hands, then offered to build a fire in the fireplace.

"I just finished setting the hearthstones a couple of days ago." He kneeled next to the fireplace, inspected the surface of the stones, and gave a nod of satisfaction. "Moisture from the mortar is probably making the room feel extra cold. That, and we don't have the sun warming us the same as outdoors."

While Jake slipped outside to gather deadwood for the fire, Lainie explored the room. She ran her gloved hand across a rounded wall beam and along a crevice of chinking, marveling how the smoothness of the timber and the roughness of the mortar merged to create something so strong, so secure.

The ceiling and the floor were a matched set of planks the color of comb honey. Lainie guessed the eight rounded beams spaced across the ceiling were ten, maybe twelve feet long. It must have taken sheer grit and might and tenacity to secure the beams in place.

Boulders, amassed into a handsome fireplace, were engraved by wind and rain and heat and ice, and now they would stand as protectors from those very elements.

It was a storyteller's home, filled with the balladry of the land.

She wondered which rocks and beams had been placed by Jake in happier times when hope filled his horizon in the form of two children and a loving wife. She studied the fireplace and realized the cruel twist of fate that its hearth—the symbol of home and comfort—had been set by a mourner's hands.

How many other elements in the home had Jake constructed over the past few days? Weeks? Months? Had this cabin been the place he'd turned to when the weight of grief and misfortune was too big a burden to carry?

Jake walked in with the firewood and built a fire while Lainie explored the kitchen and the bedrooms.

"Thank you for building the fire. It feels warmer in here already. And your cabin is beautiful, Jake. Simply beautiful."

He stammered out a thank you and quickly turned his attention back to the fire.

"May I sit on the hearth?" she asked. "Or does the mortar need more time to dry?"

He checked the raised hearth for stability. "Seems fine," he said and motioned for her to sit down.

Lainie sat on the hearth next to where Jake knelt on the floor. She slipped off the gloves and held her hands close to the warmth of the flames. From the corner of her eye, she watched this towering man of strength, of determination, of weakness, of grief. She watched how he studied the fire and how his eyes darkened and how his face aged as the flames danced across glowing embers. She turned away when his features turned brittle, as if fate had ensnarled him in a bitter winter storm.

She supposed fate had done just that.

In time, Jake aimlessly nudged the burning logs with one of the sticks he'd brought in as kindling. Lainie chanced a look in his direction and dared not decipher the subtle yet remarkable change crossing his face.

A flush of warmth slowly returned to his skin. Reflections from the flames flecked color to his eyes. Wavering light spilled pleasing shadows across his stubbled jaw, his cheeks.

When the end of the stick caught fire, he blew out the fresh flames and watched the wisps of smoke as they swirled into the air.

"I have a timber in mind for use as a mantel." Jake murmured, his eyes still focused on the fire. "I spotted it just the other day. Would you like to see it?"

He paused, then finally looked into her eyes. "It means going back outside when you were just starting to get warm. We don't have to go."

"I don't mind. When we come back in, we'll appreciate the fire's warmth even more."

Jake led her outside and to the back of his property. He held her hand, once again gloved, and they crossed the uneven ground and stepped over boulders and downed tree limbs as they walked several feet through the stand of evergreens.

As they walked, he described how the purple camas lilies of spring would soon dot the land.

"Snow Owl will be happy to teach you how to harvest and cook camas bulbs," he added.

He also spoke of orange hawkweed. "You'll enjoy its spark of color, but it's got meddlesome ways." He described purple lupines as swaying dancers that are gone too soon and paintbrush as prairie fire you never want to douse.

"Balsamroots are my favorite flower of the land," he said. "When you spot them lined up along the canyon's rim, you'll see how they weave the grass and the sun."

Lainie spotted a six-inch pine cone on the ground and scooped it up. Jake gave her an amused look, to which she smiled and said, "Just a little keepsake."

They turned to quiet, each lost in their own thoughts until Jake stopped and pointed to a white pine. "This is it," he said. "Stand closer to the tree trunk and look upwards. About twenty feet up you'll see a huge burl in the trunk."

He stood behind her and softly gripped her forearms to position her closer to the tree. He pointed to an area of dense green and they both visually searched through the tree's limbs. Sure enough, a fat, round knob protruded from the trunk.

"It looks like the burl grows from the outside of the tree. In truth it grows from the inside," Jake explained. He realized how close he stood to Lainie, how natural it was to feel her arms beneath his hands. His chin brushed against the scarf she wore over her hair and he had a sudden desire to smooth his fingers over the dark curls that fell across her shoulder. He let go and stepped away from her, then cleared his throat as he refocused on their conversation. "A burl starts growing because that spot on the tree has been injured. Maybe from an arrow hitting it, maybe from a gunshot. Could be some natural source caused a problem, like a broken limb or burrowing insects. The burl is the tree's attempt to scar over and protect itself."

Lainie repositioned herself to see the burl from a different vantage point.

"How in the world did you spot the burl in the midst of all these trees?" she asked.

He shrugged. "I suppose someone needed me to see what a scar's beauty is all about."

She looked at him quizzically.

"Never mind. It's a long story. The point is, once we cut the tree down and mill it out, you'll see these beautiful twists and striations deep in the wood."

Lainie's eyes lit up. "Like a hidden treasure!"

"Yes, like a hidden treasure."

The Dance
Leeds, Idaho — April 1891

"How many pies are you baking for this shindig?" Paul asked. "Any chance you're saving a couple of them for tonight's supper table."

"Don't worry, we'll save you a pumpkin pie for home," Miss Jayne said. "And stop snitching the pie dough."

Paul waved his hand in front of her eyes. "Landamighty, I swear you can see my every move."

"I just know your every move from years of raising you."

He reached for another scrap of pie dough and Miss Jayne playfully slapped his hand.

"How in the world do you do that?" he asked, feigning serious injury.

"Face it, Cuz, Mama's some sort of soothsayer when it comes to protecting her cooking from your grubby paws."

"My paws aren't grubby. Ask Lainie. She watched me wash them."

"I sure did," Lainie said. "Last week."

"Ha ha. You just wait. When you need someone to save you from some bungler on the dancefloor, I'm simply gonna laugh," Paul teased.

"You'll be too busy dancing with your wife, silly," Lainie countered. "Besides, I won't be going to the dance."

"Malarky. Everyone in this town goes to the Spring Mingle. Last time I was around for the dance, the Donovan sisters lived in town. Remember them, Miss Jayne? Twin sisters that took over the teaching post from Ms. Winthrop?"

Snow Owl groaned as she cradled their baby boy in her arms. "You and your stories."

"And each one of my stories is legendary. Right Jake?"

Jake slapped his cousin on the back. "You're absolutely right, Cuz. I'm always so proud that you're a legend in your own mind."

297

"I spose' that's all that counts," Paul countered. "Now Jake, you sit down and hush up. This is a whopper of a story you'll wish was your own."

"Here it comes," Jake moaned.

"Back in the day, there was always more menfolk than ladies at these dances, so it was pretty much a guarantee that the gals would dance every dance." Paul let out a whoop. "We'd bounce the ladies around the dance floor from sunup to sundown."

"I'm not sure I want to hear this," Lainie said as she rolled her eyes.

"Of course, you want to hear this, so listen up. At this particular dance, since Jake had abandoned me for marital bliss, I showed up with the work crew from Harriet and Lawrence Thompson's place."

"Seven cowhands, two left legs apiece, all starved for attention," Jake said.

"Don't matter how clumsy we were, it only matters that we each danced every dance. And we showed the Donovan sisters that a small town hoodang is mighty more fun than those fancy city cotillions they were accustomed to."

Jake leaned over and whispered to Lainie. "Here comes the part where the legend makes a name for himself."

"That's right, Jake. I did indeed make a name for myself that night. Six months of planning, a couple of practice sessions on an abandoned shack, and just the right amount of foolhardiness was all I needed to pull off the best prank in this town's history."

Jake rubbed his forehead as if thoughts of Paul's story pained him.

"Me and one of the boys escorted the Donovan sisters home, safe and sound," Paul continued. "The mayor and his wife followed behind in their wagon, chaperoning us the whole time. We were perfect gentlemen, of course. After we delivered the ladies to their front door, we said our goodbyes, headed back to town in our wagon, then our crew returned to their cabin around one in the morning.

"Now that cabin was maybe ten-foot square in size, with its perch from the front door overlooking the prettiest sunsets you ever could see. My buddies and me, we pulled out our lariats, tied them around the cabin, and jerry-rigged the lariats with ropes to our horses. Once we had everything in place, we used pure horsepower to lift that cabin and spin it around, so it now faced eastward. The girls never woke up once."

"You're joshin' me, right?" Lainie asked. "There's no way you could do that."

Miss Jayne chimed in. "Those girls woke up the next morning, stepped outside to head for the privy, and had no idea where they were at. 'Tweren't the landscape they were expecting."

"Nah, can't be," Lainie said. "I know you're all making this up."

"It's all true, every last word," Paul said. "Ask Charlotte Wittenberg yourself, four farms up. She's the schoolmarm sister who took a shine to the buddy who helped me come up with the plan. They married, bought the old McKinnley place, and have a second youngster on the way."

* * *

"Miss Jayne, I have no interest in attending this dance." Lainie set three wooden boxes on the kitchen table, tucked straw in the bottom of each, then nestled jars of apple cider into the straw. "Besides, the fewer people who see me, the less likely McNally is to find me."

"It has been eight months since you arrived. And I refuse to believe that this McNally man continues to look for you," Miss Jayne said. "You are a beautiful young woman. At nearly eighteen years old, you should be going to dances and socials, meeting young men, and gossiping with young ladies instead of baking bread and darning socks with this old woman."

"First," Lainie protested, "I have no interest in gossiping with young ladies when you and Irene keep me perfectly posted of the goings-on in town. And, by the way, you are certainly not old."

Miss Jayne passed the baked pies to Lainie to stack on top of the cider.

"Second, by your very words I should be cautious of the young men in town, for in your postings you and Irene have portrayed them to be young, brutish sorts who have only three missions in life: to go about seeking a pretty girl's smile, to bum a hunk of apple pie, or to lollygag at the general store."

Lainie settled clean towels over the pies.

"And third, we both know that as soon as the weather warms more, I should be moving on."

"You're wrong, Lainie. You belong here. You belong with us."

299

"Miss Jayne, I know that I belong far away from you." Lainie grasped the woman's hand. "Far from where I can bring you or Jake harm. If McNally found me here with you and Jake, well, you can't imagine what sorts of things that man can do. Worse yet, what his wife can do."

"No more talk of those awful people. You're going to the dance with us."

Two hours later, Lainie lost the battle with Miss Jayne.

"No sense beatin' the devil around the stump," Jake said. "The iron's hot and ready to go."

Lainie groaned, leaned over, spread her hair across the ironing board, and waited for Jake to press her hair straight.

* * *

"Settle down, folks. Settle down," Heller Bayern hollered from the makeshift bandstand to the crowd. "We all know the annual Spring Mingle is our last chance to visit and dance before good weather and full-on farm chores completely take over our days."

Heller waited for the crowd's cheers to quiet before announcing thanks to all the townsfolk who contributed food, time, and talent to make the evening a success.

"Folks," he continued, "We've been holding this dance for longer than I can remember and The River Creek Band sure puts on a good show, so let's give them a round of applause."

Anton Bauer, along with two other gentleman and two ladies stepped forward with their instruments and took a bow.

"One of the River Creek band members hasn't played in public for a while," Heller announced. "Leastwise not in front of a fancy crowd like this. But he's here tonight with a song he wrote hisself. So, let's give a proud howdy-do to our very own Jake Adamsen."

Jake walked to the front of the room amid applause and good-natured slaps on the shoulder.

At the back of the room, Lainie and Jake's family stood among friends and were surprised to learn that Jake was about to perform.

Jake picked up a guitar from the stage, positioned its strap over his shoulder, and checked the tuning. When he was satisfied with the tone of the guitar, he mustered a voice that all could hear.

"Tonight, I want to share a song that I wrote for someone very special in my life," he said. "You never know how the companionship of a woman can improve your days, how her cooking can brighten the morning, or how her suppertime prayer can warm your heart. I'm hoping this song captures all this because, well, this girl . . ." His voice cracked and he nervously looked down. "This woman, well, she means the world to me. This song captures how every memory of her is making me stronger."

He played an introduction with sweet strains, lilting and mellow. When his voice reached for the first words, he faltered, paused, then began the song again.

Lainie stood waiting, one hand clasped in Miss Jayne's, anticipation rippling through her mind. She sensed Miss Jayne felt the same as she watched her son take this giant step towards reclaiming his life.

When Jake's voice finally filled the room, she tried to collect his words, preserve his lines, archive his chorus, so she could retell his song should he need to be reminded of his own healing verse.

There's no escaping yesterday,
Tomorrow's gonna come;
Words unfound, words unsaid,
Make me come undone.
But somehow on the darkest days
Sunlight lands on you,
And when I fear I've lost my way
Your dawn comes shining through.

Our fates, they met in summertime,
We struggled through our fall,
The icy winds of winter
Threatened to take all.
And now I melt into your spring,
The tempest leaves my space,
I'm earning back my seasons
To love my Lady Grace.

Lainie had felt Hannah's presence the many times she had visited the family plot. She had felt Hannah's presence at other places on the farm, too. And now, with Jake's song filling the air, she felt Hannah's presence stronger than ever. She pictured how Jake's eyes must have lit up as he walked into the cabin to be with his family after a long, hard day. She pictured his wife bringing him a tall glass of water, then tipping the brim of his hat and leaning in for a kiss. She pictured how his jawline would relax. How his shoulder strain would ease. How he'd run his hand along his wife's spine as they embraced.

She was so caught up in images of Jake during happier times that she missed part of his song. As she concentrated on the final verse, guilt washed over her, for the images now playing in her head were not of Hannah, but of herself. Instead of imagining Hannah brush her fingers across the stubble on Jake's cheek, the fingers were her own. It wasn't Hannah who slid into his arms or laughed at his jokes or touched her lips to his. Lainie had slipped herself into a daydream that wasn't hers to own.

"Stop," she whispered out loud, though no one heard her as Jake sang the last line of his song: *Yes, I'm earning back my seasons so I can love my sweet Lady Grace.*

When the last strum of his guitar held in the air and no words were said and no motion was made, Lainie returned to reality and her heart broke. The crowd simply stood as they watched Jake remove the strap of the guitar from his shoulder and set the guitar on the stage.

She watched him move off the stage and try to lose himself in the crowd. At last, one person began to clap. Her applause was followed by that of another and then another. Soon the room roared with appreciation. All eyes remained on Jake as he made his way to the back of the room. He received embraces and congratulations along the way.

Jake's skin glistened with sweat when he rejoined his mother and her group of friends.

"So, Mama, what'd you think?" he asked as he gave her a hug.

"Words can't describe, Jake. Words can't describe."

"Your pa would be so proud of you and your song," Mr. Levine said as he shook Jake's hand.

"Thanks. I felt him there, up on that stage. It felt good."

"Jake, you had all of us ladies melting on the dance floor," Irene said as she slipped her tiny grandson into Paul's arms.

"I didn't see anyone dancing while I was up there," he replied. "I was sure hoping everyone'd keep their eyes on their dance partners and not on me."

"Who could dance?" Irene exclaimed. "We were all mesmerized by your song, weren't we Lainie?"

Lainie avoided the question by turning her attention to little Margarete, who was tugging at her mother's skirt.

"Looks like folks are out there dancing now. Mama, would you mind if I take Lainie out for a whirl?"

"You'd better, before some other young man comes to sweep her off her feet," Miss Jayne said. "Lainie has been the belle of the ball."

"So I noticed," Jake said. "So I noticed."

He held out his hand and her face became the moon, pale and searching. The immediate retreat in his eyes and the slight drop of his hand when she didn't respond to his gesture sent the guilt and confusion and disgust over her newly recognized feelings into a whirlwind.

"It's only a dance," he assured, and she gave a small puff of laughter before she awkwardly took his hand in hers.

"Have you mastered the schottische yet?" he asked as he led her to the dancefloor.

"Hardly," she said, a cringe on her face. "I've injured at least three dance partners who have tried to teach me."

"Guess I'll be the fourth victim."

As they danced their way into the center of the crowd, Lainie and Jake both laughed at her missteps.

"I think I'm more suited for the two-step," Lainie called out, wondering if she'd ever master this German folkdance.

When the song ended and the guitar strums began something soft and sweet, Lainie turned in retreat, knowing a waltz with Jake was an unlikely thing.

He held out his hand. "Don't leave just yet."

She half smiled, found her courage, and placed her hand on his shoulder. Jake's hand fell to rest on the small of her back. She pinched her lips tight for fear that the kaleidoscope of butterfly wings flitting inside her would burst forth and fill the room.

They danced quietly, shyly, neither secure enough to look at the other. The excruciating silence between her and Jake tripped up her feet. She stepped on Jake's foot then backed into Judge Greely.

"I'm so sorry," she fumbled.

The old man laughed. "It's fine. Nothing a month in a splint won't fix."

Jake reclaimed her hand in his—claimed her eyes, too—and continued the dance.

Lainie's mind searched for a way to build a wall, to uncoil her dizzying spiral of feelings, to stop her unconscionable betrayal to Hannah's ghost.

"The song you wrote, that you sang . . ." She broke eye contact. "It was lovely, Jake. Quite lovely. I can't imagine a more fitting tribute to your wife."

He stopped dancing and stared at her. "It wasn't a song for my wife. This song was meant for someone else that I love."

Eyes locked again. Breaths mingled. He stepped back and kissed her hand.

"Thank you for the dance, Lainie."

With that, he was gone.

Lainie stood in the middle of the dance floor, defiant to believe the words she'd just heard. When the music stopped and she realized she was the only one on the dance floor without a partner, she raced through the room, following Jake's path through the crowd to the main door.

Outside, she gulped in cold air and searched for Jake. In the distance, a bonfire blazed, and men stood around drinking warm liquor and telling old jokes. Wagons were scattered around the building, waiting for their owners to make claim and return home. She weaved around the wagons towards their own, hoping Jake might be there. The Adamsen wagon sat empty, the horses pawing at the cold ground, eager for their evening oats. Lainie moved to O'Malley's side, hugged his neck, and buried her face in his mane.

Sparking Season

The ride back home was long, strained. The tension between Lainie and Jake was interrupted by Miss Jayne's constant banter.

"The dance was absolutely marvelous, wasn't it? Millie Crawford's pies were simply lackluster in taste compared to yours, Lainie. Wasn't Phillip Kershaw a garish showboat, swelling with pride over that suit he claims is from New York City?"

On and on she went, spilling out tidbits of gossip that would last until harvest. Lainie blocked most of it out, knowing she'd hear it again and again over the next few days. She looked off into the distance, replaying Jake's song and their dance in her mind.

"And tomorrow, Chivalry Day will be even more exciting than tonight's dance, won't it, Lainie?" The woman's odd question brought the girl back to the present.

"What exactly is Chivalry Day?" Lainie asked.

"Why, all of the young men you danced with tonight will be vying for your attention," Miss Jayne said.

"Excuse me?"

"In the old days we called it Courting Day, but a few years ago Martha Winston came up with the idea to change the name to Chivalry Day. The eligible gentlemen you danced with tonight will prove their courtesy and generosity by performing kind tasks for you. You and that Crawford girl will have plenty of excitement as the young men come to pay their visits to both of you."

"You mean those boys I danced with tonight might be stopping at the cabin tomorrow?" Lainie asked.

"Of course, it's all a part of sparking season."

"Sparking season? Jake, she's funnin' me, right?"

"Nope."

"You mean this is really going to happen?"

"Mmm hmmm."

"And I have no say in the matter?" Lainie asked.

"You can always kick them out," Jake said.
"I'll gladly borrow your sharpest pair of boots."

* * *

Lainie grimaced at the crystal vase filled with flowers. Miss Jayne had insisted that each daffodil presented to Lainie by one of her suitors be tucked into the vase for display on the kitchen table.

"That table and those flowers are all signs of fresh beginnings," the woman had said when Lainie groaned her objections.

Miss Jayne had brimmed with positivity all day long and Lainie was quite tired of it. Happy words were one thing, but this overfussed, sugarbeet sweetness to entice Lainie into choosing one of the local suitors for the purpose of matrimonial bliss was archaically insane.

Lainie snatched the daffodils from the vase, stomped out into the fading light of the front porch, and flung the flowers over the railing. A dozen or so daffodils hit Jake in the face as he rounded the corner of the cabin.

"Whoa," he exclaimed. "A man's not allowed to enter his own home without being whacked by a bunch of flowers?"

Lainie shot him a savage look, grabbed the broom from the corner, and began sweeping the porch with a vengeance.

"You've had an eventful day," Jake said. "Seven suitors in one day. That must be a Chivalry Day record."

"Very funny."

She swept harder, avoiding his teasing smile.

From the corner of her eye, she watched him stroll to the stairway, set a bucket and a lantern on the ground, then lean on the railing.

"Miss Jayne's not going to be happy that your herd of men destroyed her daffodil patch."

"Miss Jayne can't complain. It's her fault that they showed up in the first place."

She stopped sweeping.

"And you! You, mister, are in double trouble with me."

"Why am I in trouble?" Jake asked.

"You should have warned me about what was going on. Had I known a bunch of foolish, lovesick puppies would show up after the dance, I would have never attended it. Sparking season—whoever heard of such a thing?"

306

"You poor thing, being chased around by a bunch of eligible bachelors."

"More like eligible nincompoops."

Jake climbed the stairs and ambled towards her, hands in pockets, his grin a mile wide. He leaned into her as she continued sweeping and whispered into her ear, "Personally, I think you enjoyed all the attention."

She swung around and whacked the broom against his shins.

"No, as a matter of fact, I did not enjoy the attention."

He backed across the porch as she kept swinging the broom at him.

"I did not enjoy making small talk, I did not enjoy putting on a fake smile, and I did not enjoy feigning interest in their attempts to glorify themselves in front of each other. It was like watching roosters spar at an etiquette class."

"Well, I sure appreciate all the attention you got." Jake said. "Your suitors finished up a large chunk of work around here. I don't remember those windows ever having such a shine, I swear Daniel gave the chimney a spit polish, and the Schneider twins beat a good acre of dirt from those throw rugs. Fine soil like that will come in handy during planting season."

"I'm certainly glad you've gained from my agony. Now get those dirty boots off my clean porch."

She swept her way across the path he had walked, sweeping him and his mud-caked boots down the stairs.

Jake playfully grabbed the broom from her hands.

"So, you're saying that receiving a bunch of pretty flowers was downright torturous, huh?"

"Yes. And foolhardy. Seems foolish to give a lady something that's gonna die in a few days. I mean, if you want to show you're sparking for someone, wouldn't you want to give her something that will last, that she can put her eyes on and enjoy for a time?"

"You are positively right."

"Darn it, Jake, whenever I see that lopsided grin of yours, I know you're laughing at me or funnin' me."

"Not true. I absolutely think that what you just said makes sense."

"What I just said makes sense," she repeated skeptically. "Jake Adamsen, you're up to something and I'm in no mood to fall prey to one of the Adamsen boys' infamous pranks."

"I swear neither of us is prankin' you, Lainie." He set the broom aside and leaned down to pull an old tin can from the bucket he'd been carrying.

"Here, this is for you."

Lainie reluctantly took the tin can, expecting some critter to pop out at her.

"Dirt. You just handed me a tin can filled with dirt."

"That's more than just dirt. I threw in some coffee grounds and some crushed up eggshells to fertilize the soil. Figured it'd be a bit more romantic than mixing the dirt with cow dung."

"Romantic?" Lainie became even more wary of being pranked.

"In case you haven't noticed, there is a plant growing in that soil."

Her eyes darted back and forth between Jake and the contents inside the can.

"A plant? You mean those twigs in the center are a plant?"

Jake gave her a sheepish grin.

"I dug up a lilac start from the bush outside the kitchen window. That bush grew from the start Mama brought all the way from Iowa. It came from her mama's own lilac bush."

Jake planted his boot on the porch step and braced his hand on his knee.

"Gads, I'm lumping my words into a bungling mess," he said with a groan. "Look, Lainie. My gift's not fancy. I ain't got none of those fancy pots like Timberman sells from his wagon, so I emptied out rusty nails from an old tin can so I'd have something to plant this, this—" He raked his hand through his hair. "And right now, it looks like a mess of twigs that'll amount to nothing. But from nothing, it will grow into something. Something that is good. Something that will last."

"Jake, are you—wait, you're not trying to be part of this chivalry stuff, are you?"

He blushed.

"Are you?"

"I thought maybe you could plant the bush outside the kitchen window at my home—at what would be our home—down the canyon."

Lainie wrapped her arms around the tin can and sat down on the front step as she puzzled through Jake's words.

Jake paced in front of her, his hands in his pockets.

"I don't have slick words like Daniel Winston, or a fancy house in town like Phillip Kershaw can offer you. What I do have is a good home on rich soil, a family that adores you, and—"

She glanced up to catch his hesitated words.

"My heart. Lainie, you have my heart."

"Jake," she whispered.

"Don't say it."

"Jake, you've got to know."

"Don't say it."

"Jake, I've been looking over my shoulder for so long that I haven't allowed myself to think on that kind of future. I haven't allowed myself to think on any kind of future."

He nodded his understanding, retrieved the lantern from the ground, and walked off into the night.

Once he was out of earshot, she made her confession to the stars. "Since last night, all of what I just said is a huge lie."

* * *

The next morning, the tin can with the lilac twig sat atop the kitchen table with one of Miss Jayne's doilies tucked underneath.

New Girl in Town

Her first steps into a mercantile since leaving Montana nearly eight months previous left Lainie dazed with elation. The jangle of the shopkeeper's bell as she opened the door, the scent of cardamom and cinnamon and mace, the banter of two old men as they played a game of checkers at a corner table—who knew such luxuries could delight her so?

"May I help you miss?"

A young man around twenty-five or so approached.

"I have a list of things to pick up for Jayne Adamsen."

"Oh, yes, you're the young woman that's been helping out at the Adamsen place. We briefly met at the dance."

"We danced, didn't we?" She cocked her head and smiled. "Your face is so familiar, but for the life of me, I don't recall your name. I'm sorry. There were so many new faces and names that night."

"I'm Mr. Hamilton. C.F. Hamilton. Charles Franklin Hamilton. I'm rambling." He shrugged. "Most folks call me C.F."

"Well, C.F., could you point me in the direction of stationery supplies? I promised Jake I'd pick up a pocket notebook for him. Plus, I have a few items we need for the larder."

"I'd be happy to fill your list while you look around."

"Thank you, that would be wonderful."

He backed away from her, his eyes still focused on her face, and promptly collided with a counter topped with jars of peppermint sticks and black licorice.

"I'll be right . . . it will be no time at all to fill your . . . I'll get right to your list," C.F. stammered.

Lainie held back her amusement at the attention she was being paid. If only poor Mr. C.F. Hamilton knew that, just as quickly as she had become part of societal courting, she had been swiftly whisked away from it.

Jake Adamsen loved her. And she was beginning to accept that she loved him back.

* * *

With the mercantile boxes loaded, Lainie further explored Leeds. It certainly lacked the hustle and bustle of Wallace, where wagons and coaches careened through town, tearing up muck and mud and menace. No, Leeds was laid back. Easy feeling. Like a sigh on the breeze. Along the boarded sidewalk, she allowed herself to peer through windows and wave at faces she recognized from Friday's dance. The menfolk were quick to provide a greeting. The women took a bit longer to warm up to Lainie. She wasn't sure why, though she suspected it had to do with sparking season and the town's bounty of single men as opposed to its limited number of young women of similar matrimonial circumstance. All the same, she enjoyed her conversations and wanted someday to be fully be welcome in this town.

Earlier that morning, when Miss Jayne had suggested that Lainie should head into town on her own, she had protested the idea with every argument she could muster. Each protest had been blocked by Miss Jayne's notion that since she'd been formally introduced into society at the dance, she needed to better make acquaintance with the townfolk.

Lainie interpreted the woman's words as "go and find yourself a husband so you'll live in Leeds forever."

She had turned to Jake for alliance and her heart flung into her throat when he agreed with his mother.

"A trip alone will do you good," he'd said. "Give you time to settle into town and think about the future without the weight of farm chores on your shoulders."

She grimaced at his words. It wasn't the weight of farm chores he was worried about. It was the weight of his evening confession two nights previous.

My heart. Lainie, you have my heart.

Jake's words had enchanted her ever since, unfolding like tender snowdrops from winter's frozen ground.

Yet, warranted or not, she feared Jake's words and dreams and aspirations for their future would be trampled underfoot by the man with the limp.

* * *

After visiting Doc and Emmeline at their home, where Emmeline treated Lainie to a piece of custard pie, Lainie walked to the end of the street where a farrier trimmed and shoed a horse's hooves. The man was quick in his duties and the horse was content with its bucket of grain.

A wave of homesickness flooded over Lainie as she pictured her grandfather performing the same task. How she missed that man, with his tall tales and teasing smile. How she missed watching him talk to the horses as he checked their eyes, their teeth, their gait. As he diagnosed sore muscles, arthritis, sole bruises, infections. As he whistled made-up tunes while he trimmed each horse hoof with his loop knife, leveled it off with a rasp, then nailed a new horseshoe in place with the driving hammer his father had made him.

She blew a kiss to her grandfather's memory. As she turned from the farrier to make her way back to the wagon, the sharp ping ping ping of a hammer against an anvil slapped ice water into her veins.

That sound, that shrill, soul-splitting omen of a sound plummeted her thoughts towards memories of another man from her childhood: Lee Landers.

She tried to shake her thoughts free of the repulsive man who had beaten her daddy, swindled her grandparents, raped her great aunt. She wondered what other maggots had followed his memory into this town.

Lainie, distracted by this returned agitation, stumbled over a loose plank in the sidewalk. "Simmer down," she quietly scolded herself. She slowed her pace, then slowed it even more to study a man who looked all too familiar, whose stride held a slight imperfection, whose left foot was slightly off-square.

She turned around and forced herself to walk slowly to the alley between the restaurant and the barbershop. Once out of sight, she slipped her face past the corner of the building, enough to confirm her suspicions.

Niall McNally. Hat in hand. Slicked back hair. A menace dressed in a waistcoat.

He'd been walking with a lady, showing her something in his hand. The two parted and he moved on to a group of children.

Lainie wished she could hear his words.

Instead, she watched his actions.

He sat down on the bench where the children played.

McNally combed back his hair with his fingers, placed his bowler hat on his head, and began whistling.

The tune carried through the air, so familiar yet so far away. Lainie strained to place it.

Next, he made a show of pulling out a cloth bag from his coat pocket. From the bag, he pulled out something small, tossed it in the air, and caught it in his mouth. He chewed slowly, noticeably. His actions caught the eye of a child.

Seeing that he now had a captive audience member, he pulled a second piece from the bag and, like a magician, flourished it in his hand before the girl, then tossed it into the air, again catching it in his mouth.

The bait was set, the girl was lured in. She drew closer to the man.

Another treat pulled from the bag. Another flourish of charm. Two more children lured in. The trio gathered three feet in front of the man, each set of eyes intent on the bag of treats. One boy, perhaps seven years old, licked his lips.

* * *

"My, my," McNally said, "it seems you are all fans of licorice." He flashed a smile. "If only I had more to share with my new friends."

Each little face showed disappointment.

"Well, now, all of your smiles have disappeared. We can't have that." He reached into the bag. "Let me see if perhaps, just perhaps mind you, there might be a few more pieces of candy tucked inside."

McNally pulled out one piece and handed it to his first spectator.

"There you go, little lady."

"Thank you, mister!" Her angel's grin faded. "But, I can't." She handed the candy back. "T'wouldn't be fair to my friends."

McNally dropped the licorice back into the bag. "You're right, that wouldn't be fair. Let's see if we can use a bit of magic to create enough candy for all."

He twirled the bag shut, snapped his fingers three times, then let the bag spin freely. To the children's amazement, he pulled out a handful of licorice bites.

"Why, I believe we do have plenty for all. Come, children. Enjoy a nice treat before you go back to your play."

They each took a share of the candy and said their thank yous. As they turned to leave, McNally called out, "Oh, children, would you look at something for me?"

They turned back, faces full of trust.

"I have this picture. A small portrait of my daughter. I got word that she moved to these parts." He showed them the portrait his wife had painted. "I was wondering, have any of you seen her?"

They all studied the painting. Two shook their heads to the negative. One studied it again, more intently.

"Well, sir, there was a lady at the dance that looked a bit like this, and she had green eyes. But her hair was different. Long and straight. No curls. And it was dark, not red."

She looked again.

"Nah, it couldn't have been her. She's lived in these parts for a long time, taking care of the blind woman."

"Oh, that's too bad. I was sure hoping to visit with my daughter, maybe even share some licorice with her." He stood, smiled, and offered each child a bow and a handshake.

"Thank you for spending time with me. It was truly a joy meeting each of you. Now, run along and enjoy your play."

The children set off down the sidewalk. McNally settled onto the bench, stretched his legs, and thought on the sightless woman. The son. And how months ago they'd blinded him of the truth.

Unrevealed

Lainie hid in the alley, fearing at any moment McNally would discover her. It seemed hours before he walked by and headed into the hotel. Once she felt secure, she rushed to the wagon, urged the team out of town, and raced home.

Miss Jayne called to her from the front door.

"Girl, I was ready to send the cavalry out to find you!"

"I'm sorry. I lost track of time." She hefted the first box from the wagon and climbed the stairs to the front porch. "I'll finish preparing supper before I bring in the rest of the boxes."

"No worries about supper, girl. I've got everything prepared. And don't worry about those boxes. Jake can bring them in. Come and tell me about your adventures in town."

Lainie wasn't ready to talk. Her mind was still crashing through the staggering scene she'd witnessed. How could she tell Jake and Miss Jayne that their time as a family was about to end?

* * *

Jake helped his mother clear the table and wash the dishes.

"Did Lainie mention any troubles during her trip to town?"

"No. She barely said boo about her trip. I figured she'd be gushin' on and on about all the fabrics and notions at the mercantile. She was looking forward to stopping in at Brenna Olsen's bakeshop, too. But when she got home, she was fretting about putting on supper late. I told her all the food was prepared. Then she insisted on emptying out the wagon and wiping down the horses. She came in for supper a couple of minutes before you did."

"Well, something ain't right. Forget the fact that she didn't eat your fine meal. She just looked downright pale and—I don't know—disconcerted." He scrubbed at the skillet. "You don't think one of the boys from the dance tried to cause problems for her, do you? If any of

315

them tried to be fresh with her, I'd bale him tight and throw him in the middle of a longhorn stampede."

"Lainie knows how to take care of herself. If someone tried to get fresh with her, she'd be sure to stop him in his tracks," Miss Jayne assured. "She's probably experiencing a heap of melancholy. After all, this was her first trip to town—to any town—in months. Maybe the venture brought back memories of her kin and all she left behind."

"You're probably right. I'm just not sure how to handle such moods. When Hannah got all flustered and emotional, I never knew what to do. Mostly I just hid out in the barn until she seemed to feel better. But, darn it all, I always wanted to just grab her and hold her and make everything alright."

"Why didn't you?"

"I did once. She kicked my shin and told me to hightail it out of the room because she didn't want anyone seeing her cry." He set the skillet on the counter. "Good Lord, Lainie's even more spirited than Hannah was. She'd bypass a shin-kicking and put a knee straight to my groin."

"Jacob!"

"It's true, Mama, and you know it. But I can't stand her being out there, alone with her troubles."

"You love her, Son?"

"Yeah, I do." Jake turned to his mother and pulled her in for a hug. "Tomorrow, I'm going to ask her to marry me," he whispered in her ear. "Would you like that? To have Lainie be a permanent part of our family?"

"Nothing would make me happier, Jake. Now go out and show that girl how much you love her."

"Even at the risk of injury that would leave me unable to provide you with grandchildren?" he teased.

"Jacob!"

* * *

Jake grabbed his coat, lit a lantern, and set off to find Lainie. "She could be anywhere," he informed Bristle. "Criminy, she's a master at wandering through the dark."

Not knowing which direction to look first, Jake decided to follow Bristle's lead. The first path they followed led to the wagon where Lainie had earlier cared for the horses.

"No such luck, Bristle. Maybe she's inside the barn."

As the two walked, Bristle stopped and stanced alert ears towards the lower corral.

"I'll bet she's commiserating with Junior." Jake bent over and scratched Bristle's ear. "I swear that girl talks more to animals than she does to humans."

They walked quietly down the path, Jake holding the lantern high as Bristle led the way.

Jake spotted Junior standing patiently with Lainie at his side. Lainie had one arm wrapped around the steer's neck. Her left cheek was nestled against a portion of the zigzag on his rough hide.

Jake watched the two together. Eventually he strode to the fence, hooked the lantern on a post, and leaned against the fence rails.

"I suppose I should be jealous," he joked. "Me going on and on about how much I care for you. And now you, giving all your attention to another male."

Lainie didn't answer. Instead, she turned away from Jake to scratch the steer's frizzle of hair along its neck.

Jake tipped his head back and looked to the stars for guidance. He opened the gate enough to slip through, motioned Bristle to stay outside the fence line, then shut the gate. He rubbed his neck and willed the correct words to come from his mouth. He was caught off guard when Lainie spoke first.

"It's a beautiful night," she said, her stance unchanged. "Seems a long time since the stars have put on such a show."

"Orion will be traveling the sky soon," Jake mused.

"Oh," she murmured. "So, the hunter will see me after all."

"Say again?" Jake said as he laid a gentle hand on her shoulders.

"Nothing."

He pushed her hair from her face. "What's going on, Lainie?"

"Nothing. Just a hard day."

"Did something happen in town? Did someone upset you?"

"No."

"I'm just trying to make sense of tonight. I don't want you to be unhappy. And if you're angry with me, I want to make things right."

She turned to him. "No, Jake, I'm not angry with you. Nothing could be farther from the truth." She gasped in air. "Truly, it was just a hard day."

"Come here." He reached for her hands and eased her towards him, unsure of his choice, unsure of his touch, unsure of her hesitation.

And then she melted into his arms.

God, how she melted into his arms.

He memorized the scent of her hair and slowly ran his fingers across her back and through the strands of curls that had escaped her braid. This woman. This woman. So resilient, so tender. How often had this sunflower, *his* sunflower, so beautifully tattered by the storm, found light in the darkest shadows?

The dampness of her tears filtered through his shirt to touch his skin. He ached to hold her tighter, to echo her heartbeat, to build her sweetest dreams. He pressed his lips to her forehead and willed her to grow to love him as he had grown to love her.

"I love you, Lainie. Don't ever let me hurt you," he whispered. "If I ever do or say something stupid, just tell me and I'll change my ways."

Lainie gave in to a weary laugh. "Of course, you'll do and say stupid things. And I'll always . . . I'll always . . ." She tucked her head under his chin and Jake feared his heart might explode for want of three little words. "Just know that I'm going to do and say stupid things, too."

"I'll always love you, Lainie, no matter what."

I hope not, she silently prayed. *I truly hope not.*

Distance

Bristle whimpered as Lainie slipped out of the cabin.

"Hush. Don't wake Miss Jayne." She whispered her warning to him as she took off a glove and bent down one last time to scratch his ear. "Take care of her, Bristle. Just like we talked about at bedtime. You've got to take care of Miss Jayne for me."

She pulled the door shut as she stepped into the frozen night, grateful that she'd thought to oil the door's hinges when Jake was out checking the stock. Grateful that she had slipped the egg money into Miss Jayne's flour tin. Grateful that she could still feel Jake's kiss on her lips.

The midnight hour was darker than she'd guessed it would be, and she relied on Miss Jayne's guide ropes to sneak her way from the house, past the bunkhouse where Jake slept, to the barn door. From there she placed her hands along the building's rough planks to guide her steps to the backside of the barn to the trail that led to the graves.

The graves. Lainie couldn't say goodbye to Jake, to Miss Jayne. But she could say goodbye to their buried kin.

Lainie touched each grave marker as she had nearly every day since she'd arrived at the farm. "I don't know how to make this right, Hannah. I don't know how to make this right." She sat on the frosted ground and pulled her knees to her chin. "Have you got any power to protect, Hannah? Any divine, afterlife magic you can spread across this land to keep your family from danger?" Her question was asinine. "Of course, you don't, or you would have saved your son. You would have kept sight in Miss Jayne's eyes."

A rustling sound came from the stand of trees. Lainie froze in place. She scanned the distance for shadows, any hint of movement. "If you're there, come out." She eked out the words. "Come out now."

Nothing. No friend. No foe. Just darkness.

She turned her attention back to her conversation.

"I saw McNally today, in town. No sign of his henchman or that woman, that she-devil that wants me dead. McNally has to know where I'm at. There's no way an entire town can keep its silence. And everybody saw me, Hannah. Every single person in this town must have been at that dance, their eyes on the mystery girl soaking up attention. Damn it. Damn it. Damn it. Why was I so foolish? So greedy?"

She raked her fingernails through the cold, hard earth.

"I couldn't say goodbye, Hannah. Jake, Miss Jayne, Snow Owl, Paul, the baby—I couldn't say goodbye to any of them. And I can't think of any way to protect them other than to go back to McNally. So, I'm leaving. And I'm asking you, with whatever divine powers you can muster, to keep our family and friends safe. I should probably be praying to God, saying 'Thy will be done,' but I'm sick of talking to a God whose so-called will allows women to be raped and innocents to be slaughtered and families to be torn asunder by the acts of spiteful people, by the ravage nature brings."

Lainie pulled herself up and took a slip of paper from her coat pocket.

"I have something for you and the children, Hannah. It's one of Jake's songs. It was tucked inside his shirt pocket. I spotted it when I was doing laundry. I had no right to take it, but I knew you would like it."

She settled the notebook paper at the base of the cross, covered it with a stone, and whispered out the last line of the song: *I'll be watching my angels dancing in the sun.*

* * *

"Where could she be Jake?" Miss Jayne's words bled out worry as she twisted a dish towel in her hands.

"I don't know, Mama. I've looked all over the farm." Jake retrieved the lantern from the table and began his second predawn search of the cabin for some indication of where he'd find Lainie. He'd spotted her dresses—Hannah's old dresses and the dresses Doc and Emmeline had funded—hanging in Miss Jayne's wardrobe. Two of Lainie's new dresses—the ones she'd sewn herself—were freshly laundered the morning before and set out to dry on pegs by the fireplace. The only dress missing was the one she'd been wearing all day.

320

"You're sure she didn't slip in or out of the house while you were stoking the cookfire?" Jake asked, wiping sweat from his brow.

"I'm positive. She wasn't in the bedroom when I woke up. The door hasn't opened once, excepting when you came in."

The door. There was something different about the door.

Jake flung it open then shut. He opened it slowly. Closed it even more slowly.

The door made no sound. The hinges had made creaking sounds for months now, ever since he'd reinstalled the door after McNally and his crony had busted it down. He was sure the hinges had made their usual sound when he came in last night for supper. But later that night, after he came in from checking the animals, he'd noticed a change.

Jake pieced the puzzle together. The night before, Lainie had come home late, upset after her trip to town. She'd kept quiet during supper. When he wasn't around, she'd oiled the hinges. In the dark, she'd made her way to the corral and cried out her frustrations to the steer. She'd allowed Jake to hold her, comfort her. When they'd returned to the cabin, they'd held hands and bid each other goodnight and he had walked a few steps away and then hurried back and kissed her. One kiss. One long, sweet, achingly tender kiss. Then he'd walked towards the bunkhouse, turned around, and called out goodnight one more time.

What had she said in reply?

Goodnight. In a small, quiet voice she had said goodnight.

No. Her word hadn't been goodnight. Lainie had said goodbye.

Reality punched him in the gut.

Lainie had said goodbye.

"She slipped out during the night," Jake said. "I'm sure of it."

* * *

"Bundle up," Jake told his mother. "You're coming with me."

"No. You can't search the countryside toting a blind woman," she said.

"Then let me drop you off at Irene's," Jake insisted.

"That'd be a waste of time. I'm staying here at the farm, Jake. Go get our girl."

"Ma, I suspect McNally is back. I can't just leave you here."

"You don't have another option, Jake. You either leave now to find Lainie, or you sit on the losing side of an argument while you waste precious minutes. Either way, I'm staying right here until you bring her home."

"But McNally . . ."

Miss Jayne cut off his words. "Go. Now."

* * *

Jake rode his Palouse towards town at breakneck speed.

He was following a mind-maddening hunch.

Lainie wasn't trying to escape McNally any longer.

Lainie was returning to McNally. To save Miss Jayne. To save the farm. To save Jake.

And Jake had to stop her.

* * *

Jake slowed his horse. By his calculation, if Lainie had left home between ten and midnight, she could have walked this distance. Her travel would have been encumbered by darkness, yes, but in months past, darkness had proven to be Lainie's friend.

With one hand wrapped around the reins, Jake lifted the collar of his sheepskin coat to better cover his face. It was cold enough that skims of ice lay atop wagon ruts that had yet to dry from the previous week's rain, and his muscles clenched as an internal ice cave hollowed out his being.

He squinted his eyes as he surveyed the horizon, watchful of any movement, any hint of color that didn't fit the natural landscape. He reached for his canteen, then realized he hadn't thought to fill it with water.

Despite the cold, despite the mist that hung in the air, Jake's mouth was duststorm-dry. He stretched his neck to relieve the nob in his throat, then huffed out his exhaustion, his weariness, his fear that he was too late.

* * *

When Lainie had first arrived in Leeds, she had roamed in the shadows, sheltered her identity at every turn, remained unnamed, unseen, unknown. Now, she begged to be found. She prayed to be captured by McNally or delivered to McNally or dragged by demons to McNally. She pleaded for this game of cat and mouse to come to its grand end, for the trap to slam her to her final fate. She was ready to be snared. Ready to be skinned alive, if need be. Let McNally and that woman have their victory. Let them relish the spoils of their infernal war.

Just keep her family safe.

She trudged along the roadside, her legs and arms stiff from the cold, her shoulders thick with a shivering ache. She spotted a boulder at the side of the road and sat on it to remove her shoes and dump the grit and pebbles that had slipped into each as she traveled the rutted terrain.

Lainie figured she was a mile, maybe a mile and a half from town. She also figured Jake and Miss Jayne had discovered her disappearance by now. Would they try to find her? Or would they let her drift off, a thorny memory on the wind?

She should have been in town before sunup. She should have been knocking on McNally's hotel door at dawn. But she had underestimated how darkness and bitter cold would hinder her travel.

And now, with the sun casting shimmers of light on the trail before her, she needed to hasten her journey before McNally set out to track her.

Cat and mouse. Cat and mouse.

And the sound of horse hooves in the distance.

Lainie slipped from the side of the road and hid behind a patch of shrubs.

Who would be on the horse headed towards town? Cat or mouse? Foe or friend?

* * *

A flock of birds scattered from an area just beyond the bend of the road. Had something spooked them from the roadside brush? Jake gauged where the birds came from and searched the area from atop his horse.

"Lainie?" he called out. "Lainie, please, just let me know you're alright."

A drumbeat of pain echoed through Jake's head as he watched for movement, listened for the sound of rustled leaves, squinted his eyes to discern shapes and colors.

He spotted it. A haze of cornflower blue enveloped by the bronze and greens of huckleberry leaves.

Finally. Finally.

Jake slipped from his horse, his tired eyes wavering as he tried to keep his discovery in sight.

"Lainie, I know you're back there. Come on out." Jake leaned over and placed his hands on his thighs to brace his weary frame. "Please. Come on out."

* * *

Alarm hammered through Lainie's veins as she crouched among bushes and bramble. Jake stood mere feet away, calling out her name with a heartsick anguish that twisted a knife in her soul.

She crushed back words that begged to be released. *Go home. Be safe. Protect yourself. Protect our mother. I love you. I love you. Let me go. Let me go. Let me go.*

He took a step in her direction. She gritted her teeth and closed her eyes and silently beckoned him away.

When her stranglehold of despair burst forth as a giant sob, she opened her eyes, knowing Jake had found her, knowing Jake would reach for her, knowing Jake would protect her.

Instead, she watched Jake collapse to the ground.

Saving Jake

"Jake! Jake!" Lainie stumbled through the tall weeds and bramble, ran to Jake's side, and dropped to her knees.

She shoved at his shoulder to turn him over. When his back rested on the ground, she discovered his eyes were closed and a trickle of blood oozed from a gash on his head. She reached to cover the gash with her hand to try and stop the bleeding.

"You're burning up. Why are you burning up?" One-handed, she unbuttoned his coat and slipped her hand inside the sweat-soaked fleece until it covered his chest.

"Your heart is beating so fast. Too fast."

With one hand still on the gash, she unclasped the rest of the coat buttons and fanned out the front of Jake's coat to help cool him. She had to get Jake help. She clicked to Jake's horse and called her by name.

The moment Jake had collapsed and let go of Iya's reins, the horse had walked to the opposite side of the road to graze.

"Iya, please, I need you to come here. Please, Iya. Please."

The horse remained content eating her roadside breakfast. Lainie checked to see if the bleeding from Jake's headwound had stopped. It hadn't. Lainie contemplated what to do—keep pressure on Jake's wound or capture the horse before she moved off into the distance.

Lainie pulled herself up, wiped Jake's blood onto her skirt, and set off for the horse.

Iya shied away from her and stepped further into the shadow of trees. Lainie grabbed for the reins and the horse backstepped away from her.

"It's apple time, Iya," Lainie coaxed. "You know I love hiding apples in my pockets for you. Please. Please. I need you to look for the apple."

Lainie moved slowly towards the horse, holding out her skirt pocket. The horse obligingly dipped its nose into the pocket to find its treat and Lainie snatched her reins. "I promise to give you a dozen apples later, but we've got to get Jake help first."

A cragged blood clot had formed across the left side of Jake's forehead and Lainie dared not touch it for fear the bleeding would start anew. She shook Jake's shoulders, trying to wake him.

"Jake, you gotta wake up. I can't lift you onto the horse myself. Wake up, Jake. Wake up."

Several minutes later, Jake slumped against his horse with one foot in the stirrup and grabbed a fistful of the horse's mane. Lainie pushed at Jake's hip and side with all her might as he sprawled upwards to sit awkwardly in the saddle.

Lainie took Iya's reins and began to lead her to town.

"No," Jake mumbled. "Not town. Home."

"Jake," Lainie protested, "Doc's office is not far from here. We've got to get you help. Quick."

"No. Home. Promise me, Lainie. Home."

"I'm not listening to you." Lainie pulled the horse in the direction of Doc's office.

"Lainie, I swear I'll drop from this saddle if you don't turn us around." He gasped out his words.

"Jake. Please, let me take you to Doc and Emmeline." She pleaded to him with her eyes.

"We deserve our miracle, Lainie. Take us home."

* * *

By the time they made it back to the farm, Jake had collapsed across the neck of his horse with the horn of the saddle jabbed into his shoulder. The last two miles of the ride, Lainie had kept reminding Jake to hold onto the horse as she held on tight to his pant leg, pulling or pushing him to the center of the saddle whenever he began to slide.

"Miss Jayne! We need you. Quick!" Lainie repeatedly hollered out the words long before they reached the cabin.

Miss Jayne darted out the door and stood on the porch, looking back and forth with unseeing eyes.

"Where are you? Where are you?" she called out over the sound of Bristle's whimpered complaint that he'd been left inside the cabin.

"We're almost there," Lainie hollered back. "Hurry and bring out bed pillows, sofa pillows, your mattress, anything soft. Leave them on the porch."

Miss Jayne hesitated.

"Hurry!" Lainie hollered. "It's important. And don't let Bristle out. Lock him inside Jake's room."

Lainie led Iya to the cabin and positioned the horse's off side against the stair railing. She loose tied Iya's reins to a rail post, then rushed up the steps. As Miss Jayne brought out pillows to the porch, Lainie grabbed one of the woman's guide ropes and pulled the length of it towards the porch.

"Don't you dare fall from that saddle," Lainie warned Jake. "We're going to get you down nice and safe."

Lainie reached across the railing and handed Jake the loose end of the rope. "Help me slip this around your waist," she ordered. He lifted himself upright long enough to clumsily slip the rope around his waist. As he slumped forward, Lainie tied the rope off to secure him.

"What's going on, Lainie?" Miss Jayne struggled to drag her mattress through the doorway.

Lainie grabbed a corner of the mattress to help get it to the porch, then dragged it down the stairs as she explained.

"Jake's sick. Injured. He's on his horse and we're going to help him safely get down."

"How bad off is he?" Miss Jayne cried out.

Lainie hurried back up the stairs and pushed Miss Jayne against the logs of the cabin. She wrapped a length of rope around Miss Jayne's arm, then positioned the next section of rope into the woman's hands.

"Brace yourself with your legs and hold tight to the rope. The other end of the rope is tied around Jake's waist. When I tell you to pull back, pull with all your might and don't let go. You'll be holding all of Jake's weight while I help to lower him from the horse onto the mattress."

"He's that bad?"

"I'm fine, Ma." Jake let out a moan as he tried to sit upright, then laid his head back down on the neck of the horse. "I can get down myself, Lainie."

"In a pig's eye," Lainie said as she positioned the pillows next to the near side of the horse. She settled the mattress on top of the pillows. "Don't need you landing on your head again, Jacob Adamsen."

"Jake landed on his head?" Miss Jayne braced her legs, intent on keeping her son safe.

"Hold on tight, Miss Jayne. I'll let you know when to inch forward to ease Jake from the horse to the ground." Lainie stood in front of Iya, who was getting skittish from all the commotion. She rubbed the horse's cheek and sent her a look of trust. Lainie then moved to the near side of the horse, settled her feet in front of the mattress, reached her left arm towards Jake's waist, and braced herself to take on his weight.

"Balance yourself as best you can in the stirrup, Jake. I'll support you as you dismount."

He lifted his head a few inches and dropped it back down. "Dizzy," he whispered. "Everything's spinning."

"Just keep your head low and ease yourself off the horse," Lainie whispered back, then called out instructions to Miss Jayne.

"Jake's getting off the horse now. Once you feel his weight pulling against the rope, hold tight to the rope and ease forward real slow."

The saddle creaked as Jake shifted his weight and dragged his right leg across its leather. His low groan further spooked the Palouse and she tossed her head twice, throwing Jake off balance. Lainie feared the horse would bolt and drag Jake off with his boot caught in the stirrup. As she felt his weight fall against her, she wrapped her arms tight around him and pulled him backwards, hoping to dislodge his foot.

Lainie's and Miss Jayne's strength were no match for Jake's weight. Lainie and Jake tumbled backwards, landing haphazardly on a portion of the mattress.

Iya reared up on her hind legs. The reins slipped free of the rail post as the horse bolted towards the barn.

Miss Jayne leaned against the porch rail, flushed and scared.

"What now, Lord?" she prayed. "What now?"

* * *

"Miss Jayne, what can we do?"

Lainie kneeled next to Jake, who was sprawled in a feverish sleep on the front room floor.

The women had been able to help Jake up the stairs and inside the cabin. Once inside, his knees buckled, and he dropped heavily from their supportive arms.

"You said his clothes are drenched. We need to get him changed into something dry."

Lainie retrieved dry clothes from Jake's trunk in the bunkhouse and the two women worked to slip Jake's heavy coat across his shoulders and arms.

"Maybe you should take over from here," Lainie said when Miss Jayne began unbuttoning Jake's shirt.

"It's not the time to be acting shy," Miss Jayne said. "Besides, you're going to be marrying my boy."

Lainie's stunned silence earned her a "pshaw" and orders to unhitch Jake's suspenders from his trousers.

"I can tell he's got a fever," Miss Jayne continued. "You'll have to tell me if you spot any rashes or blisters or such. I don't know if he's dizzy from being sick or from hitting his head or both. We've got to narrow down what he's suffering from."

"I don't see any marks on his arms or chest." Lainie pushed Jake on his side and checked his back. "Nothing."

The women continued their medical examination. "Do you see any patches of white or gray in his throat or on his tonsils," Miss Jayne asked.

"No," Lainie said, "but his throat looks raw."

"We'll keep watch," Miss Jayne said. "White patches could mean infection, maybe the beginning of rheumatic fever."

"And gray patches?" Lainie asked.

"Diptheria."

* * *

Jake's fever raged. The women had helped him to his bedroom, where he sunk onto the mattress Lainie had been using since she arrived at the farm, the one now riddled with frayed out holes from being torn from the wall tacks and dragged across the floor and ripped on an errant nail sticking out from the wall as it was returned to its original home.

Over the hours, Jake swung from the depths of tormented sleep to the ruthless fury of wakefulness. He'd flail his arms to clear himself of sweltering blankets. He'd cocoon himself deep in the darkness of their ineffective warmth. He'd sleeptalk unclear words then fall into the eerie silence of the near-dead.

Miss Jayne propped his shoulders on pillows and covered his injured forehead with wet washcloths to help cool his temperature, and when his teeth chattered louder than hail pelts against the roof, Lainie feared he'd bite a portion of his tongue clean off.

In Miss Jayne's judgment, Jake suffered from a violent form of influenza. For three days, she urged her son to sip willow bark tea and water with cinnamon oil for the fever. She tucked sachets of camphor crystals on each side of his jaw to alleviate his wheezing. She ground mustard seed and mixed it with flour and water and vinegar and spread it across muslin and murmured a healing prayer each time she set the sheet of poultice on her son's chest. When the poultice wasn't in place, she wrapped kitchen towels around flasks filled with scalding water and placed them across his chest and against his ribs to loosen his lungs.

Through it all, Lainie hovered nearby, awaiting instructions, pledging repentance, anticipating ambush.

Miss Jayne didn't know it, but Lainie roamed from room to room toting Jake's loaded rifle like a soldier on the front lines. And one night, as Miss Jayne slept and Jake endured a particularly violent fit of coughing, Lainie confirmed her vow of penance.

She eased Jake back on the pillows and stroked his hair until he fell asleep.

"I brought this plague to your land," she whispered. "I'll be sure to wipe it out."

* * *

Lainie plunged the towel into the blistering hot rinse water, pulled it out, and wrung out the water. She pinned the towel to the clothesline to dry.

Outside the cabin, springtime was inching its way across the land. Inside the cabin, Jake's fever still soared, and Miss Jayne feared the influenza had turned to pneumonia.

Regardless of disease, regardless of fear, food still needed to be cooked, animals still needed to be fed, and laundry still needed to be done.

Bristle slept on the grass near the washstand, his left ear twitching each time a pesky fly landed on it.

When she finished with the wash, Lainie picked up the rifle she'd tucked between the laundry tubs on the wooden stand and leaned it against the clothesline base so she could dump the water.

She tapped Bristle's hip with her foot.

"Wake up, lazy bones. Unless you want to get soaked."

Bristle's head popped up and he looked expectantly at her.

"Forget it, pup, you're not getting any more food until suppertime."

She picked up a stick and tossed it. Bristle took off after it, then a rabbit in the distance caught his attention and he gave chase.

Lainie hefted the first tub and cringed as the backsplash of water further soaked the muddy edge of her skirt.

"Well, that's a shame." A man's voice sent shivers down Lainie's spine. "That's why I glory in having servants. I never have to do the dirty work. Well, except in the case of killing you. But I'll stand far enough away to avoid blood spatter on my suit."

Lainie spun around. She recognized the hint of Irish in the man's voice. She knew McNally would be aiming a gun at her.

"You found me." She eyed Jake's rifle, just out of her reach. "Took you long enough. I thought maybe you had slunk back to that overlord of a wife with your tail between your legs."

"Aren't you charming, darling daughter," McNally said. "My wife doesn't direct my actions, though she pompously presumed she did. Once I found out she and my business associate were having romantic interludes, I shot him in the head and barred her up inside the lunatic asylum."

"Is that business associate the same henchman you sent after me?"

He gave a wry grin.

"He proved more than once that he was worthless."

Bristle came loping back to Lainie. When he spotted the stranger, he shifted from a playful pup to a snarling hackle of warfare.

"Shut that creature up," McNally demanded, pointing his gun at the dog.

Lainie reflexively grabbed the rope collar around Bristle's neck. The dog pulled against her, vaulting his body towards the intruder. Lainie pulled back with all her might and begged McNally to let her tie the dog up.

She dragged Bristle to the clothesline post that one of Miss Jayne's guide ropes was attached to and fumbled to fasten the rope around the dog's collar. "Shut up, Bristle," she growled, "or you'll get us all killed."

When the dog pulled against the rope collar still held in her hands, she gave him three low, threatening commands to sit. Be quiet.

The dog finally heeded her instruction, though he remained ready to strike.

* * *

Miss Jayne heard Bristle's bark and knew there was trouble. She moved closer to the kitchen window, which was half open to air out the house, and tried to catch sense of what was bothering the dog. Bristle finally stopped barking and Miss Jayne could hear baritone words.

"Where are the man and the blind woman?" she heard the man ask.

"They're both sick. Bad sick." Lainie's voice. "Got the influenza. I doubt either of them will make it through the night."

She heard Jake fall into a coughing fit, as if on cue.

"Is that so." The man gave a mocking laugh. "The whole damn town is dying from influenza while you're out here washing your dainties." There was a pause in the conversation. "My, my. By the look on your face, darling daughter, you weren't aware of the epidemic."

Darling daughter? Miss Jayne's hand flew to her mouth as she realized the man talking was McNally.

"So, leave us all alone and let us die of our own accord," she heard Lainie say.

"Perhaps I should put them out of their misery, this man and this blind woman." McNally cursed. "A bullet through the head is a swifter way to die than drowning from your own lungs. Of course, I will also put you out of your misery, but only after I've taken care of them."

"Or perhaps I should put you out of your misery," she heard Lainie say. "You're sick with it, aren't you? I see the beads of sweat trickling down your face. I hear the huskiness in your voice. And you are leaning hard against that shade tree. I'll bet you can barely stand up straight."

Keep him talking, Miss Jayne thought as she slipped out of the cabin, carrying the closest weapon she could find.

* * *

"You haven't shot me yet," Lainie stated, her voice low, controlled.

332

"That will come. In time." McNally kept his pistol aimed at her as he removed his hat and set it on the ground. He pulled a handkerchief from his trouser pocket and dabbed sweat from his face. "I thought we should enjoy a nice chat first. We didn't have much time to chat when you visited my home. After all, you were too busy murdering my son."

"You murdered your own son. You may not have pulled the trigger, but you set the deadly rounds in motion."

"And you murdered your own mother," McNally retorted. "If she had born me a son like she was supposed to, we wouldn't be in this quandary."

"Quandary? Is that what you call this bloodthirst? This business of butchery?"

"Your birth was worthless once I had a male heir. Your death was inconsequential to my world. And then you showed up at my home, grown up and the spitting image of your mother." He coughed, then spit phlegm onto the ground. "I can tell you every singular, gory detail of how your mother died. Of how she vomited on the staircase as she was led to the hanging noose. Of how Stut tied boulders to your mother's ankles to weight her down so the noose would snap her neck." Lainie flinched at that. "Of how your mother begged to hold you in her arms and Stut cowered from his executioner's duties and Mother Damnable scooped your lifeless body into her arms and how she and her floosies buried you and your mother in a pine box purchased with hootch money. Alas, your burial turned out to be a lie."

McNally observed the look of confusion on the girl's face.

"Yes, I know that Mother Damnable helped you escape. Twice. Allow me to enlighten you of the first time she saved your body from death's ghastly grip." He dabbed the handkerchief at his chin as he conjured memories. "I do wish I had hired a photographer to capture the image of your mother holding you, her precious newborn, with that rope dangling around her neck as she said her final goodbye. And those women, Mother Damnable and her illicit troupe of dancers, bawling their eyes out and howling out words of comfort. It was quite the rousing sight. And the sound of the trapdoor as it unexpectedly opened, then the gasp of the crowd as your tiny body slapped against the floorboards, then dropped through the hole, eight feet to the ground. Those sounds still fill my mind." He laughed. "A part of me was glad when Stut refused to pull the hangman's lever. I took great pleasure in performing that task, in watching my gallows swallow both of your lives."

The man began coughing just as Lainie spotted Miss Jayne inching around the corner of the house with her left hand spread against the wall to help map out her course.

"I've grown bored." McNally cleared his throat as he motioned to Lainie with his pistol. "Shall we set off for the riverbank? Its stand of cottonwoods will serve as a lovely backdrop for your last moments on earth. I also observed a pleasant knoll about half a mile from here. Perhaps you'd prefer to die overlooking the valley?"

"Charming offers. I'll pass."

"You're right. I've romanticized this event far too long. I just never imagined a menial laundry line would hang above your dying ground."

Lainie swallowed hard as she watched Miss Jayne shift her steps towards the laundry line. Her pulse quickened as she realized the weapon Miss Jayne held in her hand.

"Do you know what kind of tree you're standing under?" Lainie blurted out.

"Darling darling darling. You shan't delay the inevitable."

"Do you know what kind of tree you're standing under?" Lainie repeated her question louder and with more force.

"Alright. I'll play your game." He reached up and plucked a leaf from a branch and twirled it between his finger and thumb.

"It's an alder tree," he said as he dropped the leaf, then crushed it with his boot.

"Do you know what an alder tree represents?" Lainie pelted out the words.

"I'd speculate this one would make a good hanging tree."

"And I would speculate that you are wrong, Mr. McNally. This tree? It was brought here by the woman who owns this farm." Lainie near cried out her message. "Her father, Hérr Links, gifted it to her on her wedding day, and she kept it alive for weeks as she and her new husband traveled across prairies and mountains to begin their new life in the West." Lainie watched Miss Jayne move a few steps to her left, obviously understanding the hint she'd shared in German. "She continued traveling with the tree and protected it with all her might, and when they bought their land and they staked out boundaries for the cabin, she planted this alder and watered it every drought-filled day to make sure it would survive and thrive in the very spot you are standing."

McNally placed his free hand over his heart and tapped the space three times. "Your story is a light to my troubled soul."

"This tree, the one you are leaning against *right* now in all your brazen glory, it was planted to provide much more than shade. It's a protector. Physically, emotionally, spiritually. Right after the wedding...*right* after the wedding," Lainie emphasized her word clues for Miss Jayne to adjust the woman's path, "the father counseled his daughter that in her journey *forward*, she would sometimes need to be a warrior. That an alder-forged weapon will defend and do battle, an alder shield will give courage and protect. A good warrior will know when to challenge things and when to hold her peace but *keep moving forward*." Lainie willed Miss Jayne to keep progressing silently towards the tree, just beyond McNally's line of sight. "She will seek enlightenment to choose the *right* course. She will know when to *step forward* and she will *step forward again and again. And again.* She will know when to lift her weapon just a little bit higher to best battle the enemy. And she will stop at nothing, *she will absolutely stop* at nothing, to take care of her own."

"Are you finished droning on? Because I have better things to be doing with my time."

"No. We've held up our shields against you long enough. *We have nothing left to lose.* It's time to do battle."

"You sound like a complete fool."

"Now!" Lainie screamed at the top of her lungs.

Miss Jayne swung the cast iron skillet at McNally's head as Lainie commanded the dog to attack.

The skillet hit hard—a thwacking blow across the back left of McNally's skull that sent him stumbling forward. His pistol went off and a bullet hit the ground a few feet from Lainie, sending up a spray of grass and dust. Bristle raced forward, his collar slipping free from the rope as intended, and his attack brought the man to the ground, with the dog sinking his teeth into the man's trouser leg. Bristle tugged until the fabric tore open, then launched a second attack when the man put a strangle hold around his neck. Bristle writhed in anger. His bared fangs pierced the man's chin and cheek and nose until blood gushed and both the man and the dog were covered in crimson carnage.

Lainie pushed Miss Jayne to safety, claimed the skillet from the ground, and swung it hard against the crown of McNally's head. The man cursed and loosened his grip on the dog. Lainie swung again. This time, the man dropped.

"Bristle, heal," Lainie commanded. "Bristle. Listen. Heal."

The dog, bloodied and panting hard, shrunk back from the man lying on the ground.

* * *

Both women, winded from heaving the unconscious intruder up planks of wood into the back of the wagon, leaned against the wagon's siderails.

"Where will you take him?" Miss Jayne asked.

"Far from here."

"To the sheriff?"

Lainie didn't answer.

"Should we tie him up more?"

"He won't break loose from those ropes," Lainie assured as she checked the wagon's tailgate latch. "Keep Bristle tied up for now. No telling what the dog will do until he calms down. I'll clean him up when I get home."

She noticed how shaken and frail Miss Jayne looked. "Shall I help you into the cabin? Back to Jake's room? He'll be needing you and your strength, Miss Jayne."

"I can make it on my own."

"I know you can." Lainie took Miss Jayne's hands into her own. "You and that dog saved all of our lives, Miss Jayne. You are the warrior your father taught you to be."

* * *

Lainie signaled the horses to turn off the road to a steep side path that led to craggy terrain overlooking the river.

When they arrived at an abandoned fur trappers camp she'd once stayed at, far from any roads or trails or buildings, she stopped the wagon, set the brake, and jumped down from the driver's box.

Lainie visually checked the bindings around McNally's hands and legs as she rounded the wagon to open the tailgate. He appeared to be unconscious, but she trusted nothing about this man or this moment.

She opened the tailgate and grabbed at the binding around McNally's boots and pulled with all her might. The man woke just as his waist slipped past the tailgate edge and gravity took over. He cursed as he landed hard on the rocky ground.

Lainie blocked out his words as she walked back to the driver's box, hitched her skirt up, and climbed into the seat. She drove the horses a few yards away and settled them in front of a stand of trees. As she tied their reins to tree limbs, she made her plea. "Lou, O'Malley, please don't get spooked and run off."

She grabbed Jake's rifle from under the wagon seat and strode back to McNally, who thrashed about like a bass out of water.

"You broke my back! You broke my back!"

"Your back ain't broke if you're kicking and squirming that way."

McNally yelled out, "I followed him. I followed him. I followed that so-called father of yours to find you. That imbecile led me straight to you, and his bloody soul went straight to hell when I shot him in the face."

"And your soul's gonna follow, once I shoot you."

Lainie positioned the rifle and aimed for his chest.

"You're spineless, just like Stut. You're going to stand there and quake and cry like a little schoolgirl. You'll piss yourself then faint into your own feces. Then you'll have to fetch that feeble sheriff of yours and when he finds me all bitten and beaten, he'll know I was attacked. You'll be the one he carts off to jail, not me."

"I'm not quaking. And I'm not crying. I'll gladly put a slug through your brain."

"Then welcome to the killer's club, darling daughter. Welcome to the killer's club. I guess you're more like me than either of us thought."

That sentence gave her pause. She didn't want to be like him, taking over fate with gunpowder. If God wanted this man dead, then God would have to be in the details.

She aimed the rifle to the left of McNally and fired off a shot.

"Holy hell," McNally shrieked.

Lainie walked past McNally towards the rabbit she'd shot in the distance. She grabbed the rabbit by its ears, offered up a silent apology, and returned to McNally after leaving the rifle propped against a boulder.

She pulled Jake's Barlow knife from her skirt pocket, opened the blade, and slit the rabbit's neck as she held it over McNally's face.

"What are you doing?" he screamed as blood splattered across his eyes and chin and trickled onto his neck and into his hair.

She set the rabbit on the ground, slit open its belly, and pulled out its entrails. She pushed the entrails inside McNally's shirt, then spread the bloody carcass across his clothes and left it in a heap upon his chest.

"We'll see who gets to you first. The sheriff, the cougar, or the grizzly."

* * *

"Doc? Emmeline? Please be here! Please be here!"

Lainie didn't knock on the Matthews' door or ring their front bell. Her mission was too crucial for such formalities. She rushed down the hall, looking in each room for her friends.

She stopped when she spotted Emmeline seated behind Doc's desk, looking tattered and faded.

"Emmeline? No. No."

"I'm recovering. Slowly. But I'm recovering."

"And Doc?"

"He's out tending to the sick."

"Jake. He's bad, Emmeline. Miss Jayne says it's turned to pneumonia."

Emmeline lifted herself from the chair and made her way to the medicine cabinet. She pulled out a half-empty bottle and pressed it into Lainie's hands.

"It will help with the cough. Miss Jayne will know how much to give him. I'll inform Doc to head out to your place as soon as he returns."

Lainie surveyed the near-empty medicine cabinet. It seemed the onrush of influenza had depleted the doctor's emergency stores. She turned back to her friend.

"Emmeline, you don't look well at all. This medicine, it's for you, isn't it?"

"I'll be fine. Others are worse off than me. Go. Go help Jake."

338

Lainie hesitated as jumbled loyalties piled up in her conscience.

"I'm on the mend," Emmeline assured, interpreting the wave of emotion that crossed Lainie's face. "I promise. Now get back home."

As Lainie embraced her friend, she silently placed the bottle of cough elixir onto Doc's desk, then swiftly made her way to the door where she remembered the second part of her mission to town.

"The sheriff. Emmeline, I need to speak with the sheriff. Is he sick? Or . . ." She feared a worse ending. "It's urgent."

"He hasn't been afflicted, though some of his family have been ill. He's out burying some of our people. We lost Mrs. Granger last night and the youngest Walther boy this morning. I suspect Sheriff Hale is still at the cemetery."

* * *

Lainie led the sheriff to McNally. What remained of the man was a torn body, slashed bite marks, and putrid devastation.

"Whatever got to him ripped part of his innards," Sheriff Hale said as he scanned the area for any remaining predators. "Smells something horrendous."

"Sheriff, I baited him."

"What'cha mean?"

"I baited him. I knew there had been sightings of a bear in this area. I didn't have the backbone to kill him on my own, so I killed a rabbit instead and covered McNally with its blood. I left this man's life in the hands of fate, nature, God, whatever you want to call it. No matter how the story's told, I killed him."

The sheriff took off his hat and studied its crown like Wallace's gypsy lady had studied her crystal ball.

"I'll take care of what remains," he finally said. "You head on home. I'll stop by your place tomorrow to check on you and your kin."

* * *

Lainie tripped as she raced up the front porch stairs at the cabin. She heard the fierce sobs and cowered at what she'd find inside.

"Jake! Jake! Oh, my son. Jake."

Lainie slipped through the door. Her leaden feet barely led her to the sofa before Miss Jayne's sobs became louder. Lainie fell to her knees.

"No. No." She cried into a pillow. "Not Jake. Please, not Jake."

What would Miss Jayne do without her son? What vulgar void would the women face without him? How would her own heart, so new to Jake's quiet, protective love, ever beat again? Lainie's stomach lurched with dread as she pulled herself up and inched towards Jake's room. She knocked softly on the doorframe and when Miss Jayne didn't answer, she walked in, her gaze cast down.

"Mama, don' t cry. Please don't cry."

The voice further bewildered the turmoil inside her and Lainie fought through a haze of confusion to determine if the words were real or imagined.

"Jake?" Lainie didn't dare believe the scene in front of her. "Jake?"

This man. This man that she had grown to treasure sat on the side of his bed, holding his mother in his arms.

He motioned Lainie to him with his hand and she walked into his tender embrace.

Field Flowers
Leeds, Idaho — May 1891

Nearly thirty people waited outside the Adamsen home. Some sat on log benches, some had brought their own stools and chairs, some milled about catching up on gossip and spring crop reports. The children were content to sit on patches of grass and daub each other's faces with dandelion blossoms while entertaining Bristle with games of fetch and pull-the-rope.

Jake moved from one conversation to the next, anxious for the wedding to begin. He shook hands with Pastor Evans.

"We sure appreciate you officiating at our wedding today, Pastor, but you didn't need to dress in your finest." Jake gestured towards his own clothing—a pale tan button-up shirt and the only pair of trousers he owned that wasn't torn. "You know we like to keep things simple. Besides, I don't own a fancy cravat like you're wearing."

"I'm afraid dressing up is part of my duties as an officiant. The cravat is the only fancy thing I own," Pastor Evans said with a laugh as he straightened the frayed silk vest he wore beneath his second-hand suit coat. "The powers that be gave me a pile of rules taller than Pike's Peak. Too bad they didn't give me any climbing boots to get to the top." He pointed to his shoes—a mismatched pair of rundown ankle boots, one of which had split out at the toe.

The two busted out in laughter. "Maybe when you're praying for manna for your congregation, you should send up a few prayers for some new footwear, Pastor," Jake quipped.

When Jake spotted his mother talking with Paul and Snow Owl, he motioned to the couple that he was returning to the cabin.

He found Lainie in her cornflower blue dress sitting on the front room floor, sifting through his mother's sewing basket.

"You know, it's been nearly an hour since I last kissed you."

"Have you been chronicling our kisses?" she teased.

"Just making sure we fill our daily quota."

He sat next to Lainie on the floor. As he watched her return items to the basket, he smoothed a strand of her hair that trailed from her headscarf.

"You know, you don't need to hide underneath that scarf anymore," he said as he playfully bumped his shoulder into hers, then laughed at her exaggerated grimace.

"I'm not sure many brides show up for their wedding with two-toned hair. Especially when it's all patchworked like mine."

Jake laced his hand with hers. "I don't care about other brides. I only care about you. And I don't care what color your hair is, but it would be nice to see these flowers tucked into your braid."

He presented her with the nosegay of yellow and white field flowers he'd hidden at his side.

"I picked them this morning at sunup. Now, I know you don't care for people plucking up flowers instead of leaving them to grow, but every bride should have flowers on her wedding day."

She beamed as she slipped the scarf from her head and set it into Jake's outstretched hand. He tossed the scarf over his shoulder and they both laughed when it landed atop a houseplant.

"Spin around. I've helped dye your hair often enough that I suppose I won't mangle it too much with these tiny buds."

Lainie turned towards the fireplace and delighted at the touch of Jake's fingers as he threaded the flowers into the wavy tendrils that were twisted and pinned at the nape of her neck.

He leaned in and kissed her neck, the curve of her jaw, the soft, hollow area beneath her chin where her heartbeat flicked its anticipation. "Beautiful," he whispered into her ear. "You are simply beautiful, inside and out."

She let out a soft moan as his lips swept across her jaw, her cheek, her temple. "I want to spin inside this moment forever," she murmured. "Let me be dizzy in love while I'm anchored in your arms."

She turned, wanting her lips to touch his, aching for the honey sweet mystery they'd share as man and wife. He traced her lips with the back of his fingers, leaned in, then pulled back ever so slightly.

The hesitation and the anticipation were maddening.

"Do you know why I moved out of the house and into the bunkhouse last winter?" Jake asked.

Lainie whispered, "No."

"Because even then, I knew I wanted to be your forever. Even then, I knew I wanted to taste midnight on your lips."

* * *

A gunshot exploded in the air. Screams followed.

Jake and Lainie scrambled across the room to peer through the bottom of the front window. They watched as two horses pulled a black carriage alongside the well. A man jumped from the driver's box and aimed a rifle at the wedding guests.

"Get back." Jake pushed Lainie away from the window. Another shot went off. "That man just shot Pastor Evans." He crouched low and took a few steps to retrieve the Winchester leaning against the wall in the corner.

Lainie followed and grabbed his arm. "No, Jake, wait. There are too many people between you and the shooter. Did you see any other gunmen?"

"I think there was someone else in the carriage." He moved back to the window and peered past the curtains. "A woman dressed in black just stepped out."

Lainie slipped open the door an inch, two inches, before Jake could stop her. "Lord, help us all," she prayed out loud. "It's McNally's wife."

The two stopped moving so they could hear what Agrippina McNally was saying.

"Oh, my, it seems you've shot the groom, Russell." They could barely make out her words. The woman walked closer to Pastor Evans, who was on the ground holding his blood-stained shoulder, and seemed to direct her comments to him. "Rest assured, no one else need be hurt. Simply tell your young bride to come out of the cabin and join us. She and I have unfinished business."

Pastor Evans spat at the woman. "I'll do no such thing."

Agrippina nodded toward the gunman, who shot a second round. Pastor Evans flinched back then grabbed his bullet-torn thigh.

"I have to stop this." Lainie said.

Jake grabbed her around the waist and pulled her away from the door.

"You are not going out there."

"I have to, Jake. That woman will kill our family and friends if I don't."

"You are staying inside." He gestured to the rifle in his hand. "I'll climb through the back window and come around the side of the cabin where I can get a clear bead on both of them."

"By the time you get out there, this will be a bloodbath. I'm the only person who can stop that from happening."

Jake clenched his jaw, his eyes wild with fury. "Fine. But I'm going with you."

"You can't, Jake. She thinks the pastor is my groom. Use me as a ploy to figure out a way to keep everyone safe."

Lainie kissed him hard. "Don't come after me, Jake. Don't you dare come after me." She slipped outside before he had a chance to argue. He knew she had no belief that she'd return. He knew there was nothing he could do or say to prevent her from offering herself as sacrifice, of becoming his family's saving grace.

* * *

The stifling air within the carriage was filled with the scent of rosewater and lavender. Lainie's stomach clenched as she remembered how this scent had filled her lungs during her first loathsome meeting with Agrippina. A year later, her wrists still burned from the ropes that had bound her to a chair. A year later, she could still feel the bristles of the woman's paintbrush as they left a trail of black upon her cheeks. And yes, one year later, she could still hear the thud of her half-brother's body as it landed in its final repose.

She feared the ending this crazed woman had planned for her and, potentially, her family and friends.

"Today would have been my son's eighteenth birthday," Agrippina said. Her hand rested on the grip of the pistol she'd settled next to her. "Imagine my surprise when I learned you would be desecrating his day with your marriage."

Lainie didn't respond. She was too busy fighting off panic and wondering if another of Agrippina's killers was murdering her family.

The woman caressed the pistol at her side with the back of her fingertips as she continued her dark and doleful monologue.

Lainie ignored the woman's words and forced her focus to the pistol. She could rip the pistol from the woman's possession. She could shoot Agrippina. The driver. She inched her hand forward. Agrippina noticed the movement, picked up the pistol, and aimed it at the girl.

Lainie dropped her hand to the seat and silently berated herself for not tucking Jake's knife into her pocket that morning.

The knife. She had persistently carried it with her as a weapon for months, nearly from the time she had used its blade to cauterize the gash in her leg. She had used it to build her courage and harness her fears and assuage the pensive expectancy that she would need to protect herself and others should McNally crash into their lives. But this was her wedding day. And McNally was dead. And this day—this day of all days—deserved to be filled with wonder, not weapons.

The driver made a sharp turn and the passengers each grabbed at their seats to steady themselves as the carriage jounced up a steep incline.

That's when Lainie's wrist banged against the small, heavy pincushion she'd retrieved from the sewing basket and tucked into her pocket. Lainie had wanted Miss Jayne to hold the bronze heirloom during the wedding ceremony as a symbol of family unity and strength. Now, she wondered if she could bash Agrippina's head with it to launch a means of escape.

"Will your husband be joining us? He is such a delightful fellow. Giving to the point of fault." Sarcasm dripped from Lainie's words. "Perhaps we can enjoy a spot of tea and some fresh pastries. I'll take my tea without poison this time."

Agrippina tilted her head. "You shouldn't deride the dead," she admonished.

Lainie feigned innocence. "No, don't tell me. Mr. McNally is dearly departed?"

The woman's eyes flashed with contempt. "My husband didn't deserve to die in that manner," she snarled.

"Such sentimentality for a man who locked you up in a lunatic asylum."

Lainie had taken a chance in throwing out that piece of information, for she had no idea if McNally's revelation had been true.

By the look on Agrippina's face, the verbal jab hit. And it hurt.

The woman, with all her grandiose gestures and finery, visibly shrank in her seat.

Agrippina looked out the window and Lainie was shocked to see a sheen of tears on the woman's cheek. "He told the doctors falsehoods.

And some truths, I suppose. His rationale for my admission into the asylum was lengthy. Dissolute habits, imaginary female trouble, menstrual derangement, overaction of the mind, egotism, novel reading. Oh, and the death of our son. It seems a woman can't menstruate or contemplate without being called crazy. And heaven help us if we show any signs of intellect or resourcefulness."

The woman turned back to Lainie and swallowed hard before continuing. "Add to that a mother's grief, and the husband has the governmental right to report a conclusion of lunacy."

Lainie could add several legitimate rationales to that conclusion of lunacy. After all, she had been poisoned, taken captive, and tortured by this woman.

"But, as you can see, I am no longer a prisoner of my husband's guile. He forgot all too often that I own the people who hold the keys to every building in my mining town. And I own political officials with great reach. Great enough reach to free me from that madhouse Niall put me in."

"Thank goodness for that," Lainie gibed.

"Thank goodness for that," Agrippina agreed, unable to finish her words as Lainie threw herself across the narrow aisle between them and dug her fingers into the woman's eyes and smacked the bronze pincushion against the woman's head once, twice, three times. The carriage rocked violently as both women clawed and kicked and bit to win the battle. The pistol fell to the floor and Lainie sprawled across Agrippina's legs to reach it. She knew that the one who held the gun would hold the victory.

Just as Lainie's fingertips touched the barrel of the pistol, the carriage hit a deep rut and the pistol slipped out of reach. Agrippina shoved at Lainie's waist until the girl fell to the carriage floor. The woman dropped down on top of her, grabbed the girl's hair, and repeatedly bashed her head against the floor and the seat frame.

The carriage came to a stop. The driver flung the door open to find the women battling to reach the pistol. He used his rifle to fire a warning shot into the air and their battle came to a halt.

"Drag her out of here," Agrippina ordered as she lifted herself from the girl.

Russell pointed his rifle towards Lainie's head as Agrippina descended from the carriage.

"Shall I commence with the plan, ma'am?" he asked.

"No, Russell, I want to kill her myself."

Agrippina ordered Russell to stay at the carriage to watch for intruders that might come to rescue the girl. Then she marched Lainie at gunpoint around the bend towards the site where her husband had died.

"Recognize this place? Recognize this place?" Agrippina slapped Lainie's cheek. "You murdered my husband here. And now I will murder you."

Lainie spit out blood. She had a raging headache, her eye was swelling shut, and her legs wobbled beneath her.

"Go ahead, Aggie." The woman blanched at the use of McNally's nickname for his wife. "Put your pistol to my head, Aggie."

"Don't call me that."

"Why not, Aggie? Aggie, Aggie, Aggie. Such an ordinary name for an ordinary woman."

The woman slapped Lainie again. "I am not ordinary. I am named after royalty. I am royalty."

"You couldn't rule a colony of termites, *Aggie*." Lainie knew this woman would kill her, but she vowed her gibes would take some of the murderous pleasure away.

"Aggie, you claim you should be painting in Italy, yet that rubbish you paint—you wouldn't be able to sell it on a street corner. So, there your art sits in that mansion of yours, collecting fly specks and cobwebs. By the way, who is taking care of that mansion of yours? More importantly, who is taking care of your town? I mean, your husband was here. You are here. While the two of you have been hopscotching around the wilds of Idaho trying to find me, who has been taking care of business, Aggie? Who has been taking care of business?"

"My manager and my attorneys are taking quite good care of my business and my financials," Agrippina said with a sneer.

"Are they, Aggie? Grandma always said when the cat's away, the mice *happily* play. The mice also enjoy pocketing money when no one is looking."

Lainie wiped the trail of blood coming from her forehead, smearing it across her face.

"Face it, Aggie, your mining town is on death's doorstep. You may have wanted your son to take over your company, but I doubt you have a company to take over."

347

The woman raged. She rammed into Lainie and the two fell to the ground. She pistol-slapped the girl across the face, tossed the gun, then used both hands to grab the girl around the neck.

"It's amusing to see those brandmarks on your neck, dearie." Lainie gagged from the pressure of the woman's hands. "I remember your wretched stink as my husband's initials were scorched into your skin. And I remember vowing that you would die."

"Not. Dead. Yet." Lainie screeched out the words.

Agrippina squeezed harder, her concentration so fixed on strangling out life that she didn't hear the sounds in the distance.

* * *

Two rifles shot in synchrony. Only one man fell.

Atop Paul's horse, Jake barreled past Russell's body towards the site he expected to find Lainie.

He spotted the women in the distance. Lainie was in a losing fight against the woman in black.

He dismounted the horse before it came to a full stop, ran towards the women, and swung the butt of his rifle against Agrippina's head. She fell sideways and landed where she could reach her pistol. Jake swung again. This time, Agrippina ducked, leaving Jake off balance.

Lainie, free of the woman's death grip, fought for air. She watched as Jake swung his rifle a third and then a fourth time at the woman who now had her pistol in hand and aimed at Jake. Lainie grabbed a handful of dirt and pulled herself to her feet. She ran towards Agrippina and threw the dirt into the woman's face. The woman faltered, giving Jake enough time to grab Lainie by the hand and race towards the horse.

Jake mounted the horse, then pulled Lainie up behind him as Agrippina, still partially blinded by the grit in her eyes, shot off five rounds towards them. Her gun emptied of ammunition and she reloaded it with bullets she pulled from her skirt pocket.

The horse raced down the trail as Jake blew off a shot towards Agrippina. He thought the bullet hit her in the shoulder, but he couldn't be sure.

As they neared the carriage, a gunshot came from its direction. Russell lay on his stomach, steadying his rifle to shoot another round.

"Shit," Jake cursed, "I thought he was dead."

Jake reined the horse into a rollback, then urged it up the craggy terrain. Lainie held tight to Jake's waist, still dizzy and winded from Agrippina's attempt to strangle her.

As they crested a ridge, Paul's horse let out a terrible snort as his front right leg lost its footing. The horse began to topple and Jake and Lainie slid off and rolled away before the sweaty giant could land atop them.

Jake retrieved the rifle that had dropped from his grip. Lainie spotted a trail of blood behind them. "Jake, the horse has been shot."

They didn't have time to confirm the injury. They had to leave the downed horse and keep climbing. They had to gain distance and find a means of escape. Or prepare for the next battle.

* * *

"Useless fool." Agrippina picked up the rifle from the dead man's hands and checked to see if it was loaded. She unhitched one of the carriage horses and mounted it like she had as a child when she snuck out to ride her father's horses bareback. She'd spotted the blood in the trail and saw how it snaked up the mountainside. With the loaded rifle in hand and her pistol tucked into the back of her waistband, the woman set off in pursuit of her prey.

* * *

They'd climbed as far as Lainie could go. Behind them, two killers. Up the mountain, treacherous terrain. In front of them, a cliff high above the river. Opposite the cliff, steep slopes with jagged rocks. And within this area of the mountain, too few places to hide.

The wind whipped around them as Lainie and Jake inspected their surroundings for options—an animal's den, a cavity in the mountain, a hidden trail, anything, anything that would help them escape. Defeated, they huddled behind a solitary white pine.

"Was anybody else hurt? At our wedding, I mean." Lainie's teeth chattered as she spoke.

"Beyond the pastor? Not that I know of."

"You shouldn't have followed me, Jake."

"Don't go there, Lainie."

"You should have stayed to protect our mother, our kin."

"Paul, Anton, and half a dozen other men took up arms. My place is with you."

"And the pastor?"

"Doc and Emmeline will take care of him."

She sucked in and blew out air like an overworked bellows. Jake kept watch for any movement coming up the mountain, his rifle at the ready.

"How many rounds of ammunition are left in your gun?" She heaved out the question.

"Not enough."

* * *

Lainie and Jake were still winded and dripping with sweat when they spotted Agrippina crest the slope on a horse.

Jake aimed his gun at the woman's chest. He pulled the trigger.

Nothing.

He pulled the trigger again. Again. He banged his fist at the rifle chamber then aimed and pulled the trigger once more.

The rifle was jammed. And Agrippina had spotted them.

"What now?" Lainie whispered as she watched the woman pump the lever of the rifle she carried.

"The river. We jump into the river."

"Absolutely not. It's too long of a drop into the water. And who knows if there are rocks just below the water's surface."

"We can't continue up or down the mountain. There's no cover and she'll outmaneuver us on that horse."

Lainie took another desperate look at their surroundings. No bramble to hide behind. No other form of cover.

"Maybe she'll run out of ammunition," Lainie offered, knowing they were easy targets regardless of the amount of ammunition Agrippina had with her.

Agrippina shot at them. The bullet hit the tree trunk. Splintered bark whizzed past Jake's face.

Jake dropped his rifle and grabbed Lainie's hand. "Do you know how to swim?" he asked. She nodded. "Then we run for the edge of the cliff and jump. Don't stop running, no matter what. We need the speed to launch us past any boulders jutting out of the mountainside. Keep hold of my hand. You've gotta keep hold of my hand." Lainie

350

promised she would. "And whatever happens, let the water carry us far enough downstream that her gunshots can't reach us."

The two raced from behind the tree. A bullet zinged the ground just behind Lainie as they bolted across the outcropping of rock towards the edge of the cliff. "Jump!" Jake barked out the word as they neared the jagged precipice and they pushed off and they plummeted into the current below.

* * *

Lainie hit the frigid water with her feet together, but the current pulled her right leg behind her and she was momentarily suspended, a freefalling acrobat in the water's belly.

Jake landed in the river at a bad angle and the water walloped his gut, his shoulders, his face. The crushing pain left him gasping and he swallowed up water and its stranglehold left him panicked, disoriented. His underwater pleas were deceptively quiet as his hand slipped free of Lainie's.

Lainie saw Jake's wild-eyed fear, his gaped mouth, his powerless arms. Her ungainly swim strokes to reach him were at odds with the river's current which propelled them both forward, but apart.

She surfaced from the water, filled her lungs with air, then plunged back into the current to save Jake.

* * *

Paul and Anton chased after Jake, following sifts of trail dust until they found the empty carriage and the driver, dead on the ground. They trailed spilled blood, disrupted rocks, hoof marks. They bypassed Paul's downed horse—it still snorted in pain—and crested a bank of chiseled rock and witnessed two people—a man and a woman—hurtle off the mountain. They witnessed the woman in black dismount a horse and dash to the edge of the cliff and shoot at the falling couple. They each levered their rifles and hollered for the woman in black to stop shooting. And when the woman in black turned and fired off shots at them, at their horses, they ended her deranged rampage.

* * *

Agrippina McNally's body was never found. She careened off the mountain into the watery depths below. Hardly any blood spilled to the ground from the bullet holes Paul and Anton had put in her.

It took two days for the search party to find Lainie who, after being washed up on a sandbar, was battered. Broken.

It took three days of searching the river and its banks to find Jake.

The Lilac

Lainie kneeled on the ground and traced the edge of the tiny lilac leaf. What had once seemed a lifeless twig thrown into some dirt in an old rusted can had grabbed hold of the soil and held on to it for dear life.

Five leaves. Her precious lilac now had five leaves.

She worried the place she'd planted it—where Jake would see it every day and the scent of future blossoms would drift across the land—would be too harsh on the tender branchlets of growth.

Would naive buds wither in the heat? Would steadfast roots drown in the storm? Would branches break under burden?

But the original plant this shoot had branched from wasn't protected from unyielding winds or the sweltering sun. It had, in fact, triumphantly faced the blights and the burdens known to lead the toughest of creations to implore for relief.

Succoring, calming, renewing relief. The balm of grace. The hand of mercy. The testament of fading storms.

Today, after she planted the lilac Jake had gifted her near his and Hannah's graves, she stretched her arms to the heavens and called out her fervent plea, her imploration, her desperate prayer.

Then she fell to the ground and carved her name within the testament of grief.

A Letter for Hannah

Dearest Hannah,

I meant to tell you, to say the words out loud, the story of how Jake died. But the words got tangled up inside me and I couldn't set them free. I'm using this paper now—the last of Jake's song paper—to tell his story, though I suppose you already know.

They found Jake in a tree snag, Hannah. It took three days of searching before the men found him downriver, draped out and peaceful looking. I suppose peace is the last thing Jake expected to gain from the river.

I didn't know he was scared of water, that he didn't know how to swim. Oh, hell, Jake wasn't just scared of water. He was terrified of it. I didn't know until Mother—Miss Jayne—confided that fact to the pastor.

He saved me twice with water, Jake did. Once he plucked me from it, once he convinced me to dive into it. I wish I could have saved him. I wish I could have saved him.

You need to know something, Hannah. You and the children were never less alive inside of Jake. He carried your stories and your musings and your enchantments with him like the sky carries the sun, the moon, the stars. Sunup, sundown, you were each with him.

I'm not sure why God let those memories rain down so hard on Jake. Then again, I'm not sure why God puts on floods and fires and fearsomes and fights. Why he severs love and loyalties. Why he scoops up babies and tells them they're not meant to roam the earth.

I know memories of those we've lost aren't meant to up and die and land inside their own graves, yet I wonder, for those left behind, if life would be easier if they did.

In time, the sharp edge of your death's blade dulled some, and it wasn't twisting inside Jake as much the past few months. Though, there were moments. Hard, soul-starved moments.

When I first met him and your deaths festered inside him and he was reaching for gunpowder to end the pain, I blamed you for trying to claw him up to heaven and I'm ashamed of thinking that. I'm ashamed that while I was grappling with

354

my own grief and demons and looking for my own answers and leaving no stone unturned, that I came up with such a horrible thought. That wasn't right of me and for that I am so very, very sorry.

Absolution seems to be calling my name, but I'm not ready for that. I'm not sure I'll ever be ready for that.

I promise to be good to Miss Jayne, Hannah, and I promise to help take care of her, if she'll let me. She and I had a rocky start, no doubt about that. We had some good times, too, just before more of life got mangled. Just before I caused Jake's death. I was beginning to feel like her daughter. Now, I'm not sure I'll ever be someone's kin.

I'll be taking my leave now, Hannah. I appreciate all the good talks over the past year or so. You've been a good friend—someone to share my secrets with when no one else could hear them. Maybe we'll talk again. More likely, we're departing ways.

Thank you for letting me love Jake.

—Lainie

Epilogue: Sonnenblume
Leeds, Idaho — June 1891

"I'm not taking that with me."

Lainie set the rocking chair back on the floor.

"What do you mean, Miss Jayne? You've had this rocking chair since . . ."

"Since Jake was a baby." The woman shrugged. "The chair belongs to this room. It's part of this home. And tomorrow, this home will belong to Paul and Snow Owl. The rocking chair will become part of their child's story. Besides, Mr. Levine is a fine woodsmith. He'll build me a new one, for our new life together."

Lainie reached for the woman's hand and squeezed it tight. "I'm so happy that you and Mr. Levine are together, that tomorrow you'll become husband and wife."

"We've known each other for a dozen years or more. I suppose courting season isn't meant for just young people."

"I suppose it's not."

The two joined Mr. Levine, who busily adjusted the ropes that secured the last of Miss Jayne's furniture in place within the back of his wagon.

"My girls," Mr. Levine called out. "Are the two of you ready to journey to your new home? I'm sure Bristle has explored every nook and cranny of his new yard. He'll be anxious to have you both back by his side."

He gently tugged Miss Jayne to him and whispered a flirtation in her ear. The woman blushed and giggled and for the first time since Jake's death, Lainie spotted a staunch eagerness in the woman's spirit.

"Sonnenblume." Mr. Levine turned to Lainie. "Sonnenblume, is there anything else you'd like to bring for your new room? You've packed so little."

"I have everything I need, Mr. Levine." She handed him the last of her belongings to be packed into the wagon—the tin can Jake had given her, which now held a second plant that she'd pruned from the wild-growing roots of Miss Jayne's lilac bush. "Thank you for your generosity. And please remember that Doc and Emmeline have invited me to live with them as I take part in my medical training."

Miss Jayne lifted her hands, as if to ward off Lainie's words.

"Tell her," Miss Jayne whispered.

"Darling, you should be the one . . ."

Miss Jayne turned away. "The words, they are too hard. Tell her."

Mr. Levine grimaced at his future wife's obstinance. "Yes, my love. Of course, I'll tell her."

The man pulled a handkerchief from his pocket and dabbed the sheen of sweat from his forehead.

"Lainie, there's something you should know. Jayne and I have held many discussions about your future, and we've held many prayerful moments."

"Stop," Lainie said, knowing that her relationship with Miss Jayne was near severed by Jake's death. "You don't need to say another word. I'm to blame for the death of your son. You don't need to pretend that I'm welcome in your home. You don't need to put on this façade anymore."

Mr. Levine held up his hand to interrupt her words.

"Lainie, are you familiar with scripture?" he asked.

"Some."

"My Jayne and I have been discussing the Book of Ruth for some time now. Her with her Christian canons, me with my Hebrew text. The story shares how Ruth and her widowed mother-in-law, Naomi, experienced tremendous grief and hardship when Ruth's husband—Naomi's son—perished. Naomi knew she needed to return to her home country, for the rights of a widow, especially one in a foreign society, were few. And she bade Ruth . . ."

"She bade Ruth to return to her people, her family, her gods. I know the story, Mr. Levine, and I understand why you want to be rid of me, Miss Jayne. I'll make arrangements with Doc and Emmeline to stay with them."

"Be my Ruth." The woman blurted out the words. "I want you so much to be my Ruth."

"What?"

357

"Jake is gone, yes, but his death wasn't your doing." The woman's words spilled out, fresh rain to parched earth. "You, you are my daughter. My child. My future. My hope. And when you marry—yes, you will again find love—and when you do, I want you to fill our home with your children, and I want your children to be our grandchildren. I want my days with you, with Mr. Levine, with all of our family to be filled with—what is the Hebrew word you shared with me last night?"

Mr. Levine answered. "Hesed. Sweet Jayne, the word is hesed."

"Yes, hesed. I want our world to be filled with hesed, with a love so steadfast, so enduring, that it mends brokenness and surrounds us with grace as we move through troubled times."

Lainie grabbed hold of the wagon's siderail to steady herself.

"Hesed?" she asked, dazed by Miss Jayne's words and this sudden glimpse of her future. "Hesed," she repeated.

She looked to Mr. Levine and then to Miss Jayne.

"I want that. I want that very much." Lainie stepped forward and wrapped her arms around Miss Jayne. "Entreat me not to leave thee," she whispered into her mother's ear. "Whither thou goest, I will go. And thy people shall be my people, and thy God my God."

Lainie stepped back and laughed with joy. "I'm sorry, I don't remember the rest of the scripture. But I do remember the spirit of it."

"We can't wipe away pain, frustration, or anger, sweet daughter, but with the spirit of hesed, we can transform it."

* * *

After Mr. Levine assisted Miss Jayne into the front of the wagon, he proffered his hand to Lainie.

"May I assist you into your seat?"

She bit her lip.

"What is it, child?"

"I believe I'm forgetting something."

"Is there a box I can retrieve for you? A chore that needs to be done before we leave?"

"No, no. I just need to check something. I'm not sure why."

Mr. Levine looked at her with concern. "Certainly, we can wait. As long as you need, Sonnenblume."

Lainie slipped away and entered the bunkhouse where Jake had slept the past few months, knowing there was nothing left in there

358

beyond two made-up cots and the wood stove. An overwhelming sense compelled her to stand on each cot and search the rafters, to crawl on her knees and check for loose floorboards, to search each mattress for an opening, a hidden safehouse for something she was being led to find.

Her search was futile. She moved on to the cabin and as she ascended the stairs, she was watchful of clues to the mystery looming before her.

Inside, her eyes roamed the room, taking in the lace curtains, the rocking chair, the sofa. Much of the Adamsen family's furniture remained for Paul and Snow Owl to use. Later, some of it would remain for the hired hands to use once Paul and Snow Owl moved into the nearly completed home Jake had built. The only piece of furniture Miss Jayne had insisted on keeping was the banged-up kitchen table Lainie had rescued.

Mr. Levine had balked at Miss Jayne's request to use the table in what would be their home. "The table I have is quite elegant," he'd assured. When she explained that she needed her table's scars to remind her to be resilient, to nourish others and herself, he gently touched her face and suggested the symbolism went beyond resilience and nourishment. "Scars are beautiful, sweet Jayne. Scars are beautiful."

Lainie shifted past that memory and searched the loft and each bedroom for whatever mystery she knew she had to uncover. She found nothing but dustlight and defeat.

She allowed her thoughts to tug her to the location in the home that she both feared and revered. Standing atop the floorboards where the kitchen table once stood, she imagined Jake and his son sitting at their table, eating breakfast, playing games, reciting fairy tales. How precious those moments must have been. How profound, those ties of trust between a father and his child.

Her thoughts turned to Jake's devotion to his wife. A few weeks before, as Lainie and Jake nestled beneath a cottonwood tree, he had shared stories about his wife, their love story, and he had shyly confided that he and his wife had once made love beneath the kitchen table. This intimate detail didn't elicit jealousy from Lainie. Instead, it helped reaffirm the depth of love this man possessed. And now, though she had never known his touch, had never been wrapped in his intimacy, she felt a warm rush of gratitude for the timeless bonds they had shared in the short time they had known each other.

Lainie let out a frustrated sigh. "I don't know what you want me to see, Jake. What is it you want me to see?"

She sat down on the floor and scanned the room again. "What do you want me to see?" Her eyes flicked to the floorboards, where older, darker boards butted up to newer boards not yet stained by age. She traced the joinery pattern with her eyes. Something was missing. Four of the floorboards were missing nails.

She pried one plank up with her fingernails and felt the cool, musty ground air filter into the room. She pulled up the remaining boards and sobbed when she spotted an old toolbox nestled between the floor joists.

Lainie pulled the box up and set it on the floor beside her. She lifted the lid. The box was filled with Jake's song paper, each covered with snatches of words and rhymes.

She scanned the pages, caught glimpses of his heart.

On a page dated July 27, 1890, he'd scrawled *my grief is the ugly and crippling kind*. One sheet had *I want my little guy back* written in capital letters across the entire page. The message for December 23 was simple: *Happy birthday, Mother. I love you*. On January 1, 1891, *I feel forever's heartbeat once again* had been written next to a charcoal sketch of Lainie.

A particular passage made her weep for the non-existent time Jake's baby girl had on earth. *Life isn't a constant, easy stride. We slip, we slide. We climb, we fall. Sometimes our steps are small, sometimes they fall short. And sometimes we can stride so large and far that fulfilled dreams seem just a glimpse away. But not every day. Not every moment. And certainly not every life*. At the bottom of that page: *Dedicated to Baby Girl Adamsen. I loved you from the start*.

Lainie read through others until she came across pages devoted to the words of his song. Her song. *I melt into your spring, my Lady Grace*.

She rocked back and forth as she hugged the pages to her. "We didn't get all our miracles, Jake, but we got a few of them." Her eyes settled on the rocking chair sitting in the corner and she thought about that first day they'd hauled it to the field so Miss Jayne could help with the harvest.

"What a day that was. What a day that was." She sorted through more of Jake's papers, not reading them, just pondering, wondering about the future. "Your mama and I, we're going to be fine. We'll both be obstinate and ornery and thrash out our gripes now and then, but we'll coax out the peaceful parts and let love do the rest."

She slipped each paper back into the box, closed the lid, and rested her fingers across the initials carved across the top. JDA.

"Jacob Durrant Adamsen," she whispered, "I give to you my love, my heart, my promise to find laughter and light. You've given me roots, Jake, deeper than any I've ever known, and these roots are tenacious and strong. Who knew that such untamed loneliness could land in an abounding field of wildflowers? Who knew that loneliness so fierce could reach for the sun to become a wildflower herself?"

Lainie placed a fingertip kiss upon his initials. "I'll take care of our roots, Jake, and I'll cherish them, too."

She thought of Miss Jayne, Paul, Snow Owl, and the baby as she nestled the box back into its hold. She slipped the floorboards in place as she tacked the names of Doc and Emmeline, the Bauers, Halifax, Pastor Evans, and Miss Jayne's new husband to her growing family tree. Her family included animals, too, for Bristle, the steer, and Miss Priss had truly claimed her heart. And, of course, there were her grandparents and auntie, her birth mother, a beautiful dancer named Kate, and Mother Damnable.

And Stut. He would be her father always and forever, for he had given her life, her name was formed from his. Lainie. The composition of her parents' initials—Louisa Adele Ingman, Nicholas Ian Edwards—gave her new hope.

Lainie.

She stood up and crossed the room to look out the kitchen window. Miss Jayne stood beneath the alder tree, twirling one of its leaves within her fingertips. "Mama," Lainie whispered as she watched Mr. Levine approach his bride-to-be and kiss her on the cheek. Lainie's spirit raced with pain and regret and happiness at the sight. She knew this upcoming chapter with Miss Jayne—with her mother—would be difficult for both, but the bonds they'd built, that they could build again—whether they were carved from stone or sprouted from seeds—would be fulfilling, rewarding. A harvest with no end.

She also knew her promise to Jake to find laughter and light would be the hardest task she would ever take on, for laughter and light were masters of hide-and-seek when a heart was on the mend. But she had watched Miss Jayne succeed. She had watched Jake succeed. Now it was her turn.

She touched her forefinger to the tears on her cheek, then used the moisture to writes Jake's name on the window.

"Go on and dance with your angels, Jake," she whispered. "Dance with your beautiful angels."

As Lainie slipped out the front door, she made one last request of Jake. "Every once in a while, if you don't mind, let us hear the music you're dancing to. And if it's a song you've written, whisper the words into my ear to courage me up for the roads ahead. You'll know where to find me. I'll be setting my roots in the shadow of wildflowers."

Acknowledgements

In all likelihood, this book would remain securely enrobed within the silver encasement of my HP Envy if it weren't for my husband. "When are you going to get that book done?" truly is a loving phrase when said in his handsomely teasing tone. Thank you, sweet Tomcat, beholder of wuv, twue wuv. I needed the verbal reminders, even if they drove me insane. You've sacrificed much for your family—we are eternally grateful.

Thanks, also, to our daughters who never gave up on their mom's dream of completing a novel. (And yes, Charlee and Lindsee, the first two novels will remain hidden. Forever. But that's okay. Sometimes the goal needs to change as the person changes and grows.) I'm so proud of both of you and your families. Thank you for growing up to be my best friends.

To my sister Glenette, seven simple words: You raise me up. I love you.

To her sons, Spencer and Alex, you are loved more than you can ever know.

To Darlene, Lloyd, and all of my husband's family, thank you for becoming my family, too. And Darlene, only a grace-filled soul could create such cherished memories for her children, grandchildren, and great-grandchildren. Beautifully done, sweet lady. Beautifully done.

Morgan High School teachers Kathy Egbert, Sue Valcarce Brough, and Linda Morrison—memories of your classes, your encouragement, and your dedication to students still inspire me.

To my friends and extended family members, thanks for putting up with this outspoken introvert over the years. I'm especially grateful for my pals at work and in our neighborhood. Three longtime friends have been especially supportive of this writing endeavor and life in general. Kelli, Melissa, and Jerry: the first sunny day of spring, vintage Farmalls, and chocolaty s'mores cooked over a fire are pretty amazing. Your friendship is even better.

363

Editor Elizabeth Lyon, thank you for your insights. Your workshop made me want to work with you, your editing guidance confirmed that inspiration.

Now, for a trip down memory lane. As a junior in high school, Ken and Marie Adams provided me an opportunity to write for *The Morgan County News*. I am beyond grateful for this experience, and I loved every moment of documenting local news and interviewing members of our community.

Each week for nearly two years, my parents would gently prod me to sit at the electric typewriter and finish my article so they could hand deliver it to the news office. And yes, most weeks, I procrastinated because procrastination is one of my God-given talents.

Six years into this book, I suppose Mom and Dad continue to prod me from heaven.

Thanks, Glen Edward Spencer and Alta Jean Adams. I'm glad Nette and I chose you from heaven.

With love and appreciation, RaeJean Spencer Hasenoehrl
(Writing under the name of Alta Ione)

Author's Notes

The Shadow of Wildflowers is not based on a real-life story, but it does evolve around details discovered in several historical documents.

Idaho's Camas Prairie served as inspiration for much of this book's backdrop. Generations of my husband's family have lived on and worked this land since the 1800s. I am indebted to the Hasenoehrl and Wessels families for sharing the rich stories of their ancestors and the land.

For a glimpse of life on the Camas Prairie in the late 19th century and the 20th century, volumes 1 and 2 of *150 Years: Our Story* is replete with histories and photographs collected from dozens of families from Cottonwood, Ferdinand, Greencreek, Keuterville, and surrounding areas. The books, which helped me describe farming and ranching practices of the late 1800s, were sponsored by the Cottonwood Lions Club, the Cottonwood Chamber of Commerce, and The Historical Museum at St. Gertrude's. As of March 2021, the books are available for purchase through the museum and online at www.stgertrudes.org.

If you ever visit the panhandle of Idaho, I highly recommend a visit to St. Gertrude's. The museum is fascinating, the grotto garden is peaceful, and the chapel is filled with architecture of yesteryear. The Benedictine sisters and their chaplain are welcoming and vibrant about their mission to sustain the land and support their community.

The Northwest Room at the Everett Public Library in Washington State proved to be a tremendous source for rare histories and journals. Its online digital collection of photos and documents, along with that of the University of Washington, the University of Idaho, the Idaho State Archives, and the National Park Service NP Gallery, among others, provided a variety of historical details that I have interwoven into the story. Additional sources of inspiration include the Facebook pages for Potlatch Historical Society and Historic Wallace Preservation Society Inc.

Photographer Linda Lantzy has captured hundreds of stunning photos of Northern Idaho. Her online collection helped me to capture memories of the scenery I've enjoyed during my many visits to the Camas Prairie and its neighboring communities. Her custom art prints, books, and gifts can be purchased at www.idahoscenics.com.

My fascination with old windmills began when I was a child, and our family would take trips to visit the desert ranch my father grew up on. I always wondered how the towers of steel ended up in such a remote region. Building a storyline around a windmill seemed a natural progression for this book. *Still Turning, A History of Aermotor Windmills* by Christopher C. Gillis helped answer many of my questions, and I turned to this book often in my research.

I adopted the term "windmiller" from the online article *Windmills Helped Settle the West*, written by Betty Thomason. This term was used by her to describe modern-day windmill technicians who specialize in repairing and refurbishing old windmills. She also used the term "windmill boss" to describe the head of a team of windmill men and well diggers "who migrated across the plains from the Dakotas to the Pecos to follow their trade."

Leaning into the Wind, edited by Linda Hasselstrom, Gaydel Collier, and Nancy Curtis, proved to be a valuable resource for gleaning information about the important role women held and continue to hold in working the land. The book's opening page says it all: Dedicated to all the High Plains women, whose stories, told or untold, sing like the prairie winds. I admit, I fell in love with the book's phrase "miniature, majestic lakes" and used it in the chapter titled "Hidden Treasure."

Descriptions about mud apples, the cattle and sheep in the lightning storm, the fire in Wallace Idaho, and the knife injury during a rooster fight were developed from true stories.

Regarding the use of Nimiipuu language, please forgive me for any inaccurate Nez Perce names, words, or phrases—I did my best to aim for authenticity and relied greatly on *A Dictionary of the Numípu or Nez Perce Language,* by a Missionary of the Society of Jesus, in the Rocky Mountains, Part I, printed in 1895. Beth Erdey, archivist and research center director at Nez Perce National Historical Park, graciously helped me sort through ideas to include in this book. She also shared that Snow Owl is likely not a name that the Nez Perce used in the 1800s, but the name called out to me, so I kept it in the text.

My father-in-law grew up next to St. Joseph's Mission in Slickpoo and enjoyed friendships with some of the children who lived there. The chapel, built in 1874, still stands as of the writing of this book and is listed on the National Register of Historic Places. I've included photos and a brief history of it on my website, altawrites.com. The mission closed in 1958 and its other buildings, which included a school, a convent, and a children's home, no longer exist. A landmark sign remains on the property.

This book includes many harrowing and heartbreaking moments. Themes are built around loss, grief, depression, and suicide. For anyone coping with any of these difficult struggles, a horizon of hope can be terribly difficult to see. Optionb.org is an excellent resource to turn to, whether you are facing a challenge, supporting someone else, or building everyday resilience.

I hope this story inspires you to find laughter and light no matter your circumstance. I hope this story inspires you to set your roots in the shadow of wildflowers, and to become a wildflower yourself.

Reading Group Guide
Discussion Questions
for *The Shadow of Wildflowers*

Dear Readers,

The Shadow of Wildflowers is an ideal novel for reading groups. Among its themes are family and identity, grief and despair, resilience and recovery.

If you haven't yet read the novel, please note that this reading group guide gives away aspects of the plot.

I hope you enjoy your discussion of *The Shadow of Wildflowers* and find value in each character's growth.

Warm wishes,
Alta Ione

1) Scars have a ubiquitous presence throughout the story. What symbolic significance do scars hold for each of the characters?

2) Grief is one of the most universal human experiences. All too often, no one talks about it. In what ways does Jake externalize and internalize his anger and grief? In Chapter 27, how do Anton's words about loss and grief affect Jake?

3) Miss Jayne admits that her feelings towards Lainie are like yellowjackets, biting down hard then plunging in their stingers. Why is her reaction to Lainie so extreme?

4) Jake comments that Lainie talks more to animals than she does to humans. In what scenes do we see Lainie relying on animals for companionship? How do the animals help stabilize her intense conflicts and emotions? How do the animals add conflict to the story?

5) Lainie has lost a mother figure in her life multiple times —her birth mother, Mother Damnable who twice helped save her life, and her grandmother. At the farm, she tries to carve out a relationship with Miss Jayne. What significant events help to build trust between the women? At what point of the story does their relationship evolve into that of a mother and daughter?

6) Compare and contrast each man's role as a father: Jake the protector, who couldn't save his family; McNally the magnate, who would do anything to have a male heir; and Stut the downtrodden, who sacrificed everything to save the child he couldn't keep.

7) What does the windmill represent for Jake and Miss Jayne? For Lainie? For Paul and Snow Owl?

8) When the cattle are killed in the lightning storm and the townspeople harvest the meat for their own food, Jake

expresses, "If God's gonna make something good happen through suffering, it doesn't need to be through blameless animals." Keep in mind, these animals were meant to someday be sacrificed as food. Is Jake's statement about God killing animals filled with hypocrisy?

9) Were you surprised to learn that Niall McNally's wife was involved in the pursuit of Lainie and the hanging of her mother? Who do you consider to be more ruthless: Niall or Agrippina McNally?

10) Secondary characters play an important role in developing backstory, setting, conflict, intrigue, and relief. What secondary character did you most enjoy meeting? What attracted you to this character?

11) A prominent theme throughout the novel is that of starting over after experiencing loss. With this theme in mind, is your interpretation of the ending optimistic or pessimistic?

12) How do wildflowers play into the theme of resilience? Is Sonnenblume, which means sunflower, an appropriate description for Lainie? In what ways did Lainie become a wildflower?

About the Author

Hushed histories. Truths swept under the rug. Facts secreted away because they didn't meet the status quo. These are the stories that speak to author RaeJean Spencer Hasenoehrl, who uses the pen names of Alta Ione for historical fiction and Florence Ione for inspirational non-fiction.

RaeJean's stories center around working-class people. She's not afraid to write about difficult subjects such as grief, depression, and hardship. Each story may have heartbreak at its core, but hope is dauntless, and so are her characters.

The author grew up in Morgan, Utah, which has a rich pioneer heritage, and now resides in Northwest Washington. Much of her writing is shaped by information from old newspapers, journal entries, and other historical documents. Her timeless themes speak of grit, determination, hope, grace, and love.

Visit altawrites.com for beautiful photography, inspired messages, and updates about future novels and inspirational nonfiction books.